SMITHBURY SKELETON

SMITHBURY SKELETON

To Karen,
A tad on the wild side and something different, but it is me.
Love,
Ed

Ed Matthews

Copyright © 2004 by Ed Matthews.

Cover design by Sonia Landwehr and Kevin Eichner

Library of Congress Number: 2004090152
ISBN: Softcover   1-4134-4506-3

All rights reserved. No part of this book may be reproduced or transmitted in any form or by any means, electronic or mechanical, including photocopying, recording, or by any information storage and retrieval system, without permission in writing from the copyright owner.

This is a work of fiction. Names, characters, places and incidents either are the product of the author's imagination or are used fictitiously, and any resemblance to any actual persons, living or dead, events, or locales is entirely coincidental.

This book was printed in the United States of America.

To order additional copies of this book, contact:
Xlibris Corporation
1-888-795-4274
www.Xlibris.com
Orders@Xlibris.com
23728

Also by Ed Matthews

Frontenac
Harkers

ACKNOWLEDGEMENTS

I offer a sincere thank you to my wife, Carol for continually supporting my writing efforts.

To Kitty Parnell, a teaching colleague and friend, and to my son, Dr. Tom Matthews for their corroboration and sensitive guidance.

1

Formerly a neighborhood of the rich, Ford Ashland sat majestically astride a hill overlooking the city of Bridgeton, Virginia. The city of some 600,000 was strategically located near the mouth of the Rappohanock River. After World War II, its wealthy residents moved from the picturesque setting of this hill top community to develop clusters of elegance in the newly developing suburbs west of the city.

Young struggling couples looking to buy class on a shoestring replaced those who abandoned Ford Ashland. What they lacked in money, they made up for in sheer confidence and determination. The new pilgrims rehabilitated the neighborhood into a stately showcase, reminiscent of its former elegance. If an early rising sea gull flying over Ford Ashland were to peer through the dense heavy air of this still and silent morning, he'd see the patio lights of one house burning brightly.

Four in the morning found Jack O'Brennan drinking coffee on his patio. Thoughts about the anticipated weekend in front of him filled his mind.

Now retired from the Bridgeton Police Department, O'Brennan continued to follow an early morning ritual. He believed the earlier a man got up, the clearer he perceived the world around him.

Last's night's eleven o'clock weather report did not portray an inviting Thursday morning. Dampness and an overcast sky seemed to dictate what the afternoon would bring. A glorious Virginia spring weekend was forecast for Red's wedding, and it seemed only appropriate after two weeks of rain and unseasonably cool temperatures.

On Friday, the Group would head to Charlottesville for Red's wedding on Saturday to his long-time girl friend, Betty Green. As a follow-up to what looked like an exciting Saturday, Red would graduate the following day from the University of Virginia Law School.

The Group, as they so off-handedly called themselves, consisted of three other close friends. John Lloyd, whom he had been a rookie with on the city police force was his closest friend. He retired with Jack, and became Chief of Security at the massive Bridgeton Auditorium. Ten years prior to his retirement, John's wife died from cancer, and after his loss, he never regained his familiar carefree attack on life.

Cal Redout, formerly the city's Chief Pathologist resigned after the Freddie Gill case and accepted a position on the faculty at Bridgeton University School of Medicine. He taught Pathology, researched violent crimes, and like John and O'Brennan had earlier lost his wife. Unlike John Lloyd, who never picked up with a lady friend, Cal, at the conclusion of the Gill case started dating Dr. Vivian McGregor. They quickly became an item and their relationship continued to flourish.

The third member was Karl Eichner. Once head bartender at Bridgeton's most elite hotel and restaurant, the Ritz Plaza, he currently served as head cook at the *Red Squire* Restaurant in the small hamlet of Spenser, east of the city. Karl's boss, Jeanette Purchase, was the owner and more importantly, was Jack O'Brennan's main squeeze. From their initial meeting Karl's wife, Phyllis became Jeanette's closest friend.

One day while gathered in the park, John Lloyd suggested they were a group of old guys sitting around talking about the old days. Somehow they picked up on calling themselves the Group and never thought much about it after that.

Red wandered onto the Group some eight or nine years ago, as if lead by the hand of destiny. He took a seat on the Bench without introducing himself and after that returned daily to just sit and listen. The others viewed the thirty-two year old with interest, but didn't include him in their conversation until finally accepting him as a regular six months after first arriving.

The mystery of Red Ted continued as the days turned into months. He had no visible source of income, yet always carried plenty of money around. Red was a child of the street who walked around in clean but rumpled clothes. It appeared his special function in life was drinking beer from morning into the late night. His background surfaced during the Gill case when Jack O'Brennan and the Group were muddling through the Freddie Gill case.

In the summer of 1952, a sailor stationed at the Bridgeton Naval Hospital had been murdered in the notorious Harkers neighborhood.

Thirty-two years later, Jack O'Brennan received an out-of-state call asking him to investigate the unsolved killing of a sailor named Freddie Gill. Harkers, the slimy neighborhood adjacent to the naval base had yielded to the wrecker's ball in the early sixties. This once sleazy playground for the Navy's Atlantic Destroyer Division now served as official residence for the new and sparkling government center. Under urban renewal, this hole-of-holes vanished if by the stroke of a master magician. Where to begin was the problem faced by O'Brennan.

The embryo of the Gill case grew out of the rip and bang of a cesspool called Harkers. This playground of evil accommodated the sailor's needs from booze to pursuing the flesh, with a stopover for drugs, gambling, and other activities to drain the sailor of his last dollar.

It was in this setting that the circle of friends called the Group and O'Brennan would solve the Gill case and along the way this collection of odd parts would reconstruct their lives with newfound romance. Like a sporting event, each team needed an opponent, and in the Group's case, "The Circle of the Shamrock" provided just that. Freddie Gill stole whiskey from the naval hospital and sold it in Harkers. Sally Ralston a young college girl paid her education expenses by selling her lovely body as a call girl in the employ of the Greenbriar Escort Service. Fritz Hansen, a destroyer-based corpsman's special proclivity lay in the sale of narcotics, as they were called in the fifties. The fourth member, and brains of the friends, would turn out to be Andrew Kenmore,

Senior Senator from Virginia. More important than his Senate position was his apparent lock on his party's upcoming presidential nomination.

The Shamrock Bar was their home base and origin of their mark of distinction. Members wore a green quarter-sized C tattooed on their upper left arm. They were placed in such a way to form the upper part of a shamrock leaf. Kenmore's green stem completed the shamrock picture.

When O'Brennan undertook the Gill case, this treacherous crew was solidly entrenched in the world of drugs on the East Coast. All members of the gang, except Freddie Gill who rested peacefully on a shady hillside in Bell Hills, Tennessee, were deeply intertwined in the operation.

To Jack O'Brennan, the centerpiece of the investigation was Jeanette Purchase. At one time, this ex-madam from Harkers ran the Greenbriar Escort Service and featured Sally Ralston as one of her top girls. At the conclusion of the case, Jeanette and O'Brennan became a steady item, and their friends assumed they some day would marry.

She was the youngest looking mid-fifties lady O'Brennan had ever seen. Her gray-auburn hair, relatively unlined face, and brilliant smile dramatically displayed her nearly six foot with a soft casual look. To call her willowy was an apt description.

Jeanette's legitimate life began with the elimination of Harkers. She jump-started her new career by opening a highly successful posh restaurant called the *Red Leather*. After the "Circle of the Shamrock" torched her classy eatery, she opened the *Red Squire*, a waterside restaurant in the hamlet-sized community of Spenser.

After several tours of duty in Vietnam, Red took advantage of the GI Bill and entered the University of Virginia as a finance major. His superior mind took over and he graduated three years later with top honors. Red enjoyed the stimulating academic life he led at UVa., but refrained from seeking work after finishing. Other than his collegiate experience life had not treated Red well, so he returned to Bridgeton and became a meanderer of the city. During the investigation, Red's metamorphous became complete. He changed from a roughneck rover to a goal-oriented man of forty. In the fall of eighty-five, Red entered law school, and now he had completed his legal training. Reaching to the coffee table, O'Brennan picked up Red's letter to again read his learned friend's comments.

> *Jack,*
> *I am pleased you and my friends are coming to town for the wedding and law school graduation. It's amazing how quickly the last three years have fallen away and seems like yesterday that I was a full-fledged member of the Group, and look back on the Freddie Gill case as an extraordinary experience in my life. The night you informed us of the imminent danger we each faced was one I shall never forget. I can still recall John Lloyd questioning the merit of an investigation that led to two deaths. At the time I agreed with John's reasoning when he questioned would anyone be better off for our endeavors? You pointed out that we would all gain something from our venture, and it appears your forecast was correct.*
> *This weekend, I'm to marry the only woman I've loved, and another plus is finishing law school. In retrospect, the Group as a whole added to their lifestyle by the Gill case.*
> *Enough said about past days. The reception should be something else with most of the guests being classmates and members of the faculty. You figure it out. They'll be out of their minds and like they say in law school, "That's a given!"*
> *There's a wild buddy of mine from Massachusetts who's taken over the reception. As a matter-of-fact, he's taken over the wedding as well. You'd think he was the one getting married Saturday instead Of me. His name is Colbert Martin and I'm sure you'll like him. But I must warn you he is the biggest nut case I've ever seen.*

I'm looking forward to the reception more than the wedding, but don't tell Betty Marie. Guess it's one of those little rituals we men have to go along with.

I joined the American Legion down here and met the Charlottesville Chief of Police; a guy named name Ben Hurly. Jeanette will be interested in this. He graduated from high school with her. One day we got talking about police work and the Gill case came up. When I told him about working on the case, he showed a new interest in me. When he found out I was friendly with the famous Jack O'Brennan, he got all excited.

The long and short of it is, he's been following a missing co-ed for the better part of thirty years. Her body just turned up, and the newspapers called it The Smithbury Skeleton. You probably remember, the skeleton was found in Smithbury earlier in the year. And get this; the girl had been missing since 1960. I get the feeling he's going to ask you to follow up on her case.

It may have been presumptuous on my part, but I placed Ben and his wife at your table for the reception. We can talk about it Friday at Michie Tavern when we have lunch. I've booked an eleven-thirty reservation, so let's plan on meeting then.

Your friend,
Red

Focusing on Red's letter, O'Brennan headed down the hill toward Inlet Park. He was baffled by the myriad of thoughts bouncing around in his mind. The beauty of the Ford Ashland neighborhood with its narrow tree-lined streets and continually burning gaslights went unnoticed as O'Brennan ambled down the incline. Through the early morning light, the streetlights cast mottled patterns against the nearby brick homes and sidewalks.

This morning was different. He contemplated Red's letter

and its implications. He didn't dare ask himself what he should do about the Smithbury Skeleton, though he was intrigued by the opportunity it offered. Hopefully, his friends could give him some direction. He'd arrive at a final conclusion after carefully weighing out what his buddies, Jeanette and this Hurly had to offer.

2

"Another brilliant day!" O'Brennan proclaimed upon joining his friends.

"What's so good about it?" Karl asked somewhat abrasively as he pointed to the distant clouds.

"Old Red has suddenly reentered our life and we're going to Charlottesville in the morning to see him get married and graduate, and that sounds good to me," Jack replied in an equally abrasive tone. "Why are you so exercised over this?"

Karl made a slight dismissive gesture with his hand as his eyes clouded over with a question. "There's another point I want to bring up. Why are we leaving at seven in the morning? That doesn't make sense," Karl asked impatiently.

"Your objection is duly noted. It's not a perfect world, never will be."

"Ha!"

O'Brennan directed an unyielding glance at his friend. "Karl, you're just being radical." Jack's response brought laughs from John and Cal. "It takes two and a half hours to drive over there, which shoots up the morning before we begin. We're to meet Red at *Michie Tavern* for lunch at eleven-thirty, so by the time we check into the motel and drive out to the mountain, we won't have much time left."

"Here's another thought for you with the prickly attitude. Plan on eating a light breakfast because you won't believe the quality of the lunch served. Right, Cal?" John said.

"Absolutely, when Vivian and I took Red to UVa. for his law school interview, we ate lunch there and found it incredibly good.

Whatever they charge isn't enough. By the way where are we staying?" Cal asked.

"At the Best Western Cavalier Inn on the corner of University and Emmet Street. Red made the reservations last winter, so we should have good rooms. We can walk to the wedding, reception and graduation from there."

"If we arrive a little early, so what? We can take a tour around the campus and check out the co-eds. You'd like that wouldn't you, Karl?" John said.

"Enough is enough! You guys are sporting me this morning," Karl said with a laugh.

"Yesterday afternoon I got a letter from Red. Let me read it and see what you think." After reading the letter, Jack took off his glasses and asked his friends their opinion.

"The reception should be fun, but the Smithbury Skeleton sounds even more inviting," Cal said.

"I agree, Cal. I need a little something different and this may be it. My dreams sometimes lead me by the nose and my own selfish reasons are pointing me at this girl. Earlier in the morning I arrived at some thoughts I'd like to share with you. Obviously I'm going to make the final decision but I'd like to hear your thoughts on the matter." O'Brennan smiled, "and I can't forget Jeanette."

Karl impatiently signaled O'Brennan to continue with a get-on-with-it gesture.

"I'm pretty good at detective work and maybe could find the killer; with your help of course."

"You're wasting our time being humble," John said with a smile.

"Need I remind you that I'm not Sherlock Holmes?"

"There are times when I don't believe one word you say and this is one of them."

Changing the line of discussion Cal offered, "Finding something that far back is like trying to grab a drop of mercury. You'd be facing overwhelming odds against recovering leads. I'm talking about entering uncharted waters and you know what that means."

"If I'm equipped to proceed, then I feel I should, but you, my friends, came too close to danger to suit me. Should I again place you in harm's way?"

"Jack, for the sake of argument, this disappearance has a shady side. Far be it from me to discourage you from undertaking this investigation; in fact, I'll be with you all the way; but what are the chances?" John Lloyd asked.

"How will Jeanette handle your news?" Cal asked.

"My relationship with Jeanette has never been better and has grown into a more than serious romance, which I'm sure will soon lead to marriage. Why jeopardize that?

"What's the reason for all this uncertainty you're displaying?" Cal said.

O'Brennan looked past Cal at the sparkling inlet water as his mind drifted away to other thoughts.

"To be honest with you, I get the feeling things aren't meshing together like I'd want them to be. It feels like I'm walking on sand."

"Whatever gave you that idea? Your life isn't going down the tubes like you infer. Your life is not built on beach sand. I detest the cliche, 'It's time to stop and smell the roses', but there's nothing wrong with sitting back and enjoying yourself. If you enjoy chasing some killer, then go for it! As you point out, our life styles are getting a little bland, but is that all bad?"

"I agree with what John said, you are an excellent detective and so is he, so I'd call that a plus for the good guys," Karl said without preamble. Another feature is you have friends who are willing to help. Now about the Freddie Gill case, after backing off the investigation, I have lived with my own personal misery since. When I returned to the case, you had pretty well put it to bed. I'm not proud about my previous actions, but if you decide to pursue this Smithbury Skeleton case, you can count on me." Karl said.

"Thanks, Karl, but I can't help remembering there were too many people hurt."

"I agree there were too many people hurt during the case. Two people met their deaths because of the investigation, but that's carrying a point a little too far. They died by the hand of some bad guys in that damn case. Granted, if you hadn't initiated the investigation, they'd probably still be living. Taking a hard-ass view, does society miss them? I believe not. You must remember they were bad people. At least Sally Hunter was, though Billy Olsen wasn't a bad sort," Doc Readout said.

"I can buy what you just said Cal, we were hurt. But I'm going against the grain when I point out we gained a hell of a lot for our troubles. We're going over to see old Red and Betty get married Saturday. He's graduating the next day from law school, now how bad is that? Great things are going to happen to that couple and that's a bonus that came out of the Gill case. You're going to Charlottesville with Jeanette and you must admit she's been a remarkable addition to your life. Cal has Vivian McGregor and a great teaching job. What the hell, he was killing himself working as chief pathologist for the city. He now has a job he truly loves. Am I right?" John Lloyd glanced in Cal's direction.

"You're right, John."

"I'm the only guy in this lash-up that hasn't seen much change, but I have a feeling my life is going to improve shortly."

"It's nice that your life will be on the upswing, John. I worry about my friends coming too close to real danger."

"Let me answer that, Jack. I think that's our decision to make and ours alone. About this harm's-way nonsense, how much harm is there going to be out there?" Cal smugly said.

"We thought that about the Gill case, and look what happened. You know yourself, Cal, we were squeezed until our tongues were hanging out," Jack said.

Cal focused on O'Brennan with a scholarly stare. "If you believe lightning will strike twice, then I know where there's a bridge for sale that crosses the East River."

Karl and John laughed at Cal's suggestion of a fire sale up north.

"What is harm's-way, Jack? What the hell, I may find it crossing the street to get in my car. We're a bunch of idle old men talking about nothing. I like the way it sounds. To say I'm not interested would not be true. This is an old-fashioned case, or her disappearance date makes it so. I think all of us," Cal included the others with a sweep of his hand, "can measure up. Experts we're not, but I believe we can help you deliver the goods. It boils down to we'll do whatever has to be done," Cal proudly offered.

"If you say so. I think my main concern is my relationship with Jeanette. You all know it's become full blown, and I'11 soon ask her to marry me. Why should I jeopardize that?"

John quickly responded, "You're asking a question we can't answer. Talk with her, and believe me, I know what her answer will be."

"Jack, let's cut to the bottom of this and find out what you really think. What's your position?"

"Cal, I guess I want to do it. Of course the final decision will be based on what Jeanette says but you're right, she'll buy it. I 'm going out to Spenser to see her now."

"Jack, don't get talked into something you can't handle."

O'Brennan laughed. "John, you're always quick with the advice. Now getting back to the more serious side of this conversation, let's talk about tomorrow. Karl, John is riding with you so come over to the house around seven. I'll pick up Cal and Vivian and meet you there. I'll see you in the morning." Jack said.

O'Brennan walked through the dining room of *the Red Squire* on his way to Jeanette's office and found her working on restaurant business for the weekend.

"Good morning. Are you ready for tomorrow?" Jeanette asked.

"I just left the guys at the park and we're all set. What time are you coming in tonight?"

"Not much before eight. I'm all packed but have much to do before I leave. With both Karl and me gone, it puts me in a little bind."

"Do you want to go out for dinner?" Jack asked.

"O'Brennan, why not stop at Vic's sandwich shop and pick up a submarine."

"We have to talk. I went over it this morning with the Group but I need your thoughts. I received a letter from Red and it's somewhat of puzzler. Here, you take a look at it."

Perusing Red's letter, Jeanette looked at Jack. "What makes this different from any other mystery you ever encountered?"

Jack replayed the discussion he had with his friends earlier. "This could be the setting for a disaster," he said not knowing how prophetic his words would prove to be. "What's your take on this?"

Impatience betraying her previously calm demeanor, she asked, "What do you want from me, O'Brennan? You have a gift so why not use it? Of course you should get involved, it's what you do. You already knew what my answer would be, didn't you?"

"Yeah, I guess I did. John said the same thing."

"O'Brennan, be gone with you. I can't chit-chat with you all morning. I have too much to do." Jeanette summarily released Jack with a slight dismissive gesture of her hand. "See you tonight." Her sly smile sent O'Brennan back to Bridgeton on a happy note.

3

The weatherman was right: the morning was gentle and beautiful. Riding in O'Brennan's cream and red 1957 Chevy convertible helped make it so.

"Jeanette, now that you have the *Squire* going full tilt, are you still putting in the hours you did at the *Red Leather?*" Cal Redout asked.

"No. It's a very different operation with Karl running the food operation. The hostess takes care of the reservations, and Nickie, my head bartender, runs the drink operation. When Karl came to work at the Squire, he vowed he'd never work a strip again because he was soured on bartending. He did show Nickie all the twists of the bar business, and that was the key.

"Work wise, I'm spending less time at the *Squire* and that's how I like it. The operation is doing well and incidentally, I'm making more money now than I ever did before."

"Do you enjoy the *Squire* as much as the *Leather?*" Vivian McGregor asked.

"I was beginning to tire of the *Leather,* especially the eating arrangements. I was sick of catering to people who could afford outrageous prices. Before I opened the *Squire,* I told O'Brennan anyone coming into my restaurant would never be embarrassed by my prices because of their limited means.

"We're probably serving the cheapest and best food on Chesapeake Bay. When you come to the *Squire* for dinner, you're eating, no; make that dining at reasonable prices. We even provide table cloths and cloth napkins and that's unheard of in my type of operation. I'm proud of the operation and love it because I've made it work."

"What do you think about Jack getting into this Smithbury Skeleton business?" Vivian McGregor asked.

"I hope he goes ahead with it. I came in at the very end of the Gill case and things were happening in a hurry. O'Brennan and I are sixty-two and it's high time we got into something different. There should be no down side to this investigation; well certainly not like the Gill case," Jeanette said.

"Can you assure me that won't happen? Many things can go wrong on such an investigation as this," Jack replied.

"Nothing's perfect, my honey."

"If you say it, then it must be so."

"O'Brennan when I try to be serious you come up with something stupid." Her infectious laugh followed.

Jack shrugged. "I hate to tie myself down, but you're right, maybe we do need a little diversion in our lives."

"When will you move on this?" Cal asked with more than a casual interest.

"I honestly don't know. Probably after I talk to Red's friend. I assume Red will bring him to lunch at Michie Tavern and we can go from there."

"Jack, you've known John for a long time, how is he doing?" Vivian asked

"We were rookies on the force in 1960, which was about the time the girl disappeared in Charlottesville."

"Did you know his wife?"

"Yeah, Vivian, she was a quality lady. After she died, he never made it back," Jack said.

"What's this 'never made it back' business?" Jeanette asked.

"Lloyd was so extroverted, he appeared to be wild. When he lost Allison, I think he lost a major part of himself. Oh, he's still a great guy to be around, but as far as fully rounded, I'd have to say no. John is a carbon copy of me before I met Jeanette."

"O'Brennan, there are few honest men left in the world and you may be one of them," Jeanette said, as she flashed her patented brilliant smile.

"Jeanette, a good sailor needs keen direction and I guess you're my compass."

"Good grief, that's some reply. Where did you dig that up? I wish I'd come up with that one myself." Everyone laughed at Cal's faint display of humor.

"Cal, do you remember the day we sat on my patio talking about the Gill case? That was the first time you mentioned Vivian. Well, John alluded to a friendship with a junior high teacher from Southside that same day. He apparently went out with her on a steady basis. Then one day, she picked up and left town. End of romance, end of story. I've never seen him with a woman since. I'm sure he still likes the ladies, but he hasn't shown it. If I didn't know better, I'd say he was going a little odd on us,"

"O'Brennan, he may find someone who will change his life, so you shouldn't give up on him. We're all members of the same club, it just takes some longer to join than others. Remember, tomorrow will take care of itself, and we'll never know until it happens," Jeanette said.

"Of course you're right, tomorrow will take care of itself. My main interest is what this Hurley has to say," Jack said.

In the other car-heading west, John Lloyd and Phyllis and Karl Eichner rode to Charlottesville. They reversed the process and talked about the other driver, Jack O'Brennan.

"John, what do you think about Jeanette and Jack tying the knot? Will it ever happen?" Phyllis asked.

"That's a puzzler, Phyllis. If you recall, he had a difficult time committing to his relationship with Jeanette. I still think he's haunted by Mary's memory. Deep down I bet he still has a problem with another woman in his life. To be honest, I really don't know. What do you think?" John said,

"I feel the same way. Jeanette and I have become close friends since she opened the restaurant in Spenser. You must remember they've been going together for three years and Jeanette isn't at all happy with the dilemma she faces. She wants to marry Jack, but presently feels like a kept woman because of their living arrangements. On the other hand, she doesn't want to lose him either. Who's to say?"

"I think they'll get married, but what the hell do I know," Karl said.

"Seeing I'm being so nosey this morning, what about Cal and Vivian?"

"Phyllis, what I'm telling you is the straight scoop. The Freddie Gill case was an odd phenomenon. It changed everybody's life; well practically everyone's, except mine. At that time, Cal was Chief Pathologist for Bridgeton and was working himself to death. This little affiliation with Vivian picked up a head of steam when we concluded the case.

"Cal was offered a teaching position at Bridgeton Medical School and accepted the offer. Since changing jobs, he's different and laid back. He likes teaching and much of this turn-around I put in the hands of Vivian. What are your thoughts on the matter, Phyllis?" John asked.

"She's been great for him and I believe that ah . . . yes, they'll end up married," Phyllis said.

"As I look at the last couple of years, I think everyone's lifestyle has changed for the better except mine. What the hell, nothing's different for me." John Lloyd said.

"You never talked about it, but again I'm being nosey. John, you used to date that teacher over at Southside Junior High. What happened?" Phyllis asked.

"It never worked out. She's a heck of a lady, but when Lucy retired, she just up and moved out West."

"Again, this isn't any of my business, but, ah . . . have you gone out with someone else since then? Is there anyone else you might like?"

"Phyllis, I'm a man of considerable patience, but don't you ever give up?" Karl said.

"Think nothing of it, Karl," John said with a laugh. "You're right Phyllis, it isn't any of your business, but if it's that important, I'll tell you. No, I haven't dated in two years and am amazed at how much time I spend by myself. I'm doing the very thing I hate most, and that's being alone, and believe me that emptiness is overwhelming."

"There has to be someone out there for you."

"You may be right, Phyllis. My intuition tells me I'm going to end up with somebody."

"What makes you say that?" Karl said as he looked over at John.

"Did you ever get a feeling; intuition if you like, that something was going to happen down the road and then it happened? I feel that may be true in my case. I honestly believe I'm going to meet someone and it will be the real thing. I hope it's sooner rather than later because this lifestyle of mine is the pits. There is one thing I know; when the right one comes along, it won't take me long to figure it out."

"I don't know anything about your love life, but I know one thing, you drive like Lucky Teeter," Karl said to Lloyd.

"Can you give me a clue as to who Lucky Teeter is?" Phyllis asked.

Traffic was light with few cars heading toward Charlottesville while Phyllis' question went unanswered.

Finally, she spoke up from the back seat. "I remember now, he was that daredevil that did those car stunts when we were kids."

"The very same," Karl said.

"There is one thing I should bring up," John said. "This Smithbury Skeleton Jack talked about is going to be a bitch."

"How so?" Karl asked.

"This one I can smell. Don't ask me why, but there's more to this missing co-ed than meets the eye." John said.

"There may be something in what you say, but I'm hungry. That coffee wasn't enough to carry me to noon. What time is it? I forgot to bring my watch," Phyllis said.

"It's nine-thirty. Remember what Cal said about eating before we go to the Michie Tavern. No use ruining a good thing," Karl said.

While traveling the last fifty miles to Charlottesville, the discussion drifted to the upcoming weekend events. One of their own had made it big and the very thought thrilled his friends. Red Ted was getting married and becoming a lawyer on the same weekend.

4

As John Lloyd headed for the land of Thomas Jefferson, the architect of a long list of murder mysteries was hard at work in his Smithbury study designing a conclusion for another sinister tale. His most fruitful and productive work was done in the morning and this morning was no exception.

The blackberry brandy he consumed triggered a rush of words and phrases that only Martin Jeffreys could create. Moving toward the conclusion of his latest work, *Time was of the Essence*, Jeffreys had not yet designated his next victim.

He walked from the solid cherry desk in my study to the full-length windows that looked out on the beauty of his backyard garden. The multi-colored flowers that abounded along the back lawn perimeter continually provide great satisfaction every time he viewed the magnificent setting.

While enjoying the view, his thoughts centered on why he was rushing ahead with reckless abandon toward completion without designating a victim. He'd never know.

In the past the killers I created displayed sensitive figures while their victims covered the broad spectrum of body and mental types. Young, pretty, homely, short, tall, heavy, thin; variety has always been my formula. I'm intrigued by the image of a woman with a physical disability or psychological infirmity. I choose a drinker, an egomaniac, a stutterer and other types but my greatest kick was the retarded lady, and I must say, she was smashing! I know the reading public will view my use of the word, retarded as politically incorrect and think of me as insensitive for using it, but so what.

Another glass of brandy is the answer. My killer will be debonair, analytical, relentless, and, have the greatest quality of all, cunning. Finally, the gimmick of all gimmicks others didn't experience; he will get away with the murder.

Getting back to the woman of my dreams, I have to create an unflawed victim, at least as unblemished as I can make a fifty-year old. I want her tall, five-ten or better with a great figure. She must be good looking and the hair style and color, . . . that I can't come up with. Minutes passed before a message from his subconscious answered the dilemma. Yes, I know what I want. Her hair must be short like they wore in the fifties. What about coloring? Damn, I find myself groping for the right word. It's easier to write a book than make decisions such as this. I saw a woman in the library yesterday with frosted hair. If it's good enough for her, then it's good enough for Martin Jeffreys.

Excellent, Martin, you've done it again. Your new prospect is going to look like a dream. She'll be very tall, have frosted short hair and be around fifty. I can't top that!

Finding a woman along the lines I've drawn will be difficult, but that's the mystique of undertaking this whole operation. I'm working against a submission date, and that makes it more challenging. The horse show at *Flat Run* is the last opportunity I'll have to find my dream. It was self-limiting to choose women only at horse shows, but it makes the chase so stimulating, and after all, isn't that the challenge of it all?

In the past my fictional killers have displayed an ingrained compulsion to fail and do so. I won't allow that to happen with Ted Nasket. I want him to display a single, no, make that numerous characteristics of an antisocial personality but with considerable charm. He must exploit people and exhibit intense ruthlessness, yet display a fragile side. He is roughneck of sorts, although not a bully. My killer deals easily with others and likes the people he contacts in his daily routine. I'd like him to show a gentle side but at the moment, I feel like a man who has fallen in love . . . totally dedicated to controlling the object of his affections, yet not knowing quite how to achieve success.

Preparation for my real personal killing is well under way except for one major obstacle; I have to choose the designated victim at the *Flat Run* race. My killing will occur the following week at the *Saxon Hunt*, the final event of the season here on my estate and this seems to be out of character for me. It may appear like a coincidence, but there's no such thing when logic is applied. My next murder will be for real while my fictionalized murder in each of my past novels have been based on my personal killing experience, and that I find confusing. Ted Nasket, the main character and killer in my latest novel comes from a totally different mold and is everything I'm not. I feel comfortable writing about the horse set, but Nasket is a yachtsman, a member of a sport I'm totally unfamiliar with, and I find this personal shortcoming annoying.

The author ran his hand through a closely cut brush cut sorting out his thoughts on how to conclude the novel. The problems I'm experiencing with this exercise have never manifested themselves in my previous novels. I find myself venturing into an unfamiliar sport, and secondly, I have yet to define the identity of my next victim.

This dialogue I'm having with myself is taking me no place in a hurry. I might consider this folly on my part, but that's not the case. The process of killing a woman then applying the experience to the novel I'm working on has been a correct one thus far, and I see no reason to change it.

Returning to his desk, Martin Jeffreys began reading from a text he had earlier authored.

Ted Nasket is the guardian of the Hartford social line and has gained a renowned reputation based on his medical prowess as a highly respected surgeon and even more as a yachtsman.

In this novel, *Time was Of the Essence*, Nasket considers the police trying to catch him as a bunch of incompetents. Because of his brilliance, he is stirred to find the brightest detective in the Hartford Police Department and challenge him to a duel of intelligence. Nasket, the killer is possessed by the desire to make a fool out of the police and outmaneuver the system.

By reading past issues of the *Hartford Courant*, Nasket determines that Ralph English is the most productive detective in the department. Nasket based this assumption on the glowing praise that police brass lavished on English then leaves a note at his latest death scene that reads:

> "Dear Chief, I want you to assign Ralph English to lead the investigation of my most recent elimination because I am smarter by far than he is."

Nasket orders the low cut version of the Maine Hunting Shoe moccasin through the L. L. Bean catalogue. He drives to Freeport, Maine and pays cash for an identical pair of hunting boots at their retail store. He now has two pair of boots to carry out his artfully crafted scheme. He uses a belt sander to give each pair of shoes an identical wear pattern. One pair, he cuts a gouge in the tread of the right shoe, then wears that pair the night of the killing. After completing the murder, he intentionally leaves a partial print at the scene, displaying the pattern with the gouge in the sole.

Detectives led by Ralph English cast the print and quickly determine the shoe came from L.L. Bean. Nasket had been equally busy. Returning home, he destroyed the sander, sand paper belt and the pair of shoes with the gouge.

English's investigation eventually comes to settle on Nasket. He decides to brace Ted Nasket at the playground of the wealthy, the Hartford Yacht basin. The policeman finds Nasket holding a hose directing a stream of water on the superstructure of his boat. After some rather mundane conversation about the water and fishing, English forges ahead unabashed.

Confronting Nasket. The detective is certain the shoe will seal his fate.

"Show me the sole of those hunting boots," English ordered. Nasket with a cold and obliges, showing him a boot with no gouge. English's case is completely wiped out.

"You killed her, you bastard! There's nothing I can do about it, but I know you did it."

The author nods yes with an unaffected smile and mouthed to the detective, "I did kill her and you will never catch me".

Beautifully crafted I must say.

I'm now approaching the conclusion of my latest novel and I'm thrilled with the direction it has taken. I have escalated my own expectations of what I can do with the written word. F. Scott Fitzgerald had it all wrong when he said, 'Show me a hero and I'll write you a tragedy'. My hero is Ted Nasket and he's not a tragedy by any stretch of the imagination. He, like I, will successfully pull off his killing without a hitch.

This dialogue I'm having with myself is taking me no place in a hurry. I should consider this folly on my part but that's not the case, My formula has been a correct one thus far, and I see no reason to change it.

Martin, I'm amazed you've have made Ted Nasket an extension of yourself. It's a shame I can't share the very genius of it all with someone who would appreciate my cunning. Oh, well, I'll have to live with my little secret.

A rush of excitement overtook Jeffreys as the fact finally hit home. He has to dedicate himself to make writing a newfound religion, though he foresees a complicated future ahead for himself. He would make due until that time comes. Jeffreys made a dismissive gesture with his hand and reached in one smooth movement for the blueberry brandy, the answer to all problems.

5

Michie Tavern, the 'Inn of the Presidents', rests on the side of a mountain occupied at the top by Thomas Jefferson's famous *Monticello*. Pulling into the parking lot, one immediately becomes aware of the awesome view of Charlottesville and its surrounding suburbs. The centerpiece of this magnificent setting is the University of Virginia once called, "The grounds" of Mr. Jefferson's "academic: village."

As Red introduced his Bridgeton friends, O'Brennan instantly identified the best man. Within minutes, Colby Martin had blanketed the gathering with incessant chatter reserved for a bull stable. This curious little man talked non-stop as he made the rounds.

"Red, what's the story on this Colby character? Is he all there?" Jack said.

"Absolutely. He's a smart one, ranks near the top of the class."

"Maybe, but like you said, he surely is different," Jack replied.

Jeanette and Charlottesville Police Chief were rehashing high school days when O'Brennan and the redhead approached. "Ben Hurley, this is the famous Jack O'Brennan, Bridgeton's answer to Sherlock Holmes." A smiling Red Ted declared.

"Jack, it's nice to meet you, and I might add, your reputation precedes you. You've become a legend in your own time," Hurley said.

"Is that like a living legend?" Jack asked.

"I do believe you're correct." It was obvious Hurley and O'Brennan liked each other from the start.

"Let's adjourn to lunch," Red prompted.

The tavern's Bill of Fare known as the "Ordinary" proved to

be as enjoyable as portrayed by Cal. Over coffee, the long awaited discussion with Hurley started.

"Ben, give me a rundown on this UVa. co-ed," O'Brennan encouraged.

"I was a detective at the time, and a missing person crossed my desk back in 1960. I was assigned the case and never got out of the starting blocks with it, and that failure has continued to haunt me to this day. In January of that year a university student left Memorial Gym after a basketball game and inexplicably disappeared. She was headed for her sorority house to meet her boyfriend and never showed up. When Shana Barber first disappeared I requested dental records from her hometown dentist in Leesburg. Over the years, I followed up on the several skeletons found in the area, but to no avail.

"The first and only break came when Red and I got talking at the Legion. He subscribed to the Bridgeton *Citizen-Tribune* and mentioned reading about the skeleton unearthed in Smithbury.

"After hearing his story, off I went to Smithbury to check with the Richmond County authorities. At the times the skeleton was discovered, they couldn't identify the body so it was labeled a Jane Doe. Sheriff out there checked. I had forensics do a comparative analysis of the skeleton with the Barber girl's records, and that's when we made a positive ID.

"Now that we've found the first leg of the mystery, it gives us our first break. I can't pursue this because it's out of my jurisdiction, but I do have all my notes. I'd like you to take a look. I apologize for this imposition, but as you can see, I'm still driven by the thought of the Barber girl," Hurley said.

"Ben, that's a puzzler. I'm not the person you think I am. I got lucky with the Gill case; it's that simple, but this," O'Brennan shrugged, "I don't know."

"I'd say you're understating your contribution, but please consider taking a look."

After lunch, the Group adjourned to Clem's Place on East High Street. Red thought Clem's would be a fine place for an after lunch drink.

"Red, why would you come to a place like this?" Phyllis Eichner asked.

"Colby and I used to study here in the afternoon. We also dumped in some cold ones, right Colby?"

"Right you are, my dear redheaded friend. Let me tell you folks one thing. People in high places should occasionally drink in bars like Clem's. One sees the real world through the eyes of a workingman. It always has a settling effect on me."

"Don't be coy with me, young man. I repeat, why would you come to a place like this." Phyllis asked.

"I guess it's because I like to drink beer, ma'am."

Departing Clem's Place an hour later, Jack said: "Ben, we're staying at the Cavalier Inn across the street from Memorial Gym. Why don't we meet on the front steps at three."

Later, Jack walked across the street to the gym where he found Ben waiting.

"Jack, let's start in the gym and go through her disappearance step-by-step. It will give you a better picture about what happened. This is the old gym where varsity basketball games were played for years until they moved up to University Hall in the eighties."

Entering the ancient gym, O'Brennan was struck by the smell of yesteryear. The combined scents of sweat, wax, floor oil and the musty smell of days gone by confounded his senses. The grand odors finally came together in a collage of memories. The outdated gyms of past years came to mind as his thoughts drifted back to earlier days. Though larger, the setting reminded Jack of his collegiate days at Elon College. Walking around the gym's interior, Jack contemplated how certain smells are quickly forgotten if you're not constantly around them.

"As you can see, the bleachers have been removed, but back then they ran up to the running track." Hurley pointed to the track some twenty feet above the playing surface.

"How many people could they seat in here? Two thousand, twenty-five hundred?" Jack asked.

"I'd say that was about right. When the Atlantic Coast Conference was founded in the fifties most of the teams played in small gyms much like this one. The one exception was N.C. State in Raleigh. That one is still in use and probably seats fourteen thousand or so. Why do you ask?"

"What size crowd did they have at the game?"

"They had a full house that night for a seven-thirty game with William and Mary. Assuming the game lasted two hours, the crowd would have left at roughly nine-thirty."

"Did this Barber girl go to the game by herself?"

"No, she attended with two sorority sisters. I recently reviewed my notes and when I interviewed them, they indicated she had hung around after the game. They returned to the sorority house never to see Shana again.

"They also told me Shana had been dating a kid from her hometown, a guy named Andy Hamlin. He was a hell of an athlete down here; in fact, the last three-sport letterman at the school."

"That's unusual even back then." Hurley nodded.

"Shana and this Hamlin grew up together in Leesburg and started dating in the summer before their senior year. From all appearances, the relationship was very serious, or so her friends said. The sorority sisters also mentioned that Hamlin was picking Shana up at the house after the game. From there, they were going to the *Corner*."

"What's the *Corner*?" Jack asked.

"It's a block of businesses off campus that cater to the students. When I talked to Hamlin after her disappearance he was completely torn up."

"Did Hamlin talk to the girl after the game?"

"No, after the game ended, he dressed and walked to her sorority house. Not finding her there, he returned to the gym and still not having any luck again walked the return route back to the sorority house. Why don't we walk the route she would have taken that night in '60? She would have come out the front entrance, turned right at the bottom of the stairs and crossed the field. As you can see, it's a lacrosse practice field, but back then it was some type of athletic game field. She'd have walked up the right side of University Avenue to the crest of the hill, then crossed the street on her way to the sorority house."

"Ben, what's the distance from the top of the hill to Memorial Gym?

"Not much more than a quarter-of-a-mile," Hurley said. As they reached the crest, Hurley gestured with his hand. "Let's cut across University here, and walk over to Madison Lane. This should give you an idea of the route Shana may have taken." While heading for the sorority house, Hurley continued. "You can tell this is sorority row by the Greek letters. My notes indicate Hamlin returned to the Theta house about ten. Not finding her for the second time, he walked down to a joint called the *Orange*. Not finding her there he again walked the entire route. After returning to the *Orange* and still no Shana, he walked over to one of our patrol cars parked on the street and told them about Shana's disappearance."

"Let's assume it's ten-thirty by this time. They couldn't have planned for much of a date when she had to be in at eleven," Jack said.

"Normally you'd be right, but this evening was the exception. In the old days if you recall, girls had to be in by eleven, Sunday through Thursday or they 'd get campused. That Thursday was the last day of finals and traditionally the last day of the semester carried with it a one o'clock curfew.

"From the time her sorority sisters left the game no one could account for her. She walked away from Memorial Gym and just disappeared. There never was a lead.

"I'll let you take a look at my notes at the reception. Maybe you can make more out of them than I can. I have to go back to the office, so I'll see you tomorrow. Red placed me at the Bridgeton table, so maybe we can talk about it then. There is one item I completely overlooked. The Barber girl was missing her left little finger."

Returning to the Cavalier Inn, O'Brennan tried to organize

his thoughts on this Barber girl. There was an alarm that continued to sound in his thoughts that made him feel uneasy. Mention of a missing finger triggered his interest and caused him to resurrect the word serial killer from his memory bank. Although he previously had never worked such a case, he was somewhat conversant about the background of these types. The word artifact continued to bounce around in his thoughts. He knew these killers relished taking mementos from their victims. Was it conceivable the Barber girl's little finger was in the collection of some serial killer's souvenirs? O'Brennan dismissed that thought as too bizarre to consider.

Jack made his decision. Unless there was something earth shattering that settled on the horizon tomorrow, he didn't want any part of this case. There was no solid reason for his decision, but long nurtured instincts nudged his decision.

6

On a lovely spring Saturday morning, Betty and Red were married in front of the Rotunda on the UVa. campus. The Reverend Alfred C. Portland of the Ashbury Methodist Church performed the simple but beautiful service that joined this middle-aged couple in holy matrimony. It was a marriage ceremony Thomas Jefferson would have approved of.

Walking back to the Emmet Street inn, Jack said, "I knew Betty would look nice, but I never figured Red would look that slick."

"I agree, O'Brennan. His hair is neatly trimmed and everything about him sparkles. New suit, shoes, shirt and tie, what more could we ask for?" Jeanette said.

"Let's get crackin', I want to get over to the Legion and watch this Colby in action," Lloyd said.

The Bridgeton guests were on the way to a fun day and the wedding was only the beginning. Poised for action, the crowd milled around the banquet room of the American Legion with great anticipation as if waiting for a major happening they knew was on the way. Betty and Red's long awaited reception had started with the older contingent sitting back to watch the younger guests on the fly.

The little man from Massachusetts walked to the microphone and started rattling off orders like a Marine drill sergeant "Ladies and gentlemen, if I may have your attention. The bar will he closed in ten minutes, so please begin drifting to your assigned tables and be seated."

John waved toward the bandstand and asked, "Karl, what is this nonsense?"

"I honestly don't know. I've worked hundreds of wedding receptions, but never encountered anything like this. You get the ladies refills while I go after a couple pitchers of beer."

After the wedding party was seated, the diminutive lawyer asked the guests to stand for the blessing.

"Someone once said that greatness is not found but thrust upon us. This afternoon, the prayer has been thrust upon me." Laughter from his classmates swelled as Colby started his prayer.

After finishing the blessing, the pint-sized puff of insanity was off and running. "My name is Ernest Colby Martin, but everybody calls me Colby. I'm more than a can of tomatoes, yet less than something abstract; whatever that means. I was born and raised on Cape Cod in Massachusetts and am about as wild as one human can get. I joined the Marines after high school and ended up in the invasion of Grenada. After attending college at Bridgewater State, I traveled south to attend law school in this wonderful state.

"It was a good thing for Red that we became friends. If you recall, I carried him through three strenuous years of law school." A gigantic swell of laughter rose from Red's classmates as Martin returned to the attack. "Now that I let that little secret out, I must get on about my business. Red asked me to plan and oversee this reception, and I'm indeed honored to do so. I have set up ground rules for my party." Laughter again erupted from Red's fellow lawyers. "Excuse me, I meant to say for Betty and Red's party." More laughter. Colby raised his hand for silence. "What I present to you, dear friends is something I'm certain you'll understand and participate in. I've planned what I elect to call organized chaos."

Someone from the back called out, "Hey, Colby, quit jabbering and open the bar." This recommendation caused a happy response from the entire reception party.

"All of which will come in due time, Jake. Remember, even barbarians must have some degree of order."

"You never answered my suggestion," Jake offered.

Colby ignored the lone voice from the audience while continuing with his directions. "Upon completing my instructions, you will he called to the hors d' oeuvre table. After appetizers, the bar will be open for an hour. It again will be closed while you visit the salad bar. The bar will reopen for another hour after which we will be privileged to dine on the famous barbecued pork and beef from the *Red Squire* Restaurant of Spenser, Virginia."

From the rear of the room came the same voice. "Will you get serious for a minute and open the bar?" Red's classmates rose in support of this lone complainer in the crowd.

"I'd like to do that very thing, get serious for a moment, but not in the same vein you're thinking. Today and tomorrow are very important days to each and every one of us. Today, we've been honored by an invitation to our good friend's wedding reception. Tomorrow, we graduate from UVa. Law School and depart its hallowed halls of learning to embark on a lifetime journey in the discipline of law.

"We've all needed a friend or friends to help us through what may have been the most demanding three years of our young careers. Red told me about his extraordinary group of friends from Bridgeton. They were available with support when his needs were many, and that is about all one can ask. Colleagues, would you give Red's Bridgeton friends at table twelve the welcome they so richly deserve." The young lawyers roared as Colby continued. "Now, would the Bridgeton group please stand?"

Embarrassed, the oldsters stood reluctantly to the hoots and howls that flooded the hall.

"This squirrel is nothing more than a dead-beat," Jack said.

"Possibly, but he does have an ingratiating way with words," Vivian McGregor said.

"After dinner, some rather unique entertainment will be offered. After that, the top DJ in the area will serve you a menu of fun and danceable music for the remainder of the evening. Little Colby wants you to start dancing early and continue throughout the night, and that includes you old duffers from Bridgeton." More laughter swept the hall as Colby prepared to wrap up his running dialogue.

"In conclusion, there is one question I'd like to ask and one point that needs making. The first question. When you wash a dish, is it the hot water, the soap or a combination of both that destroys the harmful microorganism that has collected? Secondly, the point I'd like to emphasize is I want you to trust me. You are in very good hands, and ladies, I'm wild and the chief purveyor of mischief in this hall. I almost forgot, this guy from Massachusetts is like James Bond, he has a license to go for it."

"That guy is some piece of work and hasn't spoken a sensible word since he started. Do you know him?" O'Brennan asked Ben Hurley.

"Yeah, I do. Got to know him through Red. Colby is one hell of a guy and don't be fooled by his wild talk. He's a far cry from being a dim bulb and knows where he's going."

"Ben, how deep is he?"

"Fathoms and fathoms. You'll be amazed once you get to know him." Ben laughed at Jack's puzzled look.

After hearing more about Shana Barber from Hurley, Jack did an about face from his decision the day before and said to Jeanette, "Monday, I'm going up to Leesburg and check this Barber girl out. I know it's a spur of the moment notion, but I feel compelled to look into it. Would you like to ride along? If I decide to take the case, I'll want you along from the start. Suddenly, the feeling is right about this case. You could play an important role in this one." Jack wouldn't know till later how prophetic his words to Jeanette would be.

"I'd love to. So you've decided to go ahead. What prompted the change? Last night you told me you weren't interested, now you're interested. Any reason for that?"

"No," O'Brennan said, leaving it at that.

Pulling on his arm, Jeanette looked up with sparkling eyes and whispered, "Have I told you lately how much I love you, O'Brennan?" Jack put his hand around her shoulder and squeezed.

"And I truly love you, ex-madam lady." Jeanette laughed at Jack.

"Cut that out you two. You're acting like two teenagers talking about doing the nasty after the dance. I know I'm interrupting something wondrous, but our table has been called for hors d' oeuvres," Cal said.

The menu of the pre-dinner repast read like something out of New York's famous *21*. The pleasing array of dainties consisted of crabmeat stuffed mushrooms, hot fish pate, lobster souffle', spiced cod fish cakes and oysters Lockhart.

Standing in line, John asked Karl, "What are Oysters Lockhart?"

"John, you're such a cretin, I can't believe it!"

"A cretin I may be, but you still haven't explained what they are."

"They're broiled seafood mix over oysters on the half-shell."

Jack quizzed Red on one of his numerous table-hopping jaunts. "Red, where are you going to live?"

"We bought a house across from Jeanette, on the other side of Saints Square."

"When did you do that?"

"Closed April first."

"Do you have to do much work on it?"

"It's been completely refurbished. We bought new furniture here in Charlottesville, and trust me, the house is Betty's fiefdom."

"Jeanette, did you notice any activity across the square? Jack asked.

"Yes, but I never thought much about it,"

After Red left, John Lloyd returned to the table. "John, you've been flying around like you're on the make."

"Jack you found me out." Lloyd shrugged his shoulders and smiled. "You'll never guess what I'm going to tell you. I was talking to one of Red's classmates and he told me Red is number one in the class."

"That doesn't surprise me. Remember when those thugs were raising hell with us during the Gill case? We found him drunk on Jack's steps no less. He'd been dropped from Bridgeton Law, and that's when I discovered about his success at UVa. Isn't he something? He even outdid our expectations of him." Cal's smile looked like that of a proud father.

Later, Red wandered back to table twelve. "Why didn't you tell us you're number one in the class?" O'Brennan asked.

"I didn't think it was that important."

"We think it is. You should have told us."

"Jack, just forget it. It's a nice honor and that's that. Betty thinks more of it than I do."

"Where are you going to practice?" Karl asked.

"I have to take the state boards in August but I've already set up a practice in Bridgeton. My office is down the hall from Jack. Maybe I can throw him some business," Red said as he winked at the Group.

Shaking his head, O'Brennan threw his hands in the air. "You're incredible. Red, why do you have to be so closed mouth about everything?"

"I talk, you know better than that," Red said.

"You're right, you do talk, but never about yourself. We've been through the complete cycle with you. When you first hooked up with us, you were drowning yourself in booze. Isn't that right, fellows?" The men at table twelve nodded in agreement.

"You quieted down and helped a lot with the Gill investigation. I can still see you the Sunday you met Betty at Harbor Day. I also remember Cal saving your ass by helping get you into UVa. Law School. What you've done since is monumental, but you still don't see where I'm coming from, do you? We worry about you because you're young and we're old," Jack said.

"Jack, get off his ass. You know Red's going to do it his way . . . isn't that right, Red? Come on gang, let's sit back and enjoy. Colby called us old duffers and I guess he's right. But on the way, let's make this table the talk of the reception. We'll never see anything like today and tomorrow in our lifetime." Former city pathologist and current medical school professor, Dr. Cal Redout raised his beer glass in the air. "Here's to Betty and Red, God bless them and protect this lovely couple."

The Group responded with a sincere, "Here, Here."

"Will you have to prepare for the boards?" John asked.

"Hell no! I worked hard for three years preparing for them."

"I'm surprised you didn't go into corporate law or hook up with a big firm."

"What for, John?"

"Money, position, prestige, or anything else that crosses your mind."

"I have all that now. I'm loaded, or have you forgotten? I plan to open my own practice and that will give me the prestige of knowing the best bunch of guys in the world."

"Now, Red, you know that's pure rubbish," John said.

"Right you are," said a smiling newlywed.

"What area of law are you going to pursue?" Cal asked.

"General law specializing in veterans affairs. Both the young and old are faced with multiple problems. I have no need to earn money because of what I inherited before I went to Nam so I can really help them."

"That sounds good, real good, Red. Do you have any idea how you'll start practicing?" Ben Hurley asked.

"I know exactly how I'll do it. I'll go to the VA. I'm certain they'll direct some business my way. Then, I'll go out and canvas some bars I used to frequent. Certainly hit a pile of them wouldn't you agree?"

"How did you hit on this veterans thing?" Karl asked.

"It started in this building. One day I was getting my hair cut and started reading an article in an American Legion magazine. A congressman took the position that all veterans needed a more productive lobby. He based his premise on the reduced support veterans are getting out of Washington.

"What he said made sense, so I came down and joined this post. I'd come over and drink some beer, and gradually got to know some of the guys. When they found out I was in law school, they started talking about legal problems they had encountered. Sometimes I could help them, sometimes not, but that's where I got the idea."

"Red, what you've planned for your career is an admirable venture," Jeanette offered.

"Thank you, Jeanette. "It appears there are some down sides to the practice of law that may not appeal to me. There are a lot of poor guys out there that don't have a chance. Let me give you an example of what I mean.

"Last week when we finished finals, a couple of the older guys came over with Colby and me to let off steam. I got talking to a guy I know who was pretty well beered up. He got talking about his wife, and I thought to myself here comes one of those divorce things, but that wasn't the case. Seems she went out to Chincoteague Island to attend the *Pony Penning Days* with a couple of girl friends. Apparently they were to meet at a certain place, and when she didn't show up, her friends became alarmed. After a fruitless search, they went to the police. After an extensive investigation, a patrolwoman discovered her body in a patch of sea oats along the beach. She had been murdered.

"I told him I couldn't help; that an unsolved murder over a couple of months was tough. That's when he started crying. The poor guy sat at the bar and went to pieces. Here it was two in the afternoon and he's totally busted up. We finally got him quieted down, but he was really destroyed."

Red stopped talking to drink some beer.

"I'll never forget what followed. After getting himself under control, he turned to me and said, 'Red, what kind of a person would cut off her little toe?' How do you answer that one? I certainly couldn't."

Jack glanced at Jeanette with an incredulous look.

Cal recognized what appeared to be confusion between the two lovers.

"Are you all right, Jack? Your coloring indicates you've just seen a ghost."

Disregarding Cal's question, O'Brennan asked Jeanette, "Are you thinking what I am?"

"Yes, I am, O'Brennan."

"Yeah, Cal, I'm fine. Here's the story. I told you Thursday about Red's letter, and Ben's continued interest in the Smithbury Skeleton. We talked at *Michie Tavern* and later visited when she disappeared on campus. Ben was a detective in 1960 when this Shana Barber disappeared. Over the years, he tried to follow-up on the disappearance.

"Do you recall the body that was unearthed in Smithbury this spring? The highway department ripped down a bridge and replaced it with boat-launching ramps on each side of the river. The skeleton they dug up proved to be Shana Barber, the missing UVa. co-ed. Until now, there was nothing. Well, guess what? The Smithbury Skeleton had the little finger on its left hand missing! You take it from there, Ben."

"A young woman walks away from a basketball game and mysteriously disappears. Twenty-eight years later, her remains are found in Smithbury, some 140 miles from where she was last seen alive. Last year there's another body found with a toe missing. John, you're a detective, what do you think?"

"Has to he one of two things, Chief. It's either coincidence, or Ben, my boy, we have a serial killer on the prowl."

"This may sounds dumb on my part, what's a serial killer?" Phyllis Eichner asked.

"Phyllis, it's a killer who is accountable for a series of deaths. They may have occurred over a relatively short period of time, say months, or an extended period of years," Ben said.

The table buzzed about the latest revelation. They had whetted their appetite for adventure on the Gill case, and it appeared they were once again poised to embark on another adventure.

"What's your take on this, Ben? Do you think John is right; that we indeed have a serial killer?" O'Brennan asked

"Yes, I do. Let's hypothesize for a moment. Because her left finger was missing, I'm projecting the Barber girl as the first victim. Assuming the killer started with fingers, the woman in Chincoteague would either be the second or eleventh victim. I tentatively have to say she fits into the latter category and she's number eleven, although no evidence has surfaced that supports my conclusion."

"What do you say my friends, shall we go for it?" Jack said. Those at the table agreed they would support him any way they could.

"I like the feel of what you're about to do, and believe me, I'm looking forward to jumping in. It may he dangerous, but what excitement!" Jeanette giggled.

"This is more than a game, Jeanette. We won't know for certain what we're looking for until we account for other bodies," Jack said glancing at Jeanette.

"This is an area I can check out. I still have an attachment to this Barber co-ed, and I'd like to help. I can come up with list of deaths where a finger was missing; that is if there are such victims. You'll need a list of men and women, though I believe women are the object of the killer's lust," Ben said.

"Jeanette, let's go out to Chincoteague Island on Tuesday. We can look around and stay overnight. You'll go won't you?" Jack asked.

"I most certainly will, Jack O'Brennan. And as an added feature I'll pack a sexy little black nightie for our stay."

"You drive me wild when you talk dirty."

Laughing at Jack's comment, it was obvious Jeanette was excited about the latest turn of events.

"Karl, could you take us over to Grisfield on your boat? I want to go over to the island Tuesday but I don't want to drive around."

"Jeanette's my boss, so that's no problem," Karl said.

"Better yet, why not bring Phyllis? We can stay over and make a day of it."

Karl asked Phyllis, "What do you think?"

"Sounds like fun."

"Can we get a car over there? Jack asked.

"Absolutely. We'll pull into Louie York's marina and he'll loan us one."

"You call and make the arrangements for the car, and I'll take care of the reservations for Tuesday night," Jack said.

"Jeanette, remind me to check out this Charlottesville man who lost his wife on Chincoteague. Red, could you get his name and address?" Jack said.

"Yeah. I'll get right on it. I'm sure they'll have it at the bar."

"Jack, you'll be busy enough, so let me check the Charlottesville guy out. Plan on hearing from me sometime Wednesday."

"Ben, call after six, we won't be home much before then."

Red returned with the address. "The man's name is David Oden."

7

The reception turned from closed to open bar, then to the main course. Ben Hurley and his wife raved about the barbecue. It was excellent by all standards, but old hat for the rest of the table. After dinner, the tables were cleared, and dancing began.

"Jeanette, tell us about your trip to Rockport with Jack. I'm sure you're sick of telling the story, but this is a festive occasion, so be a sport." Phyllis Eichner coaxed her best friend, "Come on, tell it again."

"An interesting thought," Jeanette said.

Jack threw his hands up in mock despair. "Phyllis, you have been overtaken by madness and have taken this too far."

"Don't listen to him, Jeanette, let's hear it again. I love it and it makes Jack squirm so, I can't stand it," Cal said.

Jeanette turned to grin at O'Brennan with glistening eyes. "It may well have been my finest performance."

"Go ahead, Jeanette, tell your story. Holly and I are newcomers to the Group and haven't heard it," Ben Hurley added.

"Ben, I'll obey your instructions to the letter. My honey doesn't think much of it, but I get a kick out of it. I'm very pleased with the Rockport incident as I like to call it."

"Get on with it, Jeanette, the sooner, the better." Jack shook his head in a false display of displeasure. "But remember, she puts a different spin on the story every time she tells it."

"We were staying at the Sand Castle Inn in Rockport, Massachusetts, when this event happened. We've been up there several times since, but our first experience was something special.

"We went straight to our third floor room after we arrived at the inn. As we stood on the sun porch overlooking the Atlantic, it became pretty evident that Jack was doing everything possible to try and prolong going to bed with me. He certainly was nervous, I can attest to that.

"He talked about the granite shore being a gift from the sea. He then carried on about the sea gulls being different than the ones at Sands Beach, if you can believe that."

The Group laughed at Jeanette. As many times as they'd heard the story, it was still fun to hear it repeated. Each time she changed and embellished it to fit the audience.

"O'Brennan said the New England gulls were more driven than the ones down here. He talked about how nature knocked Sands Beach around while the shore at Rockport stood firm against time and how formidable and so on it was.

"I finally said, 'Jack, it's time.' I didn't know what else to say, so I told him I was going in and change. When I came out of the bathroom, Jack was in his shorts sitting on the bed with his back against the bed board. You know O'Brennan with his take-charge persona; well it failed him this time. He just looked at me with little or no reaction. I was dressed in black with a wrap-around skirt, a sleeveless blouse and heels.

"I walked over to the open doorway and looked at the water. After awhile I turned to face him and said, 'what do you have in mind?' after which I kind of gave him a simple little grin." This broke Cal up when she told the part about the grin. In fact he always laughed when she told it.

"I loosened the skirt and it dropped to the floor. That was when O'Brennan said something like, 'Well, you do whatever comes to mind', and of course I did. I guess you could call it a strip tease. Actually, it was just that."

Her friends laughed as Jeanette radiated a smile brighter than a flash of lightning as she looked around the table. It was evident in Jack's smile how he loved this woman. Each time she told the story, he appreciated her more. It didn't matter that the joke was on him.

"I was wearing a half-slip and bra, with a garter belt and stockings underneath my lacy tap pants. I looked like the merry widow all dressed in black. I looked at him, then turned and faced the water. I unbuttoned the blouse and it dropped to the floor. If I recall correctly, I said something like,

O'Brennan, you'll remember this day the rest of your life. Then after that, I turned to face the wall.

"Having read this in a novel, I thought it would be just right for the moment. With the ocean on my left and a nervous O'Brennan on the right, I turned my head and asked, 'what do you have to say?' After my last question, he just acted kind of dumb."

The Group again laughed. "I laughed myself, and figured why not, let's go for it. With that I reached down and pulled the lace panties right down. I stepped out of those babies and about that time, O'Brennan said, 'Jeanette, you're driving me crazy'. He sat there watching my little performance going on and I said, 'you haven't seen anything yet' or something like that. I reached around and . . ."

Phyllis interrupted with a laugh, "Tell them about the tattoo."

"Let me think, Phyllis." Jeanette paused for a moment then continued. "Remember the Freddie Gill case where the three people involved had a green shamrock leaf tattooed on their left shoulders? The brain of the outfit had a shamrock stem tattoo, and he turned out to be Senator Kenmore. This all came out in the trial.

"The day we went to the Senate Office Building to talk to Kenmore's Administrative Assistant Charles Bretton Hughes, he told O'Brennan everything and that solved the case. That same morning, we flew to Boston.

"On our flight from National to Logan, O'Brennan continually talked about what if situations. What-if we were wrong in our assumption the Stem wasn't Senator Kenmore? What-if the Stem got away? What-if we put an innocent man in jail? That type of thought. Apparently, this was on Jack's mind all the way to Rockport and he was having second thoughts about the case's conclusion.

"Getting back to my little strip-tease. Here I am standing in front of O'Brennan with hardly enough on to flag down a train, and is this bird nervous." Jeanette glanced at O'Brennan real quick, then looked away with a smile.

"Jeanette, you sound more like Jack everyday you're with him. Better stop hanging around him, because he may become a bad influence on you," Cal said.

"I'd been thinking about the situation for awhile, so the day before we traveled to Rockport, I went to a Five and Ten and got one of those tattoo kits the kids press on their skin. It's a make-believe tattoo that washes right off. I bought something green and cut out a little stem like the one O'Brennan had been looking for.

"While changing clothes in the bathroom, I put the stem on my left shoulder. Getting back to my burlesque act, while facing the wall I reached around and unhooked my bra. Now my routine was complete. Well, as complete as I was going to make it. I kept my left side away from him all this time so he couldn't see the fake tattoo. When I turned to get into bed, the green stem on my left shoulder showed for the first time.

"You should have seen O'Brennan, he almost fainted! You've heard him say 'Look at their eyes, the eyes never lie, they tell the whole story'. Well, his eyes told the whole story that afternoon. There was true alarm in them. All of a sudden here was the woman he loved wearing a green tattoo."

"What happened then? What did he do?" Holly Hurley asked, swept up and delighted by the story.

"He was stunned for a moment, then blurted out, 'You're the Stem. The wrong person is being sent to jail'. I walked to the bathroom and grabbed a wet face cloth. Returning to the foot of the bed, I wiped the fake tattoo off and said, 'No, O'Brennan, I'm not the Stem. I'm just an ex-madam lady who loves you very much'. And that, my friends is the end of the story."

"What happened then? Holly asked.

"I'll never tell. Is that all right with you, big man?" Jeanette replied. Jeanette displayed her magnificent smile to the Group and winked in O'Brennan's direction.

8

Red's reception was becoming a full-blown banger when O'Brennan asked, "Does anyone know who that woman is dancing with Colby? I've seen her someplace, but I can't place where."

"If it means that much to you, I'll check her out." John left the table in hot pursuit of the phantom lady.

"I've never seen John like this; what's gotten into him?"

"Jack, he told me he was in love," Cal said

"Okay, Doc, what are you getting at? You're telling me he's in love with a woman he never met."

"Exactly so. He also said, 'love takes us in strange directions'."

Returning from his table-hopping to rejoin the Group, O'Brennan asked Red, "Who is the lady dancing with Lloyd?"

"That fine lady is Professor Woodsen. She's a member of the law school faculty and one fine teacher. Jack, you getting tired of Jeanette?"

"I heard that, you goofy shit." The flush of embarrassment rose beneath Jeanette's tan as the Group laughed. "I never talked that way until I started hanging around with this savage." She glanced tenderly at O'Brennan.

John Lloyd returned to table twelve with the mystery lady. "Ladies and gentlemen, I'd like you to meet Professor Woodsen." After introducing her to the Group, John and his newfound acquaintance joined the gathering.

"Have we met? I swear I've seen you before, but can't imagine where," Jack said.

Their eyes focused on each other. "No, we've never met."

Short and to the point, Jack thought. *This woman must have taught her students how to be tough because she's pretty feisty herself. I'll bet she's around sixty years old but owns the best looking legs in captivity.* Woodsen's fair complexion was covered with freckles framed by short brown hair fighting to turn gray. A photo of her long slender hands would look great in a magazine ad. It was no small wonder John Lloyd was pursuing this fair-haired maiden like a hound dog.

"Starting next week, we'll be neighbors of sorts. I just retired from teaching and will live year-round at my cottage on Sands Beach."

"I also have a cottage on the beach and am a confirmed porch sitter. I've noticed you jogging by the cottage for years."

"You're right. As the kids say, I'm heavy into running. I've run in both the Scots Harbor and Georgetown 10 K's, and I'm going to Cape Cod in August to run in the Falmouth Road Race."

"Enough of this chit-chat, as you ladies call it. Professor, would you like to dance?" John asked in a courtly manner.

The lady professor made a let's go gesture while speaking to John "Lead on, you with the broad smile." Woodsen's response brought laughs from those at the table as she quickly rose to lead Lloyd to the dance floor.

Lloyd turned and gave the Group an okay sign, then followed the good looker out to gird his loins to the rhythms of Georgia Gibbs', *Dance With Me Henry.*

"They're an attraction of opposites if ever I've seen one," O'Brennan said.

"I don't care what you say, O'Brennan. I like her. Mark my words; something nice will come of this chance meeting, wait and see," Jeanette said.

Returning to the table, Professor Woodsen spoke to Jack. "John told me you're embarking on an investigation that may lead toward a serial killer."

"That is a possibility. We have what may be the first and last victims of a killer. As of now, we know little about it."

"I've done considerable work in the area of serial killings. Along the way, I've authored numerous articles on the subject and developed a course around the very same area. Coincidentally, Colby and Red recently finished the same course."

"Neither John nor I has ever worked a serial killer, Professor Woodsen."

"Jack, you'll find them different with a very dark side, that's a given."

"If I may, what advice could you give us on approaching such an investigation?" Jack asked.

Looking around the table, the Professor said, "I'd be pleased to help, but I don't know whether this is the time or place. Your friends want to a have a good time and such a serious discussion may interrupt the festivities."

"Professor, most of us were directly or indirectly involved in the Freddie Gill case. I'm certain you're familiar with its background and it proved to be an engaging part of our lives. Most people watch TV or movies and vicariously experience the adventure they see. The Gill case was real and provided a front row seat characterized by danger and intrigue. I speak for all of us when I say we're extremely interested. To me, this is part of one glorious day and I don't want to miss a minute of what you have to say," Jeanette said.

"We all agree with Jeanette, and time is not a problem. This party is just starting and a half hour here or there won't change a thing," Cal added.

"Fine, ladies and gentlemen, you're my kind of group. I'm beginning to enjoy your company, and why not? Serial killing is my bailiwick and I could consume the rest of your evening, but that wouldn't do. I'll try to give you some general insights of what I conceive a serial killer to be; somewhat an overview or base description of how he thinks. Before I start, please call me Liz, professor sounds a little stuffy for such a gathering, wouldn't you agree?"

A member of the graduating class on his way to a liver attack stood in the middle of the dance floor and dropped his pants. His quick flash caused the audience to shatter into laughter, including those at table twelve.

Shortly after, O'Brennan suggested Liz continue, which she did.

"Victims tend to be women or children and interracial. Thus, with two dead whites, you probably have a Caucasian killer. We know bizarre crimes have dramatically increased which points to perpetrators driven by psychological disorders.

"The two killings indicate they were stranger murders. A stranger murder is when the killer has previously not met the intended victim. I hate this, but there are exceptions. On occasion, the killer may initiate a casual contact prior to his fatal assault, and thus becomes a stalker.

"If your case truly involves a serial killer, he may do one of two things. One, he may return to the scene of an old killing and vicariously relive the excitement of the kill. His second option may be to take an artifact from the victim. How do I characterize an artifact? Usually, it's a personal item such as jewelry, a lock of hair, or a finger. That's the artifact

I'm talking about. There is . . ."

"Excuse the interruption, Liz, but could you give us a description or general pattern to our killer's social status?" Vivian McGregor asked.

Now full of herself, Woodsen continued. "Yes. He is reasonably attractive with his body make-up within the norm we tend to call average. He would have an average or above intelligence, and get this, his victims would tend to reflect a similar intelligence. The higher the killer's IQ is, the smarter the victim.

"He would come from an average or above average socio-economic base, and I'm sure you'll find a lack of bonding with family members and peers."

"Could you elaborate on this bonding point?" John said.

"Certainly. The lack of bonding I mentioned is the withdrawal of one's self from family or friends. He would tend to go his own way; be a loner if you will. There would probably be little loyalty or allegiance in any relationship he might have. Your killer would undoubtedly have a limited social life, and probably live in his own little world, so to speak."

"How would he relate to his fellow workers?" Karl asked.

"Chances are he'd interact successfully with them. You'll find he may be charming and well liked by his fellow colleagues. What do I mean by that? You would describe him as a nice enough guy, but kind of odd, difficult to get to know."

"The average person views himself as reasonably stable, pretty well adjusted, certainly consistent with what we call normal. How does the killer view us, the general public around him?" Jack asked.

"That's an interesting question, Jack, rather insightful. The killer views us, the general public, as responsible for his fate. They view authority as inconsistent and don't trust it. The type of killer I just described lives with delusion. His life of fantasy becomes real when the plundering begins. It is at this time fantasies take over and become the real McCoy. The killing is for real, and will be a carnal stimulant to his continued human destruction."

"Does he understand his predicament?" Cal asked.

"Partially. At some point, the killer is unable to recognize the difference between fantasy and reality. To sum it up, you must constantly remember that death is the last progression of the life cycle. If the killer controls this phase of the cycle, he validates his reason to continue."

"It appears your portrait of our unknown dispatcher of death is a most unhappy person," said a somber Jeanette Purchase. All at table twelve nodded in agreement.

John Lloyd could not take his eyes off Liz's face and whispered to O'Brennan, "Isn't she out of sight? I'm going to get at that, mark my word."

"John, words fail me," O'Brennan laughed.

9

Just then, the Colby Mark Show began. "Ladies and gentlemen, the University of Virginia Law School, Class of 1988 presents, for your viewing pleasure, The Red Ted Follies.

"You are now leaving the known for something out there called the unknown. Before we embark on this light-hearted venture, I'd like to tell a story. The Doctors McGregor and Redout at table twelve should enjoy this tale."

"An old man accompanied by his wife went to the doctor. Upon entering the examining room, the doctor asked, 'what is your problem, old-timer?'

'I can't hear,' responded the old duck.

After a rather cursory check-up, the doctor replied, 'I want a sample of your stool, one of your urine and a semen specimen on your next visit.'

Leaving the examining room, the old fellow asked his wife what the doctor wanted.

She answered in a very loud voice. 'He wants your shorts.'

A burst of laughter followed Colby's story.

"You know, this Colby character is some piece of work," John said.

"I personally think he's a glue sniffer. No one can get this wild without help," Jack said.

"If you ask me, he's nothing more than a wild little boy who never grew up." Those at the table agreed with Vivian McGregor's appraisal of this unruly comic.

"I don't care what you say, but when you talk about shooting the bull, this guy is magnificent," John replied.

"I don't know what kind of a lawyer this character will be, but his proper station in life should be on the stage," Phyllis said.

"Are you in the market for some first-class entertainment?" Colby called out.

"Yes," roared his amused audience.

"Excellent choice. Continuing on with the follies, our next act is of a musical nature. When I first heard this young man play, my keen analytical mind reminded me superlatives weren't needed to describe his accomplished talent. Being a patron of the arts, I arranged for this brilliant virtuoso to perform for you this evening. I defer to your apparent wisdom and present for your listening pleasure, Frank Costanza as the One-armed Fiddler. Will you please welcome maestro Costanza."

Entering the banquet room from the bar area, Costanza walked briskly to the center of the dance floor. Enthusiastic applause enveloped the short, heavy-set young lawyer. Displaying a deadpan expression, he bowed then stared at the audience until not a sound was heard in the hall.

Maestro, or Frank as he was commonly called, wore a raincoat with his left sleeve loosely suspended in a half-extended manner. A clothes hanger had been hooked to the back of his jacket collar and extended inside the left sleeve of the raincoat. His left arm was concealed under the buttoned outer coat.

"My friends, for my first number I shall play Beethoven's Sonata in C Sharp, more commonly called, Moonlight Sonata."

Frank carried the handle of a toilet plunger in his right hand. Lifting the handle he would use as a bow to the fake left arm, he began to draw it back and forth. The fiddler emitted sounds of "squeak, squawk, squeal" that glided throughout the room.

A voice from in back called out, "Hey maestro, your Sonata needs a little work, can't you play better than that?"

The fiddler's grave expression didn't change while speaking. "I shall try sir, I shall try," replied an unhappy Frank Costanza. Gathering himself for another assault on the Sonata, the unconventional sounds were again repeated.

From the back of the room, the voice again cried out as if

suffering extreme pain. "You ain't makin' it. That's the worst sound I've ever heard in my life; can't you get with it?"

Costanza once again faced his critic. "Your wish is my command." The familiar sounds of "squeak, squawk and squeal" again rose from the maestro and his withered left arm.

For his most savage attack, Costanza's adversary called out, "Maestro, do you realize your performance stinks and is smelling up the place. Can't you fix that thing?"

Frank's lips made a round "O" of surprise. "Ladies and gentlemen, the voice is correct. I shall indeed fix this thing!"

Costanza now went into action. With his concealed left hand, he pushed his index finger through the front opening in the buttoned coat. As he brought the plunger up with his right hand, he placed the handle in the waiting index finger. He then continued to the withered arm, where he appeared to adjust the make-believe violin.

Incredible as it seemed, here stood a fat little man wearing a buttoned up raincoat trying to fix a withered arm that didn't play. As he stood, the plunger was held at belt level by his index finger while giving all appearance of having his dink wrapped around a plunger handle. Laughter from the audience continued to swell as they noticed the great pecker scam.

Act followed act as young lawyers displayed their entertaining talent for those in attendance to see. The Group was amazed by the quality of the acts. The performance ran the amusement spectrum from instrumental to dance, with a stop for vocal, pantomime, and magic acts.

Of all the acts that caught the guests' attention, the impromptu one put on by Judy Webster won top honors. Overcome by a massive hops attack, the quiet and studious Ms. Webster slinked onto the floor and started to perform some minor gyrations in a sensual way that seemed unintended. The heavily endowed attorney's dance was quickly picked up by her colleague's makeshift band. Strains of *The Stripper* filled the room and turned her efforts into a full-fledged strip tease. Tossing her brunette hair around, she flashed a ravishing smile while pitching her horn-rimmed glasses on the floor as if to signal greater things would follow.

Grinding away to the salty music, this very spirited young lady danced herself into the altogether and into the hearts of those in attendance.

"I'll bet I know who gets the loudest ovation when she receives her degree in the morning," Cal said.

"This is like watching a night of the Ed Sullivan Show and Arthur Murray Show with food and drink. It's difficult to believe a bunch of kids could be so talented. That little band could play parties," Phyllis Eichner said.

"You're absolutely right, Phyllis, but you didn't mention that wild little boy masquerading as a lawyer," Jack said.

"Oh him, I think he's cute, Phyllis offered.

"Phyllis, we all have to display bad taste on occasion. Do you people realize we've been here eight hours? I'm so tired, I think I'm about to drop." Jack said.

Numerous acts followed as the night wore on. After the Red Ted Follies concluded, the DJ returned to play his earlier format of danceable music. All agreed it had been a fun-filled day and sleep would soothe if not heal their weary bodies.

On one of his many trips around the banquet room, Red found Colby entertaining those at the bar. "Colby, they're getting ready to take off. If you want to lay it on O'Brennan, you better do it now."

As the Group prepared to leave, Colby Martin again claimed the microphone and began his final assault of the evening.

"My friends, we've known each other for three years and you know I'm a man with a sterling character." Ripples of laughter started as he bowed to the audience. "Ya' know, ladies and gentlemen, I feel wronged. I'm the type of person that must deal with events as they present themselves, and this is why I'm going to be a good lawyer. It has been brought to my attention that a certain inflammatory remark has been directed at me. I feel obliged to attend to it this instant."

"If that little fellow is having as much fun as I am, then he's having a ball," Jeanette whispered to Jack.

"Colby started walking toward table twelve as Vivian commented, "Here comes that Katz and Jammer kid now. I wonder whether he's the Katz or the Jammer? I'm curious what that nasty little thing has in mind?"

Standing on the edge of the dance floor, Colby faced Jack as if preparing for the Gunfight at the OK Corral. "My friends, I'd like to introduce you to Mr. Jack O'Brennan from Bridgeton, Virginia. It's hard to believe that this so-called gentleman is Red's chief mentor. I'm crushed this pillar of his community would avail himself of our hospitality, and then turn around and maliciously defame the host. He made a false accusation against me, one that causes me true consternation."

O'Brennan saluted Red's buddy with a nod.

Colby stopped dramatically and pointed at O'Brennan. "This man accused me of having oral sex with a chicken. His cruel condemnation is a personal affront to me."

The little man's preposterous comment proved to be the showstopper of the evening. O'Brennan's comrades in arms went crazy with laughter. Jeanette laughed so hard she came close to falling out of her chair. Wanting to continue, Colby was forced to wait until the room returned to some degree of normalcy. Table twelve was beside itself as Colby prepared to finish his attack.

With a sweep of his hand, Colby returned to the attack. "The facts speak for themselves, he has attacked my character and that I cannot permit. In the near future, he shall look in the eye of the biggest defamation lawsuit in the annals of Virginia jurisprudence." Snickers rose from the wedding guests as the little man pressed on.

Turning again to confront O'Brennan, Colby brought his cupped right hand up near his mouth. In it he had a handful of finely shredded yellow tissue.

"I'm appalled this man would have the temerity to accuse old Colby of having oral sex with a chicken." Bringing his cupped hand to his mouth, he coughed and opened up his little finger. The particles of paper flew out over table twelve like a winter blizzard covering Buffalo, with much of the fake feather storm settling on O'Brennan.

Colby turned to again face an audience seized by uncontrollable laughter. "Friends, can you believe this man's effrontery to accuse me of having oral sex with a chicken?"

Covered with tiny shreds of tissue, O'Brennan looked up at the little man and laughed. Members of the Group had grown hysterical as Jack sat under a yellow feather storm. Laughing as hard as the others, Jeanette's laughter turned to sobs and tears as she said, "Good grief, I've wet my pants." Her admission caused another round of laughs louder than the first.

"Let's go back to the inn; this bird is wearing me out," Jack said as he stood to leave. "This Saturday has not been a run-of-the-mill day to say the least."

Returning to the inn, the Group talked about the fantastic day they had experienced. The thought of a serial killer poised to strike number twelve never crossed their mind.

10

Much of the drive from Bridgeton to Leesburg involved replaying the glorious two days in Charlottesville. The fun of the exciting weekend was finished, and Jack's thoughts centered on the investigation he was about to launch.

On this cloudless Monday morning, little stirred except the traffic blowing by them on their approach to Leesburg. The stately Oatland Estate was situated on the right as they approached the colonial city. Driving past the picturesque mansion, Jeanette commented on its classic elegance. They had no way of knowing as they continued toward Leesburg, that the case they were beginning would dramatically conclude in a former plantation much like the Oatland mansion.

"This strip between Warrenton and Leesburg may he one of the most beautiful stretches of road in America. Yet, people are in are such a hurry, they miss much of its beauty," Jack said.

Jack and Jeanette faced each other on benches straddling the front walk leading to the Loudoun County Courthouse

"O'Brennan, why would we come so early?" The courthouse bell rang nine o'clock as Jack replied to Jeanette's question.

"To take the pulse of a little southern city waking up. I want to see what's happening, and feel what's going on. Jeanette, look around at this delightful morning; smell the fresh cut grass and listen to the birds at their daily morning meeting. This is a close-hand look at America and we're sitting in the middle of it.

"I know what the people are feeling as they head for work. Don't ask me how, but I just know."

"What do you see that I don't?"

"I've been a detective for much of my working life, and it

will always be a part of me until I die. I'm trying to look at Leesburg as it used to be when Shana Barber walked these lovely streets. To understand what I'm looking for this morning, I must go back to yesteryear. Jeanette, there's something out there," O'Brennan vaguely waved, "that may give us some direction about this Barber girl's disappearance."

"O'Brennan, I've never heard you talk this way before."

Jack laughed as he stood up, "Come on, my honey, it's time we played detective."

After talking to the residents at 20 Mountain Street, Jack reported, "No luck. Both her parents are dead. Let's go over to the high school and see if anyone remembers her." Much of the morning was consumed looking for a Shana Barber connection. Jack was directed to the Silk and Lace dress shop in downtown Leesburg.

Parking in the municipal lot, Jack and Jeanette headed for the dress shop across the street.

"The lady at the high school told me Bobbi Jo Conlin is the lady to see. This Conlin owns the store and was formerly Bobbi Jo Greyson. She and Shana were the best of friends from childhood."

Entering the Silk and Lace, O'Brennan observed a cornucopia of subtle color tones. It didn't appeal to him, but never the less it was tastefully done. O'Brennan knew nothing of women's apparel, but he did know the display of dresses and accessories pointed to class and hefty prices.

"This is a very nice store," Jack said.

"It should be called a shop, not a store," Jeanette corrected. "I could spend all day here."

"Not today, my dear. We have things to do, and they don't include buying dresses."

A smartly dressed sales lady approached the couple as they stood near the entrance.

"Good morning. Please look around and if you need my assistance, I'll be by the resister."

"Hi, Jack replied. "We'd like to see Mrs. Conlin."

"One moment please, Bobbi Jo is in the back office."

Moments later, an attractive woman in her late forties approached the front of the store. "Good morning, I'm Bobbi Jo Conlin. How may I help you?"

"Mrs. Conlin, my name is Jack O'Brennan and this is Jeanette Purchase. I'm a private investigator from Bridgeton and, as of this morning, I'm investigating the death of Shana Barber. As you probably know, her body was discovered early this spring in Smithbury, which is some twenty-eight years after her disappearance in Charlottesville. Mrs. Tanner at the high school told me you and Shana were close friends, so that's why I'm here."

"It's a pleasure to meet you, and please call me Bobbi Jo. I'll do as much as possible to help, but that was a very long time ago. Please follow me to my office where we can be more comfortable, and we can have coffee." After she served her visitors, Bobbi Jo asked, "What can I do to help?"

"I'd like to know something about the Shana you knew. Her likes, dislikes; a capsule view of her personality."

"Shana and I were friends from the time we were little girls. She was pretty, a scholar and extremely popular. Shana liked the quiet life, and tended to stay out the limelight. She was quiet to the point of being shy. From the time she was a kid, she wanted to be a doctor and you couldn't believe how much she loved this town. She probably would have practiced medicine here if she'd lived."

"Did your friendship continue after high school?"

"Oh, yes! I attended James Madison and majored in elementary ed, while Shana was a pre-med student at UVa. We phoned, wrote letters, and visited each other at college."

"What were your feelings when you first heard Shana was missing?"

Bobbi Jo's voice thickened with emotion. "From the beginning, I believed she was dead. This spring when that skeleton was found in Smithbury, I got an uneasy feeling it was Shana. To this day, I believe Martin Jeffreys murdered Shana." She made her candor blatantly clear and left little doubt about her feelings.

O'Brennan immediately recognized the name Jeffreys as the prominent lawyer for the bluebloods of Smithbury.

"What was the connection between Shana and Jeffreys?"

"Shana dated him the summer between her sophomore and junior year in college."

O'Brennan couldn't think of a subtle way of wording the question so he bluntly asked, "Why do you think he killed her?"

"It's just a feeling I have."

"How did they get together in the first place?"

"Jeffreys was a rich kid from Smithbury. He lived on a big estate that had been converted to a horse farm. Shana and I worked in town for the Sky View Catering Service when they first met. Sky View did picnics and banquets. No, I'm wrong, they're still in business.

"They do parties for organizations such as the Masons, fire departments, Legions, and anyone who wants to throw a party. You name it they'll do it. Sky View's specialty is hunts, and I think they do most of the business in Virginia and Maryland. As an afterthought, they're big in wedding receptions and were leaders in the catering business back then as they are now."

"It sounds like you think a great deal of this Sky View."

"I do. They paid us well and treated us like first-class citizens. Sky View hired college kids; still do as a matter of fact. They have a large party house that is open all year. Between the party house and picnics, we stayed busy all summer long. With the low tuition at our state schools and the excellent summer job, Shana and I had a terrific thing going. It was a great job."

"And that's where Shana met this Jeffreys, at a horse show?" Jack asked.

"Yes, I think it was the *Saxon Hunt* in Smithbury, but I'm not certain. They started dating after that first meeting."

"What can you tell me about Jeffreys?"

"He was a great athlete and played football and basketball at William and Mary. Jeffreys won some honors for athletics and I know he was a scholar and president of the local Phi Beta Kappa chapter."

"He sounds like an all-American boy."

"Everything but."

"What happened to the romance?"

"It was just one of those things that happen. I think Shana got tired of him and the romance petered out. As the split developed, Jeffreys became more possessive, more demanding. At about the same time she started dating Andy Hamlin. By the time they returned to UVa. for their senior year, their romance had blossomed to the point where I believe they would have married; that is, until she disappeared."

"Is there anything you can tell me about this Andy Hamlin?"

"He was in our high school class . . . just the very best. He was a wonderful guy; and our very best friend and buddy. I don't ever remember Andy having a girl before Shana. It seemed he was saving himself for her.

"Andy is one of the very few people in this world that is liked by everyone. Little kids and adults, all like him."

"You've helped me a great deal with this information. We'll he back to visit you next week, and if you recall anything else, it would help. Remember, nothing is too trivial or insignificant in an old case like this."

"Did you start the dress shop when you finished college?" Jeanette asked.

"No, I taught first grade in town for five years. I quit teaching and started the shop in 1966. I decided if I was going to work for next to nothing, I could accomplish that by working for myself. The business has been a big success, but I've never understood the mentality of some of my customers."

"How is that?" Jeanette asked.

"The same people who come in here and spend outlandish money for clothes, squeal like pigs when a teacher gets a raise. That trite business about teachers being overpaid and under worked is pure garbage. That's one part of my life I've long forgotten, thank you."

"One last question. Have you ever talked to Andy Hamlin about Shana?" Jack asked.

"Yes, we've talked about her, but he's very reticent about the whole matter. Andy is a quiet guy to begin with, and although he never said much about Shana, I think he's still in love with her, or maybe her memory. Incidentally I talked to him last week."

"He's still in the area?"

"Oh yes, he runs the Village Inn over in Middlebury."

"What's the best way to get there from here?"

Conlin gave Jack directions to Middlebury, and then continued, "Once you're in the village, you'll have no problem finding the Village Inn. It's the oldest building in town and you can't miss it."

"O'Brennan, when we come back next week, we should spend the day. I want to buy some of these spiffy dresses and it will give you a chance to get a feel for the horse country in the area."

"That's fine with me," Jack said.

"Bobbi Jo, I love your inventory, and I will return ready to do business." Jeanette smiled as she reached to shake Conlin's hand. Thank you for your help, and we'll be back next week."

"I'll be looking forward to it," Bobbi Jo Conlin said as she ushered them to the front door.

The Village Inn, true to its billing, was a throwback to colonial days. Three rooms on the first floor featured dining at its best. Entering the lobby of the main dining room, Jack approached the hostess standing by the waitress station.

"I'd like to speak with Mr. Hamlin?"

"One moment please." The hostess soon returned with a giant in tow.

As the owner ambled toward them, it was obvious the world was his oyster. "I'm Andy Hamlin. Joan said you would like to talk to me."

"Yes, I would." After introductions, Jack bore straight to the point. "I'm a PI out of Bridgeton working on the Shana Barber case. I just finished talking to Bobbi Jo Conlin, and during the conversation she mentioned your name and thoughtfully suggested you might help us."

"Certainly. It's a lot quieter in the grill room, so please follow me."

They walked through the crowded dining room into an ancient barroom at the rear of the building. The old beam ceiling contrasted nicely with the rough stone foundation walls. Plank tables darkened by time and numerous coats of varnish provided dining space for customers. Red cushions placed on benches against the outside walls along with Windsor styled armchairs facing the walls on the other side of the tables appeared to guard the gentle fire stirring in a massive field stone fireplace.

"How about something to drink? I'm having coffee, but you're welcome to anything we have."

Jeanette and Jack agreed coffee would be fine. After it was served Hamlin asked, "What can I do for you?"

O'Brennan detailed Bobbi Jo's story, then asked, "Can you tell me about your relations with Martin Jeffreys?"

"Let me digress a bit. I started dating Shana the summer before our senior year in college. We'd been friends since we were kids, never dreaming we'd start dating as adults. She had dated Jeffreys for two years in college, and then suddenly dropped him. Shana told me she was sick of him, that he was too possessive during their romance. His possessiveness even carried over after they broke up."

"How did you get on with him during this period?"

"Not very well. We almost fought at the *Saxon Hunt*. At the time, I worked for Sky View Caterers and you probably know he was a member of the social register down there. It was like I wasn't supposed to date her, like she was still his."

"Was that incident your only problem with him?"

"No. Our little go-round started in high school with football in our sophomore year. He played tight end while I was a defensive tackle. Leesburg played a wide tackle six and I flopped to his side. Do you follow?"

"Indeed. I played the same position at Elon College a hundred years ago."

Hamlin laughed as he continued. "Ah, you've been there. My job was to jam him and disrupt his pass patterns. It used to drive him batty and I loved every minute of it. Jeffreys was a crybaby, sort of a whiner. The same thing carried over in basketball. He was slick while I was the bull, the enforcer type. He didn't like the hard stuff, it was as simple as that."

I've been there, Jack thought.

"Was he tough?" O'Brennan asked.

Hamlin flipped his hand forward and backward. "Not so you'd notice."

"May I ask about your relationship with Shana before you started dating her?"

"We were close friends since we were kids. It was almost as if I were her big brother."

"Bobbi Jo laid a heavy load on us when we stopped at her shop. She seems to think Jeffreys was responsible for Shana's death. Could Jeffreys have killed Shana?"

Hamlin's eyes appeared to intensify before he carefully chose his words. "Definitely not. He didn't have enough ass for that, and I still think he loved her." His face reddened. "Please excuse me, Jeanette, that just slipped out."

She waved her hand in a forgiving gesture.

"Why do you say that?" Jack asked.

"I know he was a pain in the neck, but it wasn't his nature or make-up to kill her or anyone else for that matter." Hamlin glanced at Jeanette as if to say, "I wish I could say what I really think."

"He was smart and good looking; why would he kill her? Jeffreys could have had any girl he wanted; no question about it. Could he have killed her?" Hamlin shook his head negatively. "No, I don't believe one word of it."

"What was he like, his personality I mean?"

"Martin was a quiet type yet arrogant. I'd call him a loner if anything. He never had much to do with the guys, but was terrific around the ladies."

After leaving the Inn, the two J's walked around the colonial village long steeped in the tradition of the hunt country.

Returning to Bridgeton, O'Brennan asked Jeanette, "They both seemed to answer with conviction, why such a disparity between their views?"

"I don't know, but when she talked about Jeffreys, the look on her face didn't support her words. I have a feeling she liked Jeffreys, or possibly she was mad because he chose Shana over herself. When we return to visit Bobbi Jo, let me talk to her"

"Why do you think that was a possibility?"

"Nothing concrete. O'Brennan, it's a woman's intuition you're hearing.

I'll bet I'm closer to the fact than meets the eye. There is one thing

I'm sure of, she knows more than we heard this morning, and I think she's linked with Jeffreys in some strange way."

"You may he right. Give it a try and see what comes up. At this stage, any bit helps."

"I have one thought that still puzzles me. When you talked to Hamlin about Shana, why didn't you ask him about the night she disappeared?"

"I thought of that question and you're right, it was the proper one to ask. It didn't seem so at the time, but it gives us another reason to visit the *Village Inn*."

11

The sun glistened on the mirror-like inlet waters as the Group assembled for their Thursday morning session.

"Did you hear from Hurley?" John asked, squinting against the morning sun.

"Yeah, he called last night. We may have been on target last Saturday at pretty boy's reception when we speculated about a serial killer on the loose. Hurley came up with nine unsolved murders in Maryland and North Carolina that could point to something. They occurred between the disappearances of the UVa. co-ed and the death of the Charlottesville woman last summer in Chincoteague.

That's eleven if what Mrs. Clark taught me in second grade is right."

"Jack, is it possible that could happen? How could there be eleven murders over a twenty-seven year period and no one connected them to a serial killer?"

"It happens, Karl. We're talking about three states and eleven separate police agencies. You just mentioned the killings took place over a period of twenty-seven years, and that accounts for some of it. These guys are overworked as it is and don't have time to look back. Time slips by, and that we can all attest to. Detectives are always working on something current, and without an early break, a case is committed to the back burner," O'Brennan said.

"Jack's right," Lloyd added, "without a break, past killings get lost in the shuffle. The poor victim quickly becomes a statistic. Sometimes, a single incident or word opens up a can-of-worms that may give authorities a new direction, but that's rare. Here's an example: if Red hadn't gone down to the legion post with his buddies after finals, where would we be?"

Lloyd tossed a piece of a doughnut to a passing pigeon out for his morning stroll.

"Red got talking to that guy who lost his wife at Chincoteague and her name came up. Probably would have slipped by if he hadn't mentioned the missing toe. Even if Red knew about it and didn't mention it last Saturday, we'd never know," Lloyd explained.

"We know about it now, don't we? Jack, speaking about Chincoteague, what did you find out Tuesday?" Red asked.

"We talked to a doctor who is the coroner out there. He talked about the annual *Pony Penning Days* held in July, and the discovery of the Oden woman. Death was caused by a puncture to the left ear, and her left little toe had been amputated. A horse chestnut was found next to her body. This he found unusual."

"What's so unusual about a horse chestnut? Karl asked.

"There are no such trees out there; odd, wouldn't you say? I called last night so you'd be ready to leave this morning. It appears there's a bad boy in the woodpile that has been very busy over the years. And to add insult to injury, he could make Jack the Ripper look like a choirboy."

A lone pigeon walking along stopped and looked at Red.

"You all agreed to travel to these murder sites, and that's why we're here. There's no need to reinvent the wheel when existing facts are out there. I drew up your assignments in a regional configuration. This arrangement should cut down your travel more than anything else. If you don't feel right about where you've been assigned, just speak up. I can make any changes you'd like."

No one commented.

"This is what I have. Cal, you travel to Winchester and Leesburg. Karl, you're going to Richmond. That's the closest place, and I know you have a heavy work schedule. John, you're penciled in for Frederick and Waldorf, Maryland. Jeanette and I are going to Galax, Virginia, Statesville and Winston-Salem in North Carolina. Red, you're a newlywed so you and Betty are going to

Southern Pines in Carolina on a belated honeymoon. What is your pleasure, gentlemen?"

"You don't give us much choice," Cal said gently. "You have me going to Leesburg; I thought you went up there Monday."

"Jeanette and I went to Leesburg on Monday to check on the UVa. co-ed who disappeared in 1960. Hurley's list shows another woman was discovered in Leesburg. That's the one you should check out. Any problem with your assignment?"

"None what so ever. I'm packed and Vivian will be ready when I get to her place."

"Karl, can you make it to Richmond?"

"Yeah, I'll probably go up this morning. If I have to, I'll go back tomorrow."

"Sounds good. Red, how about you?"

"Southern Pines is great. You're right Jack, this gives Betty and me a much-needed honeymoon."

"That leaves you, John. Any problem with Frederick and Waldorf?"

"None whatsoever; I talked to Liz and she can't wait to get at this thing."

"Liz is going with you?" asked an astonished Cal Redout.

"Why certainly," John said with a smug look coupled with a sweep of his hand. "She's been all over me!"

Red asked what the others were thinking. "And you're telling us she's going to sleep with you."

"It's very simple, my boy. Liz will get into bed on one side and I'll get in on the other. How's that?" John smiled modestly.

"Old friend, you're trying to tell us something, aren't you?" O'Brennan laughed at his rhetorical question.

"Indeed I am. Other than Karl and Red, I'm living in sin like the rest of you guys.

"It didn't take you long," Karl said

"At my age I don't have time to take long," Lloyd said.

"Doesn't that beat all, but enough about John's love life. Let's get on with the investigation. Ben Hurley contacted each agency involved with the individual deaths, and paved the way for your visits. The locals will provide a copy of each victim's file."

"What else do you want us to look for?" John asked more to help the others than him.

"The usual. Get copies of newspaper coverage if possible. Try to look at the site where the body was found, and, if possible, talk to any detectives around who worked the case. You'll probably have more luck with the recent murders. Just remember you're not experts so don't go off half-cocked. What the hell, do what you think is right!"

"When do we meet?" Karl asked.

"Plan on Saturday noon at my cottage. We can talk business, and then enjoy the beach, I'll pick up some steaks for supper or rather Karl will. Isn't that right old timer?"

"You're the one sleeping with my boss, not me, so check with her," replied a smiling Karl Eichner.

After his friends left, O'Brennan decided a walk around his cherished neighborhood would pass the time until he picked Jeanette up at eleven. The district was officially named Ford Ashland, but its residents affectionately called it *The Hill*.

The community is the most incredible residential area I've ever seen and I live here, he thought. *What more could I ask for?*

The early bluebloods of Bridgeton built their mansions atop the highest hill in the colonial city. To accommodate the needs of their domestics, the wealthy constructed brick row houses on the severe slope of the hill. Each home was fifteen feet wide and abutted the next house along the cobblestone streets. Eight-foot brick sidewalks rested neatly between the narrow streets and houses.

City fathers in the mid-sixties, who subsequently paid scant attention to the quiet district, determined through their infinite wisdom that the gaslights should be replaced with new styled mercury vapor lights. They further ordained the brick sidewalks should be replaced and reasoned the old walks presented a hazard to area pedestrian traffic.

The city's proposal of ripping up the sidewalks and replacing them with blacktop infuriated the *Hill's* residents. They claimed, and accurately so, the new walks and blue-hazed mercury vapors would dramatically alter the appearance of Ford Ashland. Their neighborhood was unique, paralleled only by the renowned beauty of Beacon Hill in Boston, and they weren't of a mind to have it changed.

In mass, the community moved to oppose this intrusive mandate from city hall. It was at that time Jack O'Brennan gained recognition as the unofficial mayor of Ford Ashland. Single-handedly, he rallied the residents into a tightly knit neighborhood organization. They raised such a ruckus; a compromise was struck with city council. Their success permanently bonded the residents into a coalition they fondly called *The Hill Stands Alone*.

The city agreed to keep the gaslights if the residents would refurbish the brick sidewalks at their own expense. Two brick masons residing on the hill supervised the walk restoration. Men of each street teamed to tear-up, clean the walk beds, and return the bricks to their former elegance. Once work was finished on one street, the team searched for other streets not yet completed and offered their support.

This unusual operation was most evident in the brick sidewalk patterns. Each street displayed a common colonial pattern determined by its residents. As a finishing touch, each homeowner planted a mountain ash in front of his house.

The *Washington Post* devoted a full page in its Sunday Home section to the dramatic turnaround of Ford Ashland. The story covered the renovation from its inception to completion, one month later. The most striking picture accompanying the story was a color photo displaying a sea of orange berries against a background of green mountain ash.

Jack's thoughts returned to the present and the task at hand. Although years had slipped by, some of the neighborhood's old guard continued to call him "Mayor" because of his earlier crusade to save the integrity of the Hill. The crusade he was now embarking on was much different than the restoration of the sidewalks. It involved the devils own kind and his lustful pursuit of unsuspecting women.

I better pick up Jeanette because she'll be hot to start on the trail of this killer, he thought. *She's excited about this mission, but I sense the chilling wind of fate swirling at my heels and that makes me uneasy.*

12

High tide gently invaded Sands Beach while the Group sat waiting for Betty and Red to arrive. Punctually at noon, they pulled into Jack's driveway, accompanied by a smiling Colby Martin.

"Look what we have here. Red, the last time I saw this young man, he was performing wondrous feats of lunacy at your wedding. Where did you find this fruitcake?" Jack said.

"Mr. Jack O'Brennan, say hello to your new neighbor," Red said.

"Hi neighbor," Colby responded with an impish grin.

"New neighbor?" Jack's amused smile turned to a frown.

"He's right. I bought that brown cottage yesterday." Colby turned to point to a shingled building three houses down from Jack's retreat.

They stared at each other as if meeting for the first time.

"You don't think much of me, do you?" Colby asked, a glint of amusement in his eyes.

"No, it's not that. You're so wild and different, I don't know where you're coming from," Jack said. "I thought you were going back to Cape Cod and live."

"I did go back on Monday, and that's when I started thinking about the law and my future. I'd been away too long to pick up again. My friends are scattered and I'd have to start from scratch. You know what? I didn't even unpack the car. Tuesday morning, I headed down here."

"Last Saturday, you told me how terrific the Cape was. Now here you are back already; what's the story?"

"The curtain is about to rise. Jack, I love this area and have a bunch of friends here. So, why not live here? I stopped at Betty and Jack's place, but they weren't home, so I drove out to the *Red Squire* in Spencer to see Jeanette. She wasn't there either, but fortunately for me, Karl was and set me up with a realtor."

Shaking his head, Jack turned to Karl, "You're responsible for this intrusion."

"Absolutely." Pointing toward Colby, Karl continued with an ear-to-ear grin. "Your observation is on target and I proudly take full credit for his presence at Sands Beach."

"You haven't had time to hook up with a firm yet, where will you work?" Cal Redout asked.

"You're right, I haven't hooked up with anyone, nor do I plan on doing so. I'm going to follow my old buddy's lead and launch my own private practice."

"And where pray tell do you plan on establishing this practice?" Jack asked with a sinking feeling. It was apparent he was losing control of this two-way conversation with this wild little man.

"Why, right here of course!" Colby smiled as he gestured toward the beach with his hand. "I'm going to call myself the *Lawyer of Sands Beach*."

The Group listened with considerable pleasure to the dialogue between the two mock adversaries. Colby was so quick, that if cornered, he'd say something stupid and laugh. They realized for the first time, what Ben Hurley had said about this character at the reception was true. They shouldn't be deceived by his wild and carefree style, because this young man knew where he was heading and had the intelligence to back it up.

"Jack, the old neighborhood will never be the same," Karl said.

Throwing his hands in the air, Jack replied, "Can you imagine living next to this beauty?" Jack's response brought laughter. "Well, the damage is done now. Let's get started on our reports.

"Jeanette and I went to Galax where Tammy Frame was found. She had been murdered June 5, 1964 and had earlier attended the *Shriners Horse Show*. She was found sitting on a bale of hay propped up against a horse barn with a baseball in her hand. Anything else to offer, Jeanette?"

"She was found with a missing little finger and was a very attractive local who had attended the show by herself. Her mouth and wrists had been taped. Oh yes, the poor thing had her head resting on her chest as if she were praying. I guess that's about it."

"We then went to Statesville, North Carolina where Mrs. Jennial Schemba had attended the *Tar Heal Classic* horse show. She was thirty-nine and was killed on a Saturday, April 8, 1978." Looking at his notes, Jack continued, "I forgot to mention the woman killed in Galax was twenty-four. She, like the Schemba woman, had died an a Saturday. Getting back to Statesville, the victim was found in a porta-john. When authorities reviewed the crime scene photos, they noticed a horseradish root in front of the toilet door. The john was located on the horse show grounds next to a horse barn. She also had her mouth and wrists taped.

"After Statesville, we then went to Winston-Salem to investigate a Mrs. Kersi Clark's death. She'd been killed May 2, 1985, and earlier had been seen at the *Tanglewood Park Steeplechase*. Mrs. Clark's body was discovered in a tobacco field near route 67, a highway running northeast from the city. From the pictures, she appeared to have been tucked under some broadleafed tobacco plants. The Carolina State Police identified what turned out to be a horseweed near the body, whatever that is. Incidentally, we were amazed by the amount of tobacco in the area.

"On Tuesday, Karl and Phyllis took us across Chesapeake Bay to Chincoteague Island where we checked on the woman Red mentioned at the wedding reception last week. This Mrs. Liz Oden was killed July 30, 1987 and was forty-eight, good looking, and came with two friends to attend *Pony Penning Days*.

Mrs. Oden was found in the sea oats at the top of the beach overlooking Assateague Island. A horse chestnut was found near her body and the old doctor that signed the death certificate found that strange because there are no horse chestnut trees on the island.

"That's our four stops. After our survey of dead women, I made several observations along the way. I wrote them out to make them easier to assimilate." Jack passed out a single sheet to everyone assembled. "I even made extras for any drifters that happened by."

"Thank you very much," Colby's reply brought laughs from the Group.

1. Each victim had a finger missing except the Oden woman who had her little toe amputated.
2. All had attended a horse activity of some sort.
3. All were attractive.
4. All had died of a puncture in the left ear, caused no doubt by a sharp instrument.
5. The killer is probably right-handed.
6. Each victim except Clark had her mouth taped with duct tape; their hands were secured in back of them.
7. Apparently, no valuables were taken from the victims.

After his friends had quickly studied his handout, O'Brennan made an observation. "I think our killer has been trying to play games with whoever investigates the killings. Something related to the noun horse has been found at the scene where each victim was discovered. Examples are: horseradish root, horseweed, horse chestnut and a baseball. Those of you familiar with baseball should know the ball is often called a horsehide. That covers our travels for the week. Karl, what are your findings?"

"Phyllis and I went to Richmond. Carol Barton had attended the *Deep Run Race Meet* and was killed, Sunday April 6, 1975. Her body was discovered at a location called the Jamesland Plantation. It's not far from Richmond.

"For five dollars you get a tour of this honest-to-goodness plantation; which includes the mansion and the outbuildings. This may be important. The house and grounds close at six, so she had to be dropped off after that. The Barton woman was found sitting in a rocker on the front porch. She was next to one of those big pillars at the far end of the porch. The porch, by the way, runs the full length of the building. She had a horsefly in her hair and a finger was missing. The denominators Jack mentioned hold true with this Barton woman. There's another thing that Phyllis knows more about than I do. You tell them."

Karl looked at his wife with a lost glance.

"The body was found with what appeared to be a fresh application of lipstick. The autopsy indicated small traces of smudged lipstick were found around the mouth. Karl and I concluded the killer had taped this woman's mouth and killed her. The tape was then removed and her smudged mouth wiped clean. A fresh coat of lipstick was then applied to the victim. The lipstick on the victim matched the tube in her purse. You know we'd never be without lipstick, so I'm assuming the killer used the victim's lipstick for the touch-up job."

"That's excellent. John, what did you and Liz discover?"

"We went to Frederick, Maryland to check on a Roberta Lehman. She died on Sunday April 30, 1972 at age thirty-two. She had attended the *Morgan-Arabian Horse Show* and apparently was taken from the show grounds to Hood College, primarily a woman's college in the city. This Lehman woman was found under a bush in front of Alumnae Hall. I should mention there are different names for the same building. It's also called Ad Building, or more commonly referred to as just plain Ad.

"Her body could not be seen as one entered the front entrance, but was spotted by a student leaving the same building. The report mentioned that a horse nettle was found nearby. I never heard of a horse nettle but it was in the report. Also, the left middle finger had been amputated.

"We then went to Waldorf, Maryland to check on a Mrs. Patricia Martie. She was forty-three and died June 25, 1983 while attending the *Charles County Fair and Horse Show.* We talked to a detective at the county sheriff's office who indicated she was found along the lane leading to a horse farm on the outskirts of town. She was found in a sitting position leaning against a fence post.

"I know this isn't germane to the case, but I find it interesting. This particular farm had dark stained wood fences that traditionally are white. I asked a gardener why the change? He told me the owners liked the appearance and maintenance was much less costly.

"Getting back to this Martie woman, she was found propped up against the inside of the fence. What we have is a driveway, a ten-foot strip of grass, and finally the fence. The grazing area is located on the other side, and incidentally, there were no horses in the field where she was found.

"When the morgue crew removed her body, they found it had been resting on a horseshoe. The possible denominators Jack mentioned are consistent with our experience."

"Betty and Red, how about you?"

"We went to Southern Pines. It's a terrific place to visit and we had a great time. Mrs. Donna Reader, age forty-two was found April 5, 1981 and had attended the *Stoney Brook Steeplechase Race* in Southern Pines. As you know, Southern Pines has numerous public and private golf courses, and Mrs. Reader was found at the halfway house on the Fox Brook Country Club."

"Red, what's a halfway house?" Vivian McGregor asked.

"Jack, you're the golfer in this crowd, you better explain."

"It's a building placed near the tenth tee on a golf course. You can get coffee, soda, beer and sandwiches. Traditionally, foursomes stop there for a couple of minutes before starting the back nine."

"We went out to take a look at it. What the hell, all we had to do was pull off the road and walk over to it. The second finger on her right hand had been removed. Too bad; Mrs. Reader was a beautiful woman. She'd been propped up against the side of the building. You can see in the picture. All the denominators hold true except for one. There's nothing related to a horse showing in the pictures I have. Here they are."

The Group looked at the pictures and all agreed there was nothing associated with horses. Karl was the last to check the pictures. He looked up and said, "Those are what they call horsefeathers in the picture."

"What do you mean by horsefeathers?" asked Cal.

"I'm talking about the rough cut siding which was popular in the old days. They would saw logs lengthwise an inch thick and overlap them much like we currently do with house siding. The picture shows the traditional look called horsefeathers."

"How would you know that?" Red asked.

"I know it, that's all. I've known it forever," Karl replied.

"We need more than a glib answer, Karl. Where would you find out something like that? We have nine people here who don't know about this horsefeathers business, yet you do. Any explanations?" Red asked.

Karl listened to Red with a detached pleasure. "None. I just know," Karl said with a smile. "Maybe I'm not as smart as some of the members here, but it appears I've somewhat closed the gap a little."

"Karl, my friend, you don't have to go very far to catch most of us." O'Brennan laughed as he looked at Cal. "Cal, how about you?"

"We went to Winchester where a Mrs. Rebecca Whitlow died May 4, 1986. Mrs. Whitlow, age forty-seven, attended the *Red Lion Horse Show*, which is associated with the Shenandoah *Apple Blossom Festival*. This I found interesting. Winchester is often called the *Apple Capital of the World*. There are orchards all over the area. Mrs. Whitlow was found in an orchard with a horse collar around her neck. And like the others, she had a finger missing.

"After that, we went to Leesburg to check on Ann Gardner who was twenty-eight, single and very pretty. She'd been murdered April 6, 1968 while attending the *Loudoun Point-to-Point Races*. Gardner was from Brunswick, Maryland on the Potomac River and had driven down to the Oatland Plantation for the day. She was found wedged between a dumpster and the back wall of the Loudon County Court House. I chec . . ."

"That's where we visited Monday. Oh, I'm sorry for interrupting, Cal," Jeanette said.

Cal shrugged as he continued. "I checked the autopsy report and true to form, her left ear drum had been punctured by the killer and she had a finger missing."

"Your case sounds like something I read," Colby said.

"What would that be?" Cal said.

"A mystery novel, that's all I read."

"And you're telling us you read this in a book, that's absurd. If you're serious, and I don't believe you are, tell us what the police found next to the body? Let us in on your little secret." Cal winked at the Group as if to say, watch this know it all squirm.

Colby appeared to drop off into deep thought. For the first time since the Group knew him, he appeared to be dead serious.

"Karl, it looks like your protege is in a little corner. Tell him that trash won't fly around this bunch, we're too good at it ourselves to let some rookie come in and snow us," Cal said.

"Come on, Colby, don't let me down," Karl spoke to Colby as if he were his own son. Colby was so deep in thought he didn't hear Karl's comment.

"He's so intense, he'll never hear you. I've never seen anyone with such concentration," Red said.

Displaying none of his earlier repartee, this strange little man from New England was totally engrossed in thought.

"I've got it, Cal." Colby couldn't turn his back on the challenge with which he'd been presented.

"Tell us the whole story and don't miss a beat," Cal said as he winked at the Group.

"She was wedged between a dumpster and the back wall of city hall. I'm pretty vague about the rest."

"You're not telling us one damn thing but just repeating what I said earlier about the incident. The only difference was where they found the victim. She was found against the courthouse," said an agitated Cal Redout.

"Well, it was city hall in the book," the equally annoyed little man countered. "Cal, you left out one important item, or were you going to tell us later?"

"What was that?"

"You didn't mention anything about what they found in a lunch bag next to her." Colby couldn't hide the elation in his voice nor did he try.

The Group caught Cal's incredulous look. "Please continue, Colby," Cal replied in a stunned whisper, his dazed look continuing.

"In the story, they found a new lunch bag next to the body. When the authorities opened it, they discovered a horse ball inside."

"Don't stop now, tell us more," John Lloyd said.

"I can't recall anything else. I read so many books, I can't remember much about them."

"He's right, my friends. This may give us a new direction to pursue." Cal smiled at the newest addition to the Group.

Red laughed.

"You were in on it, weren't you, Red?"

"No Jack, I wasn't, but I knew what the result would be. Though I must admit, I'm just as surprised as you about what he told us," Red patiently explained.

O'Brennan fixed Colby with a curious look. "What was the name of the book, and who wrote it? "Jack asked.

Looking at Red, Colby merely shrugged as if to say, "What do I tell them now?"

"Colby is a prolific reader. He reads every mystery and detective story written, and he's a speed reader to boot," Red said as he glanced around the Group.

"How fast can you read a book?" Cal asked.

Could this wild little man be another Red? A veritable genius masked by a facade of dim-witted humor. I'll have to observe this rascal more closely, Cal thought as he continued to observe this curly-headed newcomer.

"It depends on my mental state at the time. If I'm trying to show off, probably ten to twelve minutes., It will be fifteen to twenty minutes if I'm kind of lazy It really depends on how much I concentrate, and of course, the length of the book."

The warning bell in O'Brennan's head grew louder.

"It would help if we could find the book, and with it we'd have the author, and with the author, we'd have the killer," Karl contemplated.

"Yes, Karl, with the author, we could have the killer. Colby, is there any way to retrieve the title and author?" O'Brennan asked.

"No problem. I'll go over to the library and read the mystery section. I should have that out of the way by noon tomorrow, more or less."

"What do you mean by more or less?" Jack asked.

"A little of this, a little of that," Colby replied.

"That doesn't make any sense. Your lights are on, but nobody's home," Jack replied.

Colby shrugged as he answered, "What do you want from me, lucid thought or results?"

"You're not that fast. How can you hope to achieve such a gargantuan task in such a short time?" Vivian McGregor asked.

"I'll read a book of each author's work. When I hit the correct one, I'll know. It's nothing more than a feel for his style. Once I find what I'm looking for, I'll critique each of his books."

"We've been waiting for a savior like you, Colby," John Lloyd offered.

"By condensing each of his books, we may find a significant rhythm in his work that may redirect our efforts," Red said.

"We need to look at the whole package, not just the parts. I'm having a difficult time understanding this information. All these facts are pure gibberish to me. We have to organize this into some kind of time line." Jack suggested.

"You're right, this is a muddle. I can't make heads or tails of this mess either. We have to sort this information out, and I know just the person to do it. Betty's a genius on the computer and I'm sure she can make sense of this mishmash. Maybe the killer has developed some tendencies that will surface on a printout. Any problem with that, Hon?"

"No, Red. An hour or so should do it," Betty said.

"That makes sense. Let's plan on meeting here tomorrow at noon and review what Betty comes up with. Can you make it by noon?" Jack asked.

"No problem." Betty replied.

"Terrific. Let's forget about the case and enjoy the beach. That water needs some old bodies swimming in it," Jack said.

"Jack, wait a minute; I just thought of something. Come

over to our place tomorrow. I've hit on a new way to barbecue chicken, and I'd like to try it out. If it works, we may be able to use it at the restaurant," Karl said.

"Done. Noon it is at Karl's house. Now that we've resolved that minor business, let's get on with the afternoon," Jack said.

Colby nonchalantly headed for his car as the others prepared for an afternoon on the beach.

"Where are you going?" Red asked.

Colby exuded confidence while answering Red. "To the library in Bridgeton. Want to get a leg up on my reading. I'll see you at noon tomorrow, if the stars don't shine."

Colby's unflappable enthusiasm settled on the gathering.

Lloyd said, "Wow!"

"What do you think of his offer?" Cal asked.

"There's little that surprised me about that bird." O'Brennan rubbed his chin as if trying to gain more insight into the goings of Colby Martin. There's no doubt about it, that little rascal is more than one-dimensional and he's paradoxical. Plus, I mustn't forget he's a wild talker, but I like him."

Unanswered questions flooded O'Brennan's thoughts as he watched Colby drive away.

13

The Group anxiously settled on the front lawn of Karl's Scotts Harbor home waiting for Betty's comments.

"Betty, why not take over and review your computer list," Jack said.

"You already know there was no rhyme or reason to the material presented yesterday. I felt it difficult to extrapolate what you need to know, so I arbitrarily categorized the information into general listings. They include, victim's name, when they died, their age and circumstances concerning their death." Passing out the printout, Betty said, "That's all I have."

Shana Barber-disappeared 1/28/60, age 21 Missing after UVa./ W & M basketball game.

Tammy Frame-died 6/05/64, age 24 Found at Schriners Horse Show sitting against horse barn holding a baseball.

Ann Gardner-died 4/08/68, age 29 Found wedged between a dumpster in back of courthouse; lunch bag next to body contained a horse ball.

Roberta Lehman-died 4/30/72, age 32 Found in front of Ad Bldg on Hood College campus. Body hidden under bushes. Horse nettle found nearby.

Carol Barton-died 4/06/75, age 37 Found at restored Jamesland Plantation west of Richmond. She was placed in a rocker on the front porch with a horse fly in her hair.

Jennial Schemba-died 4/08/78, age 39 Found in porta-john on show grounds. A horseradish was found outside the toilet door.

Donna Reader-died 5/05/81, age 42 Found at FoxBrook Country Club leaning against halfway house on tenth tee. Rough siding on building is called horsefeathers.

Patricia Martie-died 6/25/83, age 43 Found along driveway on a horse farm seated against the post of a wooden fence; horseshoe was found under her.

Kersi Clark-died 5/25/85, age 45 Found in tobacco field next to road; horseweed found in her hair.

Rebecca Whitlow-died 5/04/86, age 47 Found under tree in apple orchard. Horse collar found next to her body.

Lisa Oden died-7/09/87, age 48 Found between the beach and sea oats. A horse chestnut was found next to body.

"Thanks, Betty. Your efforts should help. Let's take some time and attempt to translate this raw data into something sequential and concrete," Jack said.

For the better part of an hour, the discussion inched on about Betty's computer lists. Finally, after considerable debate, the Group appeared ready to draw some conclusions and express their observations.

"Are we ready to hear some remarks about the list?" Jack asked.

Soon a newly created list materialized that presented some interesting calculations.

1) The difference between the first and last date of death is 27 years.
2) There appears to be a distinct possibility the killer is murdering white women his own age. Starting in 1960, age 21, last year, 1987, age 48.
3) If number two is correct, that places the killer in the 48-50 bracket.
4) It appears the victims were born in or near the same year, 1938.

5) A horse related article found near or on the body of each victim.
6) The time between the murders is reducing. The second murder was in 1964 four years after the Barber girl was killed. The Whitlow woman was killed in 1986, Lisa Oden in 1987.
7) All murdered women had attended a horse-related activity.

"Liz, why such a dramatic change? If the pattern continues, we're in for another murder in the near future. Why would he kill again so soon," John asked.

"One, the thrill of the slaying has waned. The after-glow of the kill no longer burns as bright. Two, if he is writing novels as Colby's earlier disclosure would seem to indicate, the killings are the inspiration for his books. His writing skills have dramatically improved; he can probably write, revise and edit a novel in a year or less. If this assumption is true, he continually needs fresh experiences to perpetuate his writing. Thirdly, there is the continued challenge of the increased risk. Lastly, we shouldn't discount the killer's vanity. He must continually prove to himself and others that his intelligence is far superior to that of the authorities. There, John, I've tied the reasons in a neat little package for you. You may choose any or all of the above. Do you have any questions?"

"I don't like the picture you just painted of our masked man," John said.

"Like it or not, he's real. This chap probably doesn't have a clue to what happiness is. I'd like to throw out an idea about the ensuing investigation. Earlier you talked about developing a strategy for overtaking this killer. Maybe this will help," Liz said.

A slight wave of the hand from Jack indicated she had the floor.

"We have eleven isolated murders, probably considered insolvable by the local police agencies. I propose we draw a profile of our serial killer. A profile is nothing more than a calculated general description. If you choose to pursue such a venture, you must keep in mind it has it's limitations.

"Traditionally, profiling is done by psychologists and psychiatrists. You must understand there is a down side to profiling. The finished product may be too vague to help, and secondly, it can dramatically alter an investigation by sending authorities in the wrong direction. Are you with me so far?"

"Liz, may I interrupt? You may think I'm uncharitable, but I don't believe in psychological profiling. If we were going to take shots in the dark, I'd rather base them on statistical probabilities and common sense. We have here," O'Brennan swept his hand toward his friends, "a collection of very sharp minds. If we apply our smarts and instincts to the matters at hand, something may open up. But I confess to being leery of this psychological stuff," Jack said.

"I agree with Jack. I don't give a damn why she was killed, just the fact that she was killed is good enough for me," John Lloyd said.

Liz gave O'Brennan and Lloyd what looked like the start of a smile.

"Spoken like a true policeman. Do it the hard way. Hard work always pays off, isn't that right?" Liz said with a noticeable edge to her voice.

"I have no intention of debating this with you. To the contrary, we need your expertise. Lloyd and I are outmoded cops who believe in a high-level work ethic."

"Jack, that's an admirable quality we all appreciate. It must come with age because we both have a difficult time with change and new ideas. In fact, many of the ideas coming down the pike don't appeal to me either," Liz said as she extended her open hands toward O'Brennan.

Jeanette felt a swell of jealousy grab her as she listened to the conversation between Liz and O'Brennan. She initially thought the ex-professor was making a play for him, but soon realized it was her way of advancing her idea by placating the detective.

"John and I have never worked a serial killer before, and we're somewhat intimidated by it; it's that simple. I don't understand profiling and microscopic attention to facts, and I doubt John does either. Don't get me wrong, we tend to business, but this scientific approach to crime-fighting is alien to us," Jack said. "Wouldn't you agree, John?" Lloyd nodded yes.

"I appreciate your concern, but please hear me out. Help us put together a loose-knit profile and then evaluate it. If it doesn't work for you, then we'll forget it. But you must keep in mind there's no guarantee we're on target," Liz said.

"I'll buy it even though I don't like it. Anything to keep the family happy, right John?" Lloyd barely nodded his agreement with O'Brennan.

"Excellent. I've drawn some guidelines for us to follow. Let's try to get a handle on this sinister character."

For many minutes, the Group played mini-psychologist while filling Liz's profile for an abstraction known as a serial killer. Satisfied with their efforts, they were ready to analyze the results.

Classification	Profile	Reason for conclusion
1) Gender	Male	Speculative, few killers are female.
2) Race	White	Victims were white. Killers tend to be white.
3) Age	49-50	Point to killer being near victim's age at death.
4) Education	H. S. or above	Speculative
5) Sexual Pref.	Homosexual	No pre or post-mortem rape. Not sexually touched.
6) Marital Status	Single	Answered by (5)
7) Personal Habits	Neat	Manner in which he leaves victim.
8) Occupation	Clerical	Meticulous killings reflect eye-to-hand dexterity.
9) Residence	Not local	Obvious.
10) Stranger	Yes	Killer carried his own weapon. Calculated guess. related

I believe this profile may help us, but parts of it don't jibe," Jack said.

"How is that?" Liz asked.

"I see a flaw in our reasoning. In number ten, under reason for conclusion, we state the killer had not previously met his victims, but think about this. We should consider the possibility of the killer being a friend or acquaintance of the victim. That may be questionable but something we should think about. In number eleven, we point out the killer carried his own weapon. This indicates the killer is a stalker and predetermines his victims."

"You're right, Jack, I totally missed that. So, under number ten, Reason for Conclusion should be changed to, had met or made visual contact with his victim. Is there anything else? In that case, detectives, there's your profile. Where do we go from here?"

"I honestly don't know. Jeanette and I are returning to Leesburg tomorrow, but frankly, I have no idea what we'll find."

As talk was running out about what the next stop should be, Colby Martin entered the scene and announced, "The Prince of Disorder has just arrived." Crossing the front yard, he headed straight for the beer. After withdrawing two cans of suds he collapsed into a lawn chair and asked, "I'm sorry I'm late. What time are you having supper?"

"We're eating at six. By the way, you look like hell," Karl said.

Colby tilted his head to one side. "So would you if you'd followed me around since I left the cottage yesterday."

Quickly finishing one, and starting on his second beer, Colby tried to relax but was deluged by questions from all quarters.

"My terms are not negotiable at the moment so give me a break! Don't ask me any questions about what I found out because I need to relax. Information will come before the ducks start to fly; so be advised that Colby is incommunicado and is going to drink some beer until further notice."

"He'll know when the ducks start flying because he's up there with them. John, that Colby may he smart, but he has a different pitch on life," Jack said.

"You still don't see where he's coming from, do you? Colby Martin is saner than you and me. This wild stuff he passes out provides a facade to the outer world. It's not a barrier to isolate him from other people, but just the opposite, it allows him to go his own way. People like you think he's crazy, and that plays right into his hands." John said as he waved at the lonely figure sitting by the beer cooler.

The Group sat around making small talk as the minutes dragged into an hour.

Finally, O'Brennan grew impatient. "What have you learned?"

Swelled with success, Colby started to talk. "I'll give you a blow-by-blow look-see of my short safari. I drove into Bridgeton and went directly to the library and started reading. It was that simple."

"Did you read all night long?" Phyllis Eichner asked.

He couldn't stifle a smile. "Yeah. I read till ten this morning. That's when I crossed the bridge of years and found the author and his novels. I critiqued each story, then typed my report; fell asleep for an hour and came here."

"The library closes at ten, how was it possible for you to stay all night?" Jack asked.

Like an actor playing to a full house, Colby continued. "I was reading in the mystery section and got talking to a security guard. Every time he made his rounds, he'd stop and talk. He was intrigued by my speed-reading and asked me how I did it, and he wouldn't believe me and said to me, 'Look, I read mysteries myself. I don't believe you can read that quickly and want you to prove it. Let me get the novel I just finished, and we'll see whether you're fooling!' He soon returned with the book and laughed as he handed it to me. I really put on a show and read the damn thing in seven minutes. He timed me and that's how I know. After putting the book down, he asked me what it was about. I quickly critiqued it for him and that knocked him over."

"Get on with the story you little turkey," Jack said.

Colby paid scant attention to O'Brennan's comment as he continued. "He was a hell of a guy and brought me coffee, a coke, and even gave me a sandwich and a banana from his lunch. By this time the library was closed. He finished his shift at midnight and when the new guard relieved him, he asked him to let me stay as a personal favor. He introduced us, and told the new guy about my speed-reading. The new guy was as impressed as my buddy, Sid."

"You did good, Colby, but what is the name of the author?" Jack asked.

"For my next miracle, his name is Michael Rambush."

"That's a new name you slipped into the equation. What do you know about this Rambush character?" John Lloyd asked.

"Not one damn thing, but I'd guess it's a nom de plume. But when I come back from the library tomorrow, I'll have the size of his shorts." With that, Colby walked over to a lounge and fell asleep.

"Where do we go from here?" Cal asked.

"I'd say we're on hold until tomorrow night. Our newfound phenomenon currently pulling a sleeping beauty will come up with the answer tomorrow night. You can bet the farm on that," Jack said.

"Jack, what do you have planned for tomorrow? Cal asked.

"Jeanette and I are returning to Leesburg to talk to the lady in the dress shop. She thinks there's more there than meets the eye, so let's plan on meeting at my house at seven."

14

Tammy Frame June, 1964

Here it is May and I still haven't claimed a victim. I've delayed this action for no particular reason, but now realize I have to get on about my work. I'm using this tape recorder to permanently document my experiences, and that should prove helpful.

The *Shriner's Horse Show* in Galax is primarily attended by the horse set, although locals show up who are not as knowledgeable. The locals tend to be interested more in partying than observing the events.

This Tammy Frame that I'm targeting is one of the camp followers that regularly attend the shows. She like many of the regulars knows the sport and makes herself available for any casual encounter.

I'm excited about this new adventure and it deserves my fullest attention. Getting back to the hand held recorder I recently purchased, it's going to work out terrifically. I'll be able to tape my conversation and thoughts, and thus maintain a record of each new encounter. The only problem with this arrangement is I have to thread the reel, and that's a pain. In the foreseeable future, some smart person will design a gimmick that will eliminate this ordeal, but until that happens, I'll have to make do.

Having attended this meet before, I have no problem with the logistics of the event. This young woman is going to fit in nicely with my plan. I'm pleased Tammy Frame is to be my first assault because she should be easy. I worry that I won't be the first to pick her up. The word from my circle of friends indicates she's easy prey for a roll-in-the-hay. Her looseness could cause a problem because one of those Don Juans that frequent the events could claim Tammy before I get to her.

I have designed my strategy so I will always have a handicapped victim with a either a physical or mental disorder. It appears that my first venture in the lively art of homicide fits into the mental disorder category rather nicely. If she's not available, then I'll quickly vacate the premises. I have no idea how I'll approach her, but Martin Jeffreys never had a problem meeting and entertaining the ladies, and there's no reason to believe I'll have one now.

I'm glad I drove this little F-80 station wagon because it's so good in tight spots. I predict these mid-sized wagons will become very popular. Getting back to my assignment, the good feature about the wagon is its color. Gray is such a bland color, it will never be noticed.

If I have apprehensions about this venture, they're based on not knowing much about this young lady. I don't know where she lives, or what she does. The only solid fact I know about her is she's retarded. There are degrees of retardation and I would say hers is not severe.

I think as I pull into the pasture assigned as a parking lot for the horse show that there's a creature out there this afternoon who's going to be the proverbial little lamb being led to the slaughter. Ramming my pick into her ear will dispatch her in a hurry and a thrill runs through me thinking about it.

Getting out of my car, the thought sweeps over me *that people have secrets they never divulge. I also have secrets that can't be disclosed, but cleverly revealing them in future novels, I can vicariously experience and safely tell them.*

The pick I designed for these eliminations is truly a work of art. I would like others to see my handy work. It is craftsmanship in every sense of the word, but tragically, I can't show it to anyone.

Walking around the show grounds another thought hits me, I must not allow myself to fail; Martin, you have to get on with your task and see if you can find this woman. One last thought before I pursue Miss Frame; I've judicially designed a format for carrying out this meeting. Although I've built some flexibility into it, I still want to follow my original plan to the letter. The last thing I want to do is get nervous and free-lance out there. If for some reason she doesn't show, I don't know what I'll do.

Will wonders never cease? There she is now. Martin, you might as well get started on this new adventure right now. I'm walking up to her, and she's good-looking, I'll say that for her.

I turn the recorder on as I approach Tammy. "Hi, are you enjoying the jumping events?" I knew she was pretty from seeing her at other events, but never realized how beautiful this young lady really was.

"Hi, hello to you. Sure am. Nice day ain't it?"

"And whom do I have the pleasure of talking to?"

"I'm Tammy Frame. Why?"

What does she mean by "why"? I thought.

"I'd enjoy calling you by your first name. A guy like me doesn't get a chance to talk to a pretty lady like you every day. I might as well know your name."

"Yeah, I guess you're right. I am pretty, ain't I?"

"You most certainly are."

I looked down at her and had to admit she looked fresh and appealing. Wearing a blue cotton skirt, leather sandals, and a multi-colored scoop-necked peasant blouse that revealed considerable cleavage.

"And what do you do, Miss Tammy Frame?"

"What do I do? Tammy paused as if searching for an appropriate answer then made a puzzling statement. "I do a lot of things."

"Do you have a job?"

"Damn right I have a job. I'm a groom at the Cutter Farms down near Mount Airy, that's in Carolina. What do you do? Do you have a job?" She looked at me with a twinkle in her eye that indicated she knew exactly what she was doing.

"Yeah, I'm a printer and work up at the Collegiate Press in Charlottesville."

"That's nice. Do you make a lot of money?"

"Naw, I'm a working guy like everybody else. I'm not rich by any means, in fact, I'm just making ends meet, do you understand that?"

"Sure, I understand what you mean. I'm a little slow but I'm ain't dumb."

"You certainly aren't because I can see that from here."

"You know, we're talking but I don't know your name. What do people call you?" Tammy asked while crinkling her nose.

"I'm Alex Macon." After replying, I knew this was going to be easier than I figured. A dream comes true. This one here is thicker than a London fog, but I think she's on top of certain things. Let's see what she has on her mind.

"Tammy, while we were talking I got thinking. Do you have anything planned for later?"

"Are you married? What did you say your name was again?"

"It's Alex, Alex Macon."

"Ah, Alex, are you married like I asked before?"

"No, I'm not married. Hey, I'm a young guy out playing the field."

"Would you like to play this field?"

"This field. What do you have in mind?"

"Would you like to make it?"

Good grief, here I am trying to be smooth with her and she's putting the make on me. I can't believe this woman is propositioning me.

"You asked me if I'd like to play this field, then you asked me if I'd like to make it. This is fast stuff you're talking about."

"You don't really get it, do you? She laughed and that annoyed me. "Well, I'm not strange by any means, and I'll make this as clear as I can. Would you like to get laid today?" Tammy giggled as she looked up at me.

"I like the way you said that and you made it very clear. Indeed I would like to *get* laid as you so artfully put it. Do you have any thoughts as to when you'd like this to happen?"

"That's a good thing of words. Yeah, I'd like that. It will have to be at night because I don't do it in the daytime."

As I looked at this appealing woman, I realize how fortunate I was to have chosen her on my maiden project. She was falling into my little trap, and interestingly enough, it's all her design. Seeing I have an open field on this, I might as well work it to my advantage.

"Tell you what, let's meet at . . . see that building over there? Let's meet in back of that barn, and we can give it a shot. Will you go for eight o'clock? It will be dusk by then and we can really enjoy ourselves without anyone watching."

"I guess we've got a deal. One other thing, do you want me to take my panties off before I meet you?"

"No, Tammy, I'll do that. We can make that part of our foreplay."

"Foreplay, what's that?"

"Never mind. I'll take them off before we do it."

"Okay. It's time for me to leave. I've got to walk around and do some things. I'll see you later."

Feeling full of myself, I was faced with six hours to kill before I returned to meet Tammy. There was nothing for me in Galax and I couldn't stay at the show with that strange one walking around, so I decided to drive to Roanoke for a movie.

Driving back to Galax my thoughts returned to my upcoming date with Tammy Frame. What they say about her is true. She's an uncomplicated young lady, apparently happy and well adjusted, but she hasn't a clue. She's as big a half-wit as they claim, and she's hotter than a dime-store pistol.

Approaching the show grounds, my thoughts centered on where I should park the station wagon. My best bet is to park away from the estate. Parking a half-mile from the show grounds entrance, I proceed across the field to the designated meeting place.

I notice the parking lot is empty save for a beat-up Chevy, which must be Tammy's. There are no spectators around; that is a good omen. This is the right time and the right setting.

Turning the corner of the appointed barn, Tammy comes into view. Majestically seated on a bale of straw, she is waiting for her sexual encounter with this blond stranger. Sitting down next to her, I start my final dialogue.

"Tammy, I was worried that you wouldn't be here."

"I'm always where I'm supposed to be when I'm going to get laid."

"That's nice to hear."

"Do you want me to take my pants off so we can do it?"

"Can't we sit here and talk for a minute?"

"What do ya' want to talk about?"

"Oh, I don't know. We can talk about today's show, horses, whatever you want to talk about."

"I don't want to talk about horses. I'm around them seven days a week. Let's talk about diddling."

I decide not to wait any longer. To make small talk with this simpleton is proving to be counterproductive. She makes "My Friend Irma" look like a PhD. I have to eliminate her right now, and quit wasting my time. I reach into my pocket and pull out a baseball. I might as well get started with this final step.

"Tammy, do you know what this is?"

"Yeah, yeah I do. It's a ball."

"What kind of a ball?"

"It's a baseball. What are you, stupid or something."

"No, Tammy, I'm not stupid. Here take this and you can play catch with it if you wish."

As Tammy sat playing catch with the ball, I reached into my pocket and pull out my cherished killing case. The open leather case displays a stainless steel pick with the carved wooden handle nestled in a field of red velvet. Taking the pick with my right hand, I reached with my other hand into my pocket and pull out a roll of white athletic trainers' tape. I now have all the ingredients needed for a quick kill.

"What's that fer?"

"It's a pick I use to clean my ears."

"Well, that's kinda' dumb to use something sharp like that on your ears. You could hurt yourself with that stupid thing."

After her last remark, I knew I could play with this idiot, jerk her around a little before I drop the hammer. She isn't smart enough to understand what I'm doing. I'll give it a try and see what happens. This should be a great addition to my book.

"Tammy, how would you like me to clean your ear out with this little plaything?"

"Clean my ear out with that thing? No way!"

"Yeah, but this is different. I rub it inside my ear and it makes me feel good."

"Feel good?"

"Absolutely. I take it and rub it on the inside of my ear. Look, I'll show you." I took my finger and opened my ear so the inside was showing. "See, I rub the pick against this part and it makes me feel great. Am I going too fast for you?"

Tammy looked puzzled. "What do you mean by great?"

"You know, how it feels when you diddle. That's the great I'm talking about."

"That sounds jazzy. Do it to me right now."

I can't believe this event is turning into a piece of cake. I won't even have to tape her.

"Well, here goes. Tammy, you'll soon know what it's like."

I reached over with my left hand and placed it on her chin. With my right hand I brought the pick up to her ear. I decided to play out the string a little longer. I started rubbing the inside of her ear as if performing some mystic maneuver.

Tammy, I thought, *you're a heartbeat away from something special.* "How is that," I ask.

"I don't know. All right I guess."

"Can you feel anything yet?"

"No, I don't feel anything yet other than that thing rubbing on me. It doesn't feel the way it does when I diddle."

My stomach knotted up for a fleeting moment before I initiated my first heinous assault on womanhood.

"There's another thing I should mention, Miss Tammy Frame; you're going to feel something now." With one sweeping motion I covered her mouth and pushed the deadly pick into her ear. I felt disappointed in that she didn't cry out or struggle; she was dead before I withdrew it.

I propped her up against the barn and reached down to pick up the baseball she dropped during my assault. I placed it in her hand and step back to admire my work. Her lipstick appeared to be smudged so I use a handkerchief and clean her mouth. Using her own lipstick, I apply a fresh application and then wipe away the minimal body fluid that had seeped from her ear.

Starting to leave, the thought hit me; I had forgotten to take a prize from Tammy. I picked up her left hand and studied her fingers. The nail of the little finger was so small I'd have a difficult time inscribing it. I withdrew a rose pruning tool from my pocket and deftly snipped the next finger away. I placed the amputated member in a piece of foil and carefully wrapped it; my task was now complete.

I again stepped back to admire my work. This time I had it right, and now could head home to write my report. What a glorious day this has been.

Back in Smithbury, I finish typing the day's activities and read the gruesome details of my day's efforts. In it I included my impressions of Tammy, and the entire tape of the dialogue between us. As an added feature, my eidetic memory made it possible to include my impressions and thoughts that occurred during my encounter with Tammy.

Again talking into the tape recorder, I proceeded to create a conclusion to this glorious day. This material will provide a stunning backdrop for my second novel. I was stuck for a title until this moment, and now I have it. A Shriner's Nightmare.

It occurs to me that all the preparation spent on this stunning day went for naught because it was so easy. I must guard against being too complacent in the future undertakings. In retrospect, the game I played with this young lady from first meeting to my termination of her was fun. The feeling I received from that experience proved to be the zenith of my day.

In conclusion, the royalties from my first novel make me believe my effort had been well received, but basing my story on a missing person report isn't the answer. I'd call this a rewarding experience and I now have something solid to write about. I'm astounded more people don't enter into such a venture. After finishing my thesis on a quiet killing, I refill my brandy snifter, and radio sounds of the McGuire sisters singing *Goodnight Sweetheart Goodnight* drift through the room. You know, Martin, it's too bad you can't sing because if you could, you could have sung that pretty tune to Tammy upon doing your lovely thing.

15

The morning was much like the previous Monday in Leesburg. O'Brennan walked around the business section while Jeanette paid a visit to the Silk and Lace Shop.

"Good morning. I'm Jeanette Purchase and I came in with Jack O'Brennan last week. If you recall, he's investigating Shana Barber's death. I've returned to try on some dresses and talk more about Shana."

"Yes, I do remember you. I'd be pleased to show you some dresses and we can talk about Shana." Bobbi Jo led Jeanette to a rack of fall dresses.

"It felt so natural when I walked into your shop, almost as if you had designed this wonderful collection for me."

"That's very flattering but isn't the case. I have an idea of what my customers like, so when I attend the New York shows, I tend to personalize my orders."

Jeanette took her time trying on dresses she thought Jack would like. After her numerous purchases, Bobbi Jo led Jeanette to the back office.

"Last week when we talked, you mentioned how Shana met Jeffreys at the Saxon Hunt in Smithbury. Could you expand on that?"

"Certainly. Shana started dating him after our freshman year in college."

"How long did she and Jeffreys date?"

"Roughly two years."

"Then she started dating Andy Hamlin the summer before her senior year?" Jeanette asked as Bobbi Jo nodded in agreement.

"You earlier mentioned being with Shana when she met Jeffreys. Where did you fit into the picture?"

"Where did I fit in with Martin? You're coming on pretty strong," Bobbi Jo said.

"I didn't mean to sound that way, but this is my first attempt at questioning someone. If O'Brennan talked to you, he'd been more tactful, believe me."

Bobbi Jo smiled. "I understand, and I'll try my best to help."

"Did you ever date him?"

Reluctantly, Bobbi Jo began. "I did go out with him."

"Very long?"

"Several months."

"What happened?"

"I never did know. It was one of those casual arrangements that never took hold."

"Earlier, when you talked to Jack about Shana's death, you emphatically pointed a finger at Jeffreys. Do you still believe he killed her?"

"Definitely," Bobbi Jo replied. Her eyes locked onto Jeanette with a confident stare.

"Let me digress for a minute. We believe Shana's killer is a man and is probably responsible for eleven deaths. Yes, we may have a serial killer on the loose that may well have killed Shana. We have compiled a profile on the general characteristics of the killer."

Jeanette paused before continuing. O'Brennan always said to watch their eyes and Bobbi Jo displayed no sign of discomfort. Withdrawing a card from her purse, Jeanette began the critical phase of the interview.

"We believe the killer is white, and doesn't know his victims. He previously may have met them, but that's debatable. He's reasonably well educated with at least a high school diploma. He is conservative in his demeanor and life style and appears to be socially well adjusted. One other thing I should mention; he is fastidious about his dress." Jeanette paused to redirect her thoughts.

"Other than Shana, all the victims were killed by a puncture in the left ear. He is highly organized and very methodical. Serial killers tend to take artifacts from their victims, and our subject is a phalanges man. He takes a finger or thumb from each victim, with the exception of his last victim where he took a little toe."

Bobbi Jo looked over Jeanette's shoulder at a spot on the wall, not making eye contact with her visitor.

"All the victims were very attractive, and there had been no pre-or postmortem sexual intercourse with the women. That in itself tells us a great deal."

"And what would that be?" Bobbi Jo asked.

"We believe the killer is single and homosexual or with tendencies in that direction. After hearing this profile, do you still believe Jeffreys could be the one we're seeking? Could he have killed Shana?"

Bobbi Jo appeared to pull herself back from the past and guardedly began, "Much of your profile fits Martin, but I imagine it could fit many men, wouldn't you agree?"

"Yes, I agree it could fit many men," Jeanette replied, somewhat uncomfortable with the question.

"I do have a problem with parts of it," Bobbi Jo added.

"How so?" Jeanette sensed Bobbi Jo was approaching a delicate matter, and her questions should treat it as such. "May I say delicate matters present problems for all of us. What you say will be between Jack O'Brennan and myself."

Bobbi Jo nodded her head in understanding. "Your profile indicates the killer has a high school education. We both know Martin is a lawyer. Secondly, you mentioned the killer might possibly have homosexual tendencies. Martin doesn't fit that category." Nodding in Jeanette's direction, she said with finality, "I had sex with Martin on a regular basis."

The opening Jeanette sought finally arrived after which neither woman spoke. Finally, Jeanette reconnected the conversation.

"During your brief encounter?"

Conlin dropped her head then nodded. "Yes. Even after we broke up we continued to meet during the time he was dating

Shana." After Bobbi Jo revealed her past indiscretion, she appeared to become more uncomfortable.

"Did sneaking out with Jeffreys bother you?" Jeanette asked.

"Guilty like Cain. Yes, that part bothered me; still does as a matter-of-fact. I was young and sexually active back then. My secret arrangement with Martin was fulfilling for both of us, that I'm certain of."

"Would you say he was an experienced lover?"

"Indeed I would." Bobbi Jo appeared to warm to the subject as the conversation continued. "Make no mistake about that, he was the best!" She added with a smile.

A thought crossed Jeanette's mind as she stood up signaling the end of the conversation was near. *You'd think Bobbi Jo would have tempered her enthusiasm for the sex she had with Jeffreys. After all, it's been suggested he's a serial killer.*

"Based on our profile and what you told me about your affair with Martin, do you still think Jeffreys was responsible for Shana's death?"

"I guess all is not as it seems. I'd have to change my mind after hearing what you told me this morning. Martin definitely wasn't your man." Bobbi Jo's eyes twinkled as she escorted Jeanette through the shop to the front door.

"Thank you for your business and do return. I truly enjoyed your company. There are several small questions I'd like you to answer before you leave. What if your profile is incorrect? What if your serial killer is heterosexual and not a homosexual as you suggest? Where does that put your investigation of Martin Jeffreys?" Bobbi Jo asked, her voice trailing away.

Jeanette looked at Bobbi Jo Conlin as if seeing her for the first time. Did this mean a new start was needed? A puzzled Jeanette trudged away from the smiling owner of the Silk and Lace Dress Shop.

Jeanette found Jack seated in front of the courthouse.

"How did it go?" Jack asked.

"Don't bother me about the interview until my head comes around," Jeanette said.

Jeanette reviewed her morning talk with Bobbi Jo that evening at Jack's house. She felt guilty about blowing the interview with Bobbi Jo and expressed her feelings to the Group.

"Liz, what does this new revelation about Jeffreys do to our investigation?" Jack asked.

"Not one thing. Before continuing, I must comment about what Jeanette is presently feeling. The information you acquired this morning is valuable regardless of what you think about the interview. You may think you missed your chance, but to the contrary, that didn't happen. We haven't heard from Colby and I believe his presentation will be most revealing."

"Any new developments, Colby?" Jack asked.

"I've been busy most of the day, and what a day it has been. To the heart of the matter, our Michael Rambush is indeed Martin Jeffreys. Jeffreys' publisher is Balanced Books and they print both hardcover and paperbacks. By the way, Jeffreys' books are hardcover. The editor for all his books has been Judy Resin, and his agent is George Smitherly. Jeffreys has a die-hard group of readers which is indicated by the half million books sold for each novel."

"How did you come up with this information?" Jack asked.

"Well, I just came up with it. Are you suggesting I might become a good detective, as opposed to a good attorney?"

"No, neither, but for what it's worth, that's a handful of information you've come up with in one day," Jack said.

Ignoring Jack's comment, Colby started talking as he passed out handouts to the Group. "I didn't critique the novels, but I can give you the story line if needed. I've listed the year Of Publication, the title, year of the actual killing, and the origins of the title.

Release Date	Title	Death date	Title origin
1965	A CAVALIER HAPPENING	1960	Nickname for UVa. athletic teams.
1967	A SHRINER'S NIGHTMARE	1964	Victim attended *Schriner's Horse Show*.
1971	THE SADNESS AT LOUDOUN	1968	Leesburg is located in Loudon County.
1975	A HOODWINK	1972	Victim found on Hood College campus.
1978	A DEEP RUN	1975	Victim had attended *Deep Run Race*.
1981	A TAR HEEL	1978	Victim was killed in North Carolina, the Tar Heel State.

1983	A STONEYBROOK RUNS HE	1981	Victim attended *the Stoneybrook Steeplechase Race.*
1985	A COUNTY FAIR	1983	Victim attended Charles County Fair and Horse Show.
1986	A TANGLED AFFAIR	1985	Victim attended Tanglewood Steeplechase.
1987	A Sour Apple	1986	Victim was found in an apple orchard on the outskirts of Winchester, Va.

"There are several observations I'd like to make about the list. As you can see, the first book was published in 1965 and the next one in 1967, a difference of two years. From 1967 on, an irregular time sequence begins. We have four years, then another four years between books. He then goes from 1975 to his next book in three years. Again, another three followed by a couple of two-year blocks. Following *A County Fair* in 1985, his last two books are a year apart.

"There is an exception to this sequence; he won't have anything released this year. It appears he must strike soon to get back on schedule. Each novel uses an actual murder as the basis of the story line. Names are fictitious and locations have been jockeyed around. Maybe someone here can explain that business about *A Shriner's Nightmare* coming two years after his first novel, then going to four years for the next, but I can't. Each title contains a word that refers back to the site or event centered on the actual killing. The theme of each novel is a thinly disguised replication of an actual murder, but little else was changed," Colby concluded.

"Why didn't you critique the novels?" Cal Redout asked.

"I didn't add the critique to my print out because they totally reflect the actual killings they were taken from. I know this is the third print out and think that's too many, but it gives us another weapon. After analyzing the three charts, I'm convinced Martin Jeffreys is our man. There are two remaining horse events this season. The *Flat Run Horse Show* is next Sunday, followed by the Smithbury *Saxon Hunt* in two weeks. If we can somehow delay his next assault until the *Saxon Hunt*, we'll have more time to work something out. But, that's not for me to say, is it? You're the experts, so show me how it's done."

"Colby, you've just sealed it for us. Jeffreys is our man. We have to come up with something in a hurry, but I have no idea what it will be. Anyone have thoughts on the matter?" The Group offered no suggestions so Jack continued. "Anything else you'd like to add, Colby?"

Before Colby could answer, Vivian asked, "Being the prolific reader you are, how do his novels read? Are they quick reads and interesting?"

His thoughts drifted off for a moment, then he replied, "I'd say yes on all accounts. They're exceptionally good books and he definitely has a flair for the written word."

"Does he have the same central character in each book?" Jeanette asked.

"No. Each novel's main character is a detective from the local police agency involved in investigating the murder. I'd like to give you some information on Jeffreys I picked up from outside sources," Colby said.

"Let it rip," O'Brennan said.

"Jeffreys is a very interesting character. He was born November 17, 1939 and had or has a fraternal twin, Martha Ann Jeffreys. He was valedictorian of his high school class and was a star athlete. Even though he came from a wealthy family Jeffreys attended William and Mary on an athletic scholarship. He played football and basketball at college, and made the Southern Conference first team in both sports his junior and senior years in college. William and Mary played in the *Dixie Classic Basketball Tournament* in Raleigh his senior year. Back then; the Classic was the premier Christmas tournament in the country. He made the first team All-Tournament Team, and that shows you how good he was.

"Evidence of his other talents: he was president of the local Phi Beta Kappa chapter his senior year. After graduating, he attended Harvard Law School then returned to Smithbury where he set up a law practice. He slowly and discreetly assumed the legal matters of the community's four hundreds.

"Martha Ann on the other hand was an opposite to her

brother. Over six feet, she was described as heavy-set heavy, whatever that means. Martha was portrayed as not ugly, but not very pretty, either.

"She attended Sweet Briar College and disappeared after graduation. One story I heard implies that Martha went to Europe, but that was the last thing my friend knew about her. She graduated in 1960, and hasn't been on the scene since. That's all I have, but I'm sure there's more out there. I need you people to point me in the right direction."

"That's some piece of work, Colby. I'm not going to ask where you picked it up because I'm certain it's privileged. You're a real asset, and I know one thing; you could give a bloodhound a serious complex. While you were talking, I mulled over several steps that we should pursue.

"One, I have to meet this Jeffreys and try to sneak a peak into the twisted valley of his psychotic mind. He's a mystery looming ever larger on the horizon of this investigation, and I think the way to accomplish that is through golf," Jack said.

"O'Brennan, you told me you haven't played golf in years. How do you figure on playing after such a lay off?" Jeanette asked.

"At one time I wasn't too bad at the game, and it wouldn't take but a short time to get my game in order. Several years ago, Jeffreys got beat in the finals of the Virginia State Amateur Championship, and although I'm not in his league I can still play a respectable game.

"I know he plays at Fox Hills Country Club in Smithbury. Ed Giles plays there too, so when we finish, I'll have a little chat with Ed and see what I can rustle up. It's an imposition on my part, but I have to ask him. If possible, I'd like you to return to your previous visits and try to uncover something new. You may come up with a fact that could alter the direction of the investigation.

"Anticipating that Jeffreys is our man, I had copies made of his picture. If you decide to return, check around the horse set and see if they've ever seen him at their home events. This may entail talking to event officials familiar with the operation." Jack paused, and then said, "I have one last thought; be careful how you handle your questions. This is a very delicate matter and it's conceivable Jeffreys could be tipped off by someone you talk to," Jack said.

The meeting concluded with no dissent from any of the Group. They talked about returning in the morning to their earlier visits and appeared anxious to do so.

"I have one parting shot. You'll be gone Tuesday and Wednesday, so for the hell of it, let's meet at the Inlet Thursday morning, You ladies have never been down to the Bench at the Inlet, so why not come down with us? The guy on the lunch cart stops, so we can get you a good cup of coffee and some fancy pastries. Until then, let's call it a night."

16

Ann Gardner April, 1968

It has been close to four years since eliminating Tammy Frame, and I've now set a course to take Ann Gardner as my newest victim. My body seemed to twitch as I awoke to a horrendous hangover. Last night when reviewing the step-by-step procedures I would assume today, my apprehension seemed to grow. I did what I was afraid I'd do, and that was to consume a considerable amount of brandy.

The jet-like stilettos of water hammered and stung my body as if penalizing me for my romance with the bottle. Slowly, the shower erased the haze that had claimed my brain, and reminded me of today's agenda. I thought about my law practice and how demanding it had become. Sadly enough, it has left me with little else to think about except the law. It's been four years since my last novel, *A Shriner's Nightmare* came out, and although marginally successful, I'm now stirred to write again. The diary of my killing of Tammy Frame was a great aid in structuring the plot. I must be as exacting today when I encounter this new victim.

I chose the *Loudoun Point-To-Point Races* because this race is the watermark for all events on the East Coast. Ann Gardner, whom I shall pursue, may be the most beautiful woman I've seen in my life. Tall and thin, one might call her willowy. She fits the portrait I earlier drew of what I want in my victims. She walks with a severe limp and fits my need for a woman with a physical handicap. Over the last couple of years, I noticed she attends many area horse events and early on made it my business to identify her. Now I project her to be my second victim.

Entering the race grounds at Oatlands Plantation, the fact struck me that my estate and Oatlands could be twins because of their physical layouts. The weather had not been good to Virginia in the early part of the spring, and horticulturists projected a two to three week delay in the annual arrival of flowers. Although a devastating blow to the state's tourist business, I have my own priorities today, and they don't include worrying about the arrival of spring flowers.

I hadn't been at the show ten minutes when I spotted Ann Gardner. She stood tall, probably five-ten with pitch-black hair and displayed a creamy complexion. Drawing near to her, I realized how beautiful she was and what a lovely feature she'd make in my new novel.

"Hi, are you enjoying the running events?"

She turned and smiled, displaying brilliant white teeth, which only added to her stunning beauty. There is an elegant air that radiates from this dark-haired beauty.

"Yes, I am. Thank you for asking."

"It seems rather unfortunate to have such a spectacular event marred by this inclement weather."

"Yes. It feels so damp and bone chilling, and uncharacteristic for this time of the year," she said.

I concur. Driving in from Richmond this morning the weather report mentioned how the flowers will be peaking two or three weeks later than usual."

"I agree about the flowers, and I hate this cloudiness. It seems so gloomy."

"I can understand your sentiments because I'm experiencing a similar feeling."

We talked about the show's events until thirty minutes later when Ann drifted into a conversation about her personal feelings.

As I transcribe her words, my thoughts drift back to our conversation. It didn't strike me at the time, but now I'm puzzled by why Ann revealed her inner most thoughts to a stranger. Maybe she felt the need of a sympathetic ear.

"This mucky weather is driving me up a wall."

"How so?"

"I feel disheartened and that isn't good in the spring. It's something I haven't been able to shake, and I was hoping for a pretty spring day to lift my spirits. But it would appear that's not going to be the case," she said with a sigh.

"Why are you so down? A lovely person like you shouldn't feel that way."

"I'm depressed all the time. Not emotionally so, it's not a psychological problem I have. I just feel like a loser."

This lady has a reclusive personality and I should use caution in dealing with her.

"Having talked to you for only a brief time, I can see you're no loser. You know, we're carrying on a splendid conversation and haven't formally introduced ourselves. I'm Chad Seaforth from Richmond. I teach history at Robert E. Lee High School in the city. I'm single, twenty-nine and live alone and find myself not doing much with my life."

She laughed and said, "This sounds like a confession or something. Chad, it's nice to meet you. I'm Ann Gardner, and come from Brunswick, Maryland, which is just across the Potomac from here. Work-wise, I'm comptroller at the Waxby Container Company in Brunswick and am twenty-eight. Like you, I'm not doing much with my life."

"It's hard to believe that our situations are so similar. Would you like to walk around and take a casual look at the events?"

"I'd rather not, Chad. You see, I'm not much for walking."

"Why is that?"

"I had polio as a kid and it permanently damaged my right leg. Although it's not severe, I walk with a limp and find it somewhat bothersome."

"That was inconsiderate of me, and I wouldn't have asked such a stupid question if I'd known."

"That's perfectly all right; I'm used to it by now. Of course, there'd be no possible way for you to know, so don't feel badly about it, I don't." Stillness settled over us before Ann spoke again. "It feels so damp; is it possible to get a cup of coffee?"

"That's an excellent suggestion. The stand is over there, so let me scoot over and get some. Would you like something with it, a roll or pastry?"

"No, black coffee will be fine. Thank you, Chad."

While at the coffee stand, my thoughts ran to Ann and what a lovely person she was. I found myself becoming emotionally interested in her and that annoyed me. I vowed never to get involved with a victim, but Ann is such a splendid person, I find it difficult not to do so. I know this is a pitfall I need to guard against, but I feel attracted to her in a way I'm not familiar with.

"Here's your coffee."

"Thank you. I'm sure it will taste good on this gloomy day."

"Ann, this isn't any of my business, but you seem so down. To me, gloom is what we make of it. If I face adversity, I try my best to override it, to not let it overtake me. I know this isn't a very pretty day, but I'm going to attempt to do something positive. I'm going to rework your thinking and lift up your spirits one way or another. I want to make this the most eventful day you've ever experienced."

"That's nice of you, Chad, but I've lived my life under an umbrella of pessimism. When I was three, I was afflicted with polio and have walked with a limp since then. At the age of ten, my father picked up and left. I was an unexpected baby, having been born when mother was forty-eight. After dad left us, it was difficult for my mother and equally so for me."

"I spent an uneventful college career as an accounting major at Frostburg State. After graduation, I moved in with my mother and started working in Brunswick. Soon after, I began a relationship with a friend from town and it appeared we'd marry, but that wasn't the case. He went off to war and was killed in

Viet Nam. His death pointed me to a pretty dismal life. I'm now starting to get back into the flow of things, but it's difficult."

"Nothing should be difficult when a person is as beautiful as you."

"That's a lovely thought, and you embarrass me with it, but I do appreciate your kindness."

The conversation starts to drag and I find myself having a difficult time keeping it moving. This is a nice person, and I feel terrible about what I have planned for her.

"Come On, Ann, let's go for a little walk. I know you don't like to, but I couldn't care less if you have a limp or not. There are more important values in life than how one walks. Wouldn't you agree?"

I'll never forget how Ann looked at me. She appeared on the verge of tears, but gradually her appearance changed into a magnificent smile.

"Why not? If you don't care, I certainly don't."

We slowly walked around the show grounds observing the race activities. She put her arm in mine, and to all appearances, we probably looked like a couple very much in love.

"Ann, do you like horse events?" I knew she did, but I thought the question would be good to redirect our conversation.

"I do and try to attend all of them. It's about my only interest; you could almost call it a hobby. I have no background with horses, but as a young girl I acquired an interest in them. By reading all the available literature from magazines and books I acquired considerable knowledge and a love for the sport.

"The one aspect I don't much care about is the excessive high admission cost, although this event isn't bad. I suppose it really isn't much different than when a person buys a season ticket to his favorite sports team, or to the symphony orchestra, is it? To me, the music that comes from these horses is purely magical."

"You know, Ann, you have just articulated my thoughts exactly. I have always been attracted to horses. We all have dreams and I'm no exception. If I were to have an excessive amount of money, I'd buy a rundown estate. This imaginary estate preferably would be along the lines of a plantation like Oatlands. I would then refurbish it into the image I believe a horse farm should be. And what a way to spend this imaginary money!"

Ann nodded in agreement. "That's a spectacular thought, Chad. Now that you mention it, I'd probably do the same thing."

"We appear to be like that matched team of horses over there pulling the carriage; we're right in step. I got up late this morning and didn't eat breakfast. I just realized I'm hungry as a bear and could go for breakfast. How about you?"

"It's hard to believe but I was so excited about coming here this morning, I also neglected breakfast. I'm also hungry as a bear." Ann laughed.

"Enough said; shall we go over to the King's Club out by White's Ferry and have breakfast? They have a weekend breakfast buffet special, and believe me, it's a splendid offering. They have any and all breakfast foods imaginable on the buffet table. Are you familiar with this concept?"

"Not really, but it sounds inviting." Ann said."

On the way to White's Ferry, I begin to have second thoughts about killing this marvelous woman. I know this is a whim, but I should consider what is to be gained by destroying this lovely person? She's so delicate and appealing, it would literally be a crime to continue on with what I have planned. There will be other tomorrows and events where I can pursue someone else.

After a brief wait at the restaurant overlooking the Potomac, we are seated and then summoned to a buffet table that displays a large variety of breakfast foods. It is a delight watching Ann carefully choose small portions from each of the buffet dishes. As we dined, I observed how she appeared to savor everything she ate.

"I just love this sausage. Although I've never had it before, I find it delightful. Do you know what it is?"

"It's called Philadelphia Scrapple and originated in the Dutch Country of eastern Pennsylvania."

"What makes it so tasty?"

"It consists of ground pork, cornmeal and even pig's feet. I don't know why, but I have to believe the gelatin from the feet is important. Seasoning and chopped onion are added to the mix and I think that's it."

"Whatever the secret, it's wonderful. When I first met you I called this a gloomy day, it's not so anymore. Underneath the cover of those murky clouds overhead, you've brought me sunshine and joy, and for that, I thank you."

"Ann, I'm glad you're beginning to see things my way."

Our table affords us a panoramic view of the Potomac River and a small flat cable ferry crossing to the restaurant side. Ann picks up on the scene and said, "It's hard to turn your head on a setting like this. You have provided me with a remarkable experience. I'm going to take a mind picture of the scene before me and place it in my diary of memories. I've never seen that ferry before, and as I look out, I find the whole scene heartwarming. The clouds can't darken the beauty of this moment; of this I'm certain."

Muted conversations of diners drifting through the room go unnoticed. My thoughts slip back to what I had planned for her. To hell with the plans I've made. You, sweet lady, are going to escape with your life because you've displayed the softness and compassion that each member of the human race should have, including yours truly. The world we live in is bitter enough without losing a gem like this gentle lady beside me. I appreciate that my thoughts seem out of character for a killer like me, but I can't help myself.

Not bothering to return to the horse show, we spent the remainder of the afternoon looking at scenery as we drove around the back roads along the Potomac. As the sun sets, we stopped for supper at a small roadside restaurant near Middlebury.

Over coffee, I consider how I will handle the remainder of the evening. I have already decided on not killing her, and it would be in my best interests not to see her again. I might as well start the ball rolling right here and now and break this off before it begins.

"Ann, this has been a remarkable day. For someone displaying so much gloom this morning, you certainly appear to have enjoyed yourself."

"I have, Chad. We didn't see much of the horse show, but never-the-less, it was fun and isn't that the important thing?"

"Yes, it is."

"Chad, I would like to . . . this is difficult to say, but I suggest we treat this day as a very special one in our lives, and let it go at that."

A surge of indignation washes over me. "Why do you say that?" I asked.

"Because I mean it. My life has become so staid and controlled I would find it difficult to change. I'm obliged to take care of my mother, and that is the most demanding force in my life." Her dark eyes darted around as her voice began to waiver. "I was hoping I wouldn't have to say this, but it must be said. I sense a sinister quality about you that scares me. I apologize for being so candid and brusque, but those are my feelings."

I don't understand why she is turning on me, a sympathetic ear, when given her admitted state of despair. I've given her an idyllic day, one she has admittedly enjoyed yet she accuses of possessing a sinister quality. The woman has something damaged besides her polio-ridden leg. How did she find out? I asked myself.

Her statement leaves nothing to discuss. After her sharp comment, my anger continues to swell and I can't hide the agitated state I feel. Her last words had recast the die, and her elimination is back. It's too bad it had to happen to this lady, but I won't forget about her comment or her impending death. As I view this event in years to come, I'll have to believe her death was her own doing.

"I feel hurt you would think such a thing, but trust me when I say your thoughts are incorrect. I think we should head back to Oatlands and drop you off at your car, wouldn't you agree?"

"Yes, Chad, I think that's best for both of us."

As we leave the restaurant in the darkness of the night, I pull out my pick in preparation for the kill. After closing the door on the passenger side, I walked around the car and think, it's too bad my lovely that you are so frank. Starting the car, I reached over and grabbed her chin with one hand, and in a blink of an eye pushed the pick into her ear with the other. I am amazed that she didn't struggle or cry out. She just quickly died.

I returned to Leesburg and drove to the parking lot at the rear of the Loudoun County Court House. I take a finger and lodge her body between a dumpster and the back wall of the building. Before departing, I leave my little bag of goodies for the authorities to find.

Back in my Smithbury study, I take a gigantic drink of brandy to settle me down. After typing the recorded dialogue and my personal observations of the day, I file the report away, knowing full well that the memory of her fear-filled eyes will haunt me for many days.

I have to face up to the truth. I've put myself in an awful situation and am so annoyed at myself I can hardly believe it. I'm mad at Ann, and not because of her candid remarks. What she said is true, but the fact she put herself in jeopardy disturbs me. What the hell, she's dead and that's as big a jeopardy as one can face. If she had just quietly left the table and graciously made an exit, she'd be alive and home taking care of her mother at this moment. No, she had to be headstrong and tell me what she thought.

I question in what direction my life is heading. When I destroyed Tammy Frame, I found it to be an enjoyable experience. I'm still thrilled when I look at her finger. This Ann Gardner incident is going to stay with me for a very long time. Granted, I have her finger and shall place it with Tammy's in my collection, but it won't be the same.

The stupid game that has consumed me involves my personal drive for gratification. Is a human life so expendable that no remorse should be displayed? I think not. I'll not be able to face the recriminations I feel tonight, but know the answer to my problem is to drink that whole bottle of brandy. It won't lift my spirits, but it will wash away this distasteful day.

17

O'Brennan reviewed the history of the missing Charlottesville co-ed while sitting in Judge Ed Giles' chambers. He also discussed her subsequent discovery twenty-eight years later as the Smithbury Skeleton. O'Brennan tried to impress on Giles the premise that a serial killer was responsible for her death as well as ten other women.

"Ed, Martin Jeffreys is our chief suspect, and after you read these, hopefully, you'll agree."

Judge Giles studied the charts for some time before pushing his glasses up on his forehead and rubbing his eyes. "What you've told me, and what I've just read is difficult to believe. I find it hard to imagine Martin as a serial killer. I've played many rounds of golf with him and observed his performance in the courtroom. I think I know him pretty well, and find your accusations hard to accept."

"Jack, we've been friends for years, and I know you're a detective who doesn't go off half-cocked. I have rules about things like this, and find myself on the very dangerous threshold of uncharted waters. Regardless of my personal feelings, I shall not stand in the way of your investigation. So, within reason, I'm available to help you with anything I can."

"I'd like to put him under the microscope so to speak. How can I get to meet him?" Jack asked his legal friend.

"If you could play golf with him, that could be the best of all worlds. You know yourself a round of golf is an excellent barometer of a man's character, especially if he's playing poorly."

"How am I going to arrange that?"

"Have you played recently?"

"The last time I played was the week before Mary died."

"Martin is one of the best golfers in the state and plays out of my club, the Fox Hills Country Club."

"That still doesn't help me. How do I get to play with him?"

"That I can take care of. This Wednesday is the annual Men's Day at the club. It's a member-guest two-man better ball, as they so elegantly call it. You'll find it one terrific event with nine holes in the morning, lunch at the halfway house, and the back nine in the afternoon. After a cocktail hour, a steak roast follows along with awards. I hadn't planned on playing, but you can play as my guest. I'll make arrangements with Biggs Nelson to be paired with Martin."

"That's terrific, Ed. I really appreciate your help,"

"You'll need all the help you can muster. Now comes the sixty-four dollar question; can you get your game in order by then? Remember, you only have tomorrow to work or it."

"I can't guarantee anything. It will be a problem, that's obvious, but one I can manage. I'll go to the range and hit a ton of balls. I never played much when I was involved with the game, probably no more than once a week. The driving range was my secret. Every day I didn't play, I'd use a different club to hit a hundred balls. I'll go through the same routine in the morning and that should do it. It won't be pretty, mind you, but I'll be respectable. I always could move the ball, so I won't slow you down."

"The big question is, can you score?" Judge Giles asked.

"You know this from your own experience. When starting the season in the spring, the average golfer tries to meet the ball and gives up distance. No over swinging like in mid-season, and that's where I'll be, that you can count on."

Giles laughed. "You've told me how terrific you used to be, and I know you'll be prepared; but does that monster called Fox Hills know it?"

Driving out to the Fox Hills Country Club, Jack's sore hands reflected the arduous Tuesday he'd spent at the driving range.

Although not confident with his ball striking, he still felt good about his game. He was pleased to be returning to the game he once loved, and for the first time realized how much he had missed it. There was a special feeling one experienced when heading for the links. *Regardless of whether I'm playing a good or bad course, the feeling is always the same. I can't wait to get at it. What a course I'm playing today;* O'Brennan thought as he looked to his left at the back nine of this fashionable playground for the rich.

Turning left into the drive of the posh setting, O'Brennan felt stunned by its beauty. Looking right at the plush fairway of the ninth hole that snaked its way along the drive, thoughts of how he'd play this difficult course ran through his mind. He passed the Jeffersonian-styled red brick clubhouse as he headed toward the parking lot in the rear. Its elegance announced to the world that the Fox Hills Country Club was the centerpiece of prestige, power and wealth on Virginia's eastern seaboard.

Parking the Blazer, O'Brennan carried his bag past the busy putting green toward the pro shop. Waiting by the locker room, Ed Giles called out, "I have a locker for you. Let's go in and get settled."

Giles introduced O'Brennan to Martin Jeffreys and his playing partner, Ted Willard. As Jack moved toward his opponent, a nod of Jeffreys' head made a handshake unnecessary. Never having met Jeffreys, he was surprised by his size. Although six-two and slightly over two hundred, Jeffreys appeared to possess a boyish quality that Jack couldn't place.

On the way to the first tee, O'Brennan replayed his last thoughts. The idea of Jeffreys looking like a young man was absurd, although he did have a youthful look. Maybe it was his graying hair and fair complexion that provided that illusion. His brush cut along with a full mouth and lantern-like jaw made him look like Joe Palooka. Jack noticed his large forearms and their muscle development. It was obvious Jeffreys was a weight lifter.

As the foursome loosened up for the opening drives, Jack attempted to puff up Jeffreys' ego by saying, "Over the years I've followed and admired your amateur career. You've had great success."

Boredom graced Jeffreys' face as he answered, "Thank you for your gracious comment. We live our lives chasing dreams we'll never catch, and that is certainly true in my case. My dream was to be a professional golfer. A funny thing happened along the way. I found out I wasn't good enough." Jeffreys sighed as he looked away.

"As far as I'm concerned, you're a terrific golfer and I'm pleased to be in your foursome."

"Thank you, Jack. I appreciate your kind words. Shall we begin?"

Winning the coin flip, Ed Giles hit a safe but unimpressive tee shot. Jack felt anxiety build as he teed up his ball. The discipline that Jack had known his entire life took over and he quickly wiped the panic that had briefly overtaken him from his mind.

With a smooth swing, Jack produced a safe drive. After Willard hit, he evaluated Jeffreys as he approached the ball. His grooved swing produced a booming drive that found the middle of the fairway some fifty yards beyond O'Brennan's feeble two hundred-twenty yard shot.

Jack took comfort in knowing his drive was straight while Jeffreys seemed pleased he had produced the longest drive of the foursome. O'Brennan wondered how he'd react if out driven.

After six holes, Jeffreys and Willard were three under while the Judge and Jack played credibly with a one under. Jack observed the confidence Jeffreys was displaying hole after hole and felt more comfortable with his own game as each successive tee shot closed the yardage gap on Jeffreys.

Jack felt a strange phenomenon overtake him as he walked off the eighth green. Here he was pursuing what he believed to be a serial killer responsible for eleven deaths, and he was out playing golf with him.

The elevated ninth tee overlooked a pine-lined shoot that opened to a dogleg left green with a postage stamp green strategically located across the from the clubhouse terrace. Because

Willard and Jeffreys bogeyed the eighth hole, Ed Giles and O'Brennan's well-played par gave them the honors on nine. Standing on the tee, Jack looked down the treacherous dogleg and decided this was the moment to let it rip. Through the trees on the left, he could see the terrace crowded with spectators watching the action. Right or wrong, he was going to crunch the ball. Hitting the screws, Jack sent the white dot screaming down the fairway, its long flight coming to rest a short pitch shot from the green. Jeffreys abstained as Willard and Giles offered their congratulations.

While teeing up his ball, Jeffreys appeared almost humiliated by Jack's quality shot. In place of his grooved swing, he tried to overpower the ball by speeding up his disciplined swing. When most golfers attempt to kill the ball, they're faced with the kiss of death that befell Jeffreys. He hit a duck hook that dramatically turned left and rolled across the drive, coming to rest in front of the spectator-loaded terrace.

Riding down the car path of the ninth fairway, Jack said to Ed Giles, I think he's beginning to come unglued. Did you see the look on his face when he hit that hook? We'll soon see what he's made of."

Jeffreys crossed the drive to the front of the terrace where his Titleist rested. He anticipated friendly comments from the gallery but the silence grew embarrassing as he approached his ball. The hush continued as he turned what should have been a quarter wedge into a three-quarter shot that flew over the green and nestled against the back of an adjacent sand trap. Jeffreys finished the hole with a triple-bogey seven.

Walking off the green, Jeffreys appeared humiliated because of his lackluster play on nine and said in a detached manner, "Jack, now you can understand why I never became a pro." Fortunately for the team, Willard saved the hole with a par, but it became apparent his partner was a faltering golfer.

His visit to Fox Hills was to appraise Martin Jeffreys and get a feel of the man's personality. As he watched Jeffreys' game come apart, Jack's dislike of this killer started to wane. O'Brennan felt compassion toward the man as he observed Jeffreys floundering in the sand trap. He no longer disliked this man; he felt sorry for him.

Thinking Jeffreys to be the killer, O'Brennan didn't like him when they first met in the locker room and for the first several holes. However, as he finished the front nine, his feelings were beginning to change.

Ed Giles banged in a ten foot to save par, thus providing O'Brennan a run at a birdie and a shot at winning the hole. Standing over the eighteen-footer, Jack drilled the putt toward the hole with alarming speed. Approaching the cup, an unread break caused the ball to dramatically turn left into the cup. Walking off the green Jack said, "Ed, that was dumb, but the tired old cliche of I'd rather be lucky than good held up on the hole."

"We're in business, my boy," Giles laughed while tapping Jack on the shoulder with a friendly pat.

Jeffreys appeared to be sleepwalking during lunch at the halfway house. Starting the back nine, he continued to press after entering the uncharted waters of bad golf. With each stroke came unseen dangers and new challenges for him.

Approaching the fourteenth green, Jack sensed the time was right to put Jeffreys away on this par five hole. On the green in two, the moment was at-hand to ram home a long putt. If he read the break correctly, he could snuggle the ball to the hole for a safe birdie. Instead he stroked the ball like a blacksmith and much to his chagrin, it streaked to the hole with alarming speed, hit the back of the cup, jumped a foot in the air, and then disappeared. O'Brennan had just registered an eagle and put the match out of reach.

O'Brennan's character would not allow him to let up on Jeffreys. This was nothing more than a contest, but he felt compelled to destroy this opponent in a silly game called golf.

With his inexplicably bad round and O'Brennan's exceptional display of luck, Jeffreys rubbed his chin while glaring at O'Brennan. Was this a nervous gesture, or nothing more than a habit?

The fact struck Jeffreys as he walked off the green that he was going to lose to this flatfoot. *He's so dumb, he laughs at everything he hits good or bad,* Jeffreys thought as he headed for fifteen.

O'Brennan was pulling the flesh off this club champion and enjoying ever minute of it. Jeffreys' performance reminded Jack of an aging fighter making a comeback with no chance of succeeding.

What apparently triggered Jeffreys' unraveling was Judge Giles' comment at the half-way house, "I knew you were good, but it's hard to believe you haven't played in seven years," he said with undisguised envy.

Jeffreys' incredulous look told the complete story. Here was a stupid retired detective who hadn't played in seven years besting him on every shot. Three years earlier, he had reached the State Amateur semi-finals, and now he had reduced himself to losing to a second-stringer.

It rattled him that the hunted was chasing the hunter. That should never happen in golf, business, or Jeffreys' carefully orchestrated and controlled world. At this moment, a mere novice was systematically destroying him. His vanity was showing and the golf game he so treasured was self-destructing.

Jack's illusions of grandeur coupled with his brilliant effort came to a halt after his birdie on fourteen. After double-bogeying fifteen, he said to Giles in the cart, "The wheels are coming off my game, Ed, so it's about time you pick up your end of the load. I'm out-of-gas, and worse than that, my luck has run out."

"Don't worry, my man, I'll pick you up." The modest round Giles put together suddenly took off in his own display of brilliance. He birdied the last four holes that catapulted them into first place with a nine under sixty-two.

As Jeffreys stormed off eighteen, he slammed his putter into his heavy leather golf bag. Jack watched this temper tantrum and thought what a frail and pathetic figure this defeated man was as he walked away from a devastatingly poor round of golf.

This guy is on the verge of being out of control over today's failure and that goes against the grain of his profile. We indicated the killer is extremely calculating and meticulous, under control at all times. This is not the image our friend Mr. Martin Jeffreys just displayed, Jack thought.

The coolness of the locker room offered welcome relief from the torrid late spring sun as O'Brennan sat catching his breath. He understood Jeffreys' display of frustration at the lousy game he had produced. *What the hell, I've pulled more than one stunt like that myself.*

"Gentlemen, I enjoyed playing with you today but you'll have to excuse me for leaving early. I'd love to stay for the post round activities, but I have a splitting headache which probably accounts for my dismal round."

Before showering, the winners sat discussing the round while savoring cold cans of beer.

"Now that you've seen him in action, what do you think?" Ed Giles asked.

"That's a good question. There's something about this guy I can't finger. He's on the threshold of something, but I don't know what. It damn near destroyed him when we shot that course up today."

Giles gave Jack a knowing look. "Today, our round would have aggravated Arnold Palmer, and he would have needed a shrink to get over it."

Jack laughed, "We got lucky and you know it, but we were unconscious out there today." Jack again laughed.

"Now that you've played with him, are you still convinced he's your killer?" Giles asked.

"He fits the profile reasonably well. After Colby came up with the pseudonym for his books, I was pretty well convinced he was the one. But now I find myself between a rock and a hard place.

"It's tough to make an evaluation having just met him. He's a good guy and I like him, and that complicates the matter. Ed, there's one thing I know, when I go back to the Group they'll be all over him."

"How will you react to their feelings?"

"Ed, you've known me a long time and I'm one to keep the powder dry. Several facts point to Jeffreys; but maybe he's caught in some bizarre twist of fate that will eventually prove us wrong."

"Does the profile satisfy you?"

"Not entirely. The little display he put on at eighteen shows a guy somewhat out of control. Now I'm not pointing a finger at him for that, we all pull stunts like that occasionally. The other problem I have is the homosexual bit. The dress shop owner in Leesburg said she had a satisfying sexual relationship with him. How do you explain that?"

"You know better than that. Monday, you told me you didn't trust profiles," Giles said.

"I guess you're right and I still have questions that linger. We were soaked with sweat when we finished playing in the hot sun, yet Jeffreys didn't take a shower, how come?"

"Can't answer that question." Giles shrugged and finished his beer. He never takes a shower."

"Why is that? Why wouldn't he shower here?" Jack asked.

"Maybe he doesn't want people to see his pecker." Judge Giles laughed as he headed for the shower. "I'll take one for him if you wish."

O'Brennan reached for another beer. Maybe Judge Giles hit on something. Was it possible Jeffreys didn't want anyone to see him undressed? That's one thought he'd have to consider.

18

Roberta Lehman April, 1972

It has taken me four years to get over my dreadful experience with Ann Gardner. For months after her death, I felt depressed, and at a loss as to how I should redirect my listless life. It took two full years to write the novel, *A Loudon Mishap*, a story that featured Ann as the centerpiece. I later changed the title to, *The Sadness At Loudon*, feeling it was more appropriate.

I'm now rejuvenated and feel the need to strike again. The one positive aspect I learned from my experience with Ann Gardner is to never, and I mean never again, become emotionally involved with my victim. My next prospect is Roberta Lehman, a professor at Hood College. I don't know what she teaches, but know she is single. Ms. Lehman started at Hood last fall, and has attended all of the horse shows since moving to the area.

The Lehman woman appears to be a classic loner in every sense of the word. The Ann Gardner attachment taught me another important lesson, and that is to not dawdle around.

Driving to the fairgrounds in Frederick, I felt a renewed sense of urgency sweep over me. I was apprehensive about this new kill, but conversely found it equally exciting.

Entering the show grounds, I passed a sign that announced the *Frederick County Morgan Arabian Horse Show* and realized a sizeable crowd had gathered. Apparently the crowd was augmented by the warm, sweeping April breeze and sunny day.

I soon found the Lehman woman standing by the stables looking at the horses.

Approaching her, I spoke out, "Are you enjoying the horse show?" As she turned, I looked into the eyes of an attractive woman. Her long red hair framed a tanned freckled face. The tan camel hair jacket and brown pleated skirt she wore were of a conservative yet expensive cut.

She seemed to look right through me as she spoke. "Yes I am, but why would you ask?"

"I thought you might be a nice person to talk to. I came up from Lynchburg this morning and feel out of place and lonely. I have an intense interest in horses, and I need someone to share my enthusiasm."

"I find that interesting, because at work they call me a recluse."

"You don't appear to be someone who avoids people."

"No, I don't, but I find it difficult to carry on a casual conversation."

"By the way, my name is Bill Bosdoors, and like I said earlier, I'm from Lynchburg."

"Bosdoors, that's a very different name, one I don't recall hearing before. Is it spelled like it sounds?"

"Exactly."

"I'm Roberta Lehman and live in Frederick. What do you do, Bill?"

"I'm a lawyer with my own practice in Lynchburg."

"A learned man, how interesting."

"What do you do, Roberta?"

"I teach American History at the college, Hood College that is."

"Do you know much about horses?"

"Yes, I do. I consider myself an authority on them. I'm going to ask the same question, do you know much about horses?"

"I consider myself reasonably knowledgeable about them myself, but I'm certainly not an authority like you. Let's go over and sit on that bench under the tree. We can talk about them, and you'll be able to evaluate what I know."

As we walked to the bench, I knew I had her hooked. If she considers herself an authority, that's great, because I can talk word-for-word and breed-for-breed with her and not appear to be a dunce, I mused. For the next half-hour we talked about horses;

she talking much of the time. Roberta displayed charming warmth that I found appealing. As time sped by, she became more outgoing and excited about our general discussion.

"I believe you are knowledgeable about horses, but let me play teacher and you act as my student. What can you tell me about the Morgan Breeds?"

"Not much I'm afraid. I know they are occasionally used on farms for light hauling, and police use them for their mounted patrols. The Morgan is popular for pleasure riding because they have a gentle side, and continually display a strong and sturdy attitude about them. I know all Morgan horses are direct descendants of a . . . ah, damned, . . . oh, I've got it. The original stallion was named Justin Morgan and I believe his origin was in New England, but don't hold me to that. How am I doing, teacher?"

"You are conversant about horses, and I'm amazed you would know about the Morgan breed. I find that refreshing, and I'm going to let you in on my little secret. I am currently writing a book about horses. I attended Cornell University in upstate New York and had a horrendous time getting my subject approved for my doctoral dissertation. I had to prove that it was germane to the conduct of the Korean War."

"What did you write your dissertation on?" I asked

"It was called: *An Examination of Reckless's Service in the Korean War.*"

"I served in Korea but I'm not familiar with this Reckless you talk of."

Roberta laughed before she continued the conversation. "There'd be no reason for you to know. In my earlier research, I found that in the Korean War a marine platoon acquired a Korean racing mare called Reckless. This horse served as an ammunition carrier for much of that period. It was later made an honorary sergeant and given a medal for the courage it displayed."

"That's extraordinary."

"I'm currently researching for a book called, *The Role of Horses in War.*"

"I presume it would be about how horses were used in war."

"Yes, that's right. The premise for the book and title came from my experience in writing my dissertation. Would you like to see the research I've done?"

"I would."

"Fine. I have all my work at the college, so let's drive over and take a look. You might even give me some direction."

Driving to the college, pleasing thoughts swept over me how I'll give her some direction. This is an ideal set-up for me, but there is a pitfall. While at the college, if one person sees me in the company of Professor Lehman, my plan of attack should be dropped. Her future depends on whether we meet anyone at the college.

I park in back of the history building, and we head for her third story office. Entering a small but well organized work area, Roberta's methodical research is neatly placed on a worktable. Watching her arrange reams of papers in the order of their presentation alerts me to how totally consumed this woman is with the academic world around her. She appears to be alone on an island with only research her sole companion.

This is her whole life, and she is oblivious to any physical threats from me. In our discussion about horses, I'm certain she has not considered for one moment the possibility of a sexual assault from me. I'd consider it unlikely she would consider a sexual relationship with any man as feasible.

I'll be reviewing and discussing her research and that is almost reward enough. An added plus to the day will be her planned destruction. I can't miss. We spend the next four hours enthusiastically discussing her research.

I look at my watch and say, "Good grief, it's eight o'clock and dark out. We've been here for hours and I can't believe how time is fleeting. I'm hungry and certain you are as well. Would you like to go out for dinner?"

"I'd love to and find myself amazed at how quickly time has flown."

"Now you know that's not the case, don't you?" I laugh as I flip the light off.

Entering the car, I quickly strike by taping her mouth. In a flash, Roberta Lehman reacts to my initial assault like her life depends on it, which of course it does. Her strength surprises me along with the fury carried with it. Finally, I successfully tie her hands together and vainly start on her feet. Roberta kicks and thrashes her legs around for a brief moment before I can secure them. It always seems easier to eliminate my victims after they're tied up, I thought as the pick slips without ceremony into her ear. After removing the duct tape, I clean her smudged lipstick and apply a fresh coat, then amputate her finger. From there, I drive around to the side of the Ad Building and park. I lift her body out of the car and carry it to the entrance of the building. To avoid attention my route leads me between the building and the bushes that guarded it. I place Roberta under a bush next to the front steps and leave. I immediately departed the city of Frederick and head home.

Once in Smithbury, I realize how hungry I am and drive to the Hounds Inn for dinner. While dining, I relish the successful and eventful day I experienced. Martin Jeffreys had again proven that any day is perfect for a killing.

19

It was nine-thirty at the Eagle with the usual morning crowd digging into their second hour of drinking when John Lloyd eased onto a stool next to O'Brennan. Big Al Simon asked what he'd have. "I'll have the same as Jack." Lloyd gestured at the coffee his partner was having. Simon obliged and left; they were free to talk.

"How did things go with Jeffreys?"

"They didn't go right for him. You know, John, golf can be a leveler of sorts and yesterday I ripped up Jeffreys on the course."

John glanced at O'Brennan with a surprised look. "How did you do that?"

Jack replayed the scene in his head before he began.

"Jeffreys wasn't on; I was. I played a career round that every golfer dreams about."

"Forget the golf and tell me about him."

"John, he's a substantial figure, a cut above what I imagined him to be. When Ed Giles introduced us, he neglected the usual handshake, but that was no big deal. At first glance one would consider him innocuous enough but he's highly motivated and comes off as self-effacing."

"Any further impressions about him?"

"It's difficult to put a word to it, he's an anomaly if you will. He has a certain quality hard to define. I know I'm not making much sense, but it seems like he's cut from a different cloth."

A puzzled look was settling on John's face. "Could you expand on that different cloth thing?"

"Gosh, John, this isn't easy. It's almost like he's lacking in self-confidence, but I know that isn't the case. Maybe unpretentious is a better word."

Jack signaled Simon for another refill.

"You know, there's something strange about that man. His frame of mind seemed miles away. It was like he was creating a plot for a novel, one minute composing, and the next minute golfing. He's so full of energy, it's like he drank four gallons of coffee."

Lloyd laughed. "It sounds like you're describing Colby."

"Pretty close. When Ed Giles mentioned how well I was playing after being away from the game for so long, Jeffreys seemed nonplussed."

"Maybe it was Giles' news that disturbed him."

"He was obviously trying to hide a truculent mood because of his poor play, but I don't know."

"Did he display this attitude throughout the round?"

"I'd have to say no. It did surface when we approached the ninth green. I hit a terrific shot to the green and I think Jeffreys was trying too hard. He hooked his approach shot left and the ball landed in front of the outside terrace filled with members. His face turned stony with the look of someone throwing the switch. It was a very embarrassing and humiliating experience for him. But what the hell, anyone who has ever played the game has suffered through a similar encounter with the little white ball."

"I need more than a story about Jeffreys chasing a little white ball around. What's your take on this guy?"

"He lacks a common touch while he goes about life, and yet, he displays a dignity hard to explain. However, in the locker room after we finished, he talked like he was in a dream."

"You're telling me a patchwork of nothing. Jack, you haven't told me what I want to hear."

"I know," Jack, admitted, "this isn't easy. Earlier, I had incorrectly labeled Jeffreys a snob. After our round, I have to say he's a good guy. I like him."

"That's very noble of you, but you and I don't see eye to eye on this. Evil is in the eye of the beholder, and I see him as just that, evil. He's masquerading as something he's not, and it flies in the face of logic for you to talk this way." John Lloyd stared insensitively at O'Brennan.

"I don't think we can go off half-cocked on this. Wouldn't it make more sense to show a little more tolerance regarding Jeffreys?"

John rolled his eyes skyward. "What is with you? I don't like the direction you're taking. Your thinking needs reworking."

"What are you driving at?" a perplexed O'Brennan asked.

"People understand what they want to believe."

Time passed as they sat in silence while O'Brennan absently weighed his empty coffee cup in his hand. Simons ambled to a stop in front of them, offered refills that they declined, and then stood there.

Lloyd finally spoke. "So much evil in the good."

"And so much good in the evil," O'Brennan countered.

Simons took them in with a confused look. "You guys sound like Colby with a belly full of beer."

Lloyd and O'Brennan laughed, then returned to silence.

Finally, Lloyd broke the silence. "We need to have a hard honest talk."

O'Brennan opened his hand as if to say, "Get on with it".

"I appreciate how you feel, but the unvarnished truth is, we have to take sides."

"I know that."

"You really don't get it, do you?" John looked through tired eyes at his partner. "It appears we have irrefutable evidence that points to Martin Jeffreys as our serial killer." Lloyd's voice was loaded with a thinly disguised anger.

"I'm telling you this for a reason. You've become too emotionally involved, and you know damned well that isn't good police technique. You should be ashamed of yourself for even thinking Jeffreys is anything but a psychotic killer."

"I guess you're right, but you should understand he's not a bad sort. The view from here is I hope we're wrong." O'Brennan's shoulder sagged as if saying; "it was beyond him".

His voice started to waiver as he glanced at Lloyd. "This is a tough pill for me to accept, but I defer to your apparent wisdom."

The Group met at the Bench in Inlet Park with the discussion covering everything but the case. After an hour of small talk, Jack stood and said, "Ladies, now that you've seen the Bench and the Inlet from this side, let's adjourn to the cottage. We need a break, and the beach is the answer. I think I'm a much better cook than Karl, and tonight, I'm going to prove it."

"Yeah, yeah, yeah," Karl said.

Settled at the cottage an hour later, Jack tried his best to allay the Group's sentiments about Martin Jeffreys. Although he believed Jeffreys to be the killer, Jack genuinely liked him. Conversely, the Group adamantly voiced strong views on his guilt, leaving Jack as the lone voice of moderation in a hostile group of friends.

"Give us one reason why he shouldn't be our prime suspect," Lloyd said in a controlled rage.

"He appears to be a well meaning person, and we may be incorrectly pointing a finger at him. It's just a feeling I have; there's nothing to base it on."

"You're damn right there is nothing to base it on. You're hoping against hope that we're wrong about him."

"Okay John, I'll try to see it your way. Let's get on with the business at hand and focus on Jeffreys. How do you want to approach him?" Jack asked.

"The view we see is from the bottom, and from that position, our choices are limited. We should get close to him, talk to him if at all possible. Secondly, we should run an around-the-clock surveillance on him," John Lloyd said,

"Let's start with me. I played golf with him yesterday, so that takes me out of it. Cal has his picture in the paper more than Eddie Feller, so that eliminates his involvement." Jack said as he glanced in Cal's direction.

"Who is Eddie Feller?" Liz asked.

"He was a great baseball player for the Bridgeton Gulls and was inducted into the Baseball Hall of Fame a couple of years ago." Since he'd met her, this was the first occasion John had known something that she didn't.

"Cal and I are the only members of the Group who can't get near Jeffreys. Everyone else except Jeanette and Liz has indicated they would help." Annoyed with the women, Jack asked, "How come you two aren't interested in tracking Jeffreys?"

"Liz and I have discussed all aspects of the case and believe the only way to get this killer is by some entrapment scam. Both of us want to be the bait, but realize only one of us can he involved," Jeanette said.

"Now that's it! That isn't going to happen, so just forget it," Jack said angrily.

"We'd like a piece of the action, but you won't listen. What did I tell you, Liz, I knew he wouldn't go for it?" Fire appeared to shoot from Jeanette's eyes as she spoke."

"Jeanette, you can bet your life I won't buy it. Have you slipped a cog?" Jack asked.

"We're not backing away from this, and who are you to tell me what to do about my destiny? You're are acting like an overseer, and I'm not ready to be a slave to you or anyone else."

"Jeanette, don't be that way. Let's put the worst face on your little scheme and see where it takes us. You could get killed or at least find yourself at risk, and besides, this isn't the time or place to discuss this matter. Why would you give me a bad time about this?"

"O'Brennan, this is the time and place to get this in the open, air it out as you like to say! We can do it right in front of our friends; they're the only ones we have. You're not . . ."

Jack cut her off before she could continue. "But, Jeanette, this should be done when we're alone."

"We have no secrets!" Their friends looked at each other as if on the edge of a major bloodletting. "We've been going together for three years living pretty much like man and wife. Well guess what, that part of my life has passed from view. As far as I'm concerned, I'm done with you. This business of you telling me what to do has ended." Jeanette paused to take a gulp of air. "I wanted to get married, but no, you wanted no part of marriage. The only time you really cared was when you crawled in the sheets with me, and that's all you wanted out of me."

"Jeanette, Jeanette! Don't say that, that's not the way it is. Let me explain."

"Explanations aren't needed. I'll do nicely without you, thank you. You won't believe how many classy men hit on me at the restaurant."

"But Jeanette, can't you . . . you can't say that, you can't talk that way."

Jeanette hurtled on like she was in a race and displayed no inclination to be interrupted. "I just did, and O'Brennan, I'll continue to do so. This is it! Either we go the marriage route, or the blanket is split, as you like to say. I'll walk away from you forever, and that is final! You're not speaking for me any more. I've been a big girl for a very long time, and know what I'm doing. I'm not listening to your chauvinistic ideas about protecting women. You can put that myth to bed about women needing help," Jeanette said as she concluded the crisp exchange with her lover.

Jeanette's fury rivaled the day Charlie Winder brought Jack to *the Red Leather* for their first meeting. That initial meeting ended in a furious argument that paralleled this one. Her raging words spilled out on O'Brennan and embarrassed the Group.

The silence was deafening as the two glared at each other. Jack started to speak but Jeanette put her hand up resembling a school crossing-guard stopping traffic for lunch-bucket carrying first-graders. This simple gesture implied an, "I don't want to hear it attitude". The only sound to interrupt the stony silence was the Atlantic's gentle waters washing onto Sands Beach.

Colby appeared to mull his thoughts around during the silence that followed Jeanette's startling outburst. He finally broke the silence in his own inimitable way. "Allison, will you talk to me that way after we've been together three years?" The comment was so absurd, stupid, and out of place it seemed to ease the tension of the moment. Much needed laughter resulted from his impromptu comment. As mad as Jeanette and Jack were at each other, they too laughed together.

"Now you've got it right. There is something you can laugh at, even if it's me," Colby said.

"Stay out of this you little jerk! This is a serious matter we're talking about," Jack angrily replied.

"If we're going to get down to brass tacks, let's do so. You are too much in love to be hurting each other this way," Colby said.

"What makes you think we love each other? And secondly, what do you know about love, you sawed-off half-ass?" Jack's face had now turned a dangerous crimson. "As far as I'm concerned, you are persona non grata around here. Do you understand that little message, Mr. Attorney? Now hit the road!"

"O'Brennan, I believe you are the biggest horse's ass I've met in a lifetime. You must have your brains in a shoebox up in the attic. Do you honestly believe I just got off the turnip truck? I didn't, and one doesn't have to be too deep to see how much you care for each other. What the hell, even the village idiot can see that."

Their heated conversation was interrupted by John Lloyd's laughter at Colby's comment. His outburst drew icy glares from the Group and an inflamed look from O'Brennan.

"As for your second question, I know a lot more about love than you give me credit for. Before I came to UVa., I never dated anyone I really cared about. When I met this one, that all changed." Colby pointed to the redheaded Allison Williams. "Since meeting her, my life has taken a dramatic turn for the better. We've gone out for over a year, and if I have my way, we'll be married by Christmas. Another thing you better believe, I won't wait three years to ask her."

Colby's angry explosion embarrassed Allison and reddened her face. "What the hell, I might as well get this over with right now. Allison, before God and all our friends, will you marry me? I know I'm kinda' wild and all that, but I love you very much, and I'll be good to you for the rest of your life."

The tension of the moment pushed the petite redhead into giant sobs that caused her whole body to shake like a sinking ship condemned to the deep. Minutes passed before she looked at Colby through swollen red eyes. With tears streaming down her face, she said in a whisper, "Yes, Colby, I'll marry you as soon as possible." Their embrace brought applause from the Group.

At that dramatic moment, John chirped in with, "See, Jack, this Yankee showed you how to do the real thing. It's pretty easy, wouldn't you say?"

O'Brennan looked at his old buddy through a sea of anger. Turning to Jeanette, he noticed a faint smile grace her unlined face. "Jeanette, I'm being coerced into doing something I fully intended on doing later. We have an open road ahead of us, and I'm not going to jeopardize it by being the horse's ass Colby accused me of being.

"People want things they know they can't have, and I must include myself in that group. Jeanette, I'm going to change all that; the mistakes we make are with us for the rest of our lives, but this is one mistake I'm not going to make. I've been accused of being a foolish man from time to time; however, this isn't one of those times. I guess the time is right. Jeanette will you marry me?"

"O'Brennan, that was nice. I love you, and yes, O'Brennan, I will marry you, but you must understand there is one condition tied to it." The slightest trace of a smile turned into a dazzler.

"And what would that be?" Jack said in frustration. *Oh-oh here comes the condition. It's not enough that I asked her to marry me, now she wants concessions. Jack, my boy, you better get used to taking orders,* Jack thought.

"You know exactly what it is. That either Liz or I is allowed to be the decoy in this entrapment scheme, or there's no marriage."

"Jeanette, this is serious. Our man has killed eleven women and you may be next."

"I don't believe one word of it. You and John are highly skilled detectives and even better organizers and planners. If you love me as much as you claim, I'm in very good hands. Remember this, O'Brennan, if you say it's not that simple one more time,

I'll scream. Let's leave it at that and enjoy this lovely day." Once again, her grand smile overwhelmed her future husband.

Jack glanced at Colby with his arm around the little redhead. As if on cue, Colby spoke up, "Allison and I are going for a walk on the beach. You know we're getting married, so we have to make some plans. I know the wedding reception won't be as classy as Red's, but my best man won't be as slick as his either."

"You've got me there." Red's smile reflected his delight with his friend's announcement.

Jack turned to Jeanette. "I reluctantly accept your condition, but I'm not thrilled with it. To borrow a sentence from Colby, let's take a walk. We're soon to be married, so we also need to make some wedding plans." Jeanette smiled and nodded in agreement as she took Jack's hand.

"There's plenty of beer, so you can get right at it if you wish. I'm having a great supper for you tonight. The same one we had when we broke into Sally's warehouse, remember, John?"

"I sure do, Jack. I remember everything about that night. Starting with supper at the Eagle to Sally's leather bras and garter belts."

Jack laughed as he started for the beach. "You never forget anything important, or not important for that matter, do you?"

"Right again, old-timer," Lloyd said with a laugh.

After the future newlyweds returned, John Lloyd asked O'Brennan, "How did it go?"

"We're getting married, that's about all I can tell you for now."

"Jeanette, that means we're ready to run this twist on Jeffreys." Liz's voice bubbled while fingering her hair.

"You're right, Liz. My honey has finally agreed to it, but between you and me, he doesn't appear to be very happy."

After a supper of cold meat loaf, potato salad, baked beans, beef stew, chili over egg noodles, and coffee, the Group discussed the next progression in their pursuit of Martin Jeffreys.

"I think we should run a twenty-four hour surveillance on this character. Let's see if we can discern any pattern or quirks that he may have . . . sort of check him out from the shadows, so to speak. If he does anything unusual, we'll know about it," John said with authority.

"That's good. How about drawing up a schedule for the Group?"

"I have anticipated your command, and it is now in place. I drew it up when you and your honey were out talking married bliss and all that good stuff. I've already instructed the guys on how I want the shadow run," John said.

"Jeanette and I have talked this over, and we realize only one person can be the decoy. We shall approach him and hope one of us appeals to him," Liz said.

"Liz, what happens if he isn't interested?" Karl Eichner said.

"Karl, you don't really believe he'd pass both of us up, do you?" Liz asked her rhetorical question more for herself than the Group.

20

Carol Barton April, 1975

Deep Run is an upscale retreat created in rough country twenty miles north of Richmond. The complex is located in a heavily wooded area with the Deep Run Brook running through the property. The basic concept of Deep Run was to provide a facility designed exclusively to host horse events. A large clubhouse nestled in the woods provided a luxurious dining area for several hundred patrons. In addition to the wondrous setting, the accompanying two hundred-room hotel provided comfort beyond imagination for those who could afford the lofty rates.

When not in use for horse events, the Deep Run Hotel offered a perpetual dinner theater, boasting a brilliant record of the finest Broadway road shows and some of the most accomplished entertainers in the business.

This is the setting I'm heading for today, and I'm again thrilled about the trip. I would guess the reason for this excitement is my return to the attack. My last encounter with Roberta Lehman was so satisfying I feel there's nothing out there that can stop me.

I find myself thinking about my newest victim, Carol Barton as I neared my destination. She appears to be in her late thirties, and I have to believe a little different. In the purest sense of the word she would have to be called an extrovert. I talked briefly to her last October at the *Chesapeake Steeplechase* Races, so she should recognize me when I hit on her. There is one point I do remember about her; she seemed to have a northern accent. There is one drawback that continues to haunt me; what happens if she doesn't appear at the event? I have no contingency plan, so that will mean I'll have to go back to the drawing board.

I find lacking information about my victim prior to the day I kill her is intriguing. It makes for a more eventful experience and tests how adaptable I am. I make it a point of talking to as many people as possible at the event. Prior to making contact with the designated victim I want to spread myself around. I realize this is a new strategy, but one that may enhance my alibi.

Carol Barton looked as fresh as a gentle summer rain.

Making contact with her was no easy matter. She talked to everyone she saw, and laughed and walked around the course as if she were an ambassador of good will.

Finally, I found her alone and figured I had better make my move.

I walked up to her. "You appear to be enjoying the jumping events this morning."

"Yeah, I am. This is the best place in the world to have the races. It's the greatest!"

Carol was short, blonde, pretty, casually dressed and appeared to be athletic. Her race attire consisted of Bermudas, a Gettysburg College sweatshirt, white button-down shirt and leather scandals.

"You sound like you're from the North, am I right?"

"Yeah, I'm from Gettysburg, Pennsylvania."

"Are you associated with the college."

"Come On," she replied with a hearty laugh." "Naw, I have nothing to do with the college. As a matter-of-fact, I'm a gym teacher at the local high school."

"What's your name?"

"I'm Carol Barton."

"I'm Jack Pembrooke from Fredericksburg, here in the state."

"You're not very far from home. When I came down route 35, I drove by your town. This isn't much of drive for you, is it?"

"No, it isn't. How come you drove this far for the races?"

"I drive all around. I'm single, so I can do whatever I want.

Didn't I talk to you last fall at the *Chesapeake Steeplechase Races?*" She asked with faint recognition.

"Yes."

Ignoring further recall she continued. "You know, I'm bummed out about this damned event being held on Sunday. It would have been a lot easier for me if they scheduled it on Saturday; that way I'd have Sunday to get out and about. It took the wind out of my sails, but I went ahead and used two personal days. That way, I don't have to get back to work until Wednesday. Now I can get at it and give this thing a real rip. A lot of my teacher friends go south for Easter vacation, but I always take a couple of days before school is out and do my thing."

This one is a wild talker if I've ever heard one. I'll bet she skirted around the hippie fringe when she was younger. Why not ask?

"Something tells me to ask you this, and please don't be annoyed by it. Were you a hippie when you were younger?"

"I dig the way you asked. Yeah, I was. Were you offended by the hippie movement?"

"Offended . . . . Hardly. I lost my job because of it, that's how offended I was."

"How?"

"I have to lay it on the line. I was a deputy in the mid-sixties with the Prince George's County Sheriff's Department and went down to Richmond to an antiwar demonstration. Something unexpected happened and I got all doped up and burned my draft card."

"Wow, that's cool."

"Well, it wasn't so cool when they found out about it back home."

"How'd that grab them?"

"Dropped me like a hot potato. They put the lid on and canned me, if you know what I mean."

She nodded her head in a knowing fashion. "What do you do now?"

"I'm a salesman for a textbook company and call on high schools and some colleges in northern Virginia."

"You sound like you used to be a wild one."

"Little lady, I was wilder than a chicken in a hurricane. I guess I still am, and you know what? I love every minute of it."

"Crazy, you sound like my kind of guy."

"Well, maybe I am," I suggested.

Carol's face displayed a glimpse of her inner thoughts. "There are many things I can offer you and one of them is a beauty. Are you into smoking?"

"Smoking?"

"Come on! A little grass; what else is there?"

"I've smoked more joints than you've got hair on your pretty head."

"I have a lot of hair on my head, and for that matter, other places too," she said with a sly smile.

"There, you said it for me."

"I've got a couple of joints with me, want to smoke one?"

"That's the most pleasant offer I've had in awhile. Why not? Let's go over to my car."

Sitting in the car, we smoked two joints, and by the time she finished her second she was talking some kind of gibberish. I must admit I was a little high myself.

"Jack, I'm starting to enjoy the direction we're headin' in. I'll give you two choices: one, we can go back to the races, or two, we can go to my motel room and party. It's your call."

"Well, the first one is no big deal, but I sure like the sound of the last one."

"I'm in tune with your sentiments, so you're my kind of guy. Let's do it."

Home sweet home away from home. This one is not only wild, but puts a different spin on life.

When we reached her motel room, I picked up a quart of blueberry brandy from the backseat. If I was going to drink with this crazy, it would be something I liked and not some wild stuff she probably drank. Much to my surprise she had a suitcase full of booze.

Her drink was V-8 Juice, gin and tonic water. I never trusted a gin drinker and Carol was no exception.

We drank for the better part of the afternoon with tidbits of discussion intertwined part of the time, and then fell asleep. When we awoke, she said, "Ya' know, I'm feeling horny. Every time I take a nap after a bunch of booze, I feel the same way."

"What did you have in mind, Carol?"

Carol pointed to the bed and said, "Personally, I'm into kinky. It's an old habit I've had for years."

What kind of kinky do you have in mind?"

"You know, walking on the edge is good."

"No, I don't. You better be more explicit."

"I want something more, and being tied up does it for me. Is that too much to ask?"

Ah hah, now the real story comes out. I was right about this one. She is weird and her fetish will make it easier for me to take her away. If I had designed this event myself, it couldn't have come out any better.

"Nothing is impossible, and I'll gladly help you out," I said. "How do you want to do it?"

Carol reached into her suitcase and pulled out a short length of rope. "Here, you can tie me up with this."

"I know this is bizarre, but I can't wait to get it on," I said with feigned anticipation.

"Yeah, I dig the way you think, far out," she added.

"I have a suggestion. Are you familiar with that all-purpose wrapping called duct tape? I have some in the car. Why don't I go get it and then use it on you? That way when I get done with you, there'll be no rope burns or abrasions."

"Sounds good to me."

Returning with the tape I set my plan in motion. "Why don't you put your hands in back of you and I'll tape them together?"

"I've never heard of anything like that. Why do you want to tie my wrists in back of me?"

"Oh, it's no big deal, just something we're using down here."

"Sounds brutal to me."

"Baby, you don't know how brutal it's going to be."

Carol laughed. "I love the way you talk."

After securing her wrists, I add," Put your ankles together and I'll tape them."

An anxious look clouded her face. "I don't know if I like what you're doing. I've been the whole route, but I've never heard of anything like this."

"Trust me," I assured, "before we get done, this is going to knock you over."

"I'm Jake with being knocked over, so go ahead and give it a rip. Jack, this is so sick I'm after it."

Carol looked past me with her gaze settling on her secured ankles.

"I can't imagine what you're going to do, but this has to be out of sight."

I cut a shorter length of tape and in one swift motion, placed it over her mouth.

"Honey, you'll never believe what's next." It was at that moment, the twinkle left her eyes to be replaced by a questioning glance, followed by a look of pure terror.

"This is going to be your swan song, and I want you to observe me very closely." I reached into my jacket and pulled out my killing case. Opening it, I displayed my weapon of death for her to see. "Take a look at the finely tooled handle I carved. I'm very proud of it and want to show it off. The only people who ever see it are the ones I'm going to dispatch. If you don't understand dispatch, I'll give it you plain and simple. I'm going to kill you.

"I think you're a great person, a little screwy, but otherwise terrific. I write mystery novels and continually need new plots for my books. You are going to be the chief character in my next effort *A Deep Run*. Just think of it, you're going to be the star!"

As strong as I am, I have a tough time controlling her. She kicked and raised all kinds of hell before I finally got a secure hold on her chin and the side of her face.

At that moment I reached the cutting edge of thrills.

"Carol, I shall see you in my next book; now watch this. I'm going to drive this pick into your brain. Here comes the pick. Watch it as it slides into your ear with darkness written all over it."

Bang, and away she went. What the hell, I can talk like the

hippest of the hip. I wipe down everything I touched; and load her into the back seat of my car. I suppose this was a dangerous move on my part, but wasn't I playing this game for the precious few moments that provided me with so much pleasure? I drive out to the Jamesland Plantation and deposit her in a rocking chair at the far end of the front porch. Earlier I had found the security guard walked by the front of the mansion on the half-hour, so I deposited Ms. Carol Barton on the hour. I place a horse fly in her hair and now my task is complete. Driving back to Smithbury, I'm secure in knowing I have again gotten away with murder.

21

Jeanette and Liz drove through open spaces with rolling farmland on their way to the horse show.

Southern estates with tree-lined lots and classy mansions provide a unique attraction in the South. These mansions hosted the infamous plantation system and the *Peculiar Institution* called slavery. The cotton fields and slavery have long since departed, but the mystique of their former existence transcends time.

The stately manors were strategically placed on knolls overlooking rolling plots of former cotton fields. The modern estates, unlike their antecedents, define their rolling fields with white board fences.

Along the foothills of the Allegheny Plateau, many former plantations were resurrected into dignified horse farms. At this point, the former plantations reached their true majestic beauty. The roadside white fences signaled to motorists that the dinosaurs of the antebellum South had completed their metamorphous. It was apparent that something very special was happening within the confines of the white barriers.

It was just such a setting Liz and Jeanette entered as they drove into the Winston Estate, home of the *Flat Run Horse Show*. Although located in a small rural community, the horse show attracted thousands.

Driving down the fence and tree-lined dirt lane, they were directed by an attendant to turn into a parking lot normally used for grazing. Crossing the lane, the new arrivals paid their admission and entered the world of the well to do. Stonewalls, parallel bars, wide jumps, and two or more jumps positioned close together graced the rolling pasture. The show consisted of Puissance Events featuring jumping exercises.

The brilliant orange and brown outfit Liz wore appeared sprayed on, while Jeanette, on the other hand, chose a conservative brown hounds-tooth skirt with a camel hair jacket. The women's color schemes provided a dramatic contrast.

Liz and Jeanette early on designed a strategy that would provide a chance meeting with Jeffreys. They would walk around until they spotted him, and at that moment, separate, and go in opposite directions. A designed chance contact would be their goal.

"Let's hope he takes the bait. O'Brennan and I talked about this very thing, and he told me exposing Jeffreys for what he is can't be done with smoke and mirrors. My God, there's Jeffreys now!"

"Where? I don't see him?" Liz's asked, her voice betraying her inner feelings.

Jeanette said in an excited voice, "He's over by the hot dog stand."

"Oh." Liz's voice trailed off as she observed Jeffreys. She felt weak-kneed as she headed out in the opposite direction. *How could Jeanette appear so excited while the tentacles of fear and panic are sweeping over me? I feel like I'm falling into a black pit*, Liz thought as she started around the course.

Her placid trip ended when she stepped aside to allow a rider and his horse to pass by. She turned and bumped into an elderly gentleman wearing a brown Harris Tweed jacket and matching hounds-tooth checked hat. She could feel her heart thump when she realized the old man was talking to Martin Jeffreys. Again, confusion and fear reigned as she muttered, "Excuse me," and hastily retreated from the twosome with close to a catatonic gaze.

Liz felt her ability to reason quickly eroding as she walked away. *That wasn't clever of you to bump into Jeffreys that way*, she told herself. The initial shock of her first encounter with him gradually subsided, but she experienced what she perceived to be hyperventilation. Liz could feel her rapid heartbeat and the dryness in her mouth and throat. Bathed in perspiration, she experienced shaking much like that of a malaria attack, a topic she knew of only through reading. Her nervous system had received an intense bashing from this chance meeting with Jeffreys and she felt her well-ordered life crumbling.

Liz was incapable of continuing this charade and knew it. She had to get away from Jeffreys, from the show grounds, and the estate. Making her way to Jeanette's car, she plopped down in the passenger seat and emotionally came apart. Tensions of the afternoon overwhelmed her causing great sobs.

Neither Jeffreys nor his physical presence upset me, no, it is more than that, she thought. *It's the portrait the Group had drawn of the killer, an outline I myself helped design. I have to gather myself as best I can then head back to the course.*

Jeffreys wasn't in the area where she earlier bumped into him, so she continued to slowly circle the course. *I can smell my fear growing with each step I take. This is the first time in my life I have encountered an obstacle so seemingly insurmountable, I've been forced to surrender to defeat.* Liz's heart felt heavy with despair as she thought of her newly discovered shortcomings and cowardly behavior.

I've spent much of my adult existence living a life of discipline while dreaming of writing courtroom novels involving criminals. I'm retired and ready to enter into this new stage of my life, but I don't have the wherewithal to become involved. Looking to the rail she spotted Jeanette and Jeffreys talking. *I've had enough. Jeanette wanted this opportunity; well, it's in her ballpark now. I'm not ready to make that commitment! There is no way in hell that this mad man is going to kill me.*

Maybe I'll write about Jeffreys, but if I do, it will be from a distance, a very far distance. Tomorrow is another day and Elizabeth Woodsen is going to live it without the sinister shadow of Martin Jeffreys over her shoulder.

Jeanette wandered onto the scene as Liz bumped into the old gentleman talking to Jeffreys. She picked up on Liz's reaction to her chance meeting with Jeffreys. *So be it*, she thought. *I'll make contact on my own. This is sensational. I can hardly control myself knowing Jeffreys is mine. This is the most exciting moment in my life. I knew Liz wasn't up to this hoax, but I am. I wanted a one-on-one situation with this savage, and now I have it.*

After observing Liz and her brief encounter with Jeffreys, Jeanette quickly wheeled around and started a reverse turn of the course. Spotting him at the rail, she was amazed at how fearless and confident she felt while settling in next to him. There came from him a certain refined presence. Like O'Brennan, he wore the attire of college men of the fifties. Jeffreys' attire for the day consisted of white bucks, starched khaki pants, lightweight dark blue blazer, white button-down shirt, and a blue and red striped tie. At six-two, with boyish good looks, he appeared bulkier than her man.

I feel in absolute control and sense I can control his destiny. Jeanette's newly found audacity amazed her.

Jeffreys turned to Jeanette and spoke, "Hi, are you enjoying the jumping events?"

"This is my first experience at a horse show. To be honest, I don't know much about the sport. A friend told me how interesting the events are, and she was right, I just adore them!" Jeanette answered as euphoria washed over her.

"It's simple and very basic. The organizers set up," Jeffreys said with a sweep of the hand, "a course in a common pasture. The riders must navigate the jumps that vary from long and short jumps, to high jumps. There are X number of points awarded for a clean jump and points deducted for lack of style, misses or near misses."

"I surmised that, but what most impressed me is the grace and skill these riders display. How elegant they look while jumping. The horses are so sleek and beautiful, they must be the most graceful animal on earth."

"Ah, you do appreciate the finer points of the sport. Even though you don't know horses the way I do, you comprehend the beauty of the sport, and that in itself is enough."

"Yes, I believe you're right. I enjoy the atmosphere and feel very comfortable here. For some reason, I've become swept up by its intensity and feel certain it will leave a lasting imprint on me. Do you understand?" Jeanette placed her hand on Jeffreys' arm and directed an impish smile at Jeffreys.

"I do understand where you're coming from. Horse events are not marquee sports, so for you to enjoy them says a great deal. I should introduce myself. I'm Martin Jeffreys and attend most of the horse events in the state."

And you have a history of attending some out-of-state as well," Jeanette thought as she gazed at the course. *Keep talking like that and I'll seal your fate by next Sunday evening.*

This lovely is truly a dream. I wonder . . . Jeffreys thought as he continued, "I find it interesting that I met you here. And whom do I have the pleasure of talking to?"

"I'm Julie Smilker."

"Do I know you from somewhere?"

"We've never met."

"Where are you from, Julie Smilker?"

"I'm from Culpepper, just down the road."

"Jokes are made about Culpepper, but you're the first person I've ever met from there."

"You're now talking to someone from Culpepper. I was born and raised there, so you are presently looking at the real thing." Jeanette smiled as she turned to again peruse the course.

"And the real thing is very lovely, I might add."

"Thank you. That's very nice of you." Jeanette said while looking up at Jeffreys with the most ingratiating smile she could muster. As an added enticement, she ran her fingers through freshly frosted hair.

"What do you do, job-wise that is?" he asked.

"I'm a math teacher. What do you do, Martin?"

Jeanette reacted nimbly as she went along with the fraud. *I'd better be careful, but the conversation is rolling along so smoothly, why not continue? I'm certain he's creating an image of me in his devious mind, but so be it. Much of what I told him has no substance, and if he were to check, my cover would be blown. Hopefully, he won't ask me where I teach.* Jeffreys interrupted her thoughts.

"I'm a lawyer in Smithbury, but my true love is studying the history of the horses in Virginia. Specifically, I research the hunt country."

"It's obvious you know a great deal about horses."

"Yes, that's true. I do know a great deal about them. One could say, I'm a student of races, hunts and other related events."

His ego is showing, but he's not abrasive or arrogant by any standards. He displays a courtly manner and understands his numerous capabilities, yet appears almost reticent about discussing them. O'Brennan was right; this is a very nice man, and it is hard to believe he's culpable for the reign of terror we're investigating. Too bad he's such a savage. Jeanette dismissed her thoughts as she again picked up the conversation.

"You obviously appreciate the arts, and I find that refreshing. We dream in one direction, things happen and go the other way. My former husband, ignorant by any criteria, never understood my desire to learn and improve my position in life," Jeanette said nonchalantly.

Jeffreys gazed down at the Smilker woman and thought, *You are next. It's such a tragedy you wandered up to me. I've always been a student of causation and why incidents happen. I'll never know why we met, but pretty lady, you lose. You are intelligent, beautiful, and possess such a lovely personality; it is almost sinful to destroy you. Just remember one thing; don't get sentimental over this one. Martin, you must first remember your needs.*

I feel a special charge when I think of her as my next victim, number eleven. What a crowning achievement Julie Smilker shall be. Jeffreys felt aroused by the delicious thoughts racing through his mind.

"You voice my sentiments exactly. The empty-headed woman I called my wife was a world class jerk. When you talk about ignorant, Agnes had all bases covered. You are the very antithesis of that backward woman. Well, enough about her! Like you, I've grown to love the arts. Those who don't appreciate them miss the sunny-side of life." Jeffreys appeared pleased with his soliloquy about his former wife.

"The arts you talk about are a blueprint for making my life more rewarding and eventful," Jeanette said.

"My sentiments exactly."

"To be honest with you, Martin, I have the feeling I'm out of your league. It appears you have considerable wealth, and that somewhat unnerves me."

"I know this is a sign of my growing decadence, but I am what people call self-centered and am wealthy beyond your wildest dreams. Do you have a problem talking to people with money?"

"No, not really. I seldom talk to that type of person. Money has eluded me all my life, but I understand what glorious experiences can come of it."

"In the great boondoggle of life, some have more than others. It has always been that way and will continue to be. After all, money is for the rich and why shouldn't they use it on themselves?" Jeffreys glanced down at Jeanette in a condescending manner.

"Put that way, I have to agree."

"It's no big deal, so think nothing of it. I'm thrilled you cared enough to attend today's event. Speaking of events, the *Saxon Hunt* is coming up next Sunday in Smithbury. Have you heard about it? Whether you're familiar with it or not, I'd like you to be my guest. There's nothing like it."

He's taking the bait, Jeanette thought.

"I am familiar with the *Saxon Hunt*. While driving over here today, my girlfriend and I talked about attending it."

"You brought a girlfriend with you?"

"Yes, she's around somewhere, but I have no idea where. Liz is a nice person, but she really doesn't fit into this type of social function. When we entered the grounds, I realized she was uncomfortable with the setting. It was poor judgement on my part to bring her along, and you better believe that won't happen again."

"Getting back to the *Saxon Hunt*, let your heart be your guide. I'd like to be modest about this, but I can't seem to find a way. The hunt will be held on my estate west of Smithbury. I live on a farm whose mansion and out-buildings date back to the early 1800's."

Jeanette gave Jeffreys her most radiant smile. "I'm flattered you asked me."

Jeffreys didn't seem to notice her show of interest. "My dad built the horse barn from bricks taken from the old slave quarters. The barn was designed to insure the new would faithfully retain the integrity of the old," Jeffreys said proudly.

"It must be wonderful to be in your position."

"I love what I do, and having sufficient money to do what I want appeals to me. As I mentioned earlier, my first love has always been horses. What else could I ask for?" Jeffreys asked with a smile.

He was enthralled by this gorgeous woman, and pondered their brief future together. *She may be a tad outspoken, but never the less a lovely person with a great personality. She has all the qualities I'm looking for, plus she's stunning. Here stands a target that will do nicely. I'll have to design something special for her; something that will maximize my satisfaction. Whatever I plan should expeditiously send Ms. Smilker to her final reward.*

"Aren't you the lucky one." Jeanette's smile served to alert Jeffreys to something more appealing later.

"But of course you'll be my guest next week. Do this as a personal favor for me."

My attraction to Julie is unusual. I feel ambivalent about having asked her to the hunt. As I look back, I resisted the urge to take number eleven, but this breathtaking beauty wins out. It was out of character for me to take such a chance, but my increasing appetite to kill frightens me. The growing need to be stimulated is like a wind that never stops.

"Martin, I'm truly tempted, but I don't know what to do. To say I'm not interested would not be true. I couldn't think of anything nicer than to drive down to Smithbury next Sunday"

"The estate is truly magnificent. The old cookhouse, the brewery, the storage shed, and several slave quarters are away from the mansion and out-of-sight from in front. Looking at the estate from the road, the horse barns are on the right but a short distance from the main house. It's all so wonderful; you must come down and see for yourself. As an added bonus, I'll show you my summer house."

"You have a summer house?" Jeanette's feigned astonishment appeared real.

"I do indeed have a summer house. It's in back of the house facing the Rappahannock. There's a path that runs from the mansion down the hill to it. If you've ever experienced grandeur, this is it. You end up at the lagoon, and a channel that egresses to the river. I have several boats down there that I take out occasionally. The stunning part of the lagoon scene is the little finger of land that juts out into the water. That's where I built the house. I'd like to show it off to you."

I just bet you'd like to get me down there, Jeanette thought as she searched his broad smiling face. *He's decided that I'm to be his next subject; chalk one up for Jeanette. It's best I don't overplay my hand. The summerhouse is the apparent place of the kill. Isn't it dreadful to think of my possible demise like this? He's licking his chops thinking about killing me down there while I'm thinking of nailing him at the same place. I wonder who will win?*

"On second thought, I look forward to the *Saxon Hu*nt and do want to attend as your guest. How can I say no to something so enticing; it sounds like fun. Plan on me being at your place early in the afternoon. You can give me the whole tour and that I'll enjoy. If it is as secluded as you say, I'm sure we'll find it rewarding." Jeanette gave Jeffreys her most seductive smile. "I have to go now and look up my friend. I shall see you next week at your place, so let's leave it at that. If nice thoughts crossed your mind, I'm certain you'll be well rewarded. Talking to you has been fun and I look forward to our next meeting."

Jeffreys nodded yes. "Julie, I enormously enjoyed talking to you today. Incidentally, I was so involved with you I neglected to watch the competition."

"Yes, it was a wonderful afternoon for me and I shall be seeing you shortly."

Turning the tape recorder off in her purse, Jeanette proceeded to head to her car. She found Liz sitting in the front seat.

"I thought you'd never get here. What have you been doing?" Her thin lips settled in a straight line.

"What else but making contact with Jeffreys? Tell me, what happened?" Jeanette asked.

"I didn't handle it very well and things didn't go right. I just couldn't face up. When we first saw him, I thought about the women he killed. I was so unnerved after seeing him I didn't know what to do so I walked around for a turn and ran into him. I stepped aside to let a horse go by and bumped into him and an old gent. That floored me. After returning to the car, I cried like a little baby, then it came to me that you were going to meet him and that made it worse. Finally, I returned to the grounds and saw you talking to him and that was enough for me."

Liz took one last look at the show grounds and shuttered. "This has been a lousy day," she said with a pained grimace.

"Jeanette, I can't believe what happened to me back there. I felt so confident when we arrived; then it blew up in my face."

"Liz, don't blame yourself. O'Brennan once told me that confidence is something you have before you understand the situation."

On their return to Bridgeton, Jeanette jubilantly reviewed her afternoon with Jeffreys.

"Liz, this is going to be easier than I thought. I'll cut him down to size so fast, he won't know what hit him. Next week his past will bump into the present with a thump"

"Aren't you being overly optimistic?'

"Liz, like O'Brennan says, 'I'm in like Flynn.'"

22

Jennial Schemba April, 1978

I've made my decision and mean to stand by it. Prior to this engagement, I had pre-determined who my next victim would be, but on this occasion, I want to try potluck. I will randomly choose my next victim at the *Tar Heel Classic*, in Statesville, North Carolina. I know this decision may be unconventional for my tastes, but when one is overcome with a whim such as this, why not ride with it.

After spending considerable time looking over the crowd, I've decided on an extremely heavy but good-looking woman. Age-wise I would place her close to my thirty-eight years. She is standing by herself and doesn't seem to fit in with the crowd.

People who attend horse events tend to have a special air about them. The object of my attention does not fit into this category. She appears lost in thought and displays the look of a football fan rather than a horse enthusiast.

"Hi, are you enjoying the horse events?"

"Oh, hi. To answer your question, I'm really not." Her eyes swept the open field where the competition was unfolding. "I know nothing about horses and so I'm at a loss as to what is happening."

She had a pleasant face quick to smile.

"Once you get the feel of it and understand what the horse people are trying to do, you'll probably enjoy it."

"Well, maybe, but I can't believe that will be the case."

"What prompted you to come here if you'd never been to one before?"

"About a month ago I bought a ticket on a drawing for this event. A friend was selling them to benefit a children's orphanage back home so I bought one. I thought five dollars was too much, but I wanted to support the benefit, so there you are. She called Monday and informed me I had won two tickets. If you win something, you might as well use it. I asked my husband if he'd like to go, but he wanted no part of it. Couldn't even get any of my friends to attend with me, so I came down by myself. I have the other ticket in my purse, but it's not doing much good there, is it?" She made a happy laugh.

"No, I guess not. Where do you call home?"

"I'm from Chapel Hill and my husband is a professor in the School of Architecture at UNC. He's a nice enough guy, but constantly complains about parking lots at shopping malls. Fred claims, he's my husband, that architects who design them don't have a clue."

"Do you work at the university?"

"I own a wood finishing business in town, and that keeps me busy. I'm Jennial Schemba. I didn't catch your name."

"I'm Fred Leigh from Wilmington."

"So you're from Wilmington, huh. That's quite a distance for you to travel. We went down there last December for the Christmas Light Show, and we also toured the battleship *North Carolina*. We spent the weekend at Wilmington and I just love it down there, and I do know it well. Strange as it may seem, I went to college at UNC Wilmington and we used to hang out at Carolina Beach. Between us college kids, the people from the eastern part of the state, and the marines from LeJeune, it certainly was a wild place. I'm sure you go out there."

"Yes, occasionally I do. It seems that . . ."

She carried on before I could continue. "As much as Fred and I like Carolina Beach, we prefer the Crystal Coast at Morehead City. As a matter-of-fact, we own a cottage on Harkers Island. We've been going there for years, and it works out nicely because my husband has the summer off. The kids are gone now, grown up that is, but it seems as if those three kids of ours grew up on that island. What do you do in Wilmington?"

"I'm a supervisor with the state highway department."

"You work for the state? My Fred does too. Well, you can't beat working for them because of the benefits and retirement plan. That makes anyone involved with the state stand a little taller."

This one can certainly talk. I haven't said ten words to her since we started this conversation. This meeting is not working out like I planned.

"Do you see that brown horse over there? Why did I bring that up? . . . Oh, now I remember. He reminds me of an experience I had when I was a kid."

Oh, God, here goes another half-hour.

"I lived on a tobacco farm outside a little town called Battleboro, which is near Rocky Mount. Dad made a comfortable living from growing tobacco, but many of the people who lived around us were pretty poor. Back then, the neighbor down the road had a kid who was probably sixteen at the time and was a half-wit. He was crazy, no, not crazy, but he was just plain stupid. So stupid they called him Stoop. Stoop for stupid, do you get it? I must have been about eight at the time when my father told us to stay away from him or he'd get us in trouble. One day we were playing in the yard when Dad came in from getting the mail. I can remember this like it happened yesterday. He told mother, 'Do you know what that crazy Stoop did?' She of course had no idea. 'He hung the brown horse,' he said. Like I said, dad had told us to stay away from there, but as soon as he went back to the fields, over we went. We walked around in back and sure enough, there was the brown horse hanging from a big tree in the backyard, deader than a doornail. We found out later that Stoop somehow got the horse up on a corn wagon, tied a heavy log chain around its neck and tied it to an overhead branch. Then he drove the wagon away and hung the poor horse. Isn't it odd that I would think of something like that by looking at that horse over there?"

Lady, your brain must be scrambled to rattle on about such nonsense. Everything you see must remind you of something from your past; you're a master of saying words without meaning. I'll bet all you do is think about stories you can tell. I have to get away from this woman before she drives me crazy.

"That really is some kind of story. Nevertheless, it must be true because you couldn't dream up something like that."

"Speaking of dreaming." It appeared Jennial was getting ready to launch another discourse into her world of fantasy. As soon as she picked up on what I said, she was off and running. I had thoughts of how I'd come here to kill this lady, and if I didn't watch my step, she'd turn the tables around and talk me to death.

"Last week I had a dream that was the craziest thing. As I told you earlier, I have a wood finishing business, and a close friend asked me where she could get an old washstand."

I jumped in before she could start a new sentence. "What's a washstand?"

"It's a wooden bench that was used in the early days to hold a wash bowl and pitcher. Then, they used to wash their hands and face in it. It had a small drawer under the top and two towel bars on the side. I should add, these stands were popular before people had running water in their homes.

"Getting back to my dream; I dreamt I went to the circus and saw one. The part of the circus I'm talking about is where a little car comes in the show ring and a bunch of little people get out. In this case, one of the clowns got out with a washstand, and called my name. Of course I woke up, but isn't that strange?"

"It certainly is." The light has now broken through the clouds. Ten minutes ago I was ready to get the hell out of here and forget what I had come for. But now, I'm in business. It's time for me to tell this fine lady some fiction and see where it leads.

"We're on the same page. It just so happens you're talking to a person who might have an answer for you. There is an antique dealer outside town who runs a wholesale business. He sells exclusively to dealers, but I know he'll help us. You see, my friendship with him dates back for many years, and if he has one for sale, the price will be right."

"Is that a fact?'

"Absolutely. Would you like to chance it?"

"Fred, you've just made my day. I can't wait to see what he has to offer. Let's take my car."

"If you buy more than you can fit in your trunk, we can shoot back here and pick up my wagon. On my return to Wilmington, I can drop off what you buy at your home in Chapel Hill this evening."

Ten minutes ago, I was ready to run away from this talker, but now, I'll knock her over in the name of antiques. Isn't that something?

"That makes sense. Where is this warehouse?"

"It's south of Statesville in a community called Elm City."

Driving toward Elm City on Jennial's final journey down life's way, I felt pleased about how the day had shaped up. I knew the World of Antiques isn't open on Sunday, so I drove around in back of the warehouse to hide the car.

I started off by declaring the warehouse was closed. With a sweep of my hand, I patiently explained how on my last visit to Statesville, the emporium had been open, but unaccountably was closed today.

Jennial appeared momentarily lost in thought, then nodded in apparent understanding. We passed the time with small talk until a low-flying Piper Cub on its way to the local flying club field interrupted our conversation. I looked up but she didn't seem to notice.

The beauty of the day flowed around us as her face displayed the blankness of her thoughts. Somehow I had missed the obvious. Jennial is a mental zephyr who talks incessantly to mask her intellectual shortcomings.

The chill of death settled over us as I decided the time had come to strike.

I searched for the rush of excitement but it didn't appear. My beautifully orchestrated strategy that I so carefully created has gone to waste.

"Jennial, bad companions bring bad luck."
"What does that mean?" Jennial said, nonplussed.

After finishing Jennial off, waves of tiredness settled over me as I pulled the pick from her ear. I placed her in the trunk and returned to the driving range that was next door to the show grounds. I parked her car there, then walked over to get my wagon. After the show twilight settled in and I drove her car back to the show grounds, then returned to the range. To kill time until it got dark, I hit balls to get my game in order. Regardless of how much time I spent hitting balls, I'm certain she had no complaints.

To wind down the day, I returned to a spooky silence at the show ground. Darkness was quickly settling in as I removed her body from the trunk. Although heavy, I managed to carry her to a porta-john next to a horse barn.

I propped Jennial up on the seat so she looked nice. Then I placed a horseradish by the door and quickly headed for home.

The bloom is off the rose and that metaphor says it all. By placing Mrs. Schemba's body in an outdoor toilet I cross the border of good taste, but the story is more important than any of its parts. I'd call that about right, I thought.

I arrived home about three in the morning and settled in my study to record my eventful day while enjoying a goodly portion of brandy. The one unique experience about this elimination was Jennial's reaction to my assault. There wasn't any.

I smile as I look back. I had long established a style of my own, but Jennial redirected my thinking. I anticipated a cold veil of terror to seize her when took I her by the elbow. She gave a start but didn't appear to react to my touch, a rare response. It goes against the grain of logic that when unexpectedly touched by a man, a woman wouldn't react to his touch. I waited for an emotion to spill out, but none came.

I thought it funny. Certainly not ha, ha, but strange is a better word.

When I grabbed this fat woman and taped her mouth, she didn't struggle or react. Apparently, she didn't realize what I had in store for her when I brought the pick to her ear. There was no response in her eyes to what she now knew to be her apparent fate. It was if she accepted dying, and that is different to say the least. It was that simple.

The thrill from my prior episodes with death wasn't there with Jennial. She deprived me of my big rush by not reacting. I have to restructure this experience to make a smooth transition to my next novel, *A Tar Heel* and live with it.

23

After his return from Flat Run, Martin Jeffreys retreated to the study that had been featured in *Country Living*. A thirty-foot long brick fireplace occupied the outside wall with floor to ceiling windows on each end of the room. The remaining side was devoted to books with pictures and prints of horses attached to the ceiling. Red and green leather furniture abounded, with braided rugs partially covering highly buffed oak plank floors.

It was in this picture book setting that Jeffreys plotted each of his removals, as he sometimes called them. His highly successful mystery novels were also crafted here.

The start of a smile settled on his lips as he replayed in his mind the image of Julie Smilker with her gentle voice and uncertain manners. Looking through the window at the spacious flower garden, Jeffreys serenely contemplated his chance meeting with the Smilker woman earlier in the afternoon. Her beauty continued to haunt him as he refilled his brandy snifter.

She's long and lean with lines of a high profile model plus her hair and facial features are remarkable . . . no, make that magnificent. Julie definitely is something to behold. I cannot walk away from this stunning woman without a significant treasure. A toe is not enough. I must make some hard decisions about the trophy that I'm about to take. His thoughts wandered to the summerhouse. *The lagoon is a perfect backdrop for my upcoming execution.* Jeffreys laughed about the roll he was on.

Refilling his glass, Jeffreys struck on what appeared to be a perfect solution to his quandary. *I'll cut her lovely head off. I'll do it at the summer place, then place it in a solution of formaldehyde and permanently enshrine it in a glass jug. Why didn't I think of that before? This foolproof design is terrific. Yes, I like it.*

Now how to arrange this maneuver? The solution seemed to escape him while studying the backyard. Finally, a glimmer of a sketchy plan entered my mind.

I'll entice Julie to the lagoon under the guise of showing her the summerhouse. That's where I'll do the amputation, then place her body in a reed basket covered with leaves, and float it down the Rappohanock. By early morning it will be swept into the bay and drift away. Immediately his impetuous plan caused him concern.

No, that isn't right. The authorities will be able to identify the body from her fingerprints. That is no problem. I'll eradicate her fingerprints with acid, though I didn't do it with the others.

It's a splendid design and I love all sides of it. Pouring another brandy, an alarm went off in his thoughts. *Removing her head would produce an excessive amount of blood and leave evidence on the property, which in turn would pose a serious threat to my safety net. The damn blood! I have to show myself around the show grounds, thus not affording me time to clean up. That best is forgotten. How can I accomplish such a delicate undertaking?*

Another brandy brought the answer. *I'll eliminate her with the pick, then return to the show. After it's finished, I'll return to the summerhouse, move her body to the mansion cellar then preserve this lovely ornament. She's too gorgeous not to save intact.*

I can't imagine what Dad had the two big jugs down there for, but I'll use one for Julie Smilker. When I want to view my ultimate achievement, I'll go down to the cellar and observe her in a full-blown state of death. That is an excellent plan.

This is my long-sought solution for number eleven. She is the finest specimen of the lot. I'm amazed at the keen analytical mind I have. Another touch of this nectar and I'll design a plan for the stroll to the summerhouse.

A pattern was fast approaching the truth but Jeffreys had not seen it coming. His dependency on alcohol had increased at an alarming rate, and it was eroding away the very qualities that made him so superb in his day-to-day activities. A crackerjack legal secretary named Mrs. Watson did much of his legal work. His writing suffered because of his addiction to the grape, and it was she who typed his manuscript and repaired his ever-increasing errors. This deterioration began with *A County Fair* published in 1985. She knew his problem, but was amazed at his ability to craft brilliant themes for his murder mysteries. The quality golf game he valued was rapidly deteriorating. Club members attributed this change to the ravages of time and thought nothing more of it. Jeffreys almost emptied the quart of blackberry brandy and found it increasingly difficult to focus.

I know I shouldn't drink like this, but I do my best thinking when I over indulge. Getting back to next Sunday, I'll stay in the mansion and observe her through glasses during the afternoon. When Regan appears ready to leave, that will be the time to approach her. Then, the best of all worlds will embrace me.

I'll take her to the mansion for a tour. At that time I'll be positioned to move on her, let's say at five-thirty. The main problem I envision is getting Julie down the path unnoticed. I'll send her down to the summerhouse before I go down. Damn, I'm smart! This game plan is working out beautifully.

The longer he thought about his latest scheme, the more he sensed he was overlooking something. *The two domestics will be an obstacle, so why not send them home at noon? Good answer. The caretaker doesn't work Sunday, so that gives me clear sailing. I can take Julie down to the summerhouse and no one will be the wiser.*

Another brandy brought Jeffreys to a horror-stricken state. *Have I taken the wrong turn? Her car will be the only vehicle in the parking lot, and that is the real rub.* Jeffreys anguished for an answer that would resolve the obstinate question he had just raised, but one didn't come. *I have to work something out, but certainly not tonight. The brandy has taken its toll, so I better call it a night."*

Retiring to the master bedroom, Jeffreys stood in a confused state before struggling out of his clothes. A lengthy shower seemed to wash away the cobwebs brought by the brandy, but the thought of Julie's car dampened his enthusiasm. Climbing into pajamas, he wrote a note reminding himself of the potential danger the car would present. *What the hell, if I'm not in the mood to go to the office in the morning, I'll go down to the lagoon and plot something amoral and sinister.*

The shower refreshed me so much, I feel as good as new. Another brandy won't hurt, that's an excellent idea, Jeffreys thought. Filling a snifter full of the indigo colored spirits, he retired to a soft chair to savor his evening planning. The shower had remarkably pulled him back from his drunken stupor and he felt at peace with the world.

A delightful alcohol glow seemed to touch every nerve in his body. *How lax of me to forget the novel which will be my finest effort. Julie as the centerpiece, what a magnificent story I shall tell. Now that I have a subject, I need a title. Over another glass of brandy, Jeffreys concocted a title. Yes, I have it. I'll call my newest creation, A Math Beauty.*

The story is roughed in, so when I write the conclusion, my work is done. Come what may, if I have a problem with the story line, I'll go down to the cellar and view this permanently enshrined beauty in her glass tomb, that's the wonderful part.

Jeffreys looked through tired eyes grown weak from the brandy, and a thought of Julie was his last lucid thought of the evening. He had bowed to the demands of the alcohol and passed out. The glass of brandy Jeffreys was holding spilled onto the white carpet, leaving a stain much like a blood-colored Rorshack inkblot pattern.

24

Donna Reader April, 1981

After a humiliating round at my home course, I realized the inevitable. When I was younger, I could start the season without practice and immediately find myself in playing shape. Now, I need to hit buckets of balls until my hands drop off, and the important feel returns to my swing. After that, I need to play golf at a casual pace until the quality game I am accustomed to returns.

I've planned to attend the *Stoneybrook Steeplechase Races* at Southern Pines a week from today, so why not shoot a little golf and kill a female. As I headed home to plan for my next slaying, I thought my last sentence was an excellent one to put in my next novel, *A Stoneybrook Runs Here.*

I head for the study and try to think through my next outing as thoughts of that lousy round of golf continue to cloud my mind. I shot a six over par seventy-seven and that was not acceptable.

Now I have to think about Stoneybrook next week. The blueberry brandy stimulates me like an insulin surge to a diabetic. Why not go down early and play myself into shape? Looking at my activity calendar, I realize the event is scheduled Sunday, not Saturday as I originally thought. Come on, Martin, you have to get with it and bear down. You can't attack this project without getting details right. I better work out the execution plans right now while I'm in the mood.

I know I'm drifting away from my master plan, but I like the refreshing idea of making a random pick at the event like I did three years ago with Jennial Schemba. In my original master plan, I hoped each victim would bring something special to me, but that old chestnut is becoming monotonous. My writing is becoming too important for me to muck it up by being inflexible. It's the events leading to the killings that are critical in my storytelling, so I'm not going to be picky.

After a week of hitting balls at the range in the morning and playing in the afternoon, my game had become fine-tuned and I'll be more than ready for anything a golf course can bring. Now, I'm set to attend the steeplechase.

The gods provided me with another terrific Sunday morning to once again display my magic. The natural setting and warm temperatures of Southern Pines proved a welcome haven for vacationing golfers beating a hasty retreat from the harsh spring days in the North. The pines of North Carolina provided a magnificent backdrop for their golf game. But unlike the golf enthusiasts that swarmed over the numerous courses in the area, I was not down here to strike a golf ball.

The brilliant morning made spectators forget their Sunday spiritual duties for the festive mood of race day at Stoneybrook. Attending today's happening just meant doubling up on the prayers next Sunday.

The woman I spotted had the glossy look of money and appeared to be everything I sought in a victim. She had a starched look about her with not one detail out of place and appeared to have spent considerable time getting ready. Her yellow walking shorts hung perfectly as if custom designed. I know women sometimes have their clothes tailored, but I find it a stretch that they'd pay attention to their shorts. Her matching blouse and white sneakers with the low cut socks and little yellow tassel had the same meticulous appearance. Her precise dress may have indicated she needed all the embellishment she could muster to mask her pretty but rather course face.

A neat little package, she looked reserved and cool while aggressively smoking as if her lungs were impervious to the dread cancer that challenged them. The look of disapproval at a competitor's sub-performance only reaffirmed my initial appraisal of her. She had a habit-formed manner of pursing her lips like she had just swallowed an anchovy. Her blonde hair was severely cut in a DA, which gave the appearance of being a member of a biker's group. All week long I felt overwhelmed by a premonition that Sunday would be difficult, and choosing my subject had done nothing to relieve my trepidation.

"Are you enjoying the events?"

The good looker turned with a glance that suggested I was a court jester and had just displeased the queen. We measured each other before she spoke.

"It's none of your business, now stop bothering me." Indignation resonated from a voice filled with festering anger and hostility. My instincts tell me I don't like her.

I'll bet she goes through life making others unhappy. A mean one; now, I have my wish. This babe will need special attention, and I'm certain she's not one to be smooth-talked. Tough talk is what she needs and admires and I'm just the one to oblige.

"Lady, it was not my intention to bother you, and secondly, your arrogance is overwhelming your ignorance."

The word ignorance appeared to trigger a reaction that turned her stoic face a bright crimson. "You have no right to say that. I am not ignorant! As a matter of fact, I'm very intelligent; but there is one concession I'll grant you. I will concede that I am very pretty. That said, I cannot abide jerks like you hustling me," she said with a razor-like quality to her words.

How could one person be so spiteful and hateful? This conversation is taking on a texture all its own, maybe one I'm not prepared for.

"You just proved your ignorance by thinking I was trying to put the make on you. It's apparent you can not decipher between being cultivated and being rude."

She stiffened and became flustered and uncertain about where the conversation was taking her. I read her correctly when I determined she had to control everything she touched, and anything less than that would not be tolerated.

"Fools like you can't comprehend how a lady like me can be

beautiful, wealthy, intelligent and a fine athlete," she said in a bullying tone.

She didn't have to continue because her "cat that ate the mouse" look gave her away. Since we started talking, the woman gave me the closest glimpse of what she would call a smile.

"If you're as wonderful as you profess, why aren't you out there riding?"

The dubious look returned as she turned her brooding eyes to view the steeplechase course. Returning her glance to in my direction, she bit down on simply stating she knew nothing about horse events. Just my luck! I waste a contact and half the racing day for what? This bitch knows nothing about horses, so scrap this effort and try salvaging the day with someone else.

"You turkey, why are you out here if you can't ride?" I turned to leave but her next comment rekindled my interest.

With an insensitive stare she explained, "I came down here to Southern Pines to get my golf game in shape for the upcoming season and thought this would he a nice change of pace."

She just said the magic words, and at that point I knew she was mine. To add a little drama to this unpleasant conversation I turned again to leave and over my shoulder said, "You're probably as lousy a golfer as a horse person." I walked away from the distressed woman, knowing her vanity would not permit me to have the last word.

"Come back here this instant!" She commanded me like a person used to pulling strings.

I wonder how this dominating woman would react if she discovered I'm a dangerous stranger?

Turning to again face her, she appeared to become more agitated as she sputtered, "I'll have you know I'm an accomplished golfer, and at one time played three years on the LPGA Tour. I made money, but retired to get married. You're not talking to a novice, so there!" Her massive ego was all over her last statement.

"What have you done since you left the tour?" I knew my comments would stir up her competitive juices, so why not put a little tempest in this blonde's head.

"You'd be surprised."

"You're too old to he any good." I sensed my comment would provoke a reaction.

My last words caused her to flinch as her eyebrows shot up. I'm certain if it had been in her make-up, she would have attacked me in front of God and the spectators at the *Stoneybrook Steeplechase Races*.

She pointed her finger at me with authority. "Listen you, by my own definition, I am a terrific golfer. Five years ago, I made it to the semi-finals of the *U. S. Women's Amateur Championship*. If that isn't enough, I am reigning state champion of Ohio and have been for the last six years," she added in a matter-of-fact tone.

"With all due respect and regardless of how good you are; a good man will beat a good woman any day of the week."

I've seen women who would destroy many good male golfers and knew it. I did know my zinger would trigger a response, but I was surprised by what it turned out to be.

The pretty lady became so flustered and annoyed at my bizarre statement she laughed in a halting manner and then her attitude changed.

Crimson shaded a face prone to fits of rage. "Do you know what a gigantic horse's ass you are for making such a statement?" She asked in a truculent manner. "I can take you out to the links and hammer your ass until you can't stand it."

I laughed at her ridiculous statement. "You do get annoyed, don't you? Besides being rude and brash, I find your language unladylike and crass."

"So be it; it's the only way I know. When golf enters my world, gentility takes a backseat and I take no prisoners. I have a purse full of money that says I can tear you apart on the golf course. Are you man enough to accept my challenge?"

"Indeed I am. Name your poison and we'll be out of here."

"Okay, but I don't know your name. Are you smart enough to remember it, or do you need to show me your driver's license?" Her smugness turned into a full-beamed smile, along with a happy laugh.

"A dim bulb I'm not. My name is Doug Brady and I teach

psychology at Duke University. So, it should be perfectly obvious that I am indeed capable of remembering my name."

We continued to trade jibes until a flash of inspiration registered in my mind. At certain times in one's life, a person draws from far reaches of the mind an insignificant piece of data that is instantly crystallized into something meaningful. For some reason the name stuck in the recesses of the mind like it was attached to a piece of Velcro.

Donna Reader came to mind from an obscure article I'd read in the sports section of *USA TODAY*. It mentioned her name and briefly described her achievements as the reigning amateur golf queen of Ohio.

"This isn't a social gathering, Ms. Donna Reader, I'm ready if you are. Your reputation precedes you."

The testy, abrasive woman was stopped in her tracks by my last sentence. Her pretty face registered amazement as she struggled to answer.

"How . . . how could you have possibly known?"

"It's very simple, my dear. When you mentioned your golfing feats in Ohio, I was reminded of the article about you in *USA Today*."

She tried guarding against the charming smile crossing her face, but failed. "You surprise me, Mr. Brady; and yes, I'm ready to meet the challenge you just offered."

After a brief discussion, a decision was reached whereby we would drive our own vehicles to the Bright Pines Golf Center between Southern Pines and Pinehurst. Parking next to Reader's red Jaguar I noticed how intently she opened the trunk and pulled out a large leather golf bag with an attached pull cart. Sitting on the cart seat, Donna sensuously placed white golf shoes on exquisitely shaped legs.

It was the manner in which she tied her laces that caught my eye, not her legs. Her herky-jerky movement reminded me of someone being chased by a snake. It was obvious her life was consumed by the thrill of golf and the success it brought.

We played for twenty dollars a hole skin game with carry-overs. This approach means the lowest score wins the hole, and with a tie the money carries over until someone wins. Donna Reader was good, so good that at my peak game, she had provided a serious challenge.

I tried to keep myself together by shooting some quality golf. Each time I looked around, she was dogging me stroke for stroke, which in turn prompted me to turn the screws up on my game. I was no longer trying to keep the match close, but wanted to destroy her. Try as I did, I couldn't make any gain on her; and that aggravated me. From the eleventh hole on, we started a string of carry-overs that ended at the final green. The sum total of the accumulated money had reached one hundred sixty dollars.

She drilled in a twenty-foot putt that won the match and the money. I was devastated by this startling turn of events, but had to admit this woman was tougher than I'd imagined. My day at Bright Pines proved to be a very humbling experience.

Donna Reader could not contain herself after the vanity match, and displayed the excited look of success after capturing the spoils.

"Congratulations, Donna. Your game is everything you said it was plus a whole lot more. From the way you played today, I'd say you have a lock on this year's championship."

"I plan to do just that."

You may think so, but the people in Ohio can count on a new state champion this year, I thought while placing my golf equipment in the wagon.

A triumphant Donna reader again spoke with much less edge in her voice. "After you pay me that one-sixty, I'll buy you the coldest beer that lady over there has in his cooler." She pointed to the patio where a circular bar stood waiting for them.

Beer after beer crossed the table until Mrs. Reader rudely stood up without saying a word and headed for the ladies' room.

I approached the bartender whose nameplate told me her name was Rita.

"I see you're not too busy, do you have a moment to talk?"

"Certainly."

"How would you describe the woman I'm sitting with? I just can't figure her out."

"How would I describe her?" The bartender thought for a moment, and then replied, "She's pretty, but then you already know that. I . . . ah, think maybe snippy and snotty, and yes, hard like. She looks at people like she was a prosecuting attorney getting ready to push the button on a defendant."

Pretty in her own right, Rita reached down to wash some dirty glasses.

"She comes in here dressed to the nines and this is only a local place, and she thinks she's better than anybody. The lady wants a drink that has to be fancy, and naturally we don't have that in a little place like this. She has to settle for something less," Rita gestured to the beer tap, "in this case beer, and she thinks it's horrible she has to drink something less than what she's used to."

It was obvious by her answer that Rita didn't care for Donna.

"But don't you think you can find a person like her in any place, right? A place that's dumpy . . . I don't mean to infer this bar is dumpy, but . . ." Swept up in my dialogue about Donna, Rita interrupted me.

"She comes to places like this because she tries to make people feel bad, like they're nothing. Of course, there's no one around to try that on, but they'll be here soon enough. She wants to prove she's classier than the rest of us." Rita looked at me with a questioning look that begged me to understand.

"From a woman's point of view, and I must add you're all woman and then some, would a woman like her come into a place like this by herself?"

My compliment brought a slight blush with Rita's smile. "Yeah, I think so. She wants to be in a position of control, and yes, she'd do it to all men that hang here."

"Are you saying she's a control freak?"

"I would think so. She wants a situation around her so she can put people down. She thinks she's better than them."

"Hm, so . . ."

"She makes the house jump for every little thing she wants."

"So if I sit down with her, which I'm doing, why is she talking to me?"

"If you're talking about the lady you just came in with, I'm surprised she's even talking to you." Rita entertained me with a gigantic smile. "Maybe she wants to pull your pants down."

I laughed and she joined in.

"Seriously, how can you say that?"

"It's easy. She's just a bad soul."

"You don't like her, you being a woman and all."

She gave me a mischievous smile. "So what?"

"But you don't know her."

"No, I don', but she's been in here before and I can't stand her. I know her type. She knows better than someone else and the bottom line says she has a choice of being right or wrong, and chooses to be bad."

"You figured all this out by just observing her sitting at a table?"

"It's what I do, look at people and serve them drinks."

"Have you observed anything about me?"

"Honey, I've been checking you out since you walked in with that bag." Rita smiled while reaching down to wash a glass than didn't need washing. While doing that, she knowingly displayed an exceptionally expanse of cleavage. "You'll have to excuse me because I have some customers."

"Rita, it has certainly been a pleasure."

"Big boy, you can't imagine how much I've enjoyed it, but remember one thing. Right is right and wrong is wrong."

After Donna returned from the ladies' room she talked about her marriage arrangement and how her husband slept around with other women. She admitted to an occasional fling herself, and alluded to the time being right for several hours in the coolness of her dark motel room.

"I don't like you much," she casually said. Her eyes flashed something fleeting I couldn't place. "But there's a certain animal attraction about you that I find appealing. You turn me on, so let's slip away and not waste the day when we can have each other for a go."

Apparently a peculiar look settled on my face causing her to laugh.

"Do I have to draw you a picture?" Donna said with an ice-covered smile.

I wasn't sure how to reply so I didn't speak.

Reader gave me a knowing smile while rolling her eyes skyward.

"We all have our faults, and yours is not understanding one of the niceties being offered in your life. As for me, mine are few and far between." Donna followed with a bone-chilling laugh.

"There are many who play at being God, but few are as adept at it as I. Follow me and you'll have a chance to see how godly I can be."

She laughed and headed for the Jaguar with a provocative sway of her hips that promised greater rewards were in store.

In her motel room after some robust verbal sparring Donna startled me by saying, "When a beautiful woman has an itch, she can scratch it. But when she has a throb, that's a man's job."

I sensed my face displayed a surprised look. "That's a nice way of putting it."

Donna glanced at me obliquely, her face completely inanimate. "Let's get on with the more trivial pursuits of life and treat ourselves to an afternoon delight." She made a pretty smile, a rare emotion for her.

"Where do we go from here?" I asked. The hook was out; all I had to do was set it.

Donna returned to her unpleasant laugh, its taunting meaning settling over me. "And you have to ask?"

My rising euphoria is real and I fail to suppress a smile.

Donna reached down to unbutton her shorts. Allowing them to drop to the floor, she stepped out of them and turned her back to me. She bent over slightly to remove her panties when the urge to strike out at her hit me as quickly as a bolt of lightning striking.

"Your short existence with Martin Jeffreys is of this moment mortally scarred," I softly told her as I yielded the pick in an accomplished manner.

I left Donna where she fell and climbed on the bed. Exhaustion overcame me and sleep came for the next three hours.

What followed proved to be anticlimactic. I carried her to my wagon in total darkness and drove out to the Foxbrook Country Club and deposited her against the rough siding of the halfway house on the tenth tee. I had completed Donna Reader's appointed meeting with the grim reaper and I headed home to Smithbury.

25

The Sunday evening dinner prepared by Colby Martin at Jeanette's *Red Squire* restaurant consisted of spaghetti and meatballs with a green salad and garlic bread. He had again revealed another side that amazed the Group. Was there nothing this little man couldn't do? After dinner, the conversation turned to the afternoon's horse show at Flat Run.

"I'd like to start," Liz said. "Much to my dismay, the afternoon was blown because of me. Jeanette and I designed a quality plan to make contact with Jeffreys. My effort was so amateurish I'm embarrassed to say I couldn't cut it. I guess my life has been too sheltered to understand the real world.

"When we first saw Jeffreys on the show grounds my heart seemed to jump into my throat. The very sight of that animal frightened me, and I could not rationally function for the remainder of the afternoon. I was no help whatsoever. I'm sorry, but that's the way it happened."

"Liz, forget it. You've been very successful in your life and shouldn't be concerned about an incident that you couldn't handle," Jeanette gestured toward the Group. "Each of us has experienced failings and reacted differently. The very fact that you volunteered is good enough for me."

"Jeanette, that's all well and good for you to say. You are one incredible lady for assuming a difficult undertaking, and I'm damn envious of your tenacity. I have nothing to add, so you take over."

Jeanette proceeded to detail her afternoon conversation with Jeffreys step-by-step. "As I speak, I'm sure Jeffreys is designing a plot for, if you will, elimination of this frosted-hair maiden." Her comment drew uneasy laughs from the Group.

"To begin with, he has invited me to be his guest at the *Saxon Hunt* next Sunday. I believe he'll isolate me at the house. A major problem for him is how to settle me in the mansion without escorting me there."

"Jeanette, we're not clear on the physical layout of the property. What did you learn from him about the estate?" Jack asked.

"A lot. Guess I'm getting ahead of myself. The mansion sits on a knoll at the end of the front lane. As you enter the estate from the road, the horse barns are right of the house, maybe four hundred feet away. Directly in back of the mansion is the lagoon and Jeffreys' summerhouse. The lagoon is connected to the river by a narrow channel. I believe he'll attack me there."

"You haven't been to his place, how do you know these things?" Lloyd asked.

"When we talked this afternoon, Jeffreys described the entire layout. He apparently built the summerhouse on the site of the former warehouse and cotton gin. There is one obvious shortcoming that I can't resolve. I know lawyer's nothing of the lagoon, channel, or summer house."

"Well, yours truly does. I can help you with the channel and lagoon."

Colby's broad beamed smile blinded the Group.

"And what do you know about the Jeffreys estate?" Doc Redout curtly asked.

"Pretty much about what there is to know!" From a thin case, Colby withdrew a folded newspaper. "The lagoon channel had been widened and deepened by slave labor to allow seagoing freighters access. It's all in this article from the *Philadelphia Inquirer.*"

Cal looked at O'Brennan and shook his head. "Jack, you'd better raise the bridge because the lad is coming through."

Jack stared blankly at Colby before walking to the table where the page was opened. "He's right! It's the April 11, 1982 edition of the *Inquirer*, and features the Jeffreys estate. Red, how did he get his hands on this?"

Red shrugged his shoulders. "We're not joined at the hip, ask him."

"Well?" O'Brennan looked at Colby.

"Just call me Mr. Magic. Magic for short if you wish. Does it matter how or when I acquired it?" Colby replied.

"Enough of this nonsense. You have to tell us how you found this," Cal said.

"Is it that important?"

"Oh, for heaven's sake, get on with it."

"Oh ye of little faith, you already know that I'm a speed-reader. Every Sunday morning I read the big Eastern papers including the *Inquirer*. I remembered the article, it's that simple."

"What's the story about?" Karl asked,

"It's a great story. The article features the Jeffreys estate and Rappohanock River. As Jeanette mentioned earlier the estate was a plantation in the antebellum days. The existing horse barns used to be slave quarters. That's why they were located so far from the mansion. The article also mentioned the brick-making area between the lagoon and river. The owner found it cheaper to build houses of brick than use wood. The article and diagram say nothing about the summerhouse. I have no idea when it was built."

"Jeffreys said it is four years old," Jeanette said

"As you can see from the sketch, there's a road running from the horse barn to the lagoon. If you look closely, there's a path that runs down the hill from the mansion," Colby offered.

"I think we should proceed in the following manner. Let's assume Jeffreys . . ." O'Brennan never finished.

"Don't even presume to plan this little caper. My skin is on the line, not yours, so this will be my doing!"

"But, Jeanette, you don't understand. You have no idea of the danger involved. This foolish stunt could place you a heartbeat away from oblivion."

"We've been through this a dozen times. This is the way it's going to be done; no, make that the way it has to be done. O'Brennan, back in the Freddie Gill case when you caught

Kenmore's henchmen down at the Village Squire, you and John were in a world of trouble. It didn't bother you then and you know it. For goodness sake, you didn't even have a gun!"

"That was different," Jack sputtered.

"Do not tell me that again! Every time someone is losing an argument or discussion, they revert back to that hackneyed 'that's different' gimmick."

"Jeanette, you win the debate, but I have a question that continues to puzzle me. You have a successful restaurant and a happy life, yet you're single-handedly pressing forward in this perilous quest of a dangerous killer. I'm certain our friends," O'Brennan's arm swept around the gathering, "have a similar thought. Do you have an explanation?"

"O'Brennan, I'm sorry I can't give you a specific reason because there isn't one. Honey, it's something I have to do."

John Lloyd returned the discussion to some degree of sanity by announcing, "Jeanette's right; it's her show and should choose her own poison. No pun intended, Jeanette. Tell us your plan."

"I'm convinced Jeffreys will isolate me on race day. Probably get me in the mansion under the guise of giving me the grand tour."

"We can't cover you in the mansion, but I doubt if he'll strike there. Jeffreys has several domestics who work for him, and they certainly will be working race day," John offered.

"I agree. He's going to move on me at the summerhouse that I'm sure of. The lagoon is the perfect venue for him."

"Jeanette, this is related but not germane. We decided in our earlier profile that the killer was homosexual. How do you view Jeffreys. Are you for or against that image we drew up?"

"John, that was my first thought after I started talking to him. There's no doubt in my mind Jeffreys is heterosexual. He has a most pleasant way about him, and looks at you with a kindly face, though that didn't mislead me. I know this seems like superficial evidence for my conclusion, but . . ." Jeanette threw out her hands in frustration. "He's a purveyor of pain and destruction; there's little doubt about it in my mind."

"Jeanette, a homosexual looks this way too," John replied. "You'll have to trust my judgment on this."

"How do you see this coming down?" Karl asked.

"I'm sure he'll delay meeting me until later in the afternoon. Although he made a date, he won't want to be seen with me at the show. He'll play for time until late afternoon."

"Will he take you to the mansion?" Phyllis Eichner asked.

"Oh yes. It must be beautiful because he talked glowingly of it. His vanity won't allow him to not show it off, that I'm certain of. I'll get the grand tour, have a drink probably, and then he'll waste time until around seven-thirty when dusk starts to settle in. That's . . ."

"But . . ." O'Brennan tried to interrupt.

"Let me finish. That's when he'll take me to the lagoon, probably by the path in back of the mansion. I'm positive he'll strike at the summerhouse."

"Honey, there is a dark side to your plan."

"And what is that, O'Brennan?"

"If he decides to kill you at any place other than the summer house, we can't protect you. Remember, the events of this Death Day you keep talking about can't be replayed. I will give you one thing; it appears you've been thorough with your planning. Someone wins and someone loses. We can't miss a beat and you mustn't lose."

"O'Brennan, for the first time this evening I totally agree with your last comment."

"Is there anything that poses a problem for you?" Jack asked.

"There is. We don't know a thing about the summer house and that has to be resolved."

"Jeanette, Colby and I can work that out. Count on us to get that information," Red said.

"How are you going to do that?" Cal asked.

"A fellow classmate at law school lives in Smithbury. You know him, Colby. I'm talking about Jerry Chappell."

Colby nodded yes. "Doesn't he come from a boating family? I believe they race sailboats in the bay."

"The very same. They have boats of all sizes and descriptions at their river estate. We can borrow one of his smaller boats and slip up the river. Let's plan on going to the lagoon tomorrow morning," Red said.

"The sooner the better. I'll bring my wide-lens camera for pictures. I have another thought about tomorrow. Why don't I wait outside the Jeffreys estate and follow him when he comes out. We should know where he is while we're nosing around the lagoon."

"That's good, Colby, but what if someone sees you when you two are in the lagoon? Let's say a caretaker or domestic wants to know what you're up to," Jack asked.

"That will pose no problem. Colby will just say something stupid and we'll be free and clear." Red smiled.

The Group laughed and soon departed the *Red Squire* for the evening.

26

Patricia Martie June, 1983

While sitting in my study on an overcast June morning, I thought back two years ago to the day I killed that egomaniac, Donna Reader at Southern Pines. Now the need to stalk has returned. With my well-crafted ambitious killing of women my own age finely honed, I pondered how best to select a new victim. When I first ventured into this special world of mayhem, I decided not to assume the role of a stalker. However, as my success as a novelist has grown, I have the urge to more clearly define my subjects. The strategy of randomly selecting a next victim worked in the beginning, but of late, I feel a need to designate the next one.

My recent writing has taken on a more intricate feel with plots forcing the reader to the very last pages before the killer is revealed. I enjoyed killing Donna Reader because she had proven to be mean and arrogant. The thrill of using her as the victim in my latest novel, *A Stoneybrook Runs Here* provided me with a passion surge almost as strong as her real death at the *Stoneybrook steeplechase Races*.

Refilling my brandy snifter, I held it so the rays of the brilliant morning sunshine would beam blessing on the nectar. My ritual was much the same as a priest holding up the golden chalice of wine in preparation for the Blessed Sacrament of Communion. My eyes came alive as I studied the purplish brandy. For me the alcohol-laced juice served more as an hallucinate than the depressant it was reported to be.

The morning was ripe with promise as I returned to the desk to review my events calendar. I determined the *Charles County Fair and Horse Show* on June twenty-fifth would serve as an excellent time and place for number seven. That means I must attend the *Red Lion Horse Show* in Winchester next week. The two shows are considered companion events in that they match time-wise as well as geographically. The odds of my next victim attending both events favor me. I thought briefly and concluded I could further stack the deck by choosing three potentials.

I refilled my glass and walked to the open French door overlooking the multi-colored flower garden. I thought of my brilliant lifestyle; how great it was to be alive and to write novels that so many of my faithful readers enjoy.

The three-hour trip from Smithbury, although lengthy, provided additional time to mentally prepare for my next adventure. The warm June breeze brought every indication of another in the string of picturesque Eastern Shore days as I pulled into the parking lot of the *Charles County Fair and Horse show*.

It didn't take long to spot the one I had chosen earlier. I can sense she is a loner, like most of the others. Settling in next to her, it was time for my pitch.

"Hi. I trust you're enjoying the horse show. My name is Nelson Kidd and it's a beautiful morning, isn't it?"

She blankly looked at me. "I ah, ah . . . fi . . . fi . . . fine . . . find them fas . . . fasc . . . nay, nascin . . . fascinating. An . . . and you . . . you're . . . ri . . . righ . . . right . . . abo . . . about . . . the pre . . . pretty . . . day . . . day," she replied with nothing but a faint whisper.

I shook my head in surprise. Damn, what a break! I found a stutterer. That was an affliction I never thought about. I have to pay close attention to what words and sounds pose a problem for her. I became so intent on her speech impediment I failed to notice the lovely fair-skinned face framed with black hair.

"I didn't catch your name. What do I call you?"

"I'm Pat Martie."

I could see and read in her eyes how embarrassed she was of her stuttering. A sense of pity overtook me as I spoke.

"You don't talk much, do you, Pat Martie?"

"I ah . . . I don't have mu . . . ch . . . ch, have much to talk ab . . . about as you ca . . . ca . . . can see, I'm a stut . . . terer." Tears filled dark eyes as she turned away.

"Don't be so hard on yourself," I offered.

A thought crossed my mind. *This lady needs a little push.*

"You feel sorry for yourself, and if you think for one minute I'll fall all over myself telling you how badly I feel, well forget it. You're a piece of damaged goods, so why not accept it? If you don't like . . ." I felt the need to complete my thought but resisted. *Maybe I pushed too hard with the damaged goods bit and should back off.*

Her eyes displayed the sad appearance of a cocker spaniel as I forged on.

"I'm a stutterer myself, but you don't see me carrying on and feeling down."

Pat's eyes widened as she surveyed me with renewed interest coupled with awed disbelief.

"You're just saying that. Yyy . . . yy . . . our, you're no stut . . . terer."

"No, you're wrong. I'm a diagnosed stutterer, but my affliction doesn't surface in normal conversation. Only when I get excited do I stutter."

"Ye . . . yes, wh . . . wh . . . when I . . . ah ge . . . gettt excited, I doo . . . I don't stut . . . stutt . . . stutter as much." She appeared to sigh as if completing a difficult task.

"So, you see, we're different yet the same in many ways. When you get excited your stuttering becomes less pronounced. While conversely, when I get excited, my stuttering problem rears its ugly head. Does that make sense?"

"Nooo . . . no, i . . . itt doesn't."

This isn't working out. Maybe this woman isn't the answer. She seems so removed from the ebb and flow of the moment. It's like she's carrying on in a script-like manner, impersonating someone from the past. *This doesn't make sense; but I feel there's something very strange about this woman. Best to get the hell out of here,* I counseled.

"I think you feel uneasy around me, and it's best I go."

I started to leave, but much to my surprise she placed her hand on my arm and squeezed. Her strength was alarming as she spoke in a husky whisper.

"Noo . . . please do . . . don't g . . . ga . . . go."

I haven't been frightened since I was a kid, but her action fired my attention to imminent danger. I had no idea what the danger entailed, but felt the need to get away from this woman. But strangely, there was something compelling about her that provoked an opposite need to stay.

Still shaken by my reaction to her touch, I asked, "Why do you want me to stay?"

"I ah . . . I need you near, I need you near me. I'mm . . . I'm so lon . . . lonely, I cann . . . I can't stand it."

Looking at her caused something from the past to surface. Not my past but a past I couldn't account for. I studied her incredible face for the first time and saw a black page-boy hair style framing an unblemished chalk-like complexion save for a mark, perhaps from an earlier bout with chicken pox on her forehead. Her bright red lipstick outlined an angry mouth, and severely plucked eyebrows defined coal-black piercing eyes. She had the look of a character out of a 1930's horror film.

The chills again raced through me as I turned to look at the crowd. *I have to get out of here, yet there's something I must find out about this woman that she hasn't revealed. I feel moved to continue. She is so unique I'd like to write her into my next novel. But . . . not as the victim mind you, as the killer. That's it! I know I hit on the right formula. I can make her into a serial killer; that's better yet. How ironic, absolutely unique, a female serial killer. I must say this will be a brilliant coup on my part.*

"Why are you so lonely?"

"Because I recently los . . . lost my hus . . . husb . . . husband."

"I'm sorry to hear that. It must be difficult for you, being so young and pretty."

"Yes, i . . . it iss, it is. I walk wwi . . . with the shh . . . shad . . . shadow of dea . . . death around me. This isss . . . this is the thir . . . third hus . . . husband I've los . . . lost inn . . . in five years."

Her disclosure left me momentarily nonplussed and I realized our encounter was going from bad to worse. *She is making the hair on my neck stand on end.*

"You've had some pretty tough luck, but I'm certain it will change soon."

"Yes, I'mm . . . I' m sure . . . I'm sure you're ri . . . right. Bu . . . but you . . . re . . . rea . . . really . . . don't un . . . underst . . . understand, do yo . . . you?" She reached to the top button of her blue cardigan sweater and slowly unbuttoned it. A slight smile cracked her mask-like face as she popped the second button. Her teasing continued until cleavage showed between her ample breasts. I looked down, then up into black shining eyes.

I felt self-control slipping away as time raced by. This was curious because I had always prided myself on controlling difficult situations. It was like the central figure in a dream finding myself being led hand-in-hand by a disembodied spirit. I could feel her presence in a vague way, but her physical being was like a high-flying cloud. This woman is taking me down a one-way street, and I must protect myself, but how?

"I need a man, and you'll nicely fill the necessity. I'm telling you this for a reason because I've always needed men. I can't imagine spending the day without a big rugged blonde. Come, follow me." Her voice thickened with excitement as she reached for my hand and led me away from the crowd.

I was compelled to follow her lead.

What in the hell am I doing? I asked myself. Then the thought hit me with the impact of an axe hitting a man's head. *The thought of a sexual encounter excites her; she isn't stuttering anymore. What does she have in mind? I can't imagine, but I'm certain it will be nothing like what I have in store for her.*

"Nelson Kidd, ride with me in my van and I shall provide

you with the most earth-shattering afternoon delight of your life."

She laughed as she eased the van into traffic and left the spectators at the horse show unaware of the delicate ritual she was about to perform. Her laugh was a cold and chilling sound that made my flesh crawl.

She parked the vehicle in a car dealer's lot next to other vans much the same as her black van.

"Okay, handsome, the time is right for us to get on with what we came for. Get in back and we'll go from there."

Controlled anxiety gripped. I did as ordered and settled into a swivel seat facing her. She looked at me with a deadly coldness and finished unbuttoning her sweater. She removed the cardigan and carelessly tossed it to the floor. Now was my time to strike and finish up the day in style.

With her fingers pressed together across her exposed breasts, she leaned back in the swivel chair in deep concentration with eyes that looked like someone preparing to throw the switch on the electric chair.

"You can't keep from looking at my lovely chest, can you? Men like you are a dime a dozen, and you're brothers at heart. Earlier, you mentioned how we were the same but different. I do agree that we are the same in one respect; we're both mean and vicious. You look surprised by my comment, but you know it's true. Oh yes, I can see it in your eyes. As for the different, we are that, my dear friend. You have to seek out women to have your way with them for an hour, an afternoon, as long as it takes to gratify your sexual drive. I also have sexual drives, but they don't include wrapping myself around a savage like you. No, you've miscalculated the easy lay you anticipated."

She's going to do something crazy that I'm not prepared for.

That thought proved closer to the truth than I realized.

Hot blood rushed to Pat's face as she reached into her bag and withdrew a pistol. "Isn't this a magnificent piece of weaponry? This is a W.W.II German 1914 model Luger, and please note its excellent condition."

Much to my horror, the gun barrel looked small compared to the round cylinder covering it that would muffle the shot. I found myself looking into the face of a violent death and for the first time thought about the terror my victims felt. Suddenly, the thought flooded over me. *What you want and what you get are totally different.*

"My sexual relief comes from killing bastards like you. I constantly dream about it and think of the kill and the trapping it embraces."

She's going to kill me, and there's nothing I can do to alter this course of events. I must get myself under control and look for some possible escape from this cold-blooded killer.

Her heavy breathing increased as she forged ahead. "I know what you're thinking," she said with a cold, knowing smile I shall never forget. "You're trying to settle down so you can escape your inevitable fate. How do I know this you are probably asking yourself? Let me properly introduce myself. My name is Dr. Patricia Martie, and I am a practicing psychiatrist. That's right, a student of the human mind and yours is an open book." Her words just hung there.

Why hadn't I noticed the mark of cruelty around her mouth before, I questioned.

"Killing animals like you is an avocation of mine. For you see, I am what members of the print media call a serial killer. I assume you are intelligent enough to grasp the meaning of this. I have killed six gentlemen of the evening if you will, and you are destined to be number seven."

At that moment the sound of two bangs echoed throughout the van. For a fleeting instant, she looked away toward the origin of the sound, and that split-second was her undoing. The pendulum of probability was ready to swing, and its course would favor me. In a desperate gesture, I kicked the gun from her hand and sent it flying to the carpet. With a quickness that amazed me, I had her in a vice-like grip and rapidly secured her with duct tape. A sudden exhilaration overtook me and I was again in control. It was after the turbulent period following the shots I later recalled two young boys arguing about who shot whom first. If it hadn't been for their childish games, I'd have been tacked on to Pat Martie's trophy list.

The aftermath of the brief skirmish was an unsettling emotional drain that left me near prostration. I sat gathering my thoughts and energy as the lovely doctor displayed the same fear she had brought to others. *She's as mad as a hatter,* I thought while preparing to finish this macabre afternoon.

"So, my dear, you profess to be a serial killer. Well, we are closer to being the same than different. You and I are truly kindred spirits for I also am a serial killer and like you have killed six people. Each of us has six notches on our weapons, but that's not going to be true for long. Your count shall remain at six while mine will escalate to unprecedented numbers."

I withdrew my killing pick and held it up for viewing. Overhead light on the stainless steel shaft sent sparkling reflections of white light darting around the van's darkened interior. I turned the pick until flashes of light danced across her ashen face, coming to rest on black eyes. Those eyes turned away but soon returned to the object, no longer shining with anticipation. The black spots of coal displayed a strange dullness I took for fear.

"You have frightened me from our first encounter this morning. Talking to you was like looking into a long dark tunnel with no light at the end. My fear never left me during our brief encounter until this very moment. Viewing that long and dark tunnel, I now can see light at the end. You see, I also know a little about the human mind, and recognize your thoughts.

"Would you like to know about the light at the end? It's like a picture on the wall all done in sunlight with a slight mound of grass with a headstone. Yes, you're right, Dr. Patricia Martie is engraved on that piece of marble."

"This has been the most thrilling experience of my life, and I feel badly we couldn't have worked in tandem as a serial killing team, but who's to say. We both know that is impossible because I have the pick and you're taped-up. The suspense must be killing you. Hey, I just made a joke."

I reached over and brought the pick to the ear of the beautiful doctor's head. Pushing the shaft into the ear of this ex-serial killer eliminated one more menace to the wonderful world I live in.

As a fitting conclusion to my thrilling day, I returned Dr. Martie to a more fitting resting-place in a pasture. I placed her against a fence post, returned her van to the parking lot at the show, and headed home.

On my way to Smithbury I wondered whether Pat Martie was truly a stutterer or was that an act?

The dreams both good and bad visited me nightly for months. The wicked ones darted in and out of my nocturnal rest without warning. They were not of the erotic variety, but full-blown nightmares.

Faithfully I revisited the van and the white face dressed in midnight hair, eyebrows, and discerning eyes. The shiny red lips emitted a guttural sound that produced shrieks reminiscent of a banshee proclaiming a warning of misfortune. She had brought the shadow of death with her.

One moment I felt detached from the dream and in the next scene found myself included in the darkness of a van. A shadowy figure was beckoning for me to enter, but I never did. I'm no psychiatrist and don't understand dreams, but I know my mental sleep wandering is scary.

27

At seven-thirty on a fresh Monday morning the rural landscape around the Jeffreys estate was ablaze with golden rays of sun signaling the arrival of summer. Leaving the mansion, Jeffreys drove out the tree-lined lane in his tan four-door roadster and headed into Smithbury. Carrying a hangover as wide as the morning, he didn't notice the green LeBaron convertible following him.

Jeffreys' car impressed Colby. With its canvas top down, the roadster glided into Smithbury on old-fashioned white sidewall tires. Colby would later identify the car Jeffreys was driving as an open bodied Chrysler Custom Imperial Phaeton. Not a student of fine cars, the name failed to impress him, but the lines of this fifty-year plus classic did.

Following Jeffreys at a safe distance, Colby felt the three miles into Smithbury whiz by. Smithbury was home for Virginia's eastern-most hunt country, and had entertained the horse tradition since colonial days.

Although this was his first visit to tree-covered Smithbury, Colby had studied a book called *The Hunt County of Smithbury* and familiarized himself with its history. The sugar maples that abounded throughout the community enhanced the beauty of this colonial settlement and its traditional appearance.

Brighton Avenue, the community's main thoroughfare ran through three short blocks that comprised the business district. The fieldstone buildings, many of which were built in the early 1700's, housed quality antique shops and clothing stores carrying the finest designer and traditional wear found on the eastern shore.

Any community this small had to be staggering under loads of money to support four jewelry stores.

Colby followed Martin Jeffreys where he disappeared through this maze of affluence. Not finding a parking space, Colby turned into the *Hounds Inn* parking lot. Dating back to 1720, the inn had once been called an "ordinary". The word was used in colonial days to describe inns and taverns that served plain and ordinary food.

A community's buildings reflect its interests and tastes and it quickly became evident to Colby this community had all the qualities that spelled Class. He agreed with the book's assessment of Smithbury, it was still the symbol of privacy for its elite residents. The rest of the community fervently guarded its personality determined by the wealthy; and what was good for the members of the social register was good for everyone.

The little lawyer also agreed with Cal's critique of the town. Smithbury was a terrific village to visit, but he wouldn't care to live here. Colby's readings had revealed an interesting fact. Originally, foxhunting was a method of ridding farmland of a large fox population, but after near extinction the Smithbury hunters so missed their newfound sport they purchased foxes from hunters on Maryland's eastern shore. The descendents from their progenitors are currently penned in some of the finest facilities in America.

A tapping on the car window interrupted Colby's thoughts. Rolling down the window, he looked up at a young parking attendant dressed in the traditional red and black hunt wear.

"Sir, this lot is reserved for patrons of the inn."

"I'm sorry, young man, I must have been daydreaming."

Colby got out and handed the attendant two dollars. "I'm going in for breakfast. Sorry if I inconvenienced you."

"Anytime, anytime at all," the teenager replied with a smile.

An hour later, Colby left the inn and casually walked by Jeffreys' office. Through the massive colonial styled front-window he could see Jeffreys talking to his secretary. *That gives us clear sailing down at the lagoon. I better head over and meet Red before he has a fit,* Colby thought as he headed for his car.

Arriving at the Chappell Estate ninety minutes late caused Colby little concern. Directed to the family marina by a gardener, he parked his car close to where Red and Jerry Chappell were talking.

"Where in hell have you been? You're an hour and a half late," Red said.

"I stopped at the *Hounds Inn* and had the hunt breakfast," Colby casually replied.

"Doc McGregor was right, you do have a screw loose."

Colby explained his tardiness to Red's unsympathetic ears. Turning to Chappell, Colby said, "Jerry, was it something I did?"

"Colby, your friend doesn't appear to be very happy. It must have been something you ate."

"You're so perceptive. Old Red is having a little snit, but he'll get over it," Colby said.

"Red told me you're settling in the area and I think that's great. We should get together and study for the state boards. The other guy," Chappell swept his hand in Red's direction, "mentioned you're working on the Smithbury Skeleton. I know you fellows want to get going, so I'll let you go. Give me a call when you have a chance."

The morning air, hot and humid, settled on the river like a blanket as the small bass boat gracefully knifed through the gently flowing water at a leisurely pace. Moving up the river, Colby asked Red, "You never spoke of it, but what do you think about Jeanette entering into this venture? Give me an answer and don't lie to me."

"I can give you an answer but I may have a problem with the second part," Red said. "It's going to be a tough event to plan for. The choreography at the lagoon is critical, and that's why we're moving against the current this instant."

"That's all well and good, Red, but you haven't told me a thing. What about the operation, will it work?"

"This is a deadly serious stunt she's trying to pull off, but Colby, I don't believe there's a chance it will play out."

"You mean we won't get to Jeffreys?"

"Oh, we'll get Jeffreys all right, but I'm afraid he'll get to Jeanette before we can intercept him," Red said soberly.

"You really believe that, don't you?"

"I'm sorry to say, I do."

"The picture you just painted isn't pretty. Is there something we can do?"

"You heard Jeanette and Jack go at it. No, I think it's out of the question. She's committed and you know how headstrong she is. Why are you so concerned about her welfare?"

"Red, I'm not the glib, fast-talking operator people perceive me to be. I'm as sensitive and concerned about her welfare as anyone. I know she'll be in a crapshoot and our efforts and observations could greatly enhance her chances of getting out of it."

"I agree."

"I have a question you may be able to answer. I never thought much about it before; but when I trailed Jeffreys into Smithbury this morning, I asked myself what the community thinks of him?"

"Jeffreys is a big society lawyer who has earned the respect of the best families in Smithbury. He has high class clients with main line connections."

"How good is he?" Colby asked.

"He's excellent from what I hear. A social type himself, he represents the four hundreds with class and distinction. He has social position and knows how to use it. He is one of the centerpieces of Smithbury society."

"What's his temperament like as a lawyer?"

"All the people I've talked to call him a buttoned-down maneuverer who has an inflated opinion of himself. But, I give him credit for one thing; apparently he is more interested in justice than headlines. We certainly can't fault him for that, can we?"

"Red, you see good in everyone regardless if he's a serial killer or not."

A silence took over momentarily until Red said, "There's the channel leading to the lagoon." Silence once again claimed the boat as they traveled the short distance into the lagoon.

"There you are, my friend, bodda bing, bobba boom; the lagoon awaits your scrutiny," Colby said.

"Why do you say such stupid things as: bodda bing, bodda boom?"

"Because I like the sound. If it's good enough for me, it should be okay with you."

"I suppose so, but where did you hear it?"

"On TV."

"That sounds like something you'd hear on a cartoon show."

"You watch cartoons, don't you?"

"No. Would you explain why you do?"

"Because I like them." Changing the subject, Colby continued, "We shouldn't overstay our welcome. I'll take the pictures and let's split."

For fifteen minutes, Red manipulated the boat around the quiet little bay, affording Colby a breath-taking opportunity of taking pictures from every possible angle.

"I wonder who guards the fort when the general is away?" As he spoke, Colby sensed the presence of a third party in the lagoon.

From the summerhouse patio came a cold booming voice, "What are you doing in the lagoon?"

"It is my considered opinion the general is back," Red whispered. "Show me how glib and slick you are now."

"Don't worry, I'll come up with something." The master of improvisation was ready to perform. Colby smiled and waved at Jeffreys from the boat.

Red steered the fishing boat to the dock where Jeffreys stood in deck sneakers, white shorts, and the tattered remains of a gray cut-off William and Mary sweatshirt.

"Didn't you see that posted sign out by the entrance of the channel? I don't know how you could have missed it." Jeffreys looked blue with rage as he admonished the young men in the boat. His rage appeared to have originated from something he drank.

Colby couldn't think of anything to say during the awkward silence that followed. Out of desperation he replied, "I'm not lying to you when I say we didn't see it. We were talking about the beauty of the river and its immediate landscape and completely missed the sign. It was not our intention to infringe on your privacy, but we were so fascinated by the channel and lagoon, we couldn't resist taking a look."

"What are you up to? You have fishing poles but don't appear to be using them," Jeffreys said with a bristling glare hard as shoe hide.

Colby chose his words carefully. "As a matter of fact, we're not," he replied with his little boy grin. "Sir, you probably won't believe this, but we're out here studying."

Red raised his eyes to the sky but remained silent.

"You're telling me that two grown men are out here in a boat traveling along on a Monday morning studying! May I ask what you're studying?"

"Yes, sir. We're getting ready to take our state boards," Colby said with considerable satisfaction.

"And what boards would they be?" Jeffreys said with a flicker of interest.

"Sir, we just graduated from UVa. Law School and we're preparing for the boards in August."

"Lawyers, huh?" Jeffreys said with an icy stare.

"Kind of, sir. Not as yet you understand, but if we pass the boards we will be."

Jeffreys' mind drifted back to the days when he was preparing for the same exams. He probably had sounded like this young man, full of trepidation over an unknown obstacle in his life.

"I appreciate your concern about the upcoming boards, for you see, I am a lawyer as well and once went through the same scary moments that you lads are currently experiencing. I know what it's like to study and prepare for them. You hope what you cover today will be asked tomorrow. Welcome to the club that all lawyers have joined. At this moment you may not think so, but you'll remember these times as the glory days of your career.

Why don't you fellows tie that boat to the dock and come up to the patio?"

As they secured the boat, Red looked at Colby as if to say, "I can't believe we're pulling this off."

"Come over to the patio, boys. Let me introduce myself, I'm Martin Jeffreys, and your names?"

"Yes sir, I'm Colby Martin from Massachusetts. I came down to attend law school and liked the area so much, I decided to stay."

"And your friend?" Jeffreys asked.

"Sir, my name is Red Ted, and I'm from Bridgeton," Red said, feeling the discomfort of the moment.

"Come on over and have a seat. We can talk some law and enjoy the beautiful morning. Could you tell me the time?"

Looking at his watch, Colby replied, "It's about ten-thirty."

"I know it's early but enough of this poppycock. Would you gentlemen be interested in a beer? I'm going to have one; in fact I really need it. I have the coldest beer you've ever tasted; it's damn near freezing. Do you follow?"

Red nodded. "A cold beer would go nicely on this hot morning."

Jeffreys left the patio and soon returned through the glass doors of the summerhouse. "I didn't bring glasses, figured drinking out of a can wouldn't bother you," Jeffreys said carrying three cans.

"No sir, it won't," Colby replied. "I love your summer retreat. I'm especially enthralled with this flagstone patio; it's so elegant yet basic."

Red shook his head as thoughts of Colby saying enthralled settled over him.

"Yes it is. When I look at this beautiful setting, I have nothing but pleasant thoughts. I wanted nothing to detract from the beauty of the lagoon, thus the austere look. We raised it a foot to impede the ducks from climbing up here and doing their business, but that didn't discourage them. When I come out in the morning, it sometimes looks like a flock of them stayed overnight. No harm done, I just hose the surface off and leave it as is."

"Sir, this is a pretty fancy retreat. Do you spend much time down here?" Colby asked.

"Yes, from early spring to late fall. Now listen, just call me Martin. 'Sir' seems awfully formal for such a casual morning."

"There's nothing wrong with that, Martin," Colby said as the two make-believe detectives nodded in agreement.

"Yesterday, I attended the *Flat Run Horse Show* west of Fredricksburg and met the most amazing woman. Meeting her has reshaped my awareness of the true meaning of beauty. I spent a lovely afternoon with her, and much to my astonishment, she agreed to attend the *Saxon Hunt* that will be held here next Sunday. When I came home and started thinking about my chance encounter with this stunner, I felt rapture.

A duck waddled up on the patio and aimlessly walked around. Finding nothing to hold his attention, he flew into the lagoon and out of the scene playing out on the patio.

"Watching that stupid duck caused me to forget what I was talking about. Now I have it." Jeffreys laughed. "I sat down with a drink and the next thing I knew, I'd climbed into a bottle of brandy. I don't know why, but as they say in basketball I slam-dunked too much of it. Did you ever drink brandy?" He asked of no one in particular.

"Naw, Martin, never did. I drank a whole bunch of torpedo juice when I was in the Marines, but never such a refined drink as brandy," Red said.

"Trust me, don't make a habit of it. It doesn't feel so refined this morning." Jeffreys' laugh brought a similar response from the rookie lawyers. "I woke up this morning with a slight twinge of the liver but I knew that would eventually pass. Work at the office didn't go well and I thought my head was coming off. Finally, I said to hell with it and came home. I changed clothes and decided to get well down here. After last night's bout, this beer truly tastes therapeutic."

"I hope we didn't interrupt something you had planned, "Colby said.

"To the contrary, my friend, you can't imagine what comfort your visit has provided this morning. If I hadn't met this beauty yesterday, I wouldn't have this monstrous letdown now. Granted, that fermented berry juice didn't help."

"So the woman you met was classy, huh?" Colby asked.

"Possibly the classiest one I've ever met. She's gorgeous and what a body! But enough about her. Tell me a little about your background. I'm interested in your goals and what you'll do for your chosen profession. What you expect from it."

For the next two hours, Colby and Red talked with Jeffreys over cans of beer too numerous to count. They desperately wanted to get into the summerhouse, but didn't know how to go about it. They had used the powder room off the kitchen but that wasn't the answer. A move was in order so Red started the ball rolling by standing up.

"Martin, we really have to run. Maybe we helped you get over your hangover, but I'm afraid we've started one for ourselves. We hadn't planned on this stop, and with all the beer we put away, we can forget studying for the day. I'm very impressed with your lagoon and fabulous retreat. Would it be possible to take some pictures of the lagoon and use the house as a backdrop?"

"Red, you're right of course; it is terrific. This estate used to be a working plantation in the antebellum days. Right here where the house is," Jeffreys waved at the near-by structure, "was the site of the cotton gin. Freighters used to come into the lagoon and load cotton from the old wharf. You can see why I'm so attached to it. You must remember this is nothing more than a summerhouse, a retreat from the mansion. It's basic and plain but comfortable. I have a thought. Why don't you stay around for a while and we'll have another beer. After we finish I'll show you around the house. I'm very proud of it, and you can take pictures of the interior as well."

Red's casual glance at Colby disclosed his thoughts, "How could we be so lucky?"

Colby smiled at Jeffreys. "That would be terrific. I'll go down and get my camera." Red shook his head at Colby as if to say, "I can't believe you pulled this off."

The next hour Jeffreys showed off his summerhouse from stem to stern. After returning to the patio, the amateur sleuths promised Jeffreys a return visit and said their goodbyes.

Leaving the dock, Red continued to take pictures of the house and lagoon. Drifting down the river, they both agreed what promised to be a-run-of-the mill day had proven very productive.

"One last question; do you think he's on to us?" Colby asked.

"No way. You know yourself we're half bombed, but that guy is in a different league. It goes without saying he's so heavy into the booze he doesn't know where he is half the time."

"Red, don't you think that lagoon is a perfect venue for a killing?"

"I'd rather not think about it."

28

Kersi Clark April, 1985

I've now reduced the writing of novels to practically a science. The manner in which I use this tape recorder has been the difference. I record everything on the machine and transcribe it into a typed manuscript. From there, Mrs. Watson edits and revises it; actually does what she wants with it. She's a remarkable woman who knows my style and makes quick work of the rough copy.

So, now, I'm on the verge of a yearly book, which is somewhat like the mass-production found in a factory. Several problems have arisen since I initiated this increased production over the recent years. First, there are the increased odds of getting caught and I see that as a major obstacle. Second, I'm on a thin line with my drinking, which ultimately will lead me to my end. There's no way out because I've become so dependent on brandy that I can't seek help. By seeking professional counseling, I'd be exposing myself to a psychologist's meanderings and that in turn would uncover my sordid history.

After staying in Durham overnight, I felt rested and clear-headed for this new effort. The morning sun promised a splendid day for my project as I drove toward Winston-Salem on Interstate 85.

Granted, the assassins I create have emotionally found the need to be caught, and I shall continue on that story line, but there should be more. For my upcoming novel, *A Tangled Affair*, I shall have a bi-sexual male face the trauma of having an anti-social preference, plus the need to destroy members of the opposite sex. It will need refinement, but that will come.

Thinking back to the days that have been part of my killing fields, I find that each of my subjects provided me with a perfect southern day. The one exception was the day I took Ann Gardner in Leesburg, and that was a dark and gloomy overcast day. If I schedule a killing and the weather is miserable, I'm canceling out. I shall not attend the event so I won't be tempted to undertake the planned project. I don't want to get involved with something that goes against the grain of reason and that's final.

I like the practice of predetermining three possible victims before I arrive at the scene. It takes me out of the frenzied emotional feeling that came with randomly selecting a victim at the playing field.

The mysterious part of the plan is I get almost as much pleasure from going to the show and meeting my subject as the inviting thought of the kill itself. Driving through the outskirts of Winston-Salem, the anticipation of the hunt and elimination gnawed at me. A feeling of sitting in a locker room mentally preparing for an upcoming game swept over me. Nervousness nudged me as I parked the wagon and headed for the *Tanglewood Park steeple Chase*, and another eventful day.

I initiated another change-up in my game plan that I felt would replace my *modus operandi*, so to speak. Now I don't know the names of my victims because I choose to go in unprepared. However, I do know what they look like, and my first choice is standing at the refreshment stand as I speak.

Presentable but not eye-catching, Madame X, I shall call her has a neat but scattered look to her anorexic body. I don't know how better to describe her other than that. She is not attractive by any stretch of the imagination, but has a head of lusty and shiny sandstone colored hair.

I noticed the flush look of what appeared to be sunburn as I approached her. Closing the distance, there was no explanation needed. I discovered sunburn was not the cause of her rosy facial hue. She had the look of blood-filled corpuscles fighting to push through the skin's surface. People pushing sixty begin to show these tattletale signs that are inherent with age. But the look on a woman forty-five was not the exception to the rule; Madame X was a boozer.

"Hi, how are you doin' today? It's a great day for the races isn't it?"

"Nicely thank you. Yes, it most certainly is."

"I get the feeling we've met before. Do I look familiar to you?"

She shrugged her shoulders as if to say she had no idea.

"I can't recall, but what do I know?"

This one is kind of strange; I can feel it. I have to find out what her game is and that may not be that easy; better tread softly, I warned myself.

While drinking my coffee, I watched her take quick sips of juice, which was a tip-off that my early assessment of her was on target. Might as well introduce myself and get this show on the road.

"I'm Juan Wilson from Greenville, South Carolina."

"It's good to know you. I'm Kersi Clark and come from right here in Winston-Salem."

Kersi appeared to study me with a puzzled look as she spoke.

"Juan . . . Juan Wilson, you don't look like a Juan. Juan is a Spanish name, but with that blond hair, you're not Spanish."

"No, I have no Latin in me. Juan is a nickname. My real name is John, but a lot of people call me Jack. My close friends have called me Juan for years."

"Why would they do that?"

"Well, I guess I'm pretty good around the ladies."

I could see her mulling around something in her thoughts before she replied, "We'll have to see about that!" Kersi modestly smiled.

I wondered what she meant by that remark, so I redirected the conversation. "I can't believe how good this coffee is. Normally, coffee at events like this is the pits, but this is exceptional. I see you're drinking orange juice; you're not a coffee drinker?"

"I hate coffee; never drink it."

The feeling of being in a time warp swept over me. The horse events were going on; people were milling around and we were just standing there talking about coffee. I wasn't going very far with this production and needed to get off the mark.

After some small talk she finished her orange juice and said, "Damn, that was good. I think I can go for some more."

Here's the opening I need. "Let me get you another cup. I . . . I, ah . . . have to get another cup of this great coffee and it will be a pleasure to buy you another juice."

I felt as if I was walking on thin ice, not sure if I would fall through on my return from the refreshment stand. Her first gulp of the drink I passed her reduced the orange liquid considerably.

She coughed and appeared to hop from one foot to the other.

"Boy, that settles the nerves a little, but it isn't enough." She reached into her handbag and withdrew a pocket-sized flask. "Ah, this will pick up the old body a bit." She filled the cup to the brim and took a healthy sip.

"Perfect! Nothing like an eye-opener in the morning," Kersi announced. The jolt put a sparkle in her eyes.

I counseled myself to let this drinking scene play out and let it lead me. I was correct in assuming the lady is a boozer and this wasn't her first drink so early in the day.

"What do you have in that little toddy you made for yourself?"

"It's not a toddy."

"How so?"

"A toddy is a warm drink and this is what I call a cooler."

"A cooler then, I stand corrected. What did you put in the juice?"

"Gin. I love it. It's the story of my life," she said calmly which surprised me. "My husband once told me I drank too much and wouldn't let go of it, but ah . . . that's a problem no longer. I don't have to listen to him anymore."

Few problem drinkers can emotionally admit to being addicted to alcohol, yet here she stands openly declaring her fondness for the grain.

"And why is that?"

"Because I'm on my own. George left me five years ago because he couldn't stand my drinking."

"You don't appear to drink that much."

"All the time," she said with a laugh. "Fixed habits are hard to undo. To be honest, I have no control over myself.

"You can't do it all the time and work, can you?"

"Naw, I don't work."

"How can you get on without working?"

"Because Mr. Clark was very rich and feathered my nest. He left lighter than when we were together."

"How did you arrange that?"

Kersi spoke with a crooked smile on her face. "I had a very good lawyer, and he stripped the meat off Mr. Clark's bones. So you see, I live in a great house and have all the money I'll ever need. The best part of it is, George isn't around hassling me about what I should or shouldn't do. He was not easy to live with and constantly fretted about how others perceived us. George claimed I was stubborn and single minded. He wouldn't let go of it. Now I don't have to worry about that. Do you want a drink?"

"No, thank you. I don't drink that stuff."

"What do ya' drink?"

"Ah . . . blackberry brandy."

I had to make some quick calculations about this one. Kersi isn't interested in the horse show, and the only thing that excited her is getting into the gin. I'm certain she has a reserve to back up that flask and is out on a rip. Kersi Clark is like a fragile tree in a booze storm. It shouldn't be a problem to get her isolated and quickly fill her full of gin. I felt the warning in my mind go off, and I was blessed that it did. If I go out drinking with her, I'll be placing myself in jeopardy. Better go to my reserve bank of grape juice. It's good I carry the juice as a substitute for the brandy I normally consume. Now, I can play a little game of charade and act as if I'm drinking with her. Once that starts, I'll have her out in a hurry. Yes, that's a good game plan.

"Kersi, that's a pretty name by the way. Do you like the races?"

"No, I couldn't less about them," she said in a detached manner.

"If that's the case, why did you attend today?"

"I had nothing else to do, that's all. Always like to do different things, but I still go back to my main interest."

"And what's that?"

"I like to watch water . . . look at water."

"You like to look at water. What do you mean by that?"

"I love watching moving water. A big river, little rivers, streams, creeks, it doesn't matter."

"Do you have a favorite spot to watch this water you're talking about?"

"Yeah, I do as a matter-of-fact. I have a place out near home that's my special little haven. It's a trout stream called Phelps Creek and it's the best."

She laughed and danced around a bit, then poured herself another gin. By this time she was beginning to show signs of intoxication as she attacked the straight gin.

Suddenly out of the blue, she suggested, "I just thought of something. I can take you out there if you don't care anything about this crazy horse show. We can sit there and drink if you want."

I have to get her moving or she'll never make it out of here.

"Sounds great. Do you want to ride with me?"

"Naw, I got that little green MG over there." She pointed to an early fifties square-nosed sports car.

"Okay, I'll follow you out."

She appeared to have difficulty finding her keys while stumbling her way toward the car. Kersi pulled out of the parking lot, spinning wheels, and headed down the road.

She's half in the bag now, I thought while following at a safe distance. *I hope she doesn't get picked up for a DWI. As I followed Kersi, I thought the possible conclusion to this eventful day. If this spot she's talking about is in the open, I have reservations about continuing. But I guess it's reduced down to where the water she's heading for is located. I didn't drink yesterday and had nothing today, so I feel clear-headed.*

Fifteen minutes later Kersi pulled off the main highway onto a secondary road. After several minutes, she turned left on a single lane country road and shortly turned into a lane that led to the right. There was no doubt she knew where she was going and soon stopped in what appeared to be a lover's lane.

Parking next to her MG I noticed the dirt in the area had

been soften by a recent rain. There in plain sight was a clear imprint of my tires. After killing her, I must get rid of the tires, but how? The thought came to me in an instant. When I get home I'll slash the tires. In the morning, I'll call the dealer and have them send a truck out to replace them. They'll assume vandals were at work, and I'll be free and clear.

I looked around and couldn't understand why Kersi chose this site to visit. It looked like a lover's lane with beer cans, condoms and plain litter covering the area.

She stood near an opening that appeared to lead to a path through the woods. Busying myself picking up my drink case, I switched my blackberry bottle for one filled with grape juice. I was now ready.

"What do you have in mind?"

"Come on, it's down here." She waved and led the way into the pathway. I followed Kersi down a trail cut through the woods until I could hear flowing water. Soon, I entered a clearing where a low bank overlooked the rushing stream. She was smugly seated at a picnic table opening up a drink case. She had all the ingredients needed, and took out a container of ice and made a drink of gin and tonic.

"This is where I hang out. Sit down and take a load off," Kersi said while gesturing to the bench opposite her.

I sat down and she smiled. Lifting her drink, she raised it in a salute and said, "There, that should do me for a moment or so."

I opened my drink case and made a drink of ice and grape juice. The scene was indeed beautiful with the rushing water making gurgling sounds in the otherwise quiet setting.

She got up and walked to the edge of the nearby stream no wider than the length of my station wagon. "Come over to the edge, I want to show you some trout. See there's a couple right there."

I looked down at the crystal-clear water and saw two foot-long trout on the bottom waving as if fighting the streams current. Tranquility was sometimes a myth, but not so with this serene setting.

"You're right, Kersi, this is a lovely place, and I can understand why you come here. I'm dazzled by the striking beauty of your secret paradise."

"Isn't it beautiful? I come here all the time, and it pleases me to no end. This is my secret and I don't intend to be put it on loan, don't you know."

"That's an expression I've never heard before. What does it mean?" I didn't understand but let it go.

We returned to the table to talk and drink over the next hour. Kersi's eyes never strayed from the water while practically emptying the bottle. She grew incoherent and was rapidly approaching an alcohol stupor. Finally, she said in a sodden tone, "I have to sleep, and . . ." Her words drifted away as if preparing for a sleep of the just. Suddenly she dropped her head to the table and began to snore.

I brought my drink case to the wagon and returned to a sleeping Kersi Clark. This would be the easiest of my killings because there was no need to tape her. She was what I'd call a captive audience as I plunged the pick into her ear and put her down to stay. I pulled it off so quickly there was no challenge involved. From there I carried her to the wagon and started out the lane for the country road. Pulling off to the side, I carried her to the edge of an adjacent tobacco field and deposited her under some plants. I placed a horseweed in her hair and left.

Living in an uncaring society, life had mortally wounded Kersi Clark before she met me. But sadly, she never realized it. Not a pretty picture to remember.

At six in the evening, I found myself in my study finalizing a report on Kersi Clark from my tape recorder. Killing her was like reading a bad novel; there wasn't much to it. The sorry part of my experience was that it could be replayed in several paragraphs, but that wouldn't do. Her story would need considerable work, and ideally, this would be the time for my creative juices to take over. Whatever is lacking about a woman boozer I can make up and it's a challenge I'm up to.

My day hadn't been an exciting one, but I'm thrilled at how simple the task had been. It was easier than going to the local supermarket and buying groceries. I've always enjoyed observing my victims' terror before I snuff them out. But in this case, you can't have everything.

She drank gin all morning while I drank grape juice. She isn't around now, so, Martin Jeffreys, you're going to have to drink alone. With this quart of blackberry brandy, I should be able to come up with some incidental tidbits to embellish the Kersi Clark story.

29

Pulling into the Eagle parking lot, Colby spoke out. "What's a couple of beers going to do to us, we're already bombed." The pungent smell of sweat and beer that converged on the hapless duo went unnoticed as they entered the *Eagle.*

"Yes sir, gents, what can I get you" Al Simons took a second look at his new customers and smiled. "Why Red Ted, you're a sight for these tired old eyes. I haven't seen the likes of you since you left for law school."

"Hello, Al, it's good to see you. You're right of course, it has been three years since I left town. Seems good to be back with old friends. Speaking of friends, I'd like you to meet a law school buddy of mine. Colby Martin, this giant of a man is Al Simons."

After shaking hands, Colby looked up at the 300-pound bald giant and said, "You certainly are a big one." This he thought hilarious as he slapped the bar.

Simons looked from the little fellow to Red. "It would appear you gentlemen are pretty well packaged up."

"Sir, your observation is accurate; we indeed are pretty well packaged up as you so succinctly put it." Colby smiled at Simons.

"Al, don't listen to him. What can you expect from a guy who lives in Massachusetts? Colby, give the man your car keys."

After some debate, Colby passed the keys to the smiling bartender.

"Put them away until tomorrow or he'll drive you crazy," Red said.

"I hear you, Red. If this little rascal hadn't given up the keys there'd be no healing water for you two tonight."

"In that case, my drunken friend and I would like some beer." Colby made a "I want more" motion.

Over the next hour, Al and Red's quiet conversation centered on the Freddie Gill case. Finally, Al drifted away as the drunken twosome began discussing their day trip to Smithbury.

"I'm amazed we pulled it off so easily. Ya' know, that Jeffreys isn't the low life I pictured him to be. He was quite civil even on a bad day," Colby offered.

"I concur, my friend. Jack said the same thing, and I feel like he does. Do you know what?" Red said.

"No, partner, what?"

"I also liked his cold beer." Red's comment reduced Colby to extended laughter as he agreed with Red. "We must remember this bird is flying under anything but true colors."

"I think you're right. Did you notice when he was talking about Jeanette, the real Martin Jeffreys may have surfaced. For a fleeting instant he appeared to show a hard and calculating side. It was only for a moment but it was there."

"I noticed that too. We're not gum shoes like Lloyd and O'Brennan, but the pictures we took should help."

At this point of the evening the beer began taking over Simons's newly acquired guests. They were beyond anything O'Brennan could help them with this night.

"When will we get them developed?" Colby asked.

"How about right now? We can go to Toby's Photo down the street and take advantage of his one-hour developing service. We'll take them over, then come back and drink some more beer, how's that?"

"Sounds great." Colby replied.

"Al, is that Toby's Photo down the street any good?"

"He's the best there is. Why?"

"I want a rush job on some film."

"Red, I'll call to make sure he's open." Simons soon returned from his call. "He said to bring them right over."

"Big one, let me have my keys and I'll get the film," Colby said.

"No way, my friend. If you want the film, I'll unlock the car for you."

"Ah, come on, I wouldn't drive the car. You know me better than that."

"You've got that right. You won't take the car, at least tonight. Another thing, little man, I don't know you for squat."

"Come on, Red, this guy is pushing the limits of my tolerance. Let's walk down to that shop and deliver the film."

"You go down, Red. This little man is staying here. With two of you wandering around down there, the sharks are liable to get you."

Fifteen minutes later, Red returned to the Eagle. "Where have you been? Toby's is just down the street," the giant asked.

"He probably got lost." Colby dissolved in laughter at his own joke.

"I can pick them up in forty-five minutes. They're going to make 8x10's, but the turnaround time is twenty-four hours. Toby said he'd rush them through, so we'll have to make due with the little ones until early tomorrow afternoon."

"I'm going back with you to pick them up. I don't want you getting lost again." Laughter returned to the little man's body as he savored his last statement. Pointing a finger at Simons, he started again. Mr. . . . whatever your name is; you must learn to manage your anger better. If you try to stop me from going with Red, I'm going to kick your ass."

Simons rolled his eyes to the ceiling and said with an amused smile, "Put that way, tough guy, I'd like you to be my guest." Simons shook his head.

Visiting Duke Frontier's tattoo shop was a highlight of O'Brennan's week. He regularly visited Duke since the Freddie Gill case and looked forward to seeing his old friend.

Jack O'Brennan never talked much because Duke controlled the conversation. From the old school, the ancient guy twisted the facts to meet his needs but nevertheless told marvelous stories about the old Harkers and the characters that made it great. This wasn't an ordinary visit but one of a serious nature. Jack needed advice from Frontier and not his usual ration about the good old days. A remarkable geezer, Frontier was the only practicing tattoo artist in Bridgeton, and had practiced his art for over sixty years.

Looking around the memorabilia-filled waiting room, Jack called out, "Duke, are you decent?"

From the backroom came the expected reply, "I haven't been decent in seventy years." Old and shriveled, the bald little man shuffled into the waiting room.

He gave his visitor a slight nod. "Hello there, big man, how ya' doin'?"

His wrinkled old smile made O'Brennan feel good.

"Couldn't be better, Duke. I just came down to gossip a bit."

The conversation carried on for several minutes before Duke finally said, "You're acting a little strange today; got something on your mind, ain't you?"

"Yeah, you're right. You read me pretty good, don't you?" Frontier merely shrugged. "Normally when I come down here we shoot the breeze and I like that a lot. But today is different. I need some advice and you may be able to help."

"I'd rather give you a tattoo."

"You're not putting any of that trash on me! You tattooed that little green shamrock on Jeanette, but don't ever think about putting anything on me."

Duke's tired old eyes displayed a twinkle hard to forget.

"Yeah, I remember her, a pretty lady"

"Don't tell me. I know you have a memory sharp as a tack. In fact, you tell me that every time I come down here. Since the Smithbury Skeleton investigation began, I've tried to keep you abreast; I mean informed where we're going. Earlier, I told you we had a line on the killer; now we know who he is, or are reasonably certain."

"Who is it?" Frontier was all ears.

"That I can't talk about and you know why." Duke again shrugged. "We're going to run an entrapment scheme on him, and that's where you come in."

"Every time you talk to me, you use big words. What's this entrapment thing you're talking 'bout?"

"It's like I told you; this guy kills women. We've set this up so Jeanette, the one you put the . . ."

Duke cut him off. "I know, damn it. I put that shamrock on two years ago. My memory's still sharp . . ."

Jack returned the favor, "Yeah, I know, you don't have to remind me. We sound more like Abbott and Costello than they did. Getting back to Jeanette, she's going to be the bait, and we're running this scheme at the killer's house. He's loaded and lives in an old plantation mansion, and also has a summerhouse down by the river. We think he'll try to kill her down there."

"Where is the summer house by the mansion?" Duke asked.

A long moment passed before Jack shook his head at Duke's twisted question. He learned early on that Duke structured his sentences in a most unconventional way.

"The mansion is about the same distance to the summer house as from here to the Eagle. We're going to hide around the house and should have a bird's eye view of this guy and Jeanette. She's planning on having our man make his attempt in front of the house. Jeanette doesn't want him to get her inside because we can't help her if that happens.

"The killer is murdering his victims with a small pointed object in the ear. I'd say it's some kind of punch but I could be mistaken. Okay, we can get him, but he'll have killed Jeanette before we can intercept him. We can't have that. It's imperative we get it right." Duke's questioned look forced O'Brennan to retreat. "I meant important instead of imperative." Duke nodded his understanding. "We want to stop him before this happens, but how?"

The old gent shook his head. "First off, it's a damn foolish stunt to begin with, but what the hell, you already know that." Duke thought briefly, then spoke to himself loud enough for O'Brennan to understand. "Mace him!"

The unexpected answer perplexed Jack. "What do you mean by mace him?"

"Mace him. Ya' know that mace. The stuff women spray on guys that are going to rape 'em or do whatever they're going to do. Have her carry some mace and squirt him when it's time. That'll stop him. You're a dick, you should know better. You shoulda' come up with that on your own."

"Well, I didn't goddamn it! So how is she going to mace him?"

"Spray it on him!"

"Duke, this is a big man, and when he grabs her, she won't be able to do a thing. A can of mace won't work if he has her tied up. Figure that out, Mister Smart Guy."

Duke again thought out his reply. His eyes sparkled as he spoke. "I got the answer, big man. Put the mace in her hair."

"What in hell are you talking about? Put the mace in her hair!"

"All you do is run a little nylon tube up through her hair. You put the can, they have that mace in a ran, right?" O'Brennan nodded in agreement "Then when sh . . ."

"Duke, before you continue, I forgot to tell you something. When he grabs a women, he ties her up with duct tape."

"What's duck tape?"

"It's called duct tape, d-u-c-t, and it's a gray all-purpose wrapping. He tapes the victim's mouth, then her ankles and wrists. One other thing, he tapes her hands in back. Now tell me how we're going to use the mace?"

"We're going to run this little tube through her hair so it comes out here. Duke pointed to the crown of his former hairline. Ya' run it under her shirt or sweater, then you put the little can, or whatever that stuff comes in down by her ass."

"If the guy ties her hands in back, won't he see the can? How will she trigger the mace? How will she secure it, I mean fasten it?"

"Can't you keep up? Big man, you're not as smart as I give you credit for. Tuck the can in her panty stockings."

"Why do you talk so crazy? I never heard of panty stockings!"

"Ya' know, them stockings. Those ones the ladies have to pull up over their ass."

O'Brennan laughed as he recited back to Duke, "Pantyhose, they're called pantyhose."

"Yeah, yeah, that's it, pantyhose. Put the can right on top of 'em."

"You know, that's a pretty good idea. It better work because that's all we got," Jack said.

The phone rang causing Duke to amble out to the backroom. O'Brennan thought about Frontier's mace scheme and believed it might work. He'd have to work out the details, but it made sense. Duke shuffled back to O'Brennan. "It's Al Simons at the Eagle and he wants to talk to you."

"This is Jack, what can I do for you?"

"I called all over hell trying to get hold of you. I finally called Jeanette at the restaurant and she said you might be at Duke's. How about coming over to do some damage control. And while you're at it, pick up some of your loose baggage?"

"Loose baggage?"

"Red's down here with a wild bastard named Colby and they're bombed."

"Let me talk to Red?"

"They're not here. They came in a couple of hours ago and have been here ever since. I shouldn't have served them, but I did get their keys. Earlier, Red took some film down to the one-hour developing service and they just went over to pick it up. They should be back by the time you get here. When they return, I'm sure they'll want some more beer. So, my friend, you'd better come over and take care of them."

"Al, the problem with bad news is that more of it usually follows."

"I don't know about that, but like I said, you'd better come over in a hurry."

Jack walked to the Eagle and discovered his wards hadn't returned. "What's the story, Al?"

"Like I told you, they came in a couple hours ago and boy were they bombed. I didn't realize it at the time, but you know Red, he's so quiet, you'd never know he was cocked. But he was with this Colby guy. Jack, that guy has a screw loose and is the wildest little son of a bitch I've ever met." O'Brennan laughed as

Simons started waving his arms. "You can laugh all you want, but I've never heard such wild talk in my life. His mouth runs like a whippoorwill's ass."

O'Brennan again laughed. "Al, I'm surprised to hear that. That may be a bit overstated, but I admit he'll bear watching. Colby is just a wild young man hurrying to grow up, and a blowhard he's not. He's harmless and doesn't mean anything by his incessant chatter, but I'll grant you one thing, he does have a bunch of bullshit."

"Here they are now. I can't wait to hear how you manage these turkeys."

Just then the whippoorwill spoke. "Look who's here, Red, it's Uncle Jack O'Brennan. What are you doin', Uncle Jack, slummin'?" Colby's eyes wildly blinked as he spoke.

"Listen to the mouth on him," Al said.

"There you are, you bad boys. I've been looking all over for you."

"Come on, Jack, we want to show you our pictures. We got pictures of the lagoon, the summerhouse and the channel. We got some more pictures of the river, of the birds, of the bees, you name it we got 'em." Colby laughed at his attempted comic relief. "Isn't that right, Red? We got 'em all."

Red didn't laugh or answer, but instead absently looked at the little attorney.

"That's it, boys. Say goodnight to Uncle Al and we'll be on our way." Jack winked at Al as he started for the door "Colby, did you drive?" he asked.

"I certainly did; got that hot LeBaron outside in the parking lot. But that bad man there, that big ugly one in back of the bar," Colby pointed at Simons, "he got my keys and won't give 'em up. I told him I was going to kick his ass but he just laughed at me."

By this time, the good-sized bar crowd had drifted over to listen to this lively exchange. The little guy was far more entertaining than the re-runs on the TV, and a lot funnier.

"I don't blame him one bit. You're coming home with me, young man, and I'll drop Red off at Saints Square on the way. Where's your car, Red?" Jack asked.

"I don't know. Do you, Colby?"

"I don't know either. Maybe that ugly guy has it." Colby started laughing, as did Red, followed by Jack and the bar patrons. Finally, Al Simons broke down and laughed so hard, tears flowed down his cheeks. Wiping the tears with a bar towel, he threw his hands in the air saying, "Where would I be without you? If you want to act like a child, be my guest. You win, you little rascal, and come back when you can make more sense and we'll talk."

"I hate to love and leave you, but there's something that needs attending to. Come on, children it's beddy-bye time for you two. Thanks for baby-sitting my two delinquents."

"That's what friends are for."

"Uncle Jack, another beer would help me along," Colby suggested.

"I'll help you along but it will be without any more beer."

O'Brennan turned to face Simons. "There's not much I can do about this one." Jack motioned at Colby. "But Betty is going to kick old Red's ass when he gets home. The next time you see him, be won't he so feisty."

Red hunched his shoulders and laughed.

On the way out Colby turned to O'Brennan. "Why is that big guy so pissed at me?

You'll understand it better in your next life, my son."

30

Rebecca Whitlow May, 1986

The *Red Lion Horse Show* is a popular event on the spring horse calendar. What makes it even more stunning is the backdrop of the *Shenandoah Apple Blossom*
Festival, the annual event that celebrates the apple crop in and around Winchester, Virginia.

Thoughts of the selection process I'd previously used to determine victims came to me while I threaded my way around the horse grounds. Choosing mentally and physically handicapped subjects has been good to me, but at some point in everyone's life, the pot has to be stirred and the spice changed.

I had covered my tracks over the last nine killings, but how would I ever know until the hammer fell? I have concentrated on women too long, and my stories are beginning to take on a sameness that must be eliminated.

The new direction I have considered is the correct one and ingenious if I say so myself. I shall pursue gays and it shouldn't be difficult to go up to Richmond and pick one up. Now that the homosexuals have come out of their closets, there is an openness that never existed before. I'm more convinced than ever that it wouldn't be difficult to find a likely subject in a gay bar.

I have no objection to the different persuasion the gay community embraces, and could objectively choose a subject without emotion. When you're a neuter like me, these decisions are much easier to make. But that's for another day, and this morning I must seek out number nine.

Almost immediately after starting the search for a victim,

my target for the day came into view. She was a large woman, large in many ways. Tall, heavy-set with ponderous breasts, she looked to be the moderator on a television cooking show. Even though I think that, there may be a possibility my new strategies aren't for today.

Wearing deck shoes, a large ground-flowing granny skirt and sweatshirt, she was dressed in gray. The same shade of gray threatened to invade her pitch-black hair limply hanging to her shoulders. When she looked through half-glasses attached to a gray string around her neck, her gray eyes appeared as manhole covers. My attraction to this unpretentious woman centered on the lettering on the shirt. It stated for all to see:

SMARTEN UP
READ BOOKS

Obviously the lettering had a special attraction for me. She was talking to another man so I laid back and waited until their conversation ended. I approached her and initiated a conversation.

"Excuse me, but I'm very intrigued by the front of your sweatshirt."

"How could you be so crass?" She crinkled her nose as if an unpleasant smell had passed through it.

"You sound annoyed. I suppose you have every right to be. I'm at fault for not stating my thoughts. The words on your sweatshirt have great appeal to me but I've never seen such wording."

A question crossed her face as she replied, "Why do these words attract you?" She said unconsciously touching the lettering.

"I'm a writer and obviously the meaning to those words appeals to me."

"What's your name?"

"I'm Michael Rambush."

"I know you. Not personally, but I know your work. As a matter of fact, I'm a fan of yours."

"And you are?"

"Rebecca Whitlow."

Her name rang a bell and I desperately sought to recover where I'd heard it. Then it came to me. Rebecca Whitlow was a highly respected book reviewer for the *Washington Post*. She was recognized for toughness as well as fairness. Over the years, I'm certain she sent more than one writer back to his word processor to regroup and gather his thoughts.

"This is a remarkable conversation because I also know about you. Rebecca Whitlow is the book critic for the Post. You are an extraordinary writer." She seemed pleased that I would know.

Her laughter came in a pleasing rush as she replied, "Ah, the notoriety that I long have sought has finally arrived. I've met someone who knows my work." She reached into her purse and pulled out a long thin black cigarette, then fired it up with a kitchen match. Here was a woman who knew what she wanted in life and was confident in her ability and gave no regard to what people thought of her. I could appreciate how objective she could be in her book reviews.

"I like your writing style, and even more than that, you display a gentle self-effacing manner. I enjoy the way you involve the forces of darkness while creating your unforgettable characters. And I might add, you finish your stories in a smashing fashion."

"Well, thank you. I'm honored you feel this way, but I must admit at times I feel embarrassed by my efforts."

"That's nothing but folderol. However, I find you have a common thread interwoven throughout all your stories."

"And what would that be?"

"The last seventy-five pages have a sameness that I love."

"You do?"

"Yes, as you develop the story line toward its conclusion, it gives me the impression that I myself am the killer and am stalking the victim. Your style infuses each tale you tell with the same relentless lust your killers exude. I like that."

"Do you get the feeling you know my killers?"

"Indeed I do. I'm intrigued by how you direct your readers to the killer's mental set and I have a two-part question. How do you accomplish such a difficult task and where do you come up with these tales? It almost feels as if you were killing the victims yourself and transplanting the experience into a fictional world."

I laughed at her comment and thought how astute this woman was. "Well, it isn't easy to do. Obviously I don't kill to create experiences for my fictional work."

"I didn't mean to infer that you did. Then how do you do it?"

"That's easy to explain; it's a frame of mind. I love Virginia; and much of my writing deals with the state. I've ventured into Maryland and Carolina for numerous backdrops, and may very well expand my horizons into D.C. in the near future. I briefly research hundreds of unsolved murder cases until I find one that fits my needs. I start with the basic story of the killing and go from there. It's nothing more than cyclical in form," I lied.

"How can you get into the killer's head if you don't know who the killer is?"

This is a very cagey lady who has an incisive mind and I'm growing very attracted to her. I shouldn't get involved but I like her and that's good enough for me. She seems laid back and uncaring yet under the facade of indifference lies elegance I can't account for. Over a period of months I've been thinking about shifting gears and this is the time to do that very deed.

To hell with the strategy I've followed over my last nine outings. My dear, you've just bought yourself a reprieve. No, that's not the word I need to use. A reprieve is a temporary suspension of a death sentence, but in your case I have commuted your sentence. Rebecca, you are free to continue your scathing attacks on pompous writers who think the art of writing stops with them. I think a trip to Richmond tomorrow evening is in order.

"You must remember I write about a tiny speck on the face of life. That's where the fun comes in and why I write. If I have a secret, it is to choose what appears to be a premeditated slaying. Once my target case has been established, I place the evidence available in what I think to be a sequential order. From there I begin to fill in what I consider to be incidental facts that build the story. Now I have the skeleton of a homicide, and this is where my inventive personality takes over."

"What is the basis for this mental masquerade of yours?"

"At this point, I myself become the killer in absentia. I'm a prolific reader of crime and its effect on society. My information is acquired from both fiction and non-fiction writings. I concentrate on the general strategy of pursuing a criminal based on police techniques and procedures. What I just described is an oversimplification of the pro forma techniques I use. Obviously, there is much more detailed planning involved."

"Well, I must commend you for your writing style and should mention you have a hard-core collection of fan support at every turn of the page."

I had to get her off Michael Rambush and direct her thoughts to what she does for a living.

"Speaking of fans, you have a considerable following yourself."

Rebecca laughed but couldn't hide the pleasure she enjoyed from my comment. "You know, it's difficult to have a following when you are a critic. I believe the reading public views us as incompetent hacks that can criticize but not create and they feel let down by this thought. That's how the reader out there," she casually waved her hand at the spectators, "perceives our craft."

Rebecca reached for another smoke but didn't light it.

"There are writers who have terrific stories to tell but never get their first word published. Yet, these same authors turn around and read some of the trash found in bookstores and libraries. I'm certain they wonder how such inferior work could find its way through the publication maze that directs public consumption."

"Yes, I agree with you on that account."

"You find many in our industry consumed by how they use words. I think they overindulge themselves with unneeded verbiage that makes their story suffer."

"I also agree with that."

"And to add insult to injury they cross the line."

"What do you mean by the line?"

"Writers have a certain style of prose; a certain message that is appreciated by a certain group of readers. An example of this would be a writer like you who creates mysteries. He develops his series of works over a period of time based on meeting the needs of his readers. Other mystery novelists tend to write in the abstract and make the reader work hard at deciphering the intricate plot that unravels. I have no problem with that approach, and personally find it stimulating and just plain fun. But my major objection is when writers alter their style and enter another arena for which they are not suited. Many get caught up in that trap, you know."

Her thesis interested me. "Why do they change?"

"I have no way of knowing, but I would presume it's for financial advantages. One must also consider the vanity factor involved in our business.

Writers are self-centered and never content with their efforts. In their hearts, I believe they would prefer to signal the public they are more intelligent, more skilled than they really are."

"From listening to you, I can begin to appreciate how you approach your work."

A knowing smile crossed her face. "You do see don't you? That's very perceptive of you. I am considered 'The Literary Bitch of the Beltway' and that I don't have to spell out for you. The major reason for the title is my obstinate pursuit of the truth. If you will note, I am fair when dealing with writers who present works that are true to form and present a good story although very simply told. People in our business lose sight of the fact we are similar to the movie industry. We don't think so, but we are."

"The movie industry?"

Rebecca Whitlow is a smart lady, very sharp indeed; and I shouldn't entertain much more of this conversation. It's said that a person loses their objectivity if they stand too close, and maybe I am that close with this lady.

"The movie industry is a business designed to entertain as is the book industry, certainly the fiction end of it. Fiction is an escape from our mundane day-to-day task of getting by, and why should writers be presumptuous to the point of encumbering their work with material the reader doesn't want to hear?"

"I agree, but in defense of writers, we all have our faults and are swept up by the desire to embellish, to make it grow like a tulip opening in spring. I'm sure you understand our penchant for verbosity, don't you?"

She laughed, "Even you, Michael Rambush, are guilty of the very blemish I just attacked. You could have said in defense, writers are trying to improve the story. See what I'm saying?"

"Indeed I do, but you haven't answered my question. Do you fall into the same trap?"

"Absolutely. I'm sorry to say I'm as guilty as the next person sitting in front of a computer." She again emitted a booming laugh that caused me to laugh with her. *This is an honest lady, and I want to become her friend,* I thought.

"I love your laugh, Rebecca Whitlow."

"I know. When I laugh everyone around me laughs. I think they're laughing with me as opposed to what I said. But nevertheless, it's fun. Getting back to my erudite thoughts," again the happy laugh interrupted her, "give me a sixty-thousand word novel any time over a hundred and twenty thousand effort about the same story and you'll find they're basically comparable in content.

"I think it's preposterous when a writer uses a full page to describe a drumlin when he could represent that same hill in a five-sentence paragraph. That offends me and I tell my readers so."

I found myself becoming increasingly enthralled by this tough woman's hard edge.

Peering through the smoke of a freshly lighted cigarette, Rebecca displayed the start of a smile that indicated she knew or certainly surmised my secret.

"I have a supposition for you; care to play?"

I shrugged, and then nodded yes.

"What if a writer killed a person to establish a setting for his story? Maybe this same writer found the formula workable and developed a series of novels based on the same format. We know this very fact has surfaced throughout the history of literature.

What if you are that writer bent on the commission of a crime and I'm to be your next victim. What if your next novel has me as its centerpiece; what horse-related article will be found next to my body? Let me guess where you'd place my remains. Would it be under an apple tree?"

Is her thought from the subconscious? To put the worst face on it, I think she has guessed my secret but how would she know? Hopefully, I can momentarily allay her suspicions, but she possesses a searching mind far superior to mine and that I must accept. She's too dangerous to have around and I must eliminate her before she puts all the pieces together into a giant indictment of what my life is about. I have to make a strong case on my behalf and that may prove to be a litmus test of my character.

While locking eyes with Rebecca I laughed. "Rebecca Whitlow, for a minute you sounded like one of the half-baked detectives I write about in my novels. Do you honestly believe I have psychopathic tendencies that would permit me to slay unsuspecting victims for personal gain?"

"Well, no . . . I just . . . I just meant hypothetically."

"I'll give you a hypothetical. Let's say you read Tuesday in the *Post* that a woman who attended this very event was found under the same apple tree you earlier alluded to. She was murdered and they found a horse collar next to her. If that death interested you, reports would be available for you to create the framework of the killing.

"From there your imagination would take over and you'd design a reason for the killing. That accomplished; you would begin to fill the empty spots with figments of your creative ability. With your writing skill, the success of the novel would reflect your imagination and yours alone. That's what I do and I'm sure you could accomplish the very same results."

I felt delighted with my slight reprimand and wondered how she'd react.

"Yes, I see. For the first time I understand your strategy. I probably was too aggressive and insensitive to your stature as a writer and for that I apologize. End of speculation."

"That's preposterous. Please believe that I'm not offended by your supposition. Now, let's change the subject and get onto something more constructive. Since we're members of the same club that deals with the written word, I have a proposal to make."

"I'm all ears after my little faux pas." The bright pretty smile returned accompanied by a half-embarrassed look after which she accepted my suggestion with a nod. I was in business.

"On my drive in from Middlebury, I became intrigued by a small antique and used bookstore outside the little hamlet of Mister. Would you like to drive out there and look around?"

"Yes, I'd love it. This horse event holds no particular interest for me."

"Why did you come here today?"

"I come out here to Winchester every year. Just love the city-wide festival and on a whim happened out here to the horse show."

"Interesting enough, I couldn't less about horses, and like you, just came out here for the heck of it. Let's go. My wagon is over there and you can ride with me. When we finish at the bookstore, I'll bring you back here to pick up your car."

"That sounds fine except I'd like to drive."

"Do you have the feeling you'd be safer driving your car?" I laughed to help make the comment seem less abrasive.

Rebecca returned my laugh and shook her head. "No, it's nothing like that. I recently bought a 1950 two-door teardrop Chevy and this is my maiden trip with it. It cost me a fortune for the reconditioning, so my ulterior motive is to show it off as opposed to worrying about you killing me for artistic reasons." Again, the laugh signified that all was well.

The classic was everything she claimed, and I marveled how a thirty-six year old car could perform so beautifully. Mister was just a couple of houses on route 50 but it did have a used bookstore where I could readily strike her down.

Rebecca pulled the green Chevy up in front of the old building. Dirty windows signaled the shop had seen better days, but a crudely written sign indicated it was still in business. A barely legible message in the window of the front door indicated there were give-away books in the rear.

"Let's drive around in back; we may find a treasure," I suggested.

She laughed as she drove to the rear. "You're right, we may find a treasure back here but I doubt it." She stopped in front of a sheltered bookrack with hundreds of old tattered books begging for someone to cart off.

"I will say they don't appear to . . ." She never finished her sentence. I covered her mouth with my right hand and snaked the pick around the back of her head and into her ear with my left. I withdrew the life-taking rod from her ear and that ended an unsettling afternoon.

Next to the building was an apple orchard that proved an excellent resting-place for this fine lady. Placing her remains under a tree, I returned her car to the festival parking lot, wiped its interior for prints, and drove away in my wagon. Passing through Masters, I returned to the scene of my crime to place the previously planned horse collar around her neck.

Unfortunately, I drove off overwhelmed with guilt over what I had been forced to do to protect myself. When I killed Ann Gardner, the same guilt and shame was with me, but not so strongly as with Rebecca. If she hadn't been so analytical and astute, she'd still be alive to continue her service to a literary community she so enthusiastically embraced. We got along famously and developed a friendship that may have had a great future.

31

Red and Colby entered the *Red Squire* dining room on their way to Jeanette's office. "Afternoon, gentlemen, I heard you were taken by the sauce and while you were doing it entertained half of Bridgeton last night. It seems I'm always working when the good times roll," Karl said.

"Karl, our predicament of yesterday was a direct result of getting these." Red waved a large manila envelope at the head cook. "I'll grant you we did get carried away but we did good, and that's what counts. Is Jeanette in?" Red asked.

"That's a plausible explanation, and yes she's in."

From inside an adjacent room came, "Get in here this instant, you bad boys."

Standing in Jeanette's office doorway, Colby said to Red, "Mom's still mad."

Jeanette laughed then gestured to two chairs. "Sit down and tell me what you brought to the dance."

"Colby and I hit the mother lode yesterday, and it's still difficult to believe we pulled it off. The part of our excursion that you're interested in begins when we turned into the channel leading to Jeffreys' lagoon. Colby started taking pictures and hardly stopped until we left the estate," Red said.

"O'Brennan told me you met Jeffreys and drank beer with him. As a matter of fact that's where you got beered up, isn't that right?" Red nodded to Jeanette in agreement.

"Did Jeffreys mention me?"

"I was going to call your attention to that later, but yes, he certainly did. When he discovered us in the lagoon and started raising hell, Colby explained to him about us studying for our law boards. The next thing we knew, all three of us were sitting on his patio drinking beer," Red said.

"Tell her how he looked," Colby said.

"If you think we look a little rough, you can't imagine what he looked like. Right, Colby?"

"Jeffreys looked darker than the sky in a hurricane. I've never seen anyone with such a hangover."

"Get on with it, Red, I'm all ears," Jeanette said.

"After awhile he spoke about the amazing woman he met at the *Flat Run Horse Show* on Sunday. He mentioned how he spent a terrific afternoon talking to her, and to his amazement, she agreed to come down for the *Saxon Hunt* as his guest," Red said.

"It sounds like he gave you a blow-by-blow description of my meeting with him," Jeanette replied.

"From his lips to our ears. He did all that and more. Jeffreys mentioned how he came home and climbed into a bottle of brandy. He said thinking about you was almost as good as being with you. Now, I think that's a crock, but he thought so, and that's all that counts," Red said with a smile.

"It's always nice to hear someone say nice things about you even if they are second-hand."

"If you think that's cool, listen to this. Colby asked him if you were classy, and you know what he said?"

Jeanette nodded no and smiled in anticipation of Red's reply.

"Jeffreys said you were the most elegant woman he'd ever met. He also said you were gorgeous and had one great body. Colby and I agreed on that one." Red laughed as he looked at the wild man from Cape Cod.

"And what do you think about my being gorgeous and having a great body, Colby?"

"Jeanette, I totally agree with my red-headed colleague. If I were a little older, I'd be sitting on your lap whispering beautiful words in your ear."

"Little man, your libido is showing." Jeanette laughed and mustered up her four-star smile for the lawyer of Sands Beach.

"That's all we can give you on Jeffreys, but we do have pictures of the lagoon. Colby, why don't you take over from here?"

"Jeanette, we placed these 8x10's in sequence so you can get a feeling of being there yourself. I took all the pictures, so if you have a problem with them, you can blame me. I started taking pictures about halfway down the channel. You can see where the lagoon begins, and this one shows the path coming down from the mansion." Colby pointed to a full-blown view of the lagoon with the summerhouse on the left and a blacktopped walk centered in the background pines.

"That's the one I'll be coming down on *Death Sunday*."

"I wish you wouldn't talk that way."

"Why Colby, you care," Jeanette said.

"Of course I care. Getting back to the pictures, the second one was taken where the channel opens into the lagoon and gives a clear view of the path. The distance across the lagoon is roughly 400 feet, surrounded by pines.

"The next picture is taken from the same spot, and shows the summer house on the left. As you can see, it was built on a little peninsula. I'm not going to discuss the interior because the inside shots I took speak for themselves. It's your turn, Red."

"The summerhouse is the key, and when you study the photos in detail you'll find there are numerous shots from every possible angle. Here's a close-up of the patio and this is critical. It's raised about a foot above the lawn and is roughly twenty-five by forty, wouldn't you say, Red?"

"Yeah, and there's something else, Jeanette. The patio doors are hinged as opposed to sliding," Colby added.

Red returned to his summerhouse narrative. "To continue where Colby left off, there is a strip of grass about twenty-feet wide between the patio and the water. It continues along the house and the side of the woods to where the path comes down. Earlier I mentioned the patio being your key; by that I mean it will be the focal point of your deception. Our best chance at intercepting him is on the patio. It's your decision, and once you study the pictures, I think you'll agree with us."

"That's it as far as I'm concerned. If you study these pictures, and I'm sure you will, you'll know the layout as well as Jeffreys," Red added.

"Thanks fellows, your trip to Jeffreys' lagoon was very productive."

Leaving the *Red Squire*, the young lawyers crossed the parking lot to Colby's hot LeBaron, as he liked to call it.

"Ya' know, Red, when people tell me not to do something or give me hell or laugh at me for doing it, I feel compelled to do more of the same. You understand what I'm driving at?" Colby said

"Indeed I do. I was thinking the same thing and obviously great minds think alike. We better hurry down to the Eagle and get it right."

"What will Elizabeth Marie say? She's probably still pissed over our performance last night."

"When I got home, I figured Betty was going to raise hell with me, like Jack said she would. I'd forgotten she left Monday morning for a seminar at George Washington University in D.C. She won't be back until late Wednesday night, so I have a free ticket. Like the referee on the Thursday night fights says, 'Let's get it on'." And get it on they did.

Entering the Eagle, rollicking laughter rolled over the novice lawyers. The owner greeted the new arrivals by announcing to the crowd, "Fred, turn the TV off, tonight's entertainment just arrived. Look what just graced the hallowed halls of the Eagle. Forget the logic because insanity is at our doorway." The newly ordained lawyers entered the bar to applause from the patrons.

"I presume you'd like a couple of draughts. You look a little gray from yesterday's efforts, but this beer should mend your ways."

"Bless you, my son; may your cash register ring throughout the night," Colby offered.

The mountain known as Al Simons turned to his customers

to announce, "See this little turkey?" pointing at Colby, "he told me last night he was going to kick my ass. Can you imagine that? Well, here I am little man, so let's get to it."

Colby turned to the bar patrons with a sheepish grin. "My newly acquired friends, my name is Colby Martin and I've just recently anointed myself 'the Lawyer of Sands Beach'. I'm just beginning my practice and if you need a slick lawyer, come out and see me at the beach. Now that my solicitation for business is completed, let's discuss the very severe problem each and every one of us faces this lovely evening." Turning to point at Simons, the little attorney said, "This big ape can't take a joke," and to Simons, "How does that grab you, ugly one?"

The little lawyer's remark brought the house down, and along with it came free beer the rest of the evening. As the night wore on, the crowd increased as if drawn by a magnet. The main attraction came when one of the patrons asked Colby to tell a story. With this opening, he proceeded to lavish great tales of wild insanity on the ensemble of supporting players.

Observing this character, Simons realized for the first time that Colby had an affinity for drawing and entertaining others. *I'm living a dream because this little rascal is the best thing to happen to the Eagle since Prohibition ended.*

Back at the *Red Squire* after the mischievous wanderers left, Jeanette began the arduous trip of sorting through the mass of photos and eventually found herself completely at home with an overview of Jeffreys' lagoon and summerhouse.

She was now ready to formulate her projected schedule for 'Death Sunday'. The need for creating a foolproof plan was never more evident.

Jeanette continually replayed the events of her upcoming date with doom until she felt comfortable with what she anticipated would happen. By a consensus of one, she began to speak to herself as she transposed her thoughts to paper. At the top, she wrote 'Death Sunday'.

"I can't believe I chose such a heading. At the time I thought it rather cute, but it doesn't seem that way now. I mustn't get hung up on this.

"Phyllis has agreed to drive me to Smithbury so I plan on arriving at the estate around three in the afternoon. Jeffreys isn't going to make contact with me much earlier than that so it won't make much sense to arrive before then. He'll treat me like the leper who mustn't be touched until he's ready for me.

"As soon as I arrive, I'll start circulating around the show grounds to stay occupied. I have no idea when he'll show up and there's nothing I can do to control it, though I believe he'll turn up about four-thirty, maybe a little later. He'll expect me to be annoyed at his tardiness, but I won't push that one.

"There will be a sizeable crowd so he'll beg off because of hunt duties he must attend to. Jeffreys will want me out of view so I imagine he'll send me to the mansion to wait. There should be a couple of domestics around which will work in my favor. Around five-thirty, Jeffreys will come to the house and give me the grand tour. I have to play to his ego by puffing him up about how elegant the house is.

"Don't forget, Jeanette, you must control your schedule as best you can. If it varies in the beginning, the schedule will be out of whack at the end when we most need accurate timing.

"I believe he'll make his move as the shadows begin to fall. Before he invites me down to see his summer retreat, I will have intimated there will be more pleasures to follow.

"Jeffreys also has an agenda for Sunday evening and I must stay aware that he will try to play it out within its limits.

"Finally, when we arrive at the summerhouse, I must keep him outside the house. Under no circumstances can I permit him to lead me inside; that is nothing more than walking into his trap. I must pull this off by myself because the geography of the lagoon dictates that I do so. O'Brennan, the Group and authorities will be strategically placed in the pines along the water, but when Jeffreys makes his move, they won't see it coming until it's too late. You have to talk to yourself like you're doing now. Remember this; think, talk and be a careful listener. There'll be no troops to come to the rescue. That's it, I've finished and will not change one blasted thing."

Jeanette glanced down at the final agenda and shuttered. She had drawn the battle line with no recourse but to bravely see it through.

Death Sunday

3:30 PM Phyllis Eichner will drive me to *Saxon Hunt* on Jeffreys' estate. Circulate around show grounds after arrival.

4:30 PM Jeffreys will make the initial contact and probably send me to the mansion. He'll follow later, but I have no idea when.

5:30 PM Jeffreys will arrive at the mansion. He'll make same small talk and give me the grand tour of the house.

7:30 PM Around dusk he'll take me to the lagoon. I figure fifteen minutes for the short walk.

7:45 PM We arrive at the summer house. I must not allow him to get me inside. I should not have a drink under any circumstances

Rising from her desk, Jeanette prepared to close for the night. Thoughts of Sunday persisted as she headed for her car. *If this scheme backfires, it will be like a diamond expert who cuts a rough stone. One bad stroke and the gem is shattered; a miscue on my part and the life I now know is gone forever.*

The remainder of the week sped by as Jeanette made the obligatory meetings with those involved in her scheme.

She and Jack spent Saturday doing the little things couples often plan on doing, but for any number of reasons never get to. They walked around Ford Ashland, sat at Inlet Park looking at its placid waters and went to Gulls Stadium to watch the Bridgeton Gulls play the Yankees. After dinner at O'Hearns, they walked up the Ford Ashland hill to Jeanette's house. On the way,

Jack ran out of small talk and silence prevailed until they reached Jeanette's home.

"I'm not going to say anything about tomorrow; that's already been rehashed too much. For the three years I've known you, I've skirted around telling you this. Jeanette, I love you and have from the very moment I met you at the *Red Leather*. Tomorrow is going to be a difficult day for all concerned, so get this ugly matter over with as quickly as possible, because we're soon to be married."

"Yes, I know," Jeanette, replied softly.

"If you're interested, the ceremony takes place Monday morning at ten o'clock. At noon, we're hosting a little reception on the beach. Karl closed the *Squire* for the day so everyone can attend. He's putting on an old-fashioned New England clambake with all the trimmings. He got a beer permit and sent out invitations with no RSVP's required. Karl said everyone he invited will be there. You're probably thinking how many people will attend? Well, I can safely say there'll be around 150."

Jeanette looked up at O'Brennan with a flood of tears beginning to build. *The only man I've ever loved has gone ahead and made wonderful arrangements for our wedding. I'm now faced with a schoolgirl stunt that promises nothing but a death-defying conclusion to a stupid entrapment plan I designed myself. There is a way out of this, but that wouldn't do. I could never live with myself pulling out at the last minute.*

O'Brennan voice drew Jeanette back from her inner thoughts. "Jeanette, I have a topper for Monday. On Tuesday, we're flying to Logan. I hear there's a lovely inn in Rockport called the *Sand Castle Inn*. A beautiful woman I know told me it was pretty neat."

"O'Brennan, you never stop being nice to me, and for that I shall always love you."

"Jeanette, I find it pretty easy to be nice because of my love for you."

The ploy in Sunday's entrapment plan couldn't control her tears as she wheeled around and went inside. *After what O'Brennan just told me, I better get some sleep,* Jeanette thought as she climbed into bed.

The restless night Jeanette spent was not caused by anxiety over 'Death Sunday', rather by her excited thoughts centering on her marriage to O'Brennan, the beach reception after, and the wonderful *Sands Castle Inn* in Rockport, Massachusetts.

32

Lisa Oden May, 1987

I cannot believe I pulled such a stunt. Somehow I inadvertently erased two hours of transcript that would have finished my latest work. Once composed, then lost, its originality can never be replicated. This trip is getting off to a ghastly start, and I have only myself to blame.

Spring, with its horse events and hunts, has drifted away like a child's balloon rising to the sky, and I have become trapped by my own procrastination. I was negligent for not taking a subject in the spring, and now here it is July with only one chance left to conclude my latest work.

The annual *Pony Round-up and Swim Event* on Chincoteague Island is my parting shot at recovering lost time and I have to make the best of it. This event is not a horse event in the truest sense of the word, and that causes me great consternation. At this stage, however, I have no choice.

I needed a victim today and know nothing about the program. That's an obstacle I must face once I arrive on the island, and logistically speaking, I'm out in the middle of the stream without a paddle. On one of my numerous trips to the Smithbury *Hound's Inn*, I picked up an excellent brochure prepared by the Chincoteague Chamber of Commerce called, *Virginia's Chincoteague Island Adventure*. It's the usual tourist guide that includes a brief history of the island along with listings of recreation, dining and housing accommodations. This honest but sketchy publication will guide me in my quest for number eleven.

I read on page four: *"The island provides services to suit every need and taste." I wonder if that will include my particular venture?*

Traffic was backed up over the bridge that crossed the channel separating the island from the mainland. Parking was at a premium and it took half an hour of jockeying to find a spot. Frustrated and off balance, I headed for the small business district that would serve as my operations base.

I again checked the map and reread the Pony round-up article. *"Early in the week of the carnival, the firemen assume western roles and ride horseback to Assateague Island for the round-up of the ponies."*

The recesses of my mind didn't yield much about the outer island, so I sought information from the brochure. *"Protecting Chincoteague Island from the Atlantic, Assateague Island boasts more than thirty-seven miles of the widest and most beautiful beaches on the East Coast. This rare beauty is protected by the Assateague Island National Seashore Refuge."* I didn't need that nugget of information, but at least some of God's green earth is being protected.

Getting back to the brochure, I continued to read; *"They whoop and holler with enjoyment as they herd the ponies to a corral on the south end of Assateague about a mile from the Assateague Lighthouse. The ponies are rested there. On Wednesday of that last week of July, the ponies swim the channel to Chincoteague under the watchful eyes of the firemen. The crowds are gathered along the shore to witness the swim.*

"After completing the swim, the ponies are again rested before they are driven along Main Street to the carnival grounds and penned. On Thursday, the auction begins bright and early."

By the time I walked to the carnival grounds where the auction had already started under a substantial sun, I knew at best this would be a difficult undertaking because there was too much milling around among the spectators. It was a different crowd than I'm accustomed to. The usual horseshow audience is casual and laid back about their movement at an event. If they can't gracefully glide to another part of the show in a sedate manner, they won't bother.

The people here seemed to have a frenzied attitude about their activities. They're on vacation and have to telescope as much activity possible in a short few days. After looking for a prospect for what seemed like hours, I realized much to my dismay that visiting this remote area had not been the answer.

There was no Miss Eleven to be found, and I certainly couldn't produce one with smoke and mirrors. The best thing to do was to just pick up and leave. How I treat this novel is a matter that should be addressed later. My work schedule will be behind, but so what? It's better being safe than sorry.

My reasoning bounced around for some time before accepting the fact that my feeble efforts had failed. Once acceptance set in, I was ready to return home. My patience was wearing thin, but before I headed back, I thought a quiet drink on the beach would soothe my ruffled feathers.

I walked through an empty Church Street in the direction of the beach overlooking the channel and Assateague Island. The sun's amber rays caused the water to sparkle signifying another fiery July day was in store which was good for the firemen's carnival, but tough on the general comfort level of the visitors.

Finding a tree near the edge of the beach I sat down and fell into a trance while trying to gather my thoughts about my failed excursion. With my head bowed as if praying, a feeling of disillusionment settled over me. The several nips of brandy I took did little to counter the funk that consumed me.

The silence of my thoughts was shattered by what I later called a subliminal sensation. It wasn't a conscious awareness I perceived as movement heading toward the water, but rather an instinct that forced me to open my eyes and glance left.

At that moment my attention caught sight of a nicely dressed woman heading into the water some fifty yards down the beach. Strange, I thought, why isn't she watching the auction at the carnival grounds, and secondly, the blue blouse and shorts seemed inappropriate to wear swimming. Her movement interested me as I watched her continue to walk into deeper water.

The water rose to her shoulders, then her chin. She seemed to take a little skip as if she were diving into the water and appeared to be in a face down floating position. Suddenly I realized this woman was attempting to kill herself, and her suicide was taking place in front of me. I got up and ran toward the water. Inexplicably, the outlandish thought gripped me that the sand was flying into my walking shoes and spotting my legs.

I hit the water and started swimming to her with all the strength I could muster. Finally, after what seemed like an eternity, I reached out and grabbed her hair, pulling the limp face up to receive any air it would accept. I pulled her around to face me and immediately noticed her eyes rolled up into her head, giving an appearance of death.

Reaching around her waist I swam and carried her to the water's edge. As soon as we reached the beach, I placed her on the sand and looked at a woman who had just killed herself by drowning. I immediately started to administer CPR techniques until I practically exhausted myself. I was mistaken. I felt a quiver, and then realized my efforts had been successful.

Shallow breathing followed until her dull and listless eyes opened and water streamed out the side of her mouth. It dawned on me I had saved this troubled lady.

After what seemed like several minutes she started breathing regularly and looked up at me through puzzled eyes. "What happened?"

Shaking my head in a helpless gesture, I discovered my thought process had momentarily shut down. I was too stunned to answer. I helped her to her feet and held her close. Eventually I started the slow arduous task of guiding her to the top of the beach and its warm sand.

For the first time I realized we were the only two people on the beach.

Her eyes filled with tears as she hopelessly raised thin arms. Speaking in a thin whiny voice, she said, "Why did you stop me?"

"I don't know you and don't much care what you do to yourself, but you were helping yourself to an early meeting with the man with a scythe."

The lady was pretty by any stretch of the imagination and her wet blouse and shorts displayed the outline of a once spectacular body beginning to wilt under the burden of age. The lady continued to shiver so I jogged back to pick up my discarded sweater. After placing the sweater over her shaking shoulders, she started to warm up and appeared ready to talk.

"Why would a good-looking woman like you want to take her life?"

"You had no right to do the thing you did." Her comment carried a strong note of anger that strangely made her all the more appealing.

"I had every right because you were standing at death's doorway. We have so little time on earth; why shorten it by such a profound gesture?"

"My life is not working out, it's that simple."

I could sense her frustration as I noted a catch in her throat.

"Well, you damned near got what you wanted."

"If not today then tomorrow. That's the story of my life, and believe me, I never catch the brass ring." She looked at me and broke down and cried.

For the first time I observed a pretty brown-haired woman of fifty looking through the prism of hard knocks.

Minutes skipped by while we sat in silence until the thunder of applause and cheering drifted to the beach from the pony auction to interrupt the serene moment.

It was time for me to speak. "There are certain bets you can't hedge on, and that little caper you just tried is one of them."

"What is there to live for?" She replied with a slack look of hopelessness.

"You don't really believe that, do you? All troubles pass and you should consider looking at the lovely day in front of you."

"Appreciating a pretty day isn't going to improve how I feel."

"But just the thought has to be worth something?"

"Not in my life it's not."

She was obviously sick at heart.

"Where do you come from?" She was beginning to interest me in a way I would never have dreamt possible.

"I'm from Charlottesville, Virginia."

"Did you come out here alone?"

"No. I came down here with a couple of girlfriends and we planned to stay until the weekend. I just had to get away."

"Get away from what? Would you like to talk about it?"

"Away from that husband of mine."

"What's the matter with your husband?"

Her emotions spilled out in a harsh indictment of her husband. "He's no good."

"In what respect?"

"He doesn't work and spends all his time at the legion drinking. Do you think life is easy for me living with a man like that?"

"Would it make a difference if you got him help?" *Isn't that ironic? If it's anyone who needs help with alcohol, it's me,* I thought.

"Are you still cold? Are you feeling better?"

"No, I'm not cold anymore and I do feel better. I could drink a cup of coffee or something."

"I don't have coffee but I do have something that will help. This is my humble way of giving you some relief." I reached to my hip and pulled out a pint-sized flask. "Here, try drinking some of this. This is blackberry brandy and I'm sure you'll find it very pleasant."

She took several pulls on the brandy, and I think that here in front of me was a custom-made victim. I was out looking to do one deed this morning and ended up playing the role of the Good Samaritan. This lady is so unsuspecting and full of guilt; I can do her without bothering to use tape.

"I should introduce myself, I'm James Rinehart."

"Hello, I'm Lisa Oden." Lisa had a nice smile when she used it.

The brandy helped her to regain control of her emotions.

"I'd like to get back to your earlier experience this morning. Lisa, we can't change the past and must face up to our personal shortcomings whatever they may be. There are other ways of dealing with the stress we must endure and a blueprint isn't needed to guide us."

Lisa waved in a helpless gesture while looking past me at the water. "I just don't know."

"I believe I know what you're going through."

"No one could know how I hurt."

"You're wrong, my dear. The fact remains that five years ago I had trouble sorting out my own thoughts. It was at that time I tried to take my life."

A blank look settled on her face while the silence between us grew. This was the edge I needed and so I wavered. I reached for the flask she was holding and took a drink, then recapped it. When I grabbed her, I didn't want to spill the brandy. A stain on a blouse is evidence, and no matter how insignificant, it's still evidence.

I put down the flask and reached for my killing case. I opened it so she couldn't see the glistening steel shaft. Withdrawing the pick, I looked around the beach and much to my delight found it still empty. No one would see.

I reached around her head, covered her mouth, and with one swift stroke drove the shining shaft into her ear. I dragged her into the sea oats bordering the beach, retrieved my sweater and dropped a horse chestnut next to her. Then I was on my way.

Here it was before ten in the morning and the task I had originally set out to do was completed. I had anticipated something difficult, but the way it happened proved to be a walk in the park.

Normally after I finish off a victim, I feel a certain degree of guilt. Although I relish the sensation of the kill, there's still that little thread of guilt that I can never seem to shake. I don't feel the guilt this time and believe my reasoning to be sound. I'm not trying to rationalize my actions, but this woman had committed herself to taking her own life.

This morning she came to that beach for the express purpose of ending her life. All I did was gallantly returned her back to life, then carry out her desire.

On the way to my wagon, loud sounds again erupted from spectators at the auction. There is not one reason in the world to feel guilty, I thought as I crossed the unencumbered bridge to the mainland and headed home.

33

This was the afternoon of *Death Sunday*, and the order of the day assigned Phyllis Eichner as Jeanette's driver for the long awaited trip to Smithbury. Phyllis's role in the entrapment scheme was a simple but important one, to drop Jeanette at the Jeffreys estate and leave.

Riding to Jeanette's rendezvous with the grim reaper, Phyllis quizzed her friend on the anticipated step-by-step events of the afternoon. The list drawn by Jeanette contained one major flaw; she had designed it, and not the object of her ploy, Martin Jeffreys. The old adage of the best-laid plans could fit here.

Nearing the Jeffreys estate, Phyllis found cars parked for half a mile on each side of the road leading to the estate entrance.

"You be careful and don't take any unnecessary chances. There's too much life left in you to get yourself in a bad way. You'll be in awkward jeopardy from the moment you leave this car. Now remember, we can turn around right now and go back if there's a question in your mind. You don't have to go through with this," Phyllis said. Try as she might to control her emotions, tears began to fill her eyes.

Jeanette mentally ran through Phyllis' admonition.

"Yes I do. This is something I must do, and let's face it, there's no other way. If I don't carry our plan to its conclusion, Jeffreys will probably continue killing women like you and I for no particular reason."

"Here we are," Phyllis said.

"Phyllis, don't worry, everything will work out."

With tears streaming down her face, Phyllis stopped the car and reached over to whisper her support. She hugged the one true friend she ever had and for the first time realized the inescapable peril Jeanette was moving toward. Jeanette closed the door and headed for the driveway that lead to what would prove to be a very dark and troubled evening. Turning back she waved and bravely walked down the lane. Tears continued to flow as Phyllis reluctantly drove away from the *Saxon Hunt*.

Jeanette paid thirty dollars at the admissions gate, and then entered the show area. *Thirty dollars is a lot of money to watch a bunch of horses running around, but if it's what you like then I guess it isn't too much. These people are loaded so why worry about them when I have my own problems to confront,* Jeanette thought as she surveyed the hunt grounds.

Walking around provided Jeanette an outsider's view of the crowd and horses. Horses did not interest her but their grace and beauty did. O'Brennan was right about the *Saxon Hunt* catering to upper-crusters who attended because it was the thing to do.

Approaching one of the numerous refreshment stands found on the show grounds; Jeanette decided to get a bite to eat. *Better get something I like because it may be my Last Supper. I've made a pun and don't think it's one bit funny,* she thought while buying a hot dog and soda.

From the time she was a kid Jeanette loved hot dogs; especially the fat-soaked ones cooked on an old greasy grill. She found a grassy spot to sit and wait.

Time was moving slowly. Looking at her watch she felt a catch in her throat. It was twenty after four, and quickly approaching the time when Jeffreys would contact her. The game plan she so carefully deigned was on target but the wait was proving to be excruciatingly difficult.

Brushing the crumbs off her brown tweed skirt, she started to walk. Jeanette made herself as visible as possible; she stopped and leaned against a fence.

The grace and beauty of the horses and beautifully attired crowd no longer interested her. She could feel a build up of anxiety with its accompanying clammy perspiration overtaking her. *I wonder if my deodorant will hold up? Good grief, I must be mad.*

Here I am walking into the eye of a major catastrophe and I'm worrying whether I have body odor, she thought as she started walking on what she hoped to be her last turn around the grounds.

From in back came a voice, "Hi, I'm delighted to see you again and welcome to the Jeffreys estate."

At that moment she realized *Death Sund*ay under the mask of Martin Jeffreys had suddenly reentered her life. The expression was a term she flippantly invented to designate the day Jeffreys would attempt to kill her. This was it; the hour she had so shamelessly looked forward to.

Jeanette was convinced Jeffreys would hit her at the *Saxon Hunt* and the moment of reality was at hand. She was confident Jeffreys had astutely drawn and planned her elimination down to the smallest detail while she had painstakingly drawn counter measures that would neutralize his dance of death. If Jeffreys' design of deceit was flawed, it was because he didn't know that she knew.

Several minutes of small talk passed before he took her by the elbow as if to lead her away. "Julie, I have some hunt business that must be attended to. I'm certain you're tired of the events, so why don't you go up the mansion and look around. I should be up shortly."

"Very well, Martin, if that's what you want. It appears to be a lovely home from here, a mansion if you will and I'll certainly find numerous points of interest inside that appeal to me."

"There are" . . . he smiled confidently. "See you later."

With Jeffreys going one way and Jeanette heading for the house, she thought, I'll probably see you sooner than I'd like.

Entering the mansion through the massive oak door, she was overwhelmed by the beautiful entryway. The stunning oak spiral stairway, a throwback to antebellum days, gave all appearances of reaching to the sky. Something very special, the large imposing residence Jeffreys called home could easily fit the image of a restored mansion open to the public. Jeanette tried entering a room to the right of the front entryway but found it locked. At the rear of the first floor, she entered a modern kitchen. Its oak cabinets closely matched the reconditioned oak casings and trim found throughout the house.

Filling a glass with water, Jeanette retreated to a round oak table where she sat and thought about the complex state of affairs she found herself in. She was scared and could use a drink but crunch time was upon her and this was no time to seek false courage. *Death Sunday* was not a day for drink. If she made it through the day, she'd probably have several, but not now. She had to be on top of her game and wondered whether that would he enough.

Her concentration waned when she heard the front door close, followed by the sound of footsteps growing louder. Jeffreys walked into the kitchen and softly said, "I see you found something to drink, but water doesn't seem appropriate for our date. There is a variety of drinks in the refrigerator including: juice, pop, beer, or maybe a mixed drink."

Jeanette could feel her body tense as she desperately tried to review her game plan

"Thank you, Martin . . . maybe later." Placing the glass on the counter, Jeanette turned to him and smiled as if signaling for the charade to begin.

Picking up from her gesture, Martin said, "Come with me and I'll give you a tour of the house."

The minutes fell away into an hour. Acting more as a thinly disguised tour guide than host, Jeffreys escorted her around the mansion. He even unlocked his study and proudly showed Jeanette the room where he had designed her death.

How did he get where he is? Jeanette asked herself.

She was enormously impressed by the beauty of the house, and equally so the manner in which he presented it. Jeanette could now see why he was considered the guardian of the legal community in Smithbury. He was acknowledged as an excellent attorney, and she could appreciate why he formed the backbone of Smithbury's social line. He was smooth, sharp, sincere, articulate, and aware.

"Martin, where are your servants? I've never seen real live ones other than in the movies, and that doesn't count, does it?"

"They'll have enough to do tomorrow, so I gave them the day off."

Jeanette sensed her plan was beginning to unravel and *Death Sunday* had barely begun.

"Shall we go down to the lagoon and look at the summer house? We can go through the kitchen and take the path that leads down the hill. When the summerhouse was built five years ago, I had this path cut through the woods, that's the reason the trees are next to the path. I really wanted a nature trail, but for some reason, the heavy spring rains caused it to wash away. After much frustration, I had it blacktopped last summer. It destroyed some of the aesthetic beauty of the woods but resolved the water problem."

The thirty feet from the kitchen door to the path, a mere ten yards to make a first down in football seemed to be an alarming distance for Jeanette.

"I didn't expect the path to be so steep."

Jeffreys ignored her comment as he started to recite the history of the plantation that earlier graced the estate. Striding down the path of danger, Jeanette was surprisingly fascinated by Jeffreys' history lesson, even given the uncertainty of her own fate.

34

The eight-foot blacktop walkway was wide enough to accommodate a golf cart. The surface shiny with beads of moisture posed a question that Jeanette asked herself. *It didn't rain, so why is it wet?*

The air felt hot and steamy, giving her the unusual impression of walking through a tropical rain forest. *What do I know of a rain forest*, she wondered, *I've never been in one.* Looking to the sky she noticed a dramatic collogue of varying green. The fifty-foot treetops with slits of light showing through formed a shadowy canopy over the man-made tunnel.

Would this four hundred-foot walk be her last? Would there be some degree of sex involved? When he bound her hands and feet, how would she react? When he stuck the pick in her ear, would she feel the pain? How long would she hurt before she died? Jeanette asked herself these questions as she and Jeffreys started down the winding path to the lagoon and summerhouse.

Jeanette braced herself for the skirmish that would most assuredly follow. Jeffreys reached down and took her hand causing her to jump at his touch. If they were fifteen, the gesture would he considered innocent, but they weren't fifteen and this man's mindset didn't have innocent in it. Holding hands accompanied by hugging and kissing was not on this violent man's agenda. She had totally misjudged this menace.

Jeffreys turned to face Jeanette.

Mental gymnastics played in Jeanette's head as she thought, *Good grief! Now starts the fertility dance. Oh, oh, here we go.*

Death Sunday's designated killer reached under Jeanette's arms and gently drew her close. Bending down, he made an audible wheeze and passionately kissed her, causing her flesh to crawl. The moment she had dreaded was now at hand.

She was totally isolated with nowhere to run. Jeanette had to get him closer to the summerhouse where help was in place; and she had run out of the bravado she had earlier displayed.

Jeanette assumed a playacting posture and actively reacted to Jeffreys' advances. She could feel his tongue brush against her teeth, enter her mouth, and simulate the ultimate sex act.

She was appalled by her reaction to Jeffreys' heated advances. Jeanette countered his action with an open-mouthed kiss that would have challenged Linda Lovelace's accomplished erotic behavior. Jeanette feverishly pushed up and rubbed against Jeffreys as if it were her first sexual encounter.

Confused by the passion of the torrid clinch, Jeanette felt oddly removed from her body. It was a feeling an outsider might experience looking at two lovers about to embark on the most intimate reward man and woman can achieve. For the first time Jeanette sensed she had become a pawn in a stupid chess match between a cunning killer and a group of old people flirting with calamity. She's part of the group and is now literally touching danger.

Jeanette's stirring afternoon continued when Jeffreys suddenly became excited. He dropped his hands to her knees and dramatically lifted her skirt to the top of her pantyhose. His latest maneuver forced a panic-stricken Jeanette to realize her previous theatrics had failed.

We were doing this in a dream I had the other night, she reminded herself.

The name of the game is to attack and get him before he gets me, but how?

Instinctively, she reached around his waist and fiercely pulled him to her. Jeffreys gasped as he felt the heat of Jeanette's feverish body flow through her sheer pantyhose. His action reminded her of someone trying to rush good wine.

At this stage of their steamy skirmish, an alarm went off that left Jeanette devastated. Martin Jeffreys displayed absolutely no sign of arousal and that assaulted her sexuality. Here was a man who had finessed her, French kissed her, and wantonly pulled her skirt over her head. She had generally been explored from stem to stern. Now, what was left?

There was something exceedingly wrong with this man, which was the only explanation. If she couldn't excite him, it couldn't be done. Jeanette had to rethink this situation in a hurry and couldn't wait until later.

Jeanette artfully redirected his intentions. "Martin, we must stop immediately. We have to get this right and this is no place for what we have in mind. Take my hand and we'll walk down to the summer house and pick up where we left off." She gestured with her head toward the bottom of the hill.

He did just that. Martin Jeffreys followed as Jeanette led the assassin to the summerhouse and her imminent destruction.

For the first time in her life, Jeanette understood the meaning of how fast the clock runs when you're behind. After the last couple of years of watching football games with O'Brennan, she'd heard the commentators mention how quickly the game clock seems to run when you're behind. Now the game clock was pushing her to a finale she didn't want to experience.

Continuing their walk toward the lagoon, Jeffreys on his mission of death suddenly changed his demeanor. The earlier reticence he displayed at the top of the path was no longer evident.

He did not look at Jeanette as he spoke. "I love the way you looked at me and the fashion in which you shamelessly rubbed your magnificent body against mine. You're bold and provocative, and that, my dear is a quality I adore in a woman." Jeffreys' mood swing was now complete as the anticipation of the upcoming kill swept over him.

His words had Jeanette's undivided attention.

The crisp scent of lilacs permeated the area as they reached the grass at the bottom of the path. Turning right, they headed for the summerhouse.

"Come with me to the upstairs sunroom."

Jeanette thought quickly. *I can't let him lead me into the house. I'm a goner if I go in there with him.*

"Martin, I can't wait. Take me on the patio."

"You're right; I shall take you on the patio." Jeanette imaged gruesome thoughts running through Jeffreys' mind as he again spoke with strange determination. "Will I ever take you on the patio."

Jeffreys' thoughts bounced back to the incident on the path. *I don't understand why I involved myself with the sexuality that occurred on the path. Strange, I never entered into such foreplay in any of my previous killings. Whatever the reason, I'll use this experience in my current novel.*

Keep your composure and don't panic, Jeanette advised herself.

35

Jerry Chappell transported O'Brennan's friends up river to the lagoon. A casual observer viewing the loaded party boat traveling against the current would think nothing more than its occupants were out for a fun afternoon on the water. The Group's trip on the river was something far more serious.

All had taken part in the unraveling of the mystery that started with the Barber co-ed in 1960. As the boat quietly moved along, there was little doubt in anyone's mind that the investigation would end today at the Jeffreys estate in Smithbury.

The dye had been cast and there was no way out. John Lloyd, Sheriff Max Gravel and Colby along with O'Brennan settled themselves at the edge of the pines. The adjacent bush and undergrowth provided adequate cover for them. The commanding position they chose provided the closest possible vantage point to observe the patio and even seemed close enough to almost touch Jeanette and Jeffreys when they passed. She expected Lloyd and O'Brennan to be in the vicinity but didn't know their exact position.

Sheriff Max Gravel had stationed his SWAT team on the side of the lagoon opposite from the house in a position that afforded them the best possible shot at Jeffreys if the situation demanded. The remainder of the Group positioned themselves across the water from the patio, and then resolutely waited for Jeanette to make a dramatic entrance into the arena of horrors.

Time crawled as the involved observers impatiently waited for the finale to begin. From his position in the woods, Jack turned to his companions and said, "Ya' know, I don't believe we can get over there in time. I thought it possible when we first looked at the pictures, and I believed it up until now, however, looking at the patio from here, I made a tactical error and underestimated the danger involved."

"I believe you're right. We'll have to follow the lawn around about twenty-feet of water before we get to the patio. If he strikes swiftly, we're lost," Max Gravel said.

"Max, what about your SWAT team?" John asked.

"Oh, they'll stop him! There's no question that we can get him, but at what point do we do that? Our problem is king-sized and you must be aware of it," Max said.

"You mean shoot him," John said.

Max carefully measured his words. "That's right, shoot him!" he replied. "If that happens, Jeffreys has no escape save for the grave digger."

"Max, how are you going to decide that?" O'Brennan asked.

"Jack, I think you're getting the wrong idea. I'm not going to decide; it's your call. This is your operation and your decision." The sheriff passed O'Brennan a hand-held scanner. "You better practice using this with the SWAT unit because you'll probably need it. Once Jeffreys starts his assault, your call will trigger my team into action."

O'Brennan cast a jaundiced eye at Gravel without speaking a word. The heavy burden of responsibility for killing a man now rested on his shoulders. "Damn, I don't know what to do. I feel like I'm out on a limb."

"Well, it's your limb and you better start gearing up for it. Once they come down from that path, it's your decision."

How Colby ended up tagging along O'Brennan couldn't remember, but he did recall Cal and Red were with the others hiding in the trees across the water.

Colby's gift for relieving a group's tension was never more evident than at that moment, "I wish this was over and it was tomorrow. I don't much care about the wedding, Jack, but I can't wait to get at that beach party, or what you call a reception. That I'm looking forward to."

"Colby, you're either thinking of something to eat or drink.

In this case, you're going to like what we have in store," John said.

The conversation came to a halt. John's reply to Colby successfully directed Brennan's thoughts from the ongoing crisis that he faced with Jeanette and Jeffreys to his wedding in the morning.

Finally, John Lloyd said to his companions, "It's starting to get cold."

"John, I feel the same way but thought it was my reaction to the tension of the moment, but there's a storm brewing," Max Gravel said.

"You're right, Max, there's no doubt about it. I can't believe what's going on here. What the hell, it's June and the sky has gone crazy. I think we're in the middle of a cold front with this fog settling on the water. What an eerie feeling!" John said.

O'Brennan's mind seemed to wander as the thickening fog rolled in through the channel to seize the lagoon.

Part of his thoughts drifted to his wedding tomorrow while the other part centered on Jeanette's crisis.

"Along the Rappohanock, the fog drifts in like a light dusting of snow. It comes in waves much like sheets of rain that accompany a hurricane," Max said.

The scene paralleled someone trying to pour five gallons of water into a one-gallon bucket. The fog quickly saturated the lagoon and overflowed into the pines surrounding the water.

John said, "What the hell, there was nothing mentioned on the weather watch this morning. I can't even see the path leading down from the house. Max, what are we going to do?"

"We'll have to sit this out and hope it disappears before they arrive. There's nothing we can do about it," Max said.

"So it would seem," a defeated John Lloyd added.

For the next half-hour Jack and his colleagues anxiously waited for something to happen.

"There you are, our troubles with the fog are over. Look at the top of the trees."

As Max spoke, the sun's rays filtered through the pines causing the fog to disappear as rapidly as it had settled in the lagoon. After the fog cleared, the temperature started to climb and returned Smithbury's summer heat to the lagoon.

"The fog here at Smithbury doesn't stay around long. A little cold front comes through and hits the hot air thus creating fog. It leaves as quickly as it comes. We're talking about ten, fifteen minutes in duration. This baby was around thirty minutes, which is unusual. Fortunately for us, it came before Jeanette and Jeffreys arrived," Max said.

Time passed and then the moment of truth arrived. Looking out at the lagoon, Jack pointed after spotting Jeanette and Jeffreys walking hand-in-hand as they left the path and headed for the summerhouse.

It was an awkward moment when he looked at John.

"Oh, boy, here they come!" Jack said in an uneven voice as Jeanette and Jeffreys moved in his direction. He felt as if fireworks were exploding in his head.

36

There are many bad people in the world and I'm holding hand with one of them, a stonehearted killer. Jeanette thought about her immediate predicament while approaching the summerhouse patio. *O'Brennan told me to follow the Rule of Holes during my preparation for this very day. That is, when you find yourself in a hole quit digging. Well, I kept digging and look where it got me, a heartbeat away from my darkest moment. I feel like I'm in a glass house with all the people in the woods looking at me under a magnifying glass.*

The amber-toned sun had begun its descent toward the horizon as she reached the patio. Jeffreys stepped in back of her and grasped her left elbow, appearing to both lift and guide her up the one step to the raised leisure area in one effortless motion. His cavalier effort was a gesture only a debonair host would make. Jeanette and her friends stationed around the lagoon knew there was nothing gallant about this attempt at chivalry.

Inconsistent given her emotional state at the moment, the start of a smile settled on her lips as her mind shifted to Red's wedding reception and how she had wet her pants laughing when Colby blew the yellow confetti over O'Brennan.

O'Brennan shuddered at the sight of Jeanette and Jeffreys hand in hand on their way to the summerhouse. He could hear her speaking but couldn't make out the words.

This day will be like no other I've ever experienced; he thought while surveying the scene in front of him. Noticing Jeanette's pained look he silently brooded why he had allowed her to get involved with this one-man killing squad.

While moving along the grass toward the elevated patio, Jeffreys appeared larger than his six-two frame and displayed a cold and unaffected veneer like a veteran actor playing in front of a full house.

An impulse struck O'Brennan. By knocking Jeffreys into the lagoon, he could save her. But that, he rationalized, would defeat the purpose of the whole charade.

The moment they reached the patio, Jeffreys quickly lifted Jeanette to the raised patio. *Why is she smiling?* pondered an unsettled O'Brennan?

At this moment Jeffreys made his move on Jeanette. Standing on the patio, he simultaneously reached around her waist and with his free hand covered her mouth. Feverishly reacting to his efforts, she unsuccessfully tried to kick him but failed. Before Jeanette realized what had happened, her mouth, wrists, and ankles had been bound with duct tape. All this was done without benefit of conversation. He then picked her up and carried his prize catch to the doors that opened into the house. There he sat her down with her back resting against the glass doorway and stepped back to admire his newly acquired trophy.

She had totally misjudged the situation. Within seconds, uncontrollable emotion scrambled her thought process. For the first time in her life Jeanette understood the full meaning of absolute terror. *This can't be happening; he has taped my wrists in front of me. He wasn't supposed to do that, but he did. Jeffreys has always tied the wrists in back of his last ten victims, but this isn't the case with me. Why would he do that? Why would he do that?* Jeanette repeated her last thoughts as hysteria set in. She had been thrown into a panic and was now helpless. The old adage about the plans of mice and men proved true at the Jeffreys lagoon.

Images of O'Brennan flashed in her mind as she softly thought the words, *"Where are you now that I need you?"*

Her orchestrated plan was now on the backburner. The plot she and Phyllis so carefully engineered had gone awry. Phyllis had bought a cheap garter belt and cut off the garters. Fitting it over Jeanette's underwear, she had placed the mace canister inside the back of the garter belt. A fine nylon tube ran up her back, under her bra and jersey then threaded its way through her hair to the front of her head.

The mace plan was based on Jeffreys' last ten victims. Their wrists had been bound in back; something she and O'Brennan anticipated would be repeated at the summerhouse. By strategically placing the mace in back, she could trigger the canister button that would release the spray on Jeffreys. She was now forced to improvise and that scared her.

The piercing sound of a descending jet on its way to the Bridgeton International Airport ruptured the silence of the moment. The well-groomed woman of sixty didn't bother to look up. After the plane passed over she looked around the lagoon and house grounds, trying to locate her friends and surveillance team.

The scheme called for her to spray the mace that would immediately neutralize Jeffreys. At that point the Group would converge on the man and capture him on the spot. If successful, she wouldn't be the worse for wear. With her hands tied in front, a new problem confronted her.

How would the Group react to this new crisis? She assumed they would move early, but she had no control over that. Jeanette had to think in a hurry. The canister had to be activated by pushing the button on top, thus releasing the mace.

I know they're in place, but I can't see them. O'Brennan will realize my plight, but what good . . ., Jeanette wondered, her thought dying before it became a question.

O'Brennan crouched in a confused state, uncontrolled anxiety grabbing him as events dramatically picked up. His attention honed in on Jeanette and he couldn't take his eyes off her. He felt anesthetized by the scene playing out on the patio. The moment O'Brennan glanced sideways at John Lloyd their eyes locked. They could virtually read each other's minds without exchanging words. John's troubled look told him what he already knew. Jeanette was in a world of trouble.

She suddenly turned her head to the right and this movement puzzled O'Brennan. *What is she looking for? Time is her worst enemy and I've got to get her out of there.* He felt compelled to push the talk button but thought better of it. His stomach knotted up with by an intense feeling of foreboding.

At least she's a hard-nosed realist and quick-minded, he thought, *and she'll have to make something out of nothing.* Consumed by thoughts of his past days with Jeanette, O'Brennan found himself gearing up to the drama playing out in front of him until the villain's movement forced him to move his finger toward the talk button. From the look on Jeffreys' face, the end was near. He swallowed with difficulty as he felt his stomach turn over.

While steeling himself for the inevitable, his gaze now flicked to Jeanette's eyes, now beginning to tear. He anguished over losing her and hardly dared ask himself what life would be like without her. Suddenly an airline jet passing overhead interrupted his thinking. The final act was about to rise on the drama playing out in the lagoon.

Jeanette's problem was monumental; she couldn't reach her back. She twisted her head to the right and spotted what was needed. She had never seen a sliding door like that before. Instead of a common flat handle, it had cut-glass knobs.

How could I have missed seeing those knobs in the photos? Then her reasoning came around. *The French doors were hinged and didn't slide but opened, thus the glass knobs. That explains it,* she thought.

I have to be standing and somehow maneuver myself in front of the knob so I can crunch down and align the canister underneath the doorknob. I can't be wrong, because most assuredly, there will be no second chance. Once in front of the knob, I'll have to back up so the canister will be under the knob. Then I can lift up and trigger the mace. This is a plan I have to live or die by.

The knob was three feet to her right and Jeanette was confronted with several questions that had to be answered immediately. Could she raise herself up to a standing position, and secondly, would he let her do it? *Fortunately, I'm wearing sneakers that will provide added much needed traction. If he puts his hand on my head, it will be impossible to move. I have to bring my feet back underneath me as close to the door as possible. From there, I can scoot up to the glass in a standing position.*

She tried but couldn't muster enough power in her legs to push herself up. When her effort failed, an unfamiliar wave of apprehension seized her.

Seeing Jeanette's attempt at standing, Jeffreys spoke out. "Julie, I see you're trying to . . . what are you trying to do, get away? No, the lovely lady wants to stand up. You're making it easier for me, my dear. Yes, that is an excellent idea, why didn't I think of it? Obviously you can't make it on your own; here, let me help you."

Much to her surprise he reached down and lifted her to a standing position.

I can't believe he'd do that. For the first time, Jeanette understood what he was up to. *The bastard is playing a game much like a cat playing with a captured mouse. He's enjoying this exercise but he has given me another chance.*

The only way to the knob is to edge my way over a little at a time. I can move three feet. No, make that I have to move three feet. I'll move my heels, then my toes and hope Jeffreys doesn't notice my movement. Yes, I can pull this off because he's not that much concerned with what I'm doing. He really isn't aware of what's happening. Look at him, he's in such an emotional frenzy he's removed himself from the reality of the moment.

O'Brennan's excitement and fear mixed together at the same time he caught Jeanette's heel and toe action moving her toward the door knob. Two questions popped into his mind. Could she trigger the mace, and would it work?

Martin Jeffreys failed to notice Jeanette slowly inching her way to the most prized goal in her life, the cut-glass doorknob. *I'm getting near that damn knob. One more turn of my toes and I should touch it. Her last movement did the trick. There it is! It's on my right hip. One more turn and I'm there.*

Jeanette had been so attentive to positioning herself in front of the magic knob she missed much of Jeffreys' bizarre monologue. The game clock she thought about on the path was about to run out. Jeffreys withdrew a small leather carrying case and opened it. Against the red velvet background nestled a mini-sized pick with an ornate hand-carved wooden handle. Attached to the end of the handle was a two-inch pointed stainless steel shaft.

"Julie, doesn't this instrument look delicious? I'm going to run this beauty into your ear which will permanently put you in seventh heaven."

Jeffreys giggled in a crazed manner. Awestruck by this blatant display of mania, Jeanette closed her eyes to the dangers ahead. *The brain doesn't register if the eyes don't see,* she thought.

"Open your eyes, my lovely. I want to view your terror when I look into those lovely blue eyes. And my beloved, you know the terror I'm talking about.

There have been others. You'll be number eleven as matter of fact," Jeffreys said with an unpleasant laugh.

When Jeanette opened her eyes, the creature she saw standing in front of her appeared to have brought the shadow of death with him.

"There is something you must understand before departing the ultimate pleasure. You are on the verge of presenting me with not like most men. Regrettably, have been with a woman and by that I mean you know, the sexual act. When I kill a woman I get the same wonderful feeling I assume comes with a stimulating exercise like sex.

His words seemed disjointed and made little sense except for his last response. It triggered an alarm in Jeanette's mind, and then its' meaning exploded like a Fourth of July rocket in the sky. *He said I'm to be his eleventh victim, but there were eleven already. Was it possible this monster did not kill Shana Barber; that Jeffreys' eventual demise will come about because the Barber death had inadvertently guided us to him. John Lloyd was right from the beginning, Martin was their man and I'm going to be another victim.*

Jeanette's thoughts were interrupted by an abnormal voice coming from Martin Jeffreys.

"After you pass on; I like to talk this way to my subjects because it arouses me." He giggled and swept his eyes skyward. "You might call it foreplay. It doesn't do much for them, but that's not my concern, is it?" Jeffreys followed with a cross between a giggle and a low rumbling laugh.

"The toe next to your little toe is the memento I shall take. I'll preserve it, and then engrave your name and departure date on a gold plate, after which I'll secure it to the toenail. That way I'll always remember your demise."

Jeanette flinched at his words as thoughts of three happy years with O'Brennan raced through her mind. *This monster is going to take what days she and O'Brennan have left and wipe them off the face of the earth if I don't come up with something to stop him.*

"You are an intelligent woman. In your last fleeting moments, you may have thought of how is he going to engrave the plate? You will probably be impressed to know I will do my own engraving, a skill I mastered very well as a student at William and Mary. For your information, I served an apprenticeship as a silversmith at Colonial Williamsburg."

Jeanette telescoped her thoughts into one fleeting glance at the reason that she had become involved in this fiasco. Why she volunteered to be the dupe in this disaster she couldn't answer. She was on one-way street she could never get off.

Her heart thumped as Jeffreys removed the lethal-looking pick, closed the case, and carefully returned it to his pocket.

I can't hang on much longer. Why are you doing this to me? The dreary reality of it all is you're going to kill me before O'Brennan can intervene, Jeanette thought.

"Beautiful lady, your mind is an open book. You are certainly thinking, why am I doing this to you? I think I owe you an explanation and shall be candid with you. The thrill of the kill isn't as intense as it once was. The need to repeat this heavenly task continues to crowd and overwhelm me.

"When I first initiated this glorious undertaking, I'd return to the scene of my artistry. It gave me a high that was greater than the actual killing, but sadly, it gradually left. Now I must kill again and again to become aroused. It's lovely for me, but not so rewarding for my subjects. Obviously you agree.

"I feel closer to you than any of my other victims. You are the first I ever kissed, and I must admit it felt very nice. If it were possible for me to have sexual relations with a woman, you'd be the one. However, we know that's unlikely, don't we? But, my dear, that isn't enough. The time has come, there will he no tomorrows for you."

Jeanette became more confused as minutes raced by and found she was becoming mesmerized by Jeffreys' dramatic soliloquy. *I have to be mentally ready,* she cautioned herself. *I'm glad I listened to Phyllis about the canister.*

Phyllis Eichner had sewn a little pocket in the back of the garter belt Jeanette was to wear to hold the mace. Without it, the canister would slip down into Jeanette's pantyhose and not activate.

Jeanette needed time to compose herself but could sense the clock racing to zero. My life is going to fade away into darkness like the finishing shot on *Sixty Minutes* where the second hand reaches twelve, the show ends and the screen goes dark. I never thought one thing about it before, but low and behold I think of it now. Could this happen to me? Maybe a more realistic question would be; when will it happen?

Jeffreys absently lifted the pick with his right hand. Forcing her head against the glass door, he brought the life-taking rod to Jeanette's left ear. His face reflected a look of absolute euphoria and triumph, then he moaned and staggered. Saliva ran from his open mouth as he peered at her through glazed eyes.

Her heart beat so rapidly she thought it would explode. *That's it*, Jeanette thought, *he's experienced some kind of sexual experience. I have no idea what it is but it has some deviant connotation.*

Jeffreys' face turned stony while speaking in a trance-like state. "Julie, do you remember the popular *Burns and Allen* radio show when we were kids? At the end of the show, George Burns always said to his wife, 'say goodnight, Gracey'. Well, Julie Smilker, it's your turn to say goodnight. Say goodnight, Julie."

O'Brennan momentarily thought of his past days with Jeanette until the villain's movements forced him back to the moment of truth. From the look on Jeffreys' face, the end was near. Swallowing with difficulty, Jack's gaze flicked to Jeanette's eyes. She had the appearance of a person running out of hope. He anguished over the prospect of losing her and hardly dare ask himself what life would be like without her.

O'Brennan's face turned hard accompanied by lips that settled in a straight line. He could feel his hands beginning to sweat while tightly gripping the scanner. "Here goes," O'Brennan muttered while looking down at the hand-held radio. He activated the instrument by pushing the talk button. A moment later the phone clicked after which he hurriedly spoke the command, "Fire."

Jeanette could see Jeffreys' mind shifting gears as the pick closed on her ear. She shut her eyes but heard no shot. At that instant she violently lifted up, smashing the canister trigger into the doorknob. Jeanette heard the mace release followed by Jeffreys' gasp of pain. She was uncertain whether Duke's plan had worked, but she was still alive. An instant before O'Brennan's call activated the SWAT team, Jeffreys fell to the patio deck, thus canceling their assignment.

The sound of running footsteps forced her eyes open and she slumped to a sitting position against the glass door. Jeffreys was rolling around the patio moaning and rubbing his eyes as O'Brennan leapt to the patio. Confusion reminiscent of a scene in the ring of a heavyweight championship fight after a quick knockout reined. The chilling moment had ended.

Hysteria and jubilation burst simultaneously. Jeanette knew most of the people gathered around her, some she didn't. Jeffreys had been cuffed and led away.

Despite the turmoil, O'Brennan was at her side holding her and sobbing at the same time. He removed the tape and helped her shakily stand. On the other side, Phyllis Eichner was kissing her, crying and laughing simultaneously.

Jeanette's emotions overcame her and tears flowed.

After recovering her composure, she turned to O'Brennan and said, "Get me a cigarette!"

"Jeanette, you haven't smoked in twenty-five years. They're bad for your health."

"O'Brennan, I don't want to hear it! This experience was bad for my health. Now, get me that cigarette!"

Phyllis reached into her purse and pulled out a pack of red-labeled Larks. "Here you are. Smoke all of them if you want."

37

O'Brennan's patio appeared to be the final resting-place of the Smithbury Skeleton investigation. It was a festive occasion with an excited Jeanette reliving her Smithbury experience.

"Today has been my day; tomorrow will be our day, isn't that right, O'Brennan?" At that moment the phone rang before O'Brennan could reply.

He called John to the kitchen. "John, we have to go back to Smithbury as soon as possible. That was Sheriff Gravel at the Jeffreys estate and he needs to see us. He said there's a wild twist to the conclusion of the case."

Returning to the patio, Jack walked over and kissed Jeanette. "That was Max Gravel over in Smthbury and he needs John and me to help wrap up a couple of matters. I'll give you the complete story when we return. Whatever news he has should be interesting because Max sounded excited, and he's not one to go overboard."

There were so many police and official vehicles parked near the front of the mansion that Jack was forced to park on the road.

"This looks more like a police convention than a crime scene." John observed as they walked toward the house. Entering the huge mansion, a deputy directed them to the study.

"This must be the room Jeanette was talking about this evening," Jack said.

They found Sheriff Max Gravel sitting on Jeffreys' desk shaking his head.

"Max, your call brought us running. What is this new twist you mentioned?"

Uncertainty crowded the sheriff's voice as he started to speak. "Apparently Martin Jeffreys was not as he appeared. Jack, you are never going to believe this. A jail attendant checked Jeffreys in and guess what?" Max paused for effect. "Martin Jeffreys is not a man, Martin Jeffreys is a woman." His incredulous look portrayed complete bewilderment.

"Never in my thirty-eight years of law enforcement has anything even approaching this happened. Old-timers like us have been around the horn and seen it all, but this sudden turn of events has knocked me for a loop."

Silence prevailed until O'Brennan interjected some levity to ease the tension in the room. "Max you must remember things aren't always what they seem. Do you know her identity?"

"Tom, he's the deputy back at the jail, didn't know who she was. We had nothing to go on; not one clue," the sheriff said. "I had an idea we'd know more when we checked through his, I mean her personal effects. When I read through her journal," Gravel raised the book in front of him as if he were tossing it to Jack, "her identity was a mystery no more. I knew this was your baby and that's why I called. Thought it only right to bring you and John in to help clear up this new twist."

"Thanks, Max. You have a lot of class for calling us, and we do appreciate it."

"Class or no class, take a gander at this and see if it doesn't get your undivided attention in a hurry. Read the first couple of pages from her journal with care. It should fill in some of the gaps that have surfaced. After finishing, you may question your admiration for womanhood." Gravel passed O'Brennan what appeared to be a ledger book.

After finishing the journal, O'Brennan handed it to John.

"Max, bizarre does not describe what I just read. I thought I was world-wise and had seen all kinds of psychotic behavior, but this one," he pointed at the book John was reading from, "is in another league."

"If you think that's another league, take a look at the case on the desk," Gravel said.

The case Max referred to looked like a photo album but with a more chilling picture to display. O'Brennan unhooked the clasp on the side and opened the red velvet case like one would open a book. Overcoming his initial shock, he placed the case on the desk and looked at the sheriff in disbelief.

Its interior dressed in blue displayed Jeffreys' hope chest of dreams. On each side of the open container of memories, there were three rows of four concave-shaped pockets, each roughly one by four inch. A thin velvet strap secured each prize. He counted eight fingers, two thumbs, and a toe encased in the field of blue with a gold plate covering the nail of each artifact. The engraving was so small O'Brennan had to use his bifocals to read the names of Jeffreys' victims.

As Jack peered at the upper left pocket, he expected one thing but read another. It read Martin Jeffreys born November 17, 1929: deceased November 17 1963. Looking to the bottom row, the little toe read, Lisa Oden born June 10, 1939; deceased, July 9,1987.

Making a quick mental count, Jack spoke. "There was eleven deaths and eleven artifacts are in the case; but Shana Barber's finger is missing and Martins' name has replaced it."

"Before you called, I was on top of the world. Jeanette is safe and we're getting married in the morning; thought I had it all going. We knocked ourselves out solving this damn thing, and when John and I came back tonight, I anticipated finding something smooth and easy. It appears I've been living in a dream, but now I have nothing. The killer is in the can, but that isn't what it's all about, is it, Max? All we have is Martha's journal up to her return to the states in sixty-three. This is like a wind that never stops blowing."

John and Max stood motionless, hardly daring to move. Much like O'Brennan, they displayed blank looks.

"I'll have to make some assumptions about her activities after she killed her brother, and those hypotheses we'll have to live with. Since Jeanette and I first talked to Bobbi Jo Conlin in Leesburg, Martin Jeffreys has dominated my every thought. The case is solved yet he returns as a ghost. What in hell can I do to work this out, Max?"

"That's a puzzle I can't help you with," the sheriff said.

O'Brennan responded to Gravel, "This boggles the imagination; I can't believe what I'm experiencing."

Gravel pointed to the red case. "You better believe it because this is just the beginning. Let's wait for John to finish, then I'll show you reality in its starkest form."

After John finished reading the passages, he appeared to reject the journal as fiction. Shaking his head, he placed the book on the table and remained speechless.

"Now that you've digested that revelation, I want you to come with me to the cellar and look into the double-door closet."

Max Gravel led the detectives to the cellar. Returning ten minutes later, it was several minutes before anyone could talk.

"Max, I need a favor. Can I bring my friends out here to look at this? You know the gang I'm talking about. They're waiting at my house, and because they helped with the investigation I'd like them to see its final conclusion."

"Jack, under normal circumstances you know what I'd have to say. But you guys were so instrumental in solving this case . . . why not! What the hell, you solved it on your own. Sure, bring them over. Everything is wrapped so I'll secure my crew and we can stay around. To be honest, I can't wait to see Jeanette's reaction to what I have in the cellar."

After contacting Jeanette, Sheriff Max Gravel, John Lloyd and O'Brennan waited for the Group with little said about the unveiling they would later call a horror show.

Arriving an hour later, O'Brennan's friends settled in the study unaware of the emotional trauma they would experience in the next fifteen minutes. Facing his friends, Jack noticed their light-hearted banter when Jeanette asked, "O'Brennan, I'm curious why you dragged us out here."

I bet this will slow them down, he thought while preparing to speak.

"I start with no ground rules, but be forewarned that what

you are about to hear and see will rock the very foundation of your logic and mental balance. You may find the next fifteen minutes extremely distasteful to say the least. What I'm about to present is an agenda of horror that most will consider extremely offensive.

"The reason you're here is because of our friend, Max Gravel. While wrapping up the day's affairs, he received a call from the county jail. An attendant checking Jeffreys in found that Martin was not a man. Martin Jeffreys is a woman."

The room buzzed from Jack's startling disclosure. He called for quiet but little followed. "Let's hold the chatter until I finish, then you'll know exactly what I know. I'm going to take you through a three-step progression of the details we have."

As O'Brennan prepared to lead his followers into this horror-chamber, Max Gravel leaned against the bookshelves reading a book similar in appearance to the one Jack held.

"First, this is a diary, no, make that a journal of one Martha Jeffreys. I shall now read you the details."

June 1987

This is a journal and not a diary. I guess one would call it an anthology of my earlier experiences. I wanted to write this for years, but delayed because I could not accept what my life had become. Now that I'm older, I find myself more at peace, and a kind of inner bliss has swept over me. Alcohol is eroding away the very fabric of my intellect and sense of reason. My only true reward is my writing, and I question how long that will continue.

I must get on with this record of transgressions before the brandy again overtakes me. The following essay presents my feelings and how and why I suffer. I'd like to add that no human being should live through the depression and turmoil that has dogged me from my childhood. But I accept the fact a successful killer constantly lives with paranoia.

Upon birth, I drew a short stick in the world of genetics and found myself shaped in the form of a hermaphrodite, a term commonly associated with inter-sexual characteristics. Neither of my parents displayed an interest in understanding my plight, thus forcing me to diagnose my own problems when I was sixteen. Although not technically correct, my conclusion compelled me to understand the severity of the problem. Later in Holland, I was examined and found to have Stein-Leventhal Syndrome. The indicators: obesity and female chromosomes and male genetic patterns. I have an internalized penis and testicles along with the obligatory female body parts. I find myself losing control and feel my undoing is close at hand.

It was at that moment the alarm went off in O'Brennan's thoughts. *That's the difference. When I played golf with him, I felt there was something out of place. At the time, I couldn't figure it out. But damn, I was close. Now I know why he didn't shower after we played golf.*

The following is an excerpt from my high school diary

I must develop a sexual identity; though I believe gender to be nothing more than a facade. I am going to try to transcend this sexual crisis through spiritual relief gained by prayer. I have to wait to finish my senior year in high school and spend four years in college but it will be worth it.

At an age when girls start menstruating and developing breasts, I had occasional spotting and no sign of breasts and sensed I was different. I never understood why my mother couldn't see for herself what I was experiencing, but she insisted I was imaging things.

In high school I continually think about having sex with little girls. Much to my horror, this veiled obsession leads me to think I am a potential pedophile. To the layman, my disorder is what psychologists call a psychosexual personality disorder. It describes an adult who prefers children as objects of their desires. I shall suppress this desire until I graduate from high school, and at that time realize the freedom to pursue the youngsters I so desperately seek.

This next excerpt is from my college diary

I can't determine what is make-believe and what is real. More often than not I feel I'm a borderline psychotic and continually live with the sensation of being tumbled around like wet clothes in a dryer. I can't help myself.

When I have sex with a little girl, only then I know the authenticity of my yearning. When I fantasize about my next subject, the anticipation satisfies my sexual appetite.

What do I accomplish with this activity? That's easy. The most gratifying part of this maneuver is providing the rare yet stimulating experience I missed at their age. It appears I have an uncanny ability to lead these targets into face-to-face sexual encounters that they'll never forget.

I sincerely believe my strength lies in providing love and warmth to these youngsters that they lack at home. I gain a girl's confidence so completely with a simple protocol that she seldom discerns sexual activity is involved. It must be instinctive because seldom am I wrong in my choice of playmates. Although success follows me, I feel surrounded by mirrors reflecting my past conquests and see no way out.

I have steadfastly tried to rationalize my activities as simple flirtations with deviant behavior. Evil is in the eye of the beholder and I must pigeonhole my persona as a member of the devil's many followers. I am a Christian as well as a good person, but this personal syndrome of child affection is driving me down the road to destruction.

Having chosen to abandon this lifestyle, I shall go to Holland after finishing here at Sweet Briar and attempt to redirect my life. My self-imposed reticence has provided no personal contacts with others, and I feel my life has been ruined because of the option I have chosen.

Taken from my diary in Amsterdam

My whole life turned around when I hit the city of Amsterdam. I noticed a moral openness about sex, and was moved by the number of sexual deviants of all persuasion common in the city.

Turning my back on this affliction of mine isn't the answer. I decided to sever all links with my former life. The first step in reconstructing my existence was to withdraw from my past behavior and eliminate approaching young girls; and that was a painful experience. Psychiatric counseling directed me toward that end, though I never did eliminate the urge to return to that ghastly practice. I have managed to curb this desire through continuing self-discipline and control. Thank God no further incidents of it have arisen.

I found time was a harness around my neck, and at that juncture decided to attend law school. Knowing my brother Martin was at Harvard Law drove me in the pursuit of his chosen discipline.

Thoughts of Martin return each time I think about my youth. From the time I was a child, he was mean to me and made my life miserable. He made fun of me because I was different, but I believe he became that way because he was green with envy over my golf achievements. I won the Virginia Junior State Golf Championship as a ninth grader and this feat overwhelmed him. Although a superb golfer in his own right, I'm certain Martin felt devastated by the statewide success I achieved.

In Holland, the sport is not as popular as back home. I wiggled my way into a country club and won the woman's championship on my first outing.

At about the same time I started formulating a plan for my return to the states. I was always heavy and standing six-two made me look like a walking woman mountain. To counter my bulky appearance, I went on a weightlifting program that concentrated on machines and free weights. I figured I was destined to be large, so why not look good while I was at it.

It seemed diverse aspects of my life suddenly began converging into a new me. While golf and physical training took center stage, I found relative success in writing fiction. I started with short stories and gradually worked up to full-length novels. I never bothered with an agent because it was reward enough to know that I was talented enough to write. The novels, although reasonably well done, lacked stirring plots that would pique the reader's interest. This shortcoming continues to plague me and I must somehow learn to overcome it because I have confidence that writing fiction will become the central focus in my life.

    Immediately after finishing Martha's journal, O'Brennan started again. "As I told you . . . hey, get with it, you're not listening! I've mentioned this before but apparently you haven't tuned in. You have surmised that Martha Jeffreys killed her brother back in the early sixties. Please bear with me as I try to make sense of this. Hopefully, we should see light at the end of the tunnel."

    Jeanette made a nervous cough that momentarily interrupted O'Brennan.

    "My second progression is this red velvet case. To some of you ladies, it may appear to be a jewelry case, or a case for one's personal treasures." O'Brennan placed his hands on the red case, picked it up and looked at it, then returned it to the desk. "This case contains treasures, but they're not the ones you may be thinking of. Yes, some have guessed . . . it's a hope chest of artifacts."

    Jack opened the red case for the Group to scrutinize.

    Further words weren't needed for O'Brennan's friends to understand his meaning. The general discussion centered on the finger in pocket one. Speculation eventually turned to why Martin's finger was among the trophies and Shana Barber's wasn't.

    I might as well get on with this, O'Brennan thought. "Max, we're ready for the cellar."

    Still leaning against the bookshelf, Sheriff Gravel motioned O'Brennan over with a glance.

    "Jack, not yet." Gravel nervously cleared his throat. "I found this while you were talking to your friends. It's Martha's journal after she returned to the states. It's not lengthy but it is revealing. Here, you'd better read it."

38

O'Brennan's voice stopped his friends in their tracks heading toward the cellar. "Max found another journal that is dated from Martha's Amsterdam departure to when she eliminated Martin."

He proceeded to read Martha's words that would lay open the end of the investigation.

November 1963

My time in Amsterdam wound down as I prepared to return home. The plan I so carefully sculpted was now in place. As I look back, setting my agenda for the next ten years was the most thrilling feature of my life. During the years prior to my return, I thought of nothing but Martin.

From childhood he cruelly abused me. His maltreatment was not of a physical nature but an ongoing insidious demolition of my mental and spiritual state.

In one of his earlier tapes, Martin said, 'Martha, words are slow to come at a moment like this. Every time I think of Shana Barber and that's often, I might add, I'm overcome with a depression I've not previously experienced. I was shocked at hearing the news of her disappearance.

She came to the game the night we played in Charlottesville. Though I never talked to her I couldn't keep my eyes off her. She was going with that bastard from her hometown, a guy named Andy Hamlin. I never saw her after that night. I know I'm a user of women, but Shana was different, I loved her.'

I felt badly for Martin but not enough to abandon my plans. Once I set the format for my future, my preparation for the grandest masquerade of all time began. Emotionally and spiritually, thoughts of Martin overwhelmed me and he became a part of me. I had to transform myself physically into a living replica of the brother I hated.

I started shaving daily. To enhance the growth of my beard, I took male hormones. Fortunately for me, Martin had a light beard, so it wasn't that difficult to duplicate. I shaved before I went to class and used rather heavy make-up to cover any possible trace of shadow.

The next phase of the operation I rather enjoyed. I got a brush cut that matched Martin's. Even in the early sixties Martin continued with the same hairstyle even though it wasn't popular at the time. It was easy to keep clean and now I see why he preferred it. While out in public I wore a wig to hide my new identity.

My studies in law school here in Amsterdam paralleled Martin's at Harvard. In preparing for my new life in Smithbury I studied law from American textbooks. At the conclusion of my three years, I was adept at both American and European law.

The next phase of my transformation was weight training. Martin had sent a picture of himself posing in a bathing suit. From that I designed a program that would provide a physique similar to my twin. I stayed exclusively with free weights and refrained from using the new drugs called steroids. I wanted matching dimensions not bulk.

The voice proved to be perplexing. Over my stay in Amsterdam I continually worked on emulating his taped messages. After considerable effort I finally achieved a close resemblance to the voice on the tape. If questioned about it, I would offhandedly mention that my voice was slightly altered due to throat surgery done in Boston.

Ready for my greatest moment I disguised myself by wearing a brunette wig. I flew to Montreal and slipped across the border into New Hampshire. From there I had little trouble hitchhiking to Virginia. With my return to Smithbury the window of opportunity opened wide to me. I couldn't wait to kill him, and this thought wasn't a whim by any sense of the imagination. I changed wigs, and again became Martha Jeffreys.

Martin was surprised to see me and appeared happier and more considerate than I ever remembered him before. But his remarkable change of heart did not deter me from consummating my well-scripted plan.

I went to the kitchen to refill our drinks, and at that time added 45 milligrams of morphine to his blueberry brandy.

Martin was dead before he finished the large brandy I had served him. Carting him to the cellar was no small task but I persevered. As I prepared Martin for his permanent residency, I still found myself puzzled by the two glass receptacles Dad kept in the cellar. Three feet in diameter, the dome fitted over the top lid of the seven-foot high cylinder like a cup fits over a coffee thermos. I placed Martin in the jar and left him in place until morning when I bought formaldehyde to preserve him. As I viewed Martin suspended in the jar he appeared to look like a Greek God.

The one irritating obstacle that plagued me throughout my preparation was Martin's secretary. I was terrified she would notice a difference.

The adage, "I'd rather be lucky than good" never displayed itself to better advantage than in my case. It turned out Martin's secretary moved to Lynchburg and was being replaced by someone starting the next week.

Returning to Martin's bedroom, I changed into his clothes, removed my wig and brushed my blonde brush cut. Pouring a snifter of brandy; I raised the dark liquid to the full-length mirror and saluted myself. "Happy birthday, Martha, I mean Martin." It is the happiest birthday I've ever experienced, and I must say a rather eventful one for Martin as well.

Life has not been kind to me, but I'm certain that will improve in the morning. I better get a good night's rest because I want to be fresh as a daisy when I get to the office in the morning.

I'm headed toward a fabulous decade and an even more stirring career as a lawyer for the Smithbury elite. The very group of snobs that treated me so sensitively as a youth is now in my sights, and I shall legally steal every dollar I can from them. I owe it to you, dear brother; have a long and hard sleep.

As Jack finished, the buzz from the Group reached ear-shattering dimensions.

"Most psychopaths want to suffer for their killing habits. After hearing what I just read to you, I'm certain you'll believe Martha doesn't suffer that guilt trip."

O'Brennan gestured around the study. "If you haven't guessed it by now, this is where the shadow of evil created her terror. Mr. Sheriff, we are now ready for the cellar."

"That's nice to hear, Mr. Detective. If you ladies and gentlemen will please follow me, I shall momentarily enlighten you," Max Gravel said.

O'Brennan stood in front of a large double closet some eight feet high. Its doors placed side by side were hinged on the outside with brass handles on the inside next to each other.

Without ceremony, Jack swung the right door open revealing the late Martin Jeffreys suspended in clear liquid inside the glass container. An eye-level brass plate was secured to the glass tomb. It's inscription read:

Martin Jeffreys
Born November 17, 1929
Died November 17, 1963
What a prick I had for a brother!

Standing at the rear of the observers, Colby and Red watched the others reactions after O'Brennan opened the closet. Red nudged Colby. "He's the only one who knows the story other than Martha, and he took it the grave."

Without speaking, O'Brennan opened the door on the left. There sat an empty duplicate of Martin's resting-place with a brass plate secured to it.

Jeanette stepped forward to look into the closet containing her predetermined tomb. The inscription she observed was secured to the front of the glass coffin. Jeanette finally forced herself to study the epitaph that read:

Julie Smilker
Born August 17, 1930
Died June 12, 1988
The most beautiful Leo in captivity

The old standard, never let them see you sweat prevails in the game of high finance and espionage but this age-old cliche was not appropriate in the cellar of the Jeffreys mansion. Beads of sweat appeared on her forehead as Jeanette stared at this evil-looking crypt.

She started to speak, "I don't believe she'd put me in tha . . ." and fainted into O'Brennan's arms.

"Liz, I don't know about how you'll start your novel, or for that matter what you'll do with the middle, but you'll have to agree the events of the last several minutes will provide you with a sterling ending," O'Brennan said.

"Jack, what are you going to do for Jeanette?" Phyllis asked with a tremor crowding her voice.

"Phyllis, if I can wake her up, we'll be married in the morning as originally planned."

+++++